FINAL DESTINATION

DESTINATION ZERO

He was still standing there, gawping and wondering, when the sheet of glass hit him in the forehead.

Falling too fast to see, it had remained vertical, and hit him edge-on. It sliced clean through his body in an instant: through the skull, between the hemispheres of the brain, down the throat, ripping through the right ventricle of his heart, down through stomach and intestine to emerge from his groin and hit the sidewalk.

The two halves of Zack hadn't even begun to topple when the glass edge cracked against the ground, and the whole pane shattered. Blood and tiny gobbets of meat splashed across the street, mixed with the glass in a silver and red seasoning that dusted the halves where they had fallen.

The whole thing took less than a second, and it was several stunned moments longer before someone on the street began to scream.

In the same series

FINAL DESTINATION #1:
DEAD RECKONING
Natasha Rhodes

More New Line novels from Black Flame

BLADE: TRINITY
Natasha Rhodes

THE BUTTERFLY EFFECT
James Swallow

CELLULAR
Pat Cadigan

FREDDY vs JASON
Stephen Hand

JASON X
Pat Cadigan

JASON X#2: THE EXPERIMENT
Pat Cadigan

THE TEXAS CHAINSAW MASSACRE
Stephen Hand

THE TWILIGHT ZONE #1
MEMPHIS • THE POOL GUY
Jay Russell

THE TWILIGHT ZONE #2
UPGRADE • SENSUOUS CINDY
Pat Cadigan

THE TWILIGHT ZONE #3
INTO THE LIGHT • SUNRISE
Paul A Woods

FINAL DESTINATION

DESTINATION ZERO

A NOVEL BY

DAVID MCINTEE

BASED ON CHARACTERS FROM THE
MOTION PICTURE "FINAL DESTINATION"
CREATED BY JEFFREY REDDICK

For my wife Lesley, for love and support during the writing process. And, of course, your good selves, for buying the thing. Enjoy.

A Black Flame Publication
www.blackflame.com

First published in 2005 by BL Publishing, Games Workshop Ltd., Willow Road, Nottingham NG7 2WS, UK.

Distributed in the US by Simon & Schuster, 1230 Avenue of the Americas, New York, NY 10020, USA.

10 9 8 7 6 5 4 3 2 1

ISBN 1 84416 171 4

A CIP record for this book is available from the British Library.

Printed in the UK by Bookmarque, Surrey, UK.

PROLOGUE

From *Borderlands Patrol,* cover date: December 2004. The one with Elvis piloting a flying saucer on the cover.

REAPER FURIOUS, NOT JUST GRIM
By Staff Reporter

LA rock band The Vipers found themselves dancing with their namesake over the summer, when the club they were playing in collapsed. The disaster has had positive repercussions, with Governor Schwarzenegger enacting a review of building codes in Southern California in the wake of the tragedy. So far, so *LA Times*. What the regular newsies didn't print puts a new slant on things that is very different from the straightforward safety issues publicized by the Governator.

According to the band's semi-official fanclub website, further deaths were avoided because lead singer Jess Golden had a clairvoyant experience, allowing her to warn some of the potential victims. The story goes, says webmaster Skyblaze, that after the disaster, Death was so irritated at this interference that he returned to stalk the survivors, many of whom died shortly afterwards.

It's a ridiculous theory, of course, harking back to the so-called Mothman death list, the supposed spate of deaths in the biochemical research industry, or the curse on the archaeologists who opened up Tutankhamen's tomb. It seems a required part of our modern mythology that hit lists crop up after any major events. Thus confident, the *Borderlands Patrol* set out to debunk the story. And couldn't.

It turns out that several prominent survivors of what we might call the Vipers Incident have indeed died brutally in a series of so-called accidents. Club bouncer Sebastian Lebecque was immolated in a motorcycle crash, while other survivors perished in bizarre incidents such as falling elevators. the *Borderlands Patrol* was unable to contact Jess Golden for comment—because she has dropped off the face of the Earth. Her checking accounts and credit cards haven't been used in over four months. Her ATM PIN number hasn't been used in the same time. She hasn't been seen from or heard of since July.

Is she dead? Hiding? Abducted by aliens? Nobody seems to know. Not her fan club, her family, her manager, or—so they say—the police.

There is one other possibility. Could she be in protective custody—or indeed hostile custody—of the Federal Government? It's not beyond the bounds of possibility. Someone or something arranged a lot of very neat and very specific accidents for her friends. There's one other reason to suspect the motives of the authorities: according to a former LAPD patrolman, who wishes to remain anonymous, the disaster was caused by police incompetence, in the form of a drugs bust gone wrong. The LAPD rubbishes such suggestions, of course. But they would, wouldn't they.

Whichever way you look at it, Jess's disappearance has done her career the world of good. Sales of The Vipers' single abum have tripled since her vanishing, leading some fans to speculate on a publicity stunt. But those who knew—or know—Jess and The Vipers say that it's not her style, and that they believe she is hiding from something. Something that killed several of her friends and acquaintances.

The *Borderlands Patrol* has no answers for this mystery but suggests that if you ever find yourself walking away from an accident, perhaps it's wise to keep an eye over one's shoulder.

ONE

Patricia Fuller woke to the sound of rain on the roof. February in LA, she thought, when the temperature could still be below seventy, and the danger of dry brush fires turned to the danger of muddy landslips. You gotta love it, she told herself.

Patti forced herself out of bed, barely remembering to switch the coffee machine on before heading to the shower. The steam that gathered in the shower cabinet matched the weather outside. Of all the urban myths Patti had heard over the years, the one most people still seemed to believe in was that it was sunny year-round in LA. Angelenos seemed to forget the rain about thirty seconds after it had stopped.

It was also just about the only urban myth that Patti wished was true. Most urban myths were about bad things—rodents in fast food, violent gang rituals, pets slaughtered in supposedly comedic accidents.

Patti was tall and athletic, with shoulder-length dark hair that thankfully didn't frizz when rushing out to work still damp. After showering, she dressed in black jeans and a black halter-top. A leather jacket—black, of course—would keep the rain off.

The fridge was typically empty—she made a mental note to remember to do some grocery shopping sometime, then mentally round-filed it with the all the others she had made over the weekend. Her faithful steed, a little three-door Saturn, would transport her perfectly well to the Coco's she often passed on Sherman Way. It was on her way to the 101 and Hollywood Freeway anyhow, so she might as well take advantage of it.

She paused by the automobile, looking up at the ashen sky. It was solid monotone gray, as if the artist who colored in the sky hadn't shown up for work this morning, and had just left the bare firmament showing. Grimacing, she climbed into the vehicle, and set off. Normally she listened to hip-hop while driving, but about thirty seconds of Snoop Dogg today proved that hip-hop and gray rain clouds didn't go together. She stopped the disc and tuned into a news channel for the rest of her trip to Sherman Way.

The news didn't entertain her much. It was the usual round of Iraq, the economy, soccer and some so-called celebrities bitching at each other. It was as boring as the gray overhead.

A half-hour breakfast in Coco's let the traffic on the 101 thin out somewhat. Why sit and stew in the car in a tailback when you can sip coffee and eat pancakes while watching the world go by?

Patti watched the road outside, trying to judge from the traffic on the street how good or bad the traffic on the highway would be. Sometimes she wondered how many of the drivers or passengers were also her readers, and how many would be the subjects of an article by herself or someone like her. Not many, in either case, she suspected. They were mundane, and the only borderlands they were likely to cross were on a day trip to Mexico.

After enough coffee, she felt hyper enough to face the office, and work. The traffic also seemed to have eased, so she left a tip on the table, and left. It took another hour to get down to Vine and the offices of the *Borderlands Patrol.* The entrance was a narrow doorway squeezed in beside a McDonalds half a block along from Mann's Chinese Theater. Patti had often wondered how and why the magazine's offices were in the heart of tourist tinsel town when it had nothing to do with movies, but nobody seemed to know. The rumor was that the offices had been bequeathed to the company by some paranormal believer of a movie star. Since none of the qualifying stars that Patti could think of were dead, she didn't believe a word of it.

The offices of The *Borderlands Patrol* were perfectly normal. Comfortable chairs, pastel carpets, desktop workstations with flat-screen monitors, and not an "I Want To Believe" UFO poster in sight.

Patti exchanged smiles and nods with various staff writers, sub-editors and artists as she strolled through to the editor's private sanctum. She rapped on the door and Matt Lawson opened it. "Where have you been?"

"Living life," Patti told him. "That's what it's for."

The wiry, curly-haired editor grinned. Today he was wearing a Linkin Park T-shirt. "Not here. We're supposed to be professional geeks, Patti. Professional means we should be working, and geeks means we should... Well, you get that one, yeah?"

"I get it." She took a seat and pulled a sheaf of papers from the small rucksack on her shoulder. "I've brought along the notes I made on my trip to England. I've still got interviews with the witnesses to transcribe, but I think you'll like the way it's going."

"Hm-hm," Lawson said, skimming through the papers. "Yeah, it looks like it should make a great spread. Pictures?"

"I've emailed in the JPEGs. The film's in for developing."

"Cool. Well, while you're waiting, I wondered if you could help fill a gap in April's issue."

As if she was going to turn down some actual paid work. Not in this life. "What sort of gap?"

"Four-page spread. Kelly's Echelon exposé hasn't panned out–something about a hard drive crash, he says." Patti raised an eyebrow, but didn't say anything. "Anyway, I was remembering that story of yours looking back at the TR3 having been tested out of Andrews in the '90s..."

"Yeah, I remember." The most recent albatross around Patti's neck; how could she forget? "It's plausible, and there are some things in legit aviation and military magazines that would back it up, but the air force still stonewall my queries." She grimaced. "They put me on hold for an hour till I get sick of it and hang up; they lose mail."

"What about an FOIA request? You mentioned that before."

"I did, but you wouldn't authorize the fee as a legitimate expense, and I don't make enough here to be able to spare it out of my own pocket." She hoped her tone and him having brought up the subject would combine to solve that problem.

"Today I'll authorize it," he replied, sounding only slightly pissed. "I've already made an appointment to pick up files from the Civic Center tomorrow. You can go along."

"All right," she replied, not wanting to let him know how ecstatic she was at his turnaround. It didn't do to let people who thought they had influence over you know how you felt. There was only one person she immediately wanted to share her joy with, and she would see him in the evening. This time, she would have to shop for breakfast foods: enough for two. She hoped Will was having at least a good a day as she was, rain notwithstanding.

Six-two and athletic, with a neat crew cut, Will Sax looked like he should have been the squad leader of a bunch of Marines, or perhaps the pitcher for a pro baseball team, rather than the supervisor of the home entertainments section of a Circuit City store in Northridge. His height could have been intimidating, but he was lanky and laid back rather than imposing. He had a square chiseled face and hair that hadn't been its original brown since the eighth grade.

It was five minutes to opening time, and Will was jamming on an electric guitar that was plugged into the most expensive amp in stock. That was then output to the speakers concealed throughout the store's ceiling panels. They weren't the best speakers in the world–frankly, they sucked like a hooker who'd been living on a diet of lemons–but they did play to the whole store, and that was what appealed to him. In five minutes, now four, they'd start excreting the bland lift muzak that kept customers docile. Or, worse, manufactured plastic boy or girl bands.

Right now, though, they were all his. "Sir?" A voice, almost dripping with audible acne, said behind him. It was the kid in charge of the kitchen appliance section. "Mister Flanagan is in the parking lot."

Will's hand slipped on the steel strings, nearly relieving him of the eternity ring Patti had given him last Christmas. "Shit!" Panicked, praying that he could get the guitar out of the way before Flanagan, the store manager, saw what was happening. He pulled out the leads from the amp and switched it off, then, carrying the guitar, ran for the customer service office. There he switched on the regular loop for the speakers, then he ran for the staff locker room. He threw the guitar in his locker and the door closed with about five seconds to spare.

Flanagan was doing a quick tour of the store when Will got back to the home entertainment department that was his domain. "Ready for another day of the War on Skinflints, Will?" Flanagan asked.

"Ready and willing, Chief."

"Good. Let's see a continued upwards progression in targeted retail bullseyes, eh?"

"Uh, yeah," Will agreed, with no idea what the guy was talking about. Will hoped he had meant, "sell more" because that seemed like the best interpretation that he could think of.

"Good, good." Flanagan smiled. "Get to it, guys. Make me proud."

Will flipped the finger at his back. His boss's pride was nothing on earning his paycheck. He straightened his shirt and turned to face the employees of his department. He knew just by looking at his team that it was going to be a long day. Most of them were college or university students looking to earn an extra buck between classes. Most of them would quit soon to do something they found more interesting, and they already knew that. Knowing it, their hearts wouldn't be in it during their shift, and they'd just be marking time until they could get out of the store and back to having fun. That meant they'd screw up, and he'd have to work extra to cover for them.

Naturally, Will wanted to quit as well. As soon as the band got a gig or a contract that paid more than five hundred bucks, he'd be as gone as the rest of them. Well, maybe not for just five hundred.

At least he didn't have any sort of age difference issues with the team, as they were all much the same age as himself. The difference between them was that he didn't have enough money–or, if truth be told, the inclination–to go to college. Whereas his team just wanted extra fun money, he needed to keep a roof over his head.

Independence sucked, he decided. On the other hand, he didn't have to worry about mom walking in on him and Patti now that he was in his own place, so there was something to be said for it after all.

Later. The evening sky was dry and clear, the rain having spent itself as it moved inland. The streets around the City of Industry were already dry again, having barely been kissed by the damp weather.

A bone-crushing impact slammed Hal Ward sideways, his head snapping to the right sharply enough to make him see stars. His ears rang from the sound of the collision. Metal screamed in what could be taken for pain by a listener in the right mood, and glass tinkled to the floor pan under the gas and brake pedals, bizarrely audible despite the cacophony all around. The safety straps held, but painfully, and the colorful helmet he wore deflected the glass fragments away from his eyes.

Despite all of this, Hal's only reaction was to whoop with delight, and enjoy the rush of blood that he could feel throughout every vein in his body. The impact might have been jarring, but it was also exciting, hyping him up to a state where he wanted to leap out of the car and shout "HELL YEAH!" loud enough to break as many zoning ordinances as he could.

Instead, he gripped the steering wheel and twisted it hard; trying desperately to catch up with the armored muscle car that Pete Martin was riding. His helmet kept out some of the engine noise, but there was so much of it that there was really no escape. The whole of the Industry Hills circuit was filled with the roar of thousands of combined horsepower, spread out over twenty automobiles. The crowd was probably roaring too. They certainly had been before the race started. Eight thousand people all cheering on their favorite riders, or their favorite marques, and all imagining that their rider would hear his name and be inspired to win.

On the race line itself, even before the engines powered into life, the roar of the crowd was just a general roar. Even a CIA spook whose whole raison d'etre was to analyze the sounds from bugs wouldn't be able to tell who was shouting what.

There was no joy in trying to really work out how many of the crowd was cheering for a given driver, so every driver just told himself that they were all cheering for him. Maybe some of the guys secretly thought that no one was cheering them but, if so, they kept their fears to themselves.

The Industry Hills circuit was short for racing cars–it had been intended for bikes–but a demolition derby didn't require long straights of rolling road for speed. In fact, the harder it was to drive without damage, the better. That was why they called it demolition derby.

Hal was enjoying himself thoroughly by the middle of the race, and was tempted to burst into song. He resisted the urge; he had given in once, in his debut season three years ago, and the race had been stopped while fire trucks and paramedics ran rings round his automobile like Indians round the settlers' wagons in an old Western. The pit guys, when they could catch their breath from laughing so hard, had told him that everyone had thought he was on fire because of the noise he was making.

Now he only sang in the shower, after the race. He was usually still hopped up on the adrenaline for hours after the race, and didn't care what people thought of his singing then.

After a day spent in libraries and archives, Patti needed a break. Worse than that, she needed company of the sort that wouldn't mind when she kicked off her shoes and tossed her shirt aside to cool off. That was what friends and lovers were for.

She had driven up to Northridge before rush hour could really get started. Better that than end up trapped Downtown for hours. Now her Saturn was pulling into the parking lot of Circuit City. The store was closed, but Patti could hear an unstoppable beat, a panzer column of musical notes, driving out from the doors.

She went round to the staff entrance, and knocked. A moment later, Will Sax opened the door, singing along to the beat in a bad approximation of German. At first glance he looked like he might be a jock, but Patti knew he was too interested in kicking back and catching some rays to put in the effort required for athletic pursuits.

"Rammstein?" she asked.

He shook his head. "Laibach. Better than the crap we put on for the shoppers while the store's open, huh? This is how to put a shit load of the best new speakers to proper use, y'know what I mean? It gives me the shits when some couple come in to pick up a kick-ass sound system and I just know they're going to be playing, like, Celine fucking Dion or something."

"What's wrong with her stuff?" It wouldn't be Patti's choice of music to work out to with the speed bags, but she found it relaxing after delivering an article on deadline. On deadline, to the minute, rather than the date.

"Or, worse," he went on, "some kid coming in to waste one on their collection of Titney's CDs." He gave a wistful sigh. "Man, these things are made for real music."

"Like German metal."

"Or any kind of metal, or proper rock music, or anything that isn't made on a production line by prepubescent teens for prepubescent teens."

Patti grinned and kissed him. "You done here or do I have to sully my Saturn with your corporate parking lot any longer?"

"One minute," he promised. He was as good as his word, as far as Patti could tell, returning in exactly what she counted as a minute, with his guitar.

"You take that thing to work?" she asked."

"Wouldn't you?"

Patti had no idea, having never owned a guitar, nor had the urge to own one. "Let's go. I'll find a safe place for your... instrument."

The next morning, the sun had come out over Santa Monica, as the rain had passed on inland overnight. Susan Fries was more than happy about that, as it meant the weather improved as she drove down from Encino, through the Sepulveda Pass and west towards the Dolphin Auto Yard.

The auto yard was, perhaps, a rather strange legacy for a father to leave his daughter, but Susan was happy with it. She had never wanted to see the business slip out of the family's grasp, and she had loved tinkering with engines and machines since she was old enough to get her romper suit covered in oil and grease at her dad's side.

She hopped out of the Dodge Ram pickup just long enough to unlock the yard's gates, and drove in. There was a solid wooden cabin near the gate, which contained the yard office, some storerooms and a wardrobe with Susan's working clothes. At work, she discarded the slacks and velvet shirt in favor of baggy coveralls to disguise her slim legs, and not-so-slim hips and breasts. She had her near-black hair cut in like a pageboy's in an old Errol Flynn movie.

There were a couple of brightly colored surfboards propped up in one corner of the office, and she resolved to check them out later in the day. They would need waxing if nothing else. She had no idea what the weather was going to be like later on, but hoped it would become good enough to strap a board onto the Dodge and head off to the beach in the afternoon. It wasn't as if she had a boss to tell her to keep the place open at any given hour.

She busied herself with invoices and bills for the first hour of the day, then decided that the call of fiberglass and wax was too strong to resist. She was halfway through treating the first board—yellow with a red flame motif—when she heard a motorcycle pull into the yard. "Come on in, Hal," she shouted, without looking up.

A moment later, the new arrival walked into the office, looking bemused. It was a black man with a buzz cut and a grin wide enough to plow snow on a road in Alaska. His round, owlish spectacles didn't seem to go with the rest of his image. He was wearing plain leathers, black with a hint of silver trim. "How did you know it was me?" Hal Ward asked.

"You're the only customer I've got with a Kawasaki Ninja ZX-6R."

"You can't see it from here."

"I can hear it."

"You can identify a bike by its sound?"

"Yeah?" Susan grinned, her plump cheeks glowing. She could have told him about growing up around engines, and how the sound of them and the odor of hot steel were as natural to her as rock and roll and apple pie, but it was more amusing not to. "What's it today?" Susan asked.

"Was looking for some good solid shocks." He had a strong Maine accent that sounded like something that belonged on an Atlantic trawler.

"For the Ninja?"

"This is a business call. For the muscle car. Industry Hills was sweet–" He rubbed his fingertips under his nose. "But punishing."

"When do you need them?"

"Friday."

"Okay. I was gonna wash my hair then, but I think I can manage to dig up some shocks for you."

He nodded gently. "Actually, your hair's fine. Like the rest of you."

"You keep saying that, but sooner or later I'm going to have to make you put your... money where your mouth is."

He looked away, and then changed the subject. "Are you coming to the next race?"

"I could be persuaded." She tossed him a can of wax. "If you can spare an hour or two for the waves. I've got two boards here, and there's only one of me."

The waves coming into the sand over on Venice Beach, fifteen minutes drive from the Dolphin Auto

Yard, weren't too big that a beginner couldn't handle. Hal had fallen off the blue and green board three times before Susan finally said, "You've never done this before, have you?"

"No," he admitted. "Not enough horsepower for my taste, you know what I mean?"

Susan laughed. "Looks like I got me a virgin, huh?"

"Pure as the driven snow. What say I sit this one out and watch an expert in action?" And so he did. It was an enjoyable hour, catching some rays, enjoying the beach, and watching an attractive friend in a bikini. Moments like that, he decided, are what life is all about. Eventually, she rejoined him, soaked to the skin. He handed her a stripy beach robe, and nodded out to sea, where a thick charcoal line hugged the horizon. "Looks like you're done just in time. Something's coming in for us."

"More rain. El goddam Nino strikes again."

Hal just smiled, and took her hands in his. "You're beautiful, you know."

"No I'm not."

"You certainly aren't ugly."

Susan waved a hand in a fifty-fifty gesture. "I like to think of it as... just pretty enough."

"Pretty enough?" He laughed warmly. "Pretty enough for what? Anything specific?"

She pursed her lips and half-closed her eyes, one eyebrow raised. It made her look cute, in a 1940s screwball comedy kind of way. "Pretty enough to be noticed, but not beautiful enough to be harassed for it."

"Even ugly girls get harassed these days."

"They probably like it more," she said.

"I doubt it. I really doubt that." He stood up. "Let's get something to eat, and reunite me with my baby."

"You should marry that Ninja."

"Hey, she's Japanese. Would that count as one of those Asian mail-order brides?"

TWO

It rained again in the night, hiding the stars and moon. Though the rain had stopped before dawn, there were still damp patches on the roads across Downtown. Puddles were scattered throughout the otherwise dry roads like little patches of fungus.

Zack Halloran hated having to come into the Civic Center, however necessary it might be. Traffic was hell, and bureaucracy gave him, he liked to tell people, "the shits." The whole area was just too full of deskbound types, whether governmental or otherwise. He had always promised himself that if ever he got behind a desk, he would get someone to shoot him.

Still barely on the sunny side of forty, Zack was president of his own company, ZH Construction, with over five hundred employees, and he had got all that way without ever spending a day in an office. Architects and city councilmen, on the other hand, spent all their time in offices, and refused to come out to look at modifications made to building plans at the construction site. No, they had to drag decent taxpaying working stiffs down to this city of the living dead. He had come down from Van Nuys, taking a route through the clinical blue Second Street tunnel, and ended up in a tail-back on First.

He knew he was going to miss his appointment, and he knew that they pencil-dicks wouldn't just see him later. They'd insist on rescheduling, losing at least another day of actual construction. The curse that Zack was about to utter never made it past his lips. Instead, something jolted the pickup, jerking him up against the seatbelt and causing his jaws to crash together. He tasted blood, and his tongue flashed and went numb.

Zack slammed a meaty fist against the wheel and resisted the urge to scream obscenities until he was blue in the face. He glanced in the mirror and saw that the vehicle that had hit him was a fragile-looking sports job. Zack felt a little better about that, hoping it was as expensive to fix as it had been expensive to buy. That would serve the owner right for being so goddamed careless as to screw up Zack's day.

Cheered up a little, he climbed out of the pickup and walked towards the back of the vehicle. The offending car, a Ferrari, had a crumpled hood and oil was leaking out from somewhere underneath the chassis. Zack's pickup seemed to have got off more lightly, but the tailpipe was scraping the ground and, bending down to look, Zack could tell the muffler was busted as well. He might have got off lightly, but he still wasn't going to be driving anywhere else in his truck today. He'd have to call a tow truck.

The Ferrari driver had emerged by now, peeking out from inside the red car like a turtle from its shell. He was about a dozen years younger than Zack, in his mid-twenties, and had short-cropped hair gelled into spikes, and the sort of round-rimmed glasses that Gestapo officers wore in the kind of exploitation war movies Zack liked.

Ten years ago he'd have been a yuppie, Zack thought. Today he was probably a studio suit. "I'm sorry, so sorry," the guy was blubbering. Zack was immediately and inevitably reminded of the governor's "girlie-man" comment. This was, without a shadow of a doubt, a girlie-man.

"So you fucking should be. You know this is coming out of your pocket, right?"

"Yeah..." The girlie-man brightened. "Yeah, hell I can afford it." He looked at Zack's pickup. "That's, what, a '98? If that's what you're still driving I probably earn more in a month than you do in a year." He scribbled a number on the back of a business card. The card was for 'Al Kinsey, Talent Representation And Management'." "Call that number," Kinsey said, "and everything will be fine." He had recovered some of the color in his cheeks, and relaxed.

"It had better," Zack grumbled, digging out his cellular phone from his vest pocket. "You want a tow truck too?

Al Kinsey made a theatrical show of poring over his trashed hood and buckled front wheel. "What do you think?"

Patti flashed her best smile, her driving license and a stamped Freedom of Information Act return. "I was told to come along and pick up this stuff."

The bored clerk looked at the paperwork for all of a second, then checked a list out of her sight in his little cubicle. "Yeah, okay," he said. "I'll just be a minute." With that, he vanished into the mysterious recesses that Patti allowed herself to imagine contained the truth about JFK, autopsy reports on recovered alien bodies, the location of Jimmy Hoffa, and maybe the Ark of the Covenant. Or at least photocopies of all that stuff. The really cool stuff was undoubtedly kept in Washington DC, and never let out to be examined by the eyes of the public.

A minute later, the clerk was back, shoving a thick manila folder through the slot between Patti and himself. She verified that he'd given her the correct documents, thanked him and left the FOIA office. As she was waiting for the elevator back down to street level, a heavily accented voice said, "Vell done, Comrade." Startled, she began to raise a fist as she turned. She needn't have bothered, as the speaker was Will.

"What are you doing here?"

"It's my day off," he reminded her. "I came along hoping I'd catch you in time to do lunch. I know this really neat little place next to Union Station. It's only one stop over on the Metroline."

Patti hugged him. "That sounds great."

Hal Ward was coming out of a DMV office, having renewed the insurance necessary to race professionally, when he caught a glimpse of a familiar face and figure coming out of a post office opposite. "Susan!" he called, causing several people to look round to see what the fuss was all about. He ignored them and darted over a crossing that was conveniently green. "We have to stop meeting like this!"

"Should I worry that you're stalking me?"

"No, you shouldn't worry, even if I stalk you. Or are you stalking me?"

"It's the twenty-first century, man; stalking equality." She laughed. "Where are you headed now?"

"A secure parking lot. I caught the Metro in here. I ain't bringing Machiko into this mess."

"Machiko?" She looked shocked, and startled. Hal wondered if he should read anything into that. Sure, they flirted, but didn't everybody?

"The Ninja," he said.

"Oh, oh, of course. Ninja, right. Were you in at the DMV picking up a marriage license for her?"

"Yeah. You wanna be maid of honor?"

"I'm not a maid, you know."

"That's probably more information than I really needed to know at this time."

"I'm headed for the Metro as well. I guess I might as well walk you there."

"Woof, woof!" Hal rejoiced happily.

The tow trucks had been, hooked the Ferrari and the pickup like particularly gullible bass, and absorbed back into the chaos of the metropolis. Al Kinsey thought the day had sucked so far. First his babe magnet car was gone, he was late for lunch with Bruce Boxleitner, and now he was stuck in the Civic Center with some redneck. All in all, not the most auspicious start to the day.

That said, the day wasn't over yet, and Al knew he could pull some kind of rabbit out of the hat and make good use of the remaining hours. Maybe. He hoped.

First though, he'd have to get where he was going. The redneck seemed to be thinking along those lines as well, as he was looking around, muttering something about Metroline stations.

"South Hill Street's nearest," Al said aloud. "It's just round the corner."

"Cool beans."

The train leaving South Hill Street was already on the platform when Patti and Will passed through the turnstiles. They darted across the platform and squeezed aboard just in time, nearly getting squashed by the doors. Thankfully the train wasn't too full, and there were some seats free. Patti hated standing on public transport; it was cruel and unusual punishment.

She turned to Will, enjoying his eyes and smile, and opened her mouth to say something loving. The words never reached her lips.

There was a flash of light, and Patti felt her whole body jolt, slamming her into a ridged and filthy wall. The numbness that spread from her shoulders cupped the base of her skull and tried to squeeze her teeth and tongue out of her head.

Distantly, Patti heard moans and whistles, which grew into screams. Despite the howls of agony, she could somehow also hear, with shocking clarity, the tinkle and tapping of broken glass hitting the floor, just like in the movies.

She tried to step away from the filthy wall, and found that she couldn't. She turned her head, and realized that the wall was the floor of the carriage. Patti was laying facedown amongst smoldering cigarette butts and gum stains, smeared by her own blood. She couldn't tell how much she was bleeding, or where from, but she could smell it amidst the acrid smoke in the air, and taste it with a tongue that felt too large for her mouth.

Patti vaguely remembered to wiggle her toes, to prove to herself that her spine hadn't snapped like a matchstick. They wiggled, but her arms and legs still refused to obey her will to move and get up. She could only turn her head, to catch a glimpse of Vin Diesel, looking impassively down at her. Jesus, was she in a movie or something? She didn't remember being on a soundstage.

She couldn't remember when she last took a breath either.

Her vision swam, and she felt hot. Then she realized that the star looking down on her was merely gazing out from a poster advertising his new movie. It was on the wall of a Metro station, except the wall was scarred and pitted, and lit in an unusual pink and orange light. Or maybe it was red.

Patti slumped back down, trying to draw breath, but receiving only a searing pain in her lungs, that made her cry and want to scream out loud. She couldn't even do that, as she had no air to force out to make the sound. She could feel the hairs on her arms and her head begin to sting and shrivel. Her head pounded and screamed though only she could hear it. Her lungs screamed without letting out a sound. And, as the fires that tinted the Vin Diesel poster reached her, Patti–

Screamed.

Will jumped, white-faced.

"Jesus fucking Christ!" a suited, spectacled man exclaimed behind her.

Patti gasped for air, drinking in deep wracking breaths. To her surprise and relief, they didn't hurt a bit. She was leaning on a handrail on the stairwell down to the South Hill Street Metroline station. Will was looking shaken but concerned, and glancing nervously at the other people around who were all staring at her.

Patti felt the urge to crawl away into a hole and die. She didn't know any of these people, but she could be pretty sure that they all now had her noted as a complete kook. What the hell had just happened to her? Some kind of fit? Epilepsy? Bad shit at Matt Lawson's birthday party at the weekend?

"You okay?" Will asked.

"I think so," she lied.

"What happened?" He sounded terrified for her rather than by her, she hoped.

"I don't know. I was just—" Where? In a subway carriage, she realized. A trashed subway carriage. "I thought I was somewhere else."

"If we don't hurry, we're not going to be anywhere else. Not in time, anyway." He made no move to go on, instead putting his hands on her arms. "You up to it? Or do you need to go up for some air?"

She shook her head. She had to be either at home or the office in twenty minutes if she was to get her notes typed up by close of business. The office was closer. "I'm okay." She took a couple of deep breaths, trying to control her *chi*, and grinned at him. "Come on." She continued down the stairs, trying not to let her nerves show. She wasn't usually nervous about anything, but having your brain misfire so spectacularly was pretty unusual. Having it do so in public was nothing short of cringe-making.

There was a short queue at the turnstiles, and a couple of people looked back as they heard her footsteps. Their expressions were hurtful: "Oh, shit," they said wordlessly. "It's that psycho bitch." The people seemed to hurry a little more, as if to get away from her before she could infect them with her imagination.

She looked at Will, who gave her a supportive glance, then turned her attention back to the turnstile, ready to go through. A train was already pulling in at the platform beyond. That was a piece of good luck, as she hated waiting on the platforms. Then Vin Diesel caught her attention, out of the corner of her eye. He was looking across the platform out of a poster for his new movie. For an instant, Patti's breath caught in her throat. The momentary choking reminded her of smoke and heat, and blood sticking her cheek to the scarred floor. Patti froze, shaking, her hand halfway to the token slot on the turnstile.

A Vin Diesel poster. Heat. Blood. Bomb, her brain finally told her; it was a bomb. No, it will be a bomb. Worse, it is a bomb.

"What's up, Patti?" Will was asking. "You okay?"

"We can't," she said.

"What?"

"We can't go through."

"Come on, lady," a stocky middle-aged man in jeans and a Wrangler shirt was saying. "We ain't got all day."

"No," Patti said, more forcefully. "Don't go. There's–" How was she supposed to say this without sounding crazy? Who cared? If it saved lives, there was nothing wrong with looking crazy. "There's a bomb. A bomb on the train."

Will looked at her as if she had suddenly grown a spare head.

"Screw you, lady," a bespectacled man with spiky hair and a lightweight suit cried. He started to step around her, but Patti dodged, stretching out an arm to block his way. "No!" she snapped. "You'll die."

"You'll fucking die if you don't get out of my way," the man snarled. He tried to push past her, but she held him back. She knew what was going to happen. It had to be knowledge, not just a fear or a hallucination; she wasn't crazy.

Patti hoped she wasn't crazy, anyway. Then again, if she was just crazy then everyone was safe, so she let herself hope that she was crazy after all. The spiky-haired man raised a hand to slap her aside, but Will caught his wrist. "You raise your hand to a woman again," he said, "and I'll snap it off." He let go of the guy's wrist. Spiky-hair's response was to sidestep Will and throw a wild punch, but the man possessed more anger than agility. Will blocked the punch easily, and sank his fist into the bridge of the punk's nose.

"No!" Patti yelled, pulling Will back with a hand on his shoulder. "If he needs hurting I'll do it myself, all right?"

"He didn't have to hurt you," Will protested. He reached out a hand to the spiky-haired man, who was pressing a handkerchief to his nose. Dark red was spreading through the cloth, and Patti found herself horrified and thrilled by it. "Look, man," Will said. "I don't mean anything by that. I just didn't want you to hurt my girl, that's all."

"And we just want to catch our train," a muscular bespectacled black guy said. He looked and sounded more puzzled than angry. He sighed, looking beyond the turnstiles. "Too late."

Patti turned. A couple of cops were marching towards the turnstile with curious expressions, and, behind them, the Metro train was pulling away. She let out a long breath and felt the energy drain from her body. "It's okay. We're okay now."

The two cops had reached the turnstile. They hadn't drawn their guns.

"Someone want to tell me what's going on here?" one asked.

Spiky-hair snorted blood. "This nut job–" he nodded to Patti, "says there's a bomb on the train, and then her boyfriend assaulted me." His eyes lit up with what Patti would have sworn were large as life dollar signs. "And I want to press charges, and sue for compensation."

The prick, she thought.

"A bomb?" the cop echoed. He looked uncertainly at Patti.

Patti didn't need to answer the question for him.

With an ear-splitting crack, light flashed out of the Metro tunnel into which the train had just departed. The floor shook worse than in a five-pointer, and a blast of scorching air, as solid as a wall of shotgun pellets, smashed across the platform, slamming Patti to the floor. When her cheek connected with the cement, the last thing she felt was the bomb going off in the centre of her skull.

THREE

It is in an explosion's nature to burst outwards, expanding outwards in a sphere from the source of the detonation. In a confined space, the expansion is curtailed, and reflected back inwards. The pressure and blast wave can be doubled, or even multiplied many times over.

PETN is a commercial and military explosive that burns at 27,500 feet per second. A dozen pounds of it in the third carriage of the Metro train leaving South Hill Street station vaporized into plasma in a fraction of a second, burning through steel, aluminum, plastic and flesh like a blowtorch turned on Styrofoam.

The pressure wave of heated and displaced air smashed along the aisle at supersonic speed, ripping seats and people from their places. The blast burst through carriage windows and walls, and jackknifed the carriage. The carriage in front was blown off its rear wheels, forcing into the front carriage and derailing both.

Hot gases and debris bloomed from the third carriage, and hit the interior of the tunnel. The heat, flame, and shredded metal reflected back, ricocheting back into the train. Screaming, burning bodies thrashed as they were shaken around the carriages like dice in a tin cup.

It was as if the passengers were the wadding in a cannon's barrel, simultaneously scorched by fire, and pummeled by the sheer force of the blast. Less than a second later, their burnt and aching bodies were smashed and pierced by steel and glass shrapnel from the ruptured carriages.

Jim Castle smiled at his wife across the table, and kissed the finger that wore her wedding band. He was in his early thirties, with a scholarly face and clear blue eyes that seemed too friendly to go with the military buzz cut of his hair. He was in good shape, with a swimmer's broad shoulders, and wore tan slacks and a pale blue shirt. The shirt's top button was open and the knot of his tie loose. A lightweight leather blazer was draped over the back of the chair he sat in. "How goes the suit?"

Lauren gave a lopsided smile. "Ludicrous, as usual. The plaintiff doesn't have a hope in hell of winning his case."

"But you're going to represent him anyway." It wasn't a question; Jim and Lauren had been married long enough to know what the other thought and felt.

"Somebody has to, and it might as well be me." She grinned. "It pays the bills, and it's not like I'm getting rapists and murderers put back on the street."

Jim shivered at the thought. "How those shysters can..." He cut himself off. It was an old conversation, and no longer either funny or even passionate. If he had been that upset by her legal career he'd probably never have fallen in love with her, or got married.

"Be grateful," she teased. "This place is my treat from my ill-gotten gains."

"Then here's to nuisance suits." They both raised their glasses and clinked them before sipping. The Pacific Dining Car was a piece of old-style California Dream, as well as one of the finest restaurants in the state. It was dark in a warm and plush way, with leather and brass and all the glamour of the era in which it had been built.

For some reason, it had become a favorite spot for off-duty and retired law enforcement officials. Cops, FBI, whatever—when they hit a certain age they started making monthly trips to the Car for that special night out. Jim Castle was neither retired nor technically off duty, but he couldn't think of a better place to meet his wife for lunch. Lauren was in the middle of a big copyright suit and loved to tell him about the celebrity gossip she was hearing firsthand.

"Now," she said, "do you know what the studio seemed to think today—" She stopped with a sigh as his cell phone started trilling.

He gave her a sheepish look and answered the phone. "Jim Castle here. What's..." He fell silent, feeling every drop of blood drain away from him as Tony Chang quickly told him to get his ass down to Hill Street. The line was dead in ten seconds, but Jim sat a moment longer, staring in disbelief at his phone. "Fuck..."

"What, here? I'm game if you are."

"Ah, no, sorry. It's... I gotta go."

Her expression changed instantly, reacting to his stunned tone. "What's happened?"

"A bombing." He stood. "You'll see it on the news any minute." He put on his jacket and bent to kiss her. "Love you."

As he passed the long bar, he could see the first aerial shots of Hill Street on CNN, with a thick column of smoke growing from the Metroline station entrance like the beanstalk in the old kids' fairy tale.

The world that Patti awoke to was utterly alien. It was warm, and almost pitch-black. Flickers and flashes of some kind of magical energy revealed her to be in a cave of some kind.

The air was thick like soup and tasted so much of chalk and acid that she could barely breathe. When she opened her mouth to suck in a gulp of air, she could feel particles of atmosphere settling on her tongue. Her head literally buzzed, feeling as if every molecule, every brain cell, was vibrating. It made her feel as if she was seeing red, though so far she was mainly still seeing black. She couldn't hear much either. There were vague rumblings and feeble cries that could have been animals or, in such an alien environment, just about anything an SF writer could dream up.

The only time Patti could remember hearing noises like that was on the swim team, gliding underwater and hearing the other girls' exertions through it. Everything sounded as if she were underwater now, which she couldn't be because she was breathing... She didn't know what exactly, but it felt like flour and tasted like barbecue smoke.

She was lying at an angle, on a jagged slope, which, as she pushed her herself up onto shaky legs, she realized was a staircase. A man she didn't know was sitting against a buckled piece of metal, tilting his head very slowly and tenderly, as if he was afraid it might come off at any moment.

Something touched her on the shoulder and she spun round to face a figure with a gray face and hair matted with blood. She stepped back, making a fist to launch at the shambling creature's face. No zombie was going to eat her brain.

A microsecond before her fist went through the figure's face, she recognized it. It wasn't some kind of flesh eating zombie, but Will.

Will was mouthing something, but all Patti could hear was that distant sound of sea life, drowned out by a rushing of water. That's when she realized the sea life sound effects were real sounds, and the rushing was blood in her own head, passing through the inside of her eardrums.

She was deaf, or as near as, damn it. It all came back to her now: South Hill Street Metroline station. The bomb. The blast must have deafened everyone in the station, and what she had thought was weird air was smoke and dust. Patti didn't know why this had happened, or whether there were other bombs, or what sort of damage and casualties there had been. She did know that it surely couldn't be safe in here. If any of the dust and grit that she was breathing in had come from the ceiling, maybe there were cracks up there, and the whole lot might come down.

Patti looked up the ceiling, intermittently lit by harsh blue flashes of arcing electrical current. For the first time she could remember, she found herself wondering just how heavy thirty feet of rock and earth were, let alone the steel and concrete buildings on the street, and all the cars and people. It was far too easy to imagine them all pouring in on top of her, smashing, crushing, impaling–

She snapped her mouth shut, cutting off the slight whimper she had begun to hear. This wasn't the time to be scared. Shocked, yes, but not scared. She looked around for the route to the surface. Get out first and be scared afterwards, she told herself. She kept repeating it silently, like a mantra, even as she pointed to her ear and said–hopefully aloud–that she couldn't hear anything. Will nodded his understanding, and pointed to his own ear and shrugged.

"We have to get out!" she shouted, waving him towards the exit. There was a faint grayish light seeping through the square archway that had admitted them to the station, and she hoped that was a sign that there was still a route to the street. Another figure staggered past, on the way to the street exit. It was the yuppie type that Will had punched. The sight of him prompted Patti to look round for the other people who had been around.

The black guy was rising to his feet, still wearing his now-shattered spectacles. He paused to help up the vaguely familiar-looking girl. Now that she was bruised and covered in smoky dust, Patti found her even harder to place than before. One of the cops was hoisting the other one over his shoulder. The second cop had a bloodied dent in his head and Patti had no idea whether he was alive or not. Either way, she decided it would be best not to distract the cop carrying him, in case he got hostile.

The burly middle-aged guy in the checked shirt was still on the floor, and Patti knelt beside him, to check for a pulse. It was beating, but weak. Normally she'd put him in the recovery position and not risk moving him, but she didn't want to leave the guy here in case there was another bomb, a ceiling collapse, or any of the dozen other things she could think of to go wrong. She called out to Will, who had turned to look at the survivors making for the exit. He didn't seem to hear her, so she picked up a handful of concrete chippings and threw them at him. He turned with a slightly henpecked expression. She beckoned him over and, when he saw what she was doing, he joined her at once.

"Take his legs!" she shouted. Whether or not Will heard her, he understood her gesture and placed his hands under the backs of the guy's knees. Patti snaked her arms around under the man's armpits. Together they heaved him off the floor. Patti briefly wondered whether it might have been wiser to let Will take the torso while she lifted the legs, but she wasn't going to waste time changing things around for physical ease now. Besides, she was in good shape, she worked out more than Will did, so it made more sense this way round.

Hoping that they wouldn't run into the others backed up behind a blocked exit, Patti guided Will up the stairs towards the surface, the muscles in her arms now burning almost as much as her lungs. Her heart began to sink when two figures emerged from the darkness. The way out must be blocked, she thought. They would have to go looking for another exit...

Flashlight beams snapped on, playing across Patti's eyes like a movie alien abduction special effect. The figures resolved themselves into firemen, wearing bulky protective clothing and full-face masks. Patti grinned, and was so relieved that she almost dropped the guy she and Will were carrying. If fire crews had been able to get in, then there was still a way out. The two firemen spoke to Patti in voices that she couldn't have made out even if they weren't muffled by their respirators. They took the unconscious man, and led Patti and Will upwards out of the abyss, and back into the light.

It was raining outside, from a blank gray sky outside that looked as if that artist in charge of coloring in the world's background had quit work early again. Patti supposed that must be why there had been no shafts of beautiful California sun slanting down into the Metroline station to show them the way to safety. Darkness had come in off the ocean during the day, like a shroud being drawn across the face of the city. Something about the shade of it depressed her, even more than the occasional winter rain usually did. Perhaps it was because it was so uniform, and impossible to focus on. It just felt infinite.

Hill Street itself wasn't infinite, but it was cordoned off for a couple of blocks in either direction. Fire trucks and ambulances were parked nose-to-tail on either side of the street, with police cruisers jammed in where they could find a space. News choppers circled slowly overhead. Uniforms were everywhere: the dark blue of the LAPD, paramedic whites, fire crews' protective gear all yellow and orange, with glowing stripes reflecting the lights from the choppers. Civilians were dirty and bedraggled, supported by each other or by rescue workers. Only one was in Patti's mind, and that was Will. She looked around for him, and saw him leaning against the side of a fire truck, throwing up.

Someone sat Patti down on the steel footplate at the back of an ambulance, and cupped a plastic mask over her nose and mouth. Her hearing was beginning to reassert itself, though her head still buzzed from the base of the skull up, as if the top of her neck was a cattle-prod giving the brain some juice. So long as Will was okay though, she didn't mind. That was love, she realised suddenly: the feeling of "better me than him" rather than the other way round.

Dark blues were just rolling out the police line tape when Jim Castle's silver Volkswagen Vanagon rolled onto Hill Street, but sawhorses and diversion signs already sealed off both West 1st and Hill half a block in all three directions from the Metro station. At least the fire department had finished their work, so it was safe enough for the authorities to go down into the station.

Jim waved his ID to be allowed through the cordon, and parked as close as he could to the station. It wasn't very close as the road immediately outside was choked with black and whites, fire trucks and ambulances. Thankfully the cordon would keep the TV trucks out, but a news chopper was hovering overhead like a vulture. Jim gave it the finger, hoping he was in shot so the station would get fined for broadcasting the gesture.

Even in the entranceway of the station, the air was thick with the smell of dust, soot and the dead. Jim descended the steps into an extinguished hell inferno. The walls were pitted with little impact craters from shrapnel, while jagged pieces of broken tiles and plaster crunched underfoot.

Streaks of soot blackened the upper walls and ceiling. The whole place was filled with the choking scent of burnt insulation and heated metal.

Bright temporary arc lights had been set up on short poles in the tunnel, so that the cops, firemen and other law enforcement people could see what or who they were stepping in as they sifted through the wreckage. Everybody was in a uniform of some description. The fire crews were in their safety gear and patrolmen in their dark blues, while everyone else had put on navy blue service windcheaters with either "POLICE," "FBI," or "ATF" in large golden letters on the back.

"Jim!" someone called. It was Tony Chang, a wiry Asian man of Jim's own age, with slightly sad eyes and a wispy goatee. Chang was the senior agent in charge at the LA field office of the ATF.

Chang tossed Jim a spare ATF windcheater. Jim pulled it on over his leather blazer. It made him uncomfortably warm, but he knew he wasn't going to be wearing it long enough to really suffer.

"Thanks," Jim said. "What have we got?"

"A bombing, for sure. Whatever caused the blast was inside the carriage, so that rules out a gas leak in the tunnel or any kind of accident with the train motor."

"Shit." Jim felt his heart sink.

Chang bared his teeth. "No shit, it's shit. McAlman's going ape, and I can't say I blame him."

"Well he's probably worried that he'll get shit canned for not being clairvoyant enough to predict and prevent this one. Worrying about his pension makes him antsy."

Chang grimaced. "Worrying about his pension makes him an annoying prick."

"Yeah, there is that, isn't there? Well, let's see what we can do about salvaging his pension and our eardrums, you know what I'm saying? Come on, there are a couple of cops with an interesting story for us."

Chang led Jim across the rubble-strewn platform and back up to the surface. Grateful to be out of the choking oven, Jim jogged back up to street level, feeling healthier and happier with every step. Chang guided him through the emergency vehicles to a nearby ambulance.

Two wounded uniformed cops were there, one holding an ice pack to his head, the other lying on a gurney with his shirt half off, having his elbow sprayed and strapped by a paramedic. "Officer Russ," Chang said to the one standing. "We'd like a word about what happened."

"I think it was a bomb," the cop said.

"So do we. What do you remember about what happened here?"

"We were checking out a disturbance at the gate. A bunch of people were held up by this girl, who wasn't letting them through. When we asked what was up, she said there was a bomb on the train."

That set off more than enough alarm bells in Jim's head. He wanted to turn his back on these two men and run to an interview room to grill the girl, but he was professional enough to know that he had to stay and get the rest of the cops' statements. Everything had to be done methodically, so as not to miss out any vital piece of information, however small, but it was excruciatingly frustrating to not be able to talk to a possible suspect straight away.

The cop gave him a look that said they knew exactly what he was thinking and sympathized entirely. "And then?"

"Then the whole place went to hell. Whammo! At first I thought it was a quake—the Big One, you know?"

"Did you see anyone suspicious boarding the train, or even waiting at the station earlier?"

"You mean like a towel-head in a robe and vest?" He shook his head. "Nah, just the usual mix of people. But like I said, we were distracted by this..."

"Altercation?"

"Yeah."

"What happened to the people who were arguing? The girl especially."

"They were patched up. A couple of them went to the ER, the rest are off to Parker Center to give statements."

"Under arrest?"

"No way, man."

Jim looked to Chang, who stood with his eyes closed, in thought. After a moment, Chang glanced back at Jim. "Okay, Jim. You go on down to Parker Center. The dark blues should have taken the survivor statements by now... Go through the statements, and if anything looks like it needs a follow-up, you can re-interview whoever."

"Right, sir," Jim said with a nod. He handed the ATF windbreaker back to Chang, and made his way back to the van. It was only a few minutes drive to Parker Center from here, and Jim used the time to think about the girl who had said there was a bomb on the train. Could she have been a conspirator with a conscience, or even a witness of some kind who had sought out a bomber's target to try to save lives? He supposed he'd find out soon enough.

Parker Center had been the symbol and headquarters of the LAPD for decades. It was what One Police Plaza was to New York, or Scotland Yard was to London. By now, survivors and witnesses had been brought back to the LAPD's home for the taking of statements, offering of counseling, and generally keeping an eye on them so that nobody was unavailable if any of the other law enforcement agencies wanted to chat. There were a lot of agencies, so the witnesses could be waiting a long time. They weren't prisoners, though–they had each been put in an interrogation room for privacy, but the doors weren't locked, and the people were allowed to hang out in other public areas of the Center, to sip coffee or watch CNN.

Room Four-Oh-One: Zack Halloran paced irritably. Tigers in cages had nothing on him; they didn't have businesses to run, and office buildings in Van

Nuys to renovate on a deadline. Most tigers in the world also hadn't just been nearly blown to bits by some terrorist somewhere. Zack shuddered to think what might have happened if he had died. For one thing, who the hell else could run the company as well as he could?

Then there were his wife and two kids. The thought of them bereft sobered him, and made him literally weak at the knees. He sat down before he could fall down in a faint, and took a gulp of chilled water from a bottle of Arrowhead one of the cops had brought him. Husbands and fathers were supposed to live long and productive lives, he thought, then leave a good inheritance and choose a worthy successor.

They weren't supposed to go out to file an amendment to an architectural plan and get blown to bits on the Metro.

Anger flashed through him then. Anger at the cowards who had planted the bomb, no doubt to laugh about it from hiding. Anger at the lawmakers and bureaucratic desk jockeys who made him go all the way down from Van Nuys to file the changes, when he should be on site, making sure nobody put a ventilation fan in backwards or something. Anger at the prick in the Ferrari who had fucked up his pick-up and his day, and forced him to be in the damn Metroline station in the first place.

Mostly he was angry at himself for not being careful enough. He knew, intellectually, that there was nothing he could have done to predict what would happen, short of becoming telepathic, or having X-ray vision, but he had always looked out for danger before. It was the first rule of self-defense: watch your surroundings and don't put yourself in a situation that could get dangerous.

Unsure whether to wreck the room or praise the Lord for his survival, he settled for thumping the table with his fist, then sitting down and sobbing.

Room Four-Oh-Two: Al Kinsey was jabbering animatedly into the tiniest and most fragile and expensive cellular that money could buy. This was quite the coolest thing that had ever happened to him. Terrifying, yes, but the fact that he had survived told him he was a real man.

"I don't care," he was saying into the cellular. "This is real, this is happening to me now. CNN and MSNBC are carrying it by now surely? Well I'm in it, Grace. In it up to my balls. Now, you get on the horn to every studio in town and tell them that the story of the Metroline bombing, by an industry pro who was at ground zero, is up for auction." He snapped the phone shut with a flourish, and stretched with his eyes closed. "Al, baby," he muttered. "You have got it made."

Room Four-Oh-Three: Will Sax just wished they'd let Patti and himself talk to each other. He could understand why the didn't—they wanted everybody's stories unaffected by cross-contamination from each other—but that didn't make it any easier to resist the temptation to go through and hug and hold her and tell it would be all right, all in the hope that she would be able to reassure him of exactly the same things. He also wished he had his guitar with him. At least that would take his mind off being in a little gray room in Parker Center.

He could feel the stirrings of musical inspiration in his mind too. Maybe it was because of the type of music he liked, or maybe it was because trauma always seemed to inspire art. People have always sung songs about Death. In days past it was to honor the fallen, or to help the living to prepare to accept the fate of those who went before, or to prepare them for their time.

For most of human history this was the backbone of religion. Religion adopted the songs, and the songs followed the tenets of religion. In recent decades came the rock and roll rebellion, but the songs were still about death. Whether it is Verdi's "Requiem Mass", or the output of your average Goth Metal band, Death was the biggest recording star in the world.

Will was also already dreading his return to work. All the guys, from Flanagan down, would want to know what happened and what it felt like. "It felt like shit" wouldn't be what they were looking for. They'd want heroism and gore, to make them feel that they had someone special in their midst because, like most people, they could then feel special by proxy. Having someone special in the team made *them* special.

Sometimes Will thought the human race didn't deserve to survive much longer. He wasn't entirely sure whether that was some immoral and subconscious lesson that the music he liked was trying to tell him, or whether it was just that he had eyes and ears and knew how to use them.

Room Four-Oh-Five: Hal Ward put his hands palm-down on the table and tried to steady his breathing. He had just gone through some heavy shit–shit that could get into anyone's head and shake a few cobwebs loose–but he was determined to handle it. After all, it wasn't exactly as if he hadn't taken a few vehicular knocks in his time. Hell, he was practically used to it by now.

Still, those had been fender-benders and injuries where he had been in control. There was a big difference between deciding to take a hit because it would help your strategy to win, and just suddenly being down for no reason that you knew of. He flexed his hands as if they were still wrapped around a steering wheel. He was still standing–well, sitting–and that was all that mattered. He would take it, and manage it.

Room Four-Oh-Six: Susan Fries dug her nails into her palms to keep from crying. If anyone was watching her on closed circuit TV, she didn't want them to think she was a scared little girl, even though part of her was. It hadn't been the thought of her own death that had crept into her head and her heart and begun to play upon her emotional keys like a concert pianist. It was the thought of being with daddy again so soon, trying to catch each other out about the tiniest intricacies of different engines.

He had only been in the ground three months, and she hadn't been sure she was quite over what had happened. Now she knew she wasn't. That was one of the reasons she cried. The other would have been even harder to explain. She didn't have a sword in her hand. Not that she literally wanted a sword in her hand, but she had read enough about warrior cultures to know that most of them thought a person only got into Valhalla or wherever if they died honorably in battle, with their sword in their hand.

Susan's swords were her tools at the auto yard. Acetylene torches, grinders, hammers, wrenches... If she had had one of those in her hand, somehow it wouldn't have seemed so bad. Daddy had managed it, still gripping the socket wrench when that jack had collapsed, landing a jeep tire on his head. What happened in the Metroline station was a reminder that death could come from anywhere at any time. She just wanted to be able to see it coming.

Sub-Basement One: Jim Castle pulled into the Parker Center's parking lot and locked up the Vanagon. Although it was the headquarters of the LAPD, he still locked the van and put the immobilizer on the steering wheel.

The survivors from the Metroline bombing who weren't hospitalized were being looked after in a set of interrogation rooms on the fourth floor. Jim took the stairs up, since the Center was busier than usual today on account of the bombing, and there were queues at the elevators. The fourth floor corridor had plain plaster walls and a neutral beige carpet, with a series of open doors on either side. Jim snagged a passing cop and asked which room the girl from Hill Street was in. "Which one?" the cop had asked.

"The one who said there was a bomb on the train."

"Four-Oh-Four."

"Cool." Jim walked along to room Four-Oh-Four, and paused outside. He took a deep breath, and went on in.

Patti Fuller stared at the wall, imagining that she could see through it, down to the people milling around in the streets, flowing around the police cruisers, fire trucks and ambulances like water around rocks and shoals. They would be shocked, angry, curious and hungry for a taste of the day. Patti knew she could see through them too, through the road and the sidewalk, down to the Metro transit tunnels where the exploded train lay.

She had once written a *Borderlands Patrol* article about remote viewing, a secret government program in which people were trained to clairvoyantly "see" things in distant places. It must have felt like this, though Patti knew that what she was seeing in her head was a product of her memory, rather than of clairvoyance.

The only problem was, it was a memory of something that hadn't happened to her. She hadn't been in the carriage when it split. She hadn't been there when the blast shredded commuters like old documents, and cast them across the ruins. Damn, but that was freaky. Patti had heard about false memory syndrome, as the magazine had often brought up the subject when debunking witch hunts for so-called satanic ritual abuse. In far too many cases, the alleged victim's supposed memories turned out to be false memories planted—either by accident or design—by someone else. Any decent stage magician or hypnotist could do it, and people did it to themselves all the time. That was the way memory actually worked; people's memories were kept in little bits and pieces around the brain, and essentially created anew when they were consciously noted.

So where did this memory of something that had yet to happen, and which happened differently, come from? Her self-examination was interrupted by the arrival of a pleasant-looking guy who had "Federal Agent" written all over him in neon. "I was wondering when the Federal government would show up. Which are you? FBI, CIA, DIA, NSA...?"

"ATF. I'm Agent Jim Castle, and I'd just like a word with you Miss... Fuller, isn't it?"

Patricia Fuller, the name she'd given on her statement, nodded. She was striking, Jim thought. Her nose was perhaps a little too hawkish to let her be traditionally beautiful, and her voice a little deep, but she certainly made an impression.

"I always expected to see the inside of a room like this eventually," she said casually. Jim wondered if the strength in her voice was a defiance of fear, to hide her nervousness, or if she was just like that normally. "I didn't think it would be for something like this."

"What did you expect it to be for?"

"You'd know better than me. Research into the JFK and RFK assassinations, whether a jet really hit the Pentagon on 9/11, that photo article on Area 51... I've written about a lot of the things the government doesn't like to see written about."

Jim suppressed an urge to laugh. "Well, I enjoyed Oliver Stone's movie, I've never been to the Pentagon and I like science fiction. So I guess I don't have any objections to any of those."

Patti acquiesced to that with a tilt of the head. "So what did you want to ask me about?"

"You said there was a bomb on the train."

"Well, yeah. And there was, wasn't there?"

Jim pretended to wipe his glasses. "Yes, that's kind of why you're in here, if you follow my meaning. You seem to have had a quite exclusive knowledge of what was about to happen."

"I guess..."

"How did you know about the bomb?"

"I don't know."

Jim wasn't surprised to hear her say that, even though he couldn't quite figure out how it could be true. The strangest thing was that she sounded as if she genuinely believed it. "You don't know how you knew that someone had planted a bomb on a three-carriage Metro train. A bomb that detonated just after you refused to board, and which has killed..." He glanced at his Palm Pilot. "Thirty-eight people. So far." He put the Palm away and grimaced. "Actually, you sound pretty truthful to me, but you can see how this is going to look a little funny on the official statements."

She looked anguished. "Look, Agent Castle... I was just walking down into the station with my boyfriend, when I was—I felt I was—somewhere else. I was in hell. There was fire all around me, and I was being smacked around by flying metal, and cut up by glass. Then I realized I was already on the train, and it was exploding and I was dying. The last thing I saw was a poster for Vin Diesel's new movie. Then I was dead."

"Dead?" Castle looked over the rims of his glasses, eyebrows raised. "You seem to have recovered quite... well."

She forced a smile. "Dead, but then I was back on the steps into the station. We went down towards the turnstiles, and there I saw the same Vin Diesel poster. Somehow I knew that what had happened was really what was going to happen. That if I got on the train, the same thing would be happening all over again, just like it had happened a few minutes earlier, and that I really would die. And this time I wouldn't wake up again, just be walking into the station."

"And that's when you blocked the turnstile, and warned the other passengers?"

"Yeah."

"Why?"

"Well... There was a bomb, man! I mean, I knew, really knew. If you knew something like that, wouldn't you try to stop people getting hurt? If I had planted a bomb, I'd hardly warn people in advance, would I?"

"Actually, the majority of bomb attacks across the world are preceded by some sort of warning. Usually it's to the media, so that they can get there in time to view the carnage and spread the bombers' message. The warning confuses people, makes them nervous and spreads fear and terror." He leaned in with a conspiratorial smile. "That's why they call it terrorism."

The moon was baleful and yellow by the time the Metroline survivors were turned out onto the streets. Nobody wanted to use the Metro, and the network was still closed for forensic examination anyway, so the LAPD called in a bunch of yellow cabs, and it was one of these that took Zack Halloran over to Glendale.

Zack shoved the door open and went into the house, tossing his jacket into a corner with a thud. Then he noticed his wife, Irma, was curled up on the sofa and the kids were nowhere to be seen. That meant they were in bed already, and he hoped he hadn't woken them by crashing in like a furious Grizzly. He closed the door more carefully than he had opened it.

"You saw the news?"

"Yeah." Irma slid over, taking his hand as he sank onto the sofa. "Luckily the kids weren't in. I've managed to keep them off the news channels until they went to bed."

"Not too difficult; God bless cheap cartoon toy ads, huh?"

"Something like that." She grabbed hold of him, wrapping herself around him in a big bear hug. He could feel her shaking. "What's up with you? I'm okay."

She let out a squeak. "I know you're okay, but... But you nearly weren't, right? When I saw the news report I thought you were dead. I thought I'd never see you again, and how the hell was I supposed to explain to the kids in the morning why you never came home...?" Her words broke up into a jumble of sobs and tears. Eventually she gave up trying to make any sense and just held onto him.

Zack held her too, looking at the top of her head. She had a point, he realized. If it hadn't been for that crazy girl at the station, he would have been on that train, and he would have been dead about thirty seconds later. He shivered. Tomorrow, as the movie line had it, was another day.

Depressingly, it was another wet day even in Venice Beach, rain falling from a sky as cold and hard as the iron whose color it shared.

Susan Fries had a pick-up chassis to lengthen at the Dolphin Auto Yard; this involved cutting off the chassis just forward of the rear axle mounts, and patching in a new section. Susan held the cutting torch in one gauntleted hand. She had put a thick leather apron on over her usual clothes, and was wearing a full-face mask as well. The most important thing was the cutting torch, though. It was a tool, and it was, figuratively speaking, her sword.

Ready to do battle, she lowered the mask over her head like a knight's visor, and put blue flame to brushed steel. The flame bit into the metal, sinking easily thought it, and, as the smell of hot steel reached Susan's nose, she found herself biting down on a shriek. It was an odor that she, unusually, had always loved. Whether it had been the engine of her father's truck as it cooled, the scent of the hulks that baked under the sun in her yard, or the tang of a heated pistol that had just unloaded a clip into a paper target at the range. It had always been something that reminded her of her childhood, or love for her work.

She realized she was biting her lip because the odor was no longer friendly and reassuring, but carried with the stench of death on the Metro train. Today it was a smell of charred metal, burnt and blasted, not heated by honest work. She was damned if she'd let it beat her. She had work to do, money to earn and a childhood pleasure to reclaim. Anything else, she thought, would be letting the bastards who planted that bomb beat her.

Once again, the Industry Hills circuit was filled with the deafening roar of two dozen armored muscle cars, and thousands of appreciative fans who wanted to see some good old fashioned vehicular demolition.

In the second car, Hal Ward checked his gear over again, and then yet again. Something felt wrong, and he couldn't put his finger on it. Glad that the crowd couldn't see his sweaty face, he waved weakly as his name was broadcast to the stands.

Immediately, the crowd began cheering, their voices coming off the stands and across the circuit in waves of raw emotion. They shouted, they yelled and they screamed. There were ten thousand voices this time, the attendance raised by the newscasts that a survivor of the Metroline bombing was racing tonight. Ten thousand screaming voices who wanted to hail him as a fallen hero.

The helmet Hal wore was the same as always, but tonight it let through the screams. Ten thousand screams.

The pit crews did double-takes as Hal walked away. By the time he was through the barriers and into the drivers' locker rooms, he was shaking. He took off his helmet and put it on a bench, then sat down beside it. He hung his head in his hands, and wished that either the tears would flow as normal, or they would disappear and leave him alone.

"Are you...? I guess you're not okay," his manager said from the door. His head set, used for passing along instructions to Hal while he was in the race, hung uselessly around his neck. "The bombing?"

"Yeah, Marty." Hal composed himself. "I, uh, I don't think I'm as ready as I thought." The words felt uncomfortable and tasted bad. "I can't race today. It's just too soon."

Marty looked stricken. "Can't race? How much did we put into this round?"

"Too much."

"Yeah, for a guaranteed too-much return on our investment when the best driver in the Sunshine State pulls another victory out of the hat."

Hal winced. He wanted to race, and wanted to win. The money was definitely not the least of the reasons for it either. That said, there were things a man sometimes found he just couldn't do; things that were physically, mentally or even psychologically impossible. There were only two answers to finding yourself in one of those situations: half kill yourself and fail anyway, or recognize the limitation and walk away. "I just need..." Hal hesitated, wondering exactly what it was he did need. Not a doctor, or even peace and quiet. "I need to get over it in my own way. I need to not be reminded of what happened when I'm in the middle of working my magic."

"What? Who reminded you of anything?"

"Everyone, Marty." Hal rose, but didn't unbutton his racing gear. "I'll be good for Saturday at Victorville."

"Will you?" Marty sounded doubtful.

"I will if I don't screw myself up out there tonight." He closed his eyes, rolling his head back to try to work some of the tension out of his neck.

"Trying to come back too soon was a mistake. I'm not going to make it worse by pretending I'm cool with it."

Marty gritted his teeth so hard that Hal could hear it. "Okay," he said at last. "Okay. You need a ride anywhere? Someone to talk to?"

"A ride? No." Hal dangled a set of keys from his gloved hand. "Someone to talk to... I don't know. I got the feeling I'll know when I get where I'm going."

"Home?"

Hal hadn't actually thought about where he had intended to go. All he knew was he had to go away from the circuit and away from the screaming. Home sounded tempting, but somehow it wasn't quite right. It wasn't that he didn't think it would be right to go there, or that he didn't want to, but that it sounded like the wrong answer on a game show. It felt as if something had decided where he would go and hadn't told him yet. "Maybe," he said in the end. "Somewhere that feels like home, anyway."

He started to walk out of the locker room. Marty put a hand on his shoulder to stop him. Their eyes met, and for the first time tonight, Hal saw real sympathy in Marty's eyes. The guy was torn between disappointment and understanding, but understanding looked to be in control right now. Hal grasped Marty's hand tightly. "It's gonna be okay, man. I'm gonna be okay. And thanks."

Marty nodded, first hesitantly, then more with more certainty. "You just make sure you're okay,

Hal. That's what matters most." He slapped Hal's back, his voice firming up. "Go on, get outta here and get fixed up. I'll have an announcement made that you've still recovering from Tuesday's injury."

"Thanks, Marty," Hal said, relief washing over him like a tidal wave. He could almost feel it blasting the sweat out from under the Nomex racing suit.

Keeping away from public view as much as possible, Hal jogged down to the parking lot reserved for racers and circuit employees. Machiko, his Kawasaki Ninja ZX-6R motorcycle was there, a beauty of smooth purple curves and gleaming chrome mechanics. He had bought it with his first championship purse, originally thinking to take up racing bikes as well. Once he picked it up and started riding it, though, he found that the machine was just too beautiful to risk on the track. As a result, it became his personal transport. After all, since he drove for a living, where would be the pleasure in driving around from A to B?

Hal felt free on the freeway. The racing outfit probably looked a bit weird to the drivers of the cars he passed—they probably wondered where the cameras were—but it kept him warm against the airflow as he rode.

The exit for West Hollywood came up sooner than he expected; he could just go home and sleep off whatever was up with him. That was what a sensible guy would do, and Hal liked to think of himself as sensible. Contrary to what people thought of race car drivers, you didn't get far or stay in one piece by being a careless hotshot. You got six months in traction that way.

Hal pulled left, away from the exit lane.

The residential streets of Encino were quiet at this hour. Hal felt a twinge of guilt at the noise of Machiko's engine, but not too much. It was, after all, a loud and pretty much relaxing purr, rather than a raucous and aggressive roar.

Maybe the residents agreed, because no lights came on, and no dogs barked. He slowed, humming around the quiet streets with their neatly-mown lawns. Most houses had garages or driveways, of course, so he could relax enough to not worry about dodging parked cars as he searched for 1307 Woods.

He found the house by recognizing the Dodge Ram on the driveway, and pulled in beside it. He pulled off his helmet and started towards the door. He paused, unsure where to put the helmet, and settled holding it under his arm, like some old English ghost with its head in a cheap comedy. For a moment, he changed his mind, and decided to return home. It would be easy enough. Then he remembered that he must have come here for a reason, even if he wasn't entirely sure what it might be.

He pressed the buzzer.

It took a few minutes before a light came on in the house, and shambling footsteps approached the door from the inside. Susan opened the door, still on its latch chain. "Hi," Hal said, with a muted smile. He couldn't quite bring himself to put on the full cheery performance tonight. Susan took the chain off and opened the door fully. She wore a silk bathrobe and a puzzled frown.

"Hal? I thought you were racing tonight, over in City Of Industry."

"I was. At least, I was supposed to be." He slumped. "I just couldn't. Not so soon after what happened. I mean, I went, I got suited up..." He looked down at himself and smiled ruefully. "Well, that part you can see."

"Yeah." She didn't smile, but her look was understanding. "You'd better come in, it's cold out." Hal stepped into the house gratefully. In his racing gear with its various padded and fireproof layers, he hadn't noticed the chill. Susan, in just her silk robe, was visibly colder, her nipples showing under the material. Inside, he unzipped the top of his collar a bit while Susan made some coffee. By the time she brought it through, her robe had fallen open a little despite the loosely-tied belt. Hal barely even noticed. "What brings you here?" she asked softly.

"I was in the car, waiting for the signal to start the engine. That's when they introduce us, you know." He sipped the coffee. "As soon as my name was announced, the crowd... Well, they started to react."

"Unfriendly?"

"Hell, no! Friendly. Worshipful, almost. It was like being a fucking gladiator or something, in the Colosseum."

"So why did you–?"

"They were screaming, Susan." He realized he was really answering his own internal question, rather than hers. It made him feel better anyway, even if he didn't quite understand it.

"Screaming?"

"Cheering, I guess," he admitted. "Yelling. But it sounded like screaming. It sounded like what the people on the train would have sounded like if they'd had a chance to scream. It sounded like how I hear the train people."

"You too, huh?" Her voice was so soft he almost thought he'd imagined the words. He couldn't help wondering whether she realized she had actually spoken.

"Every time I close my eyes," he said aloud. "Every time I'm alone with the lights out."

She was silent for a minute or two, just looking into his eyes and clearly feeling something akin to what he felt. He could see that much in her eyes, as clearly as if he was looking into a mirror that reflected the viewer's emotions instead of their appearance.

"Maybe you shouldn't be alone when the lights are out."

There was no seduction, no attempt to impress each other, no offer of a heart or desire to win one. There was only the desire to feel life; to have one's own life be reassured and reinforced by the most intimate possible joining of life to life.

Susan held Hal tight, not sure whether it was because she was appalled by how close she had come to being taken from him, or by how close he had come to being caught in the bombing as well.

It didn't really matter which it was. What mattered was that they could both feel each other, both physically and emotionally. The warmth of an embraced lover, their heartbeat against one's chest, and the love that showed itself in how they responded to one another, were just about the most alive things that Susan could imagine.

She had never really liked the use of the f-word in a sexual context, telling whatever man she slept with that she had made love a few times, had sex more than a few, but never fucked. Today she decided that their lovemaking was a big "fuck you" to whatever shitty karma had nearly killed them.

FOUR

The LA headquarters of the Justice Department's Bureau of Alcohol, Tobacco, Firearms and Explosives was at 350 South Figueroa Street. Most people still called it the ATF, forgetting the recently-added Explosives part of their title. It was quite close to the bombed Metroline station—just a few blocks along West First Street.

Jim Castle came in for work feeling harried and looking baggy-eyed. People who knew who he worked for tended to think that it must be like on TV, with agents ever-fresh and raring to go, that vital clue just a phone call or chat with a handy snitch away. If only.

It had already been two days since the South Hill Street Metroline bombing, and there hadn't been what anyone in Southern California's law enforcement community would call a surfeit of useful information.

When Jim made his way up to Suite 800, he found a worn-looking Tony Chang in his office, looking half- asleep. Jim wondered if Tony had even been home to bed since the bombing, or whether, as it looked like, he had been catching quick catnaps in his office. Chang looked up as Jim entered, and his eyes seemed unfocussed, his goatee even more unkempt than usual. "Jim," he said, taking a deep breath. "I wanted to hear your thoughts on the survivors from South Hill Street."

Jim slung his leather blazer onto an old-fashioned hat and coat stand in the corner. "They all seem like regular people, and they all had good reason to be traveling. I doubt any of them were carrying remote detonators anyway. It's all in the report."

"What about the girl?" Chang prompted. "She seemed to know something was up."

"She says she..." Jim wished he could think of a way to put this, that wouldn't sound totally insane. It didn't help that the idea was totally insane. "I dunno, she had a vision. Saw herself dying on the train, and just didn't want to go through with that."

Chang sat back and paused, sipping his coffee. "Had a vision..."

"It sounds crazy, I know, but it–"

"It happens quite often," Chang said. "I guess we call that one a hunch."

"You believe her story?"

"That she had a vision? Not really. That she had a hunch? Pretty much. She's a journalist, right? Half of them have the street smarts of a Rampart dick." Jim laughed. Chang waved a hand. "Besides, there might have been subliminal clues her subconscious mind noticed without her having the context for her conscious mind to put them in. Perhaps there was an odor from the explosive, or an individual on the platform that she once saw on the TV news as a suspect, but doesn't consciously remember."

"And how do we check that out?"

"Trying to force her to remember or to analyze herself would probably just bury any subconscious memories deeper. I'd say give her a couple of days then go round and re-interview her. If there was something she saw or heard that tripped an alarm in her head, it might pop up in the course of things."

Jim nodded; that was exactly his thinking. Then, much as he resisted the idea, the thought of visions slipped back into his head. "And what if she's just clairvoyant?" he suggested lightly.

Chang leaned back in his chair and didn't answer for a long moment. Jim began to wonder if he was going to suggest he sought professional help for even asking. Finally, Chang spoke quietly. "A friend of mine at the NTSB has been attending crash sites for years. One night, I think it was at his brother's birthday party, he told me about how almost all the trains, planes and buses that had crashed on his watch were under-booked. I mean, there were fewer people aboard than on the same route on previous days or weeks. He said he had this theory that there was some kind of survival instinct in mankind, that made more sensitive people not show up for trips that were going to crash and burn."

Jim let that sink in, wondering whether it could be true, and what it meant. "Did he interview the no-shows and find out if any of them had visions about dying in fire on the trip?"

"No, but it makes me think that the Fuller girl is just one of those statistical anomalies that doesn't board a doomed voyage."

Castle didn't know what to say. "That's... freaky."

Chang smiled. "Somebody once said, the universe is not only freakier than we imagine, it's freakier than we *can* imagine."

Susan Fries looked at Machiko. The Kawasaki was indeed a thing of beauty; the curves of it were strangely attractive, in the way another woman might be. "No wonder you don't race her. It'd be like abuse or something."

"Exactly," Hal agreed. They were both standing in Susan's driveway in Encino. Hal was back in his racing gear, and looking a lot more self-conscious in it than he had been last night. Susan thought that was a good thing, as it suggested he had regained control. She hoped she had helped, and felt it had been fun anyway. "I do have a dirt bike as well, actually. That's a Kawasaki too, but not as beautiful."

"And what's her name?"

"She doesn't have one. I never even thought of naming a piece of aluminum and plastic until I saw

Machiko here." He looked down into her eyes, and she felt that they were still joined somehow, in an even deeper and more spiritual way than they had been last night. "I think I'll take the dirt bike out this afternoon, actually. Go out to the edge of the desert and cut up some sand."

"I wouldn't have thought motorbikes were quite the same as being in a good solid car. I mean, the feeling of being inside such a powerful machine, part of it..."

Hal laughed. "Fast cars is one thing," Hal said, "but you're still locked in a box. It makes me feel like an action figure still in its blister pack. On a bike, now... that's a different matter. There's no metal between me and nature. There are just the wide open spaces, the wind in my hair—"

"The bugs in your teeth?" she suggested.

Hal laughed. "Hey, they're protein, right? Why have to stop for lunch?"

In Suite 800 at 350 South Figueroa, all hands were to battle stations. An armored SUV had just delivered a couple of people to the basement garage, and, as far as Jim was concerned, the use of such a vehicle could only mean someone important had flown in from Washington. Tony Chang had called a meeting of all case officers for eleven o'clock in the briefing room. Jim gathered up the summaries of his reports at ten fifty-nine and headed along to the meeting.

Inside, Chang was at the head of a polished table, and a dozen local agents were there too, but it was the presence of the deputy director and a cluster of her immediate staff that made Jim straighten his back a little. The brass was indeed here from DC, which meant it wasn't a time to be casual or familiar, however loose a ship Chang normally ran.

People who had never been in the briefing room always imagined it as some hi-tech lair with lots of black and chrome, and huge LCD screens hanging from the ceiling, all controlled from sinister consoles with low-intensity lit touch screens. In fact it was a simple presentation office. Comfortable work chairs were arrayed around a normal office table, with a couple of desktop PC workstations on them. At one end was an ordinary widescreen TV on a stand, with a VCR and DVD player. An OHP and screen were at the other end, with flipcharts in two of the corners.

Dilbert would be more at home than James Bond would.

Jim took a seat, and glanced nervously at the brass. Something serious must be up to bring them all the way from DC. He checked out the faces of everyone in the room; they all wore looks of the same worry and anxiety that he felt, and none of them gave any sign of knowing what the latest development was. Jim began to have the horrible feeling that perhaps the Metroline bombing was just a teaser, and that something else even worse had happened.

Before anyone could ask any questions, Tony Chang cleared his throat. "Ladies and gentlemen, we have a new development." He held up a silver disk, either a CD or DVD. "The original of this was delivered to Parker Center this morning. Appropriate copies have been sent to the FBI, DEA and so on." With that, he put the disc in the DVD player.

On the TV screen, a black and white image appeared, of a man in combat fatigues and a tac-vest that was as common to hunters and fishermen as it was to military or SWAT personnel. A dark ski-mask hid most of his head, with Ray-Bans hiding his eyes. The monochrome image made it impossible to tell any of the colors in the room, and it occurred to Castle that this might be a deliberate choice on the terrorist's part.

When he spoke, his voice was electronically disguised, of course. The accent sounded heavy.

"Greetings to the United States. The bombing of South Hill Street's Metroline station has, I hope, your attention. Who we are does not matter, so I will not waste your time with a stupid name or set of meaningless acronyms. Suffice it to say that if you do not listen very carefully, this will not be the last you hear from us." He paused, as if enjoying the worried expressions on the faces of an audience he couldn't have seen. "I will be quick, and you can replay this message to your hearts' content. First of all, we wish for the release of prisoners at Guantanamo Bay and Abu Ghraib. You will pull your troops out of Iraq, Saudi Arabia, and Afghanistan. You will persuade the Russians to pull out of Chechnya." He paused again. "You will also deposit one hundred million dollars into the following offshore bank accounts..."

Everyone sat stunned when the clip ended. They weren't surprised, since terrorists pretty much always demanded something, but the nature and scope of the demands were obviously ludicrous. Jim tuned out the discussion that the brass from DC immediately got into with Chang, and replayed the message in his head, perfectly word for word. Something about it just didn't sound right to him, though he couldn't quite place what is was. Chang and the brass were in full flow by now, trying to decide who the terrorists most likely were. What they thought didn't really matter, Jim knew, as there were plenty of intelligence analysts no doubt already looking at the clip and listening to it with all ears, picking up every tiny clue. Computers would join in the fun, processing every pixel and analyzing all the words and the vocal stress levels used in them.

It was human nature to speculate all the same, and sometimes it paid off. Those analysts weren't field men with street-smarts, and the computers didn't have instincts. He tuned back in just in time to hear the deputy director say "The demands are pretty typical, of course."

"Typical?" Chang echoed.

The deputy director nodded, her russet bangs bouncing with the enthusiasm of it. "It's the usual, if we're looking at Islamic Fundamentalism."

Jim sat back, and took off his glasses, examining the rims. "Wait a minute. What was that about a hundred million?"

"All those Stinger missiles and foreign training don't come cheap," Chang said.

"No," Jim said. "They don't... You know, I may be jumping to conclusions, but I don't think we are looking at Islamists here."

"You don't?" The deputy director fixed him with a look that dared him to explain that opinion. Jim was happy to oblige.

"Terrorists with a cause, especially ones with a religious cause, who think God is on their side, don't care about being captured or killed. They do care about their operation being interrupted, so all their efforts at throwing off the authorities are usually directed to that end. If they're caught afterwards, they can use their trial to promote their cause, and if they're killed then they're martyrs and get their seventy-two virgins in heaven, or whatever. This group are different. They've been hiding their forensic track, which means they don't want to get caught."

"So?"

"So... They must know no administration is going to give in to their demands about prisoners and troops, and we sure as hell aren't in charge of the Russians in Chechnya, but they might think we're willing to buy them off."

"With a hundred million dollars?" Chang replied.

Castle nodded. "I think that's their only real demand. A man with a cause doesn't mind being caught or killed, but a man who wants to spend a fat pile of cash... He minds. He doesn't want to get caught, because he wants to live in luxury without working for it."

"Straightforward extortion?"

"Nice and old fashioned. This isn't a political or religious act; it's a bid for a retirement fund."

"In your opinion," the deputy director said archly.

"I think it's an informed one," Chang said to her. "It would be prudent to take any and every possibility into account. I don't think we can take a chance on overlooking any angle. This is a threat we have to neutralize as soon as possible, no matter what." Jim masked his feelings, unexpectedly touched by his boss's confidence.

The deputy director took in a slow breath, her sharp face pinched and doubtful. Then she nodded. "None of us want to overlook an angle." She turned to address Jim directly. "Keep working on your theory; I want a report on my desk by four this afternoon."

"Yes, ma'am," Jim said with a nod.

"All the same, remember the demand for the money only came after the usual Islamist demands. It might have been an afterthought."

"It might be, ma'am, but I really think the other demands are pretty much just a smokescreen, to hide the group's nature. Maybe as a sop to us to make us think we're being tough if we 'talk them down' to just accepting the cash."

"Anything's possible these days," she agreed sadly. "Bring back Al Capone, all is forgiven..."

Chang took the disc out of the DVD. "The guy disguised his own voice, but I'll have it processed to see if there's any background noise that might give us a clue to where that was shot."

The deputy director nodded. "That's about all it's useful for, I guess."

Al Kinsey bounced lightly down the steps from his Hollywood office and tore the inevitable parking ticket from his old BMW's windshield. What were the cops going to do? Shoot him for it? It would go in the glove box with the others and get paid at the end of the quarter as usual. They should be used to that by now.

The BMW was a Z8 and he supposed it was nice enough in its own way, but it wasn't his Ferrari. That would still be in the auto shop for another three or four days. Al knew he should be angry about that, but the thought of getting a movie about his experience off the ground kept him calm. He told his secretary, Grace, that it was a sure thing, because who could turn down such a story from an industry pro? It was obviously his destiny, and a better one than taking ten percent of the fee for some old 1970s TV has-been to "star" in some direct-to-video action trash.

Once out in traffic, his mood dissipated. Where Hollywood should have been a town of sunshine and bright lights, today it was muted and quiet, as if the gray had come down from the clouds and infected everyone in the city with some kind of apathy virus.

He drove over to the offices of a small production company he had made a few deals with. The prodco wasn't exactly a major player in the industry, but they churned out pictures to the video stores with reliable regularity. What more could he ask for? Apart from a major studio deal, that was. Sometimes he sat outside the gates of one of the big players or other, and dreamed of having his own office in there.

Gloria was in her office, looking at the budget figures for an Eric Roberts movie she was bankrolling, and he slumped in a seat across the desk from her. "You busy?"

"Yes," she said, waving the sheets of paper at him.

"Tough, I could use a few minutes together."

Gloria looked uncertainly at the budget figures. "It couldn't wait until you get home tonight?"

"Hey, when I got a need I got a need." He put his feet up on her desk. "What happened to 'love, honor and obey?'"

"That show got cancelled years ago, honey. This is the age of equality, even between spouses."

Al's grin vanished. "Reruns go on forever."

"What do you want anyway? A blowjob? Go to one of your floozies for that."

"Okay," Al said casually, "thanks for the advice. Anyone in particular you'd recommend?" He flashed a cocksure grin again, and saw a dim flicker of amusement in his wife's eyes. He still had it, that was all he needed to know. He couldn't just come and ask for reassurance that he was worth a damn, but he could provoke a situation to find it out.

"You're crazy," she said fondly. "That actress you put in *Dimension Hunters 2*; she sucked. If she still does, you're in hog heaven."

He put on an expression to imply that he was thinking about it, and then let out a vaguely dismissive "Nah." He canted an eyebrow at her. "I've got a better idea, okay. Picture this; a vivacious young movie producer working for a courageous indie prodco. She's no pushover, but when the passion hots up so does she, for the right man..."

"You sound like a trailer, but it sounds like a good movie. I should be home by eight, okay?"

"I'll have dinner ready," he promised.

Patti was poised on the balls of her feet, practicing side-kicks at a heavy bag hanging from the roof of her small patio. A portable stereo blasted out suitable exercise music, namely a demo CD that Will and his friends had put together to storm the halls of the music industry with. So far their storm had been little more than a light breeze.

Outside the patio, a light shower fell. The sky was watery today, and the rain dripped like the sweat Patti was working up on the bag. Thankfully it didn't smell like it. She unconsciously wrinkled her nose at the thought, surprised at her own icky thought.

Will's frantic guitar solo came on, and that brought out the joy in Patti. He was her ideal man, and this was her ideal way to relax. What could be cooler and healthier than a good cardio workout to the sound of a band that had least had real hopes and dreams, even if they didn't have the contacts or the industry savvy.

Will himself was playing air-guitar along to his own track, and volunteering the occasional "Ouch, that's gotta hurt" when she landed a particularly hard hit to the bag. Normally she wouldn't go quite so all out on the bag, but, hey, a girl could show off a tad for her other half, couldn't she? Besides, she knew that watching her was as big a turn on for Will as the workout was for her. After what had happened to them anything that was bright vibrant life was the way to go.

Eventually Will stopped her assault on the bag by putting a hand on her shoulder. "Easy, Patti, you're gonna bust that thing."

"Allow a girl some ambitions," she said, wrapping her arms around him. She kissed him. "Let's live a little."

"You took the words right out of my pants." He peeled his shirt off, and began attacking the buckle on his belt. At which point, someone rang the doorbell. Will let his head slump against the heavy punchbag. "Tell whoever that is to fuck off, will you?"

"Oh yeah," she agreed. Whoever had such a monumentally bad sense of timing had made a big mistake by indulging in it while she was still jazzed up from the workout. She felt like Bruce Lee, ready to kick ass across the city, if she had been the sort of person who thought that kicking ass could ever solve anything.

It was the ATF guy, Castle, flashing a badge. He took her state in at a glance, from bare feet reddened by impacts with the bag, up her sweat pants, to the damp halter top. Then he shrugged it all off, and said, "May I come in?"

"Uh, sure," Patti said. She let Jim in, and called out to Will. "It's the ATF guy." Will came into the living room, through the sliding glass door from the patio, pulling his shirt back on.

"Anything we can help you with?" Will asked, not managing to cover his hostility.

"I just wondered if you—either of you—had remembered anything more that you didn't tell us down at Parker Center." Patti could hear the lie in the "either of you" but let it slide for now. The only thing she really wondered was whether he wanted to see her because she was suspect, or because he was hot for her. She didn't really like either option, but would have preferred to be a suspect. The guy was good looking, but Will was love incarnate.

"Why would we?" Will asked belligerently. "We told you all we know—"

Jim made a placating gesture with his hands. "I don't think otherwise. It's just the way the human mind works; sometimes something traumatic gets buried to protect a person, and only kind of slips out later. We just wondered whether anything like that—"

"No," Will said firmly.

"I'm sorry, but he's right," Patti told Jim. If you're thinking we saw, like, a bomber or a remote control in somebody's hand... no. I don't remember anything that I didn't remember at Parker Center."

He sighed. "That's what I thought, but I had to ask. You understand, right?"

"I guess so," Jim sighed. "Sorry to bother you." He stood. "I'd better be going; I've got the rest of the witnesses to visit as well. Same question." He went to the door, and Will opened it for him. "See you around."

Hal Ward's Kawasaki KDX 200 kicked up a trail of dust as he sped along the empty desert floor not too far from Victorville. Out here, he had managed to escape the rain, and bask in the rusty and pink warmth of baking dust and stone.

This off-road bike was the complete antithesis of the cars he drove on the demolition circuit. It was lightweight despite its steel frame, and the 220cc engine was tweaked in such a way as to give the machine the performance of a 250cc bike. All of which meant it would stick to the desert trail he was blazing, jumping small creeks and the occasional Gila monster with ease. He loved the desert, probably because it was so different to the Maine coast where he had grown up. Even if it rained in LA, it was never depressingly cold and damp in the desert.

Hal had no interest in taking up motocross or stunt biking as a sport, but, as he had told Susan, this was the best stress-busting thrill ride there was. No time to beat, no opponents to get past... It was just the open skies, the colorful desert, and the massive horsepower to control between your legs. It was what being a man was all about, and Hal's good times were indeed rolling. Hell, they were rolling, sliding, jumping and doing the Superman on the long leaps.

For the first time since he took a breath from soot and bomb smoke at South Hill Street, he felt himself again. Susan had helped a great deal, but being back in control of a sports machine with no limits had finally brought him home from whatever emotional and mental shelter part of him had been hiding in.

The day was bright and hot, especially in protective leathers, but the brisk flow of air over and around him kept him cool and refreshed. He felt more awake and together than he had in a week.

Suddenly, the desert floor ahead quivered. For an instant, the scrub and rock wavered, as if the earth was out of focus, the way a person's vision went when his eye watered to dislodge a piece of grit. Then the ground simply broke, a long crack appearing in front of Hal's scrambler. He stopped in time, his eyes fixed on the black crevasse that snaked along before him. It was only a couple of inches wide and deep, but it might have thrown him if he had hit it unexpectedly. It had already stopped moving before he did, but wisps of dust were still hanging in the air above it.

The trembling that Hal felt when he put his foot down had also stopped now. Staying where he was, he dug his Walkman from his pack, and took off his helmet to put the little speakers in his ears. A local radio station was in the midst of mentioning the tremor, the announcer saying it had barely registered on the scale.

Hal was relieved, having half-thought that he had imagined it, or that it was the trauma from the bombing mounting a counterattack on his well-being, and put the Walkman away. Then he looked round, and felt something cold ascend his spine. The small crack in the earth was only one of several to either side of him. Four of the others were about the same size, and all five seemed to be branching off from a wider crack, perhaps a foot across and at least half as deep.

Four of the cracks curved around him from one side, and one from the other. The widest crack stretched away into the distance. Together, they looked like someone had taken a big stick and drawn the scraggly image of a hand in the dirt; a hand that was holding him in its grip, between four fingers on one side, and the thumb on the other.

He told himself that the image they put in his head should be funny, and deserved a photo submitted to a magazine like the *Borderlands Patrol*, but he didn't feel like laughing. He felt like curling into a ball and hiding, and he didn't know why. Instead, he got back on the bike and started off again. The rocks and scrub around him blurred pleasingly, and he was pleasantly surprised to find a track down into a creek bed. The walls of the old creek, which probably hadn't seen water since the dinosaurs died out, rose about six to eight feet on either side of him. He decided to follow this natural path, as it was pointing towards the old Route 66, and from there he could head home, or, better still, call on Susan again.

The curved and smooth walls of the former creek became a blur on either side, and he ceased to consciously decide how to control his mount. "Use the Force," he chuckled to himself, as he let instinct borne of long experience guide him. Something nagged at him despite his pleasure. A shadow was flickering over the pink wall to one side, as if a bird was flying low overhead. He looked up, but saw nothing. When his eyes returned to the creek bed, he was startled to see a sinuous coil of darkness leaping up towards him.

Even as his brain screamed "diamondback" to him, he was sliding and tumbling, losing control of the Kawasaki. It slid into a rock, and he bounced in the dust of the creek bed, blasting a cloud of fine powder into the air. He coughed, and pushed his visor up, hoping that he would see better without it. He looked around for the diamondback rattler, hoping he hadn't landed on top of the bastard. He didn't even know where to put his hands, for fear of offering the dark serpent a tasty snack.

As the dust cleared, Hal still couldn't see any sign of a snake. A Joshua tree was perched on the lip of the creek above him, its roots half out of the wall, exposed to the air in the creek bed. These were old and thoroughly desiccated, and he realized that one of these, sticking out a couple of feet above the creek bed, was the "leaping snake" had seen.

Hal caught his breath, which was ragged at first, and forced himself to calm down. He waggled his fingers and toes, to be sure that his arms, legs, or spine were broken. Then he patted himself down, but found no sign of injury. He started to remount the bike, and found that he couldn't lift his right leg off the ground.

Some of the other roots of the Joshua tree, as dry and pale as old bone were wrapped around his foot and ankle. He tried to pull free of what looked like brittle wood, but the desiccated wooden digits held as fast as a bear trap. He cursed under his breath, and grabbed the wood with both hands and tried to snap it free. Despite its brittle appearance, the wood refused to bend or break. It was like trying to bend a steel bar.

Hal cursed again, and tried to pull himself free by wiggling his foot around in search of an angle that would allow it out. His foot had got in there, so there surely ought to be a way for it to move in the reverse direction.

If there was, he couldn't find it. Disgusted with his luck, Hal threw up his arms and sat back against the creek wall. At least, he thought, things couldn't get any worse.

There was a rumble from somewhere then, vibrating up his legs from the ground. It didn't feel like the earth tremor from earlier though, but more like a convoy of eighteen-wheelers was passing by somewhere close. Maybe he was closer to the road then he thought. If so, he might be able to attract attention. The thought buoyed him for a few seconds, until the true nature of his vibration presented itself.

Hal's eyes widened, though this didn't make the sight before him any easier to accept. A wall of water, twelve-feet high, was hurtling down the canyon towards him.

The water struck Hal with the speed and force of a Greyhound bus, smashing him into the reddish rock. His shin bone wouldn't bend ninety degrees to allow his body to be knocked down while his ankle was still held by the tree roots, so it snapped cleanly instead. The pain barely registered, as the impacts all over his body conspired to smother the single point of agony. Finally, the tree-root itself tore away, releasing Hal at last. The current was already pushing both Hal and his bike along, tumbling into each other with massive force. Hal couldn't tell how deep the water was; only that he hurt everywhere, and that he had to try to get his head above water. That or drown.

His arms thrashed, trying to get a grip on the canyon walls, but when he managed to do so, the tumbling bike thudded into his back and knocked him free again. Trying to dig his feet into the creek bed only caused an explosion of pure white-hot pain in his broken shin, and he fell again.

Water was rushing into his helmet, and he was swallowing some, while more flowed down his nostrils. He kept trying, forcing himself to ignore the pain long enough to get his head about the surface, but his leg wouldn't support him, and the helmet he wore was growing heavy. Belatedly, it occurred to him to try to remove the helmet, but he couldn't stay upright long enough to get his hands on it. When he tried, he tumbled again, swallowing more water... Water was rushing down his nose and throat, and he tried to keep breathing, but his lungs were too heavy and too hot, and his shattered leg wouldn't let him fight his way free of it.

Five miles down the creek, the water subsided enough to leave man and motorbike alone on the shore.

FIVE

Susan opened up the Dolphin Auto Yard office and put on the coffee machine in the corner. She didn't feel like going out into the yard proper yet, but today the scent of warm metal in the wind wasn't as distressing as it had been before the weekend. The sense of discomfort it brought, and the memories it teased out of her head weren't gone yet, but those things were diminishing.

No, not diminishing, she corrected herself. Being assimilated and overcome. They were still there, but she was feeling more up to dealing with them, rather than letting them deal with her. That was good enough for her.

The alterations to the pick-up chassis still needed doing, and today she was able to carve up the steel like a Thanksgiving turkey. Molten droplets had rained into the earth at her feet, like the golden tears of angels, weeping for the lost souls of the city which bore their name. They had turned almost instantaneously to black when they touched the ground, as if the earth had poisoned them.

With the original chassis cut into pieces, she could go and dig out the pieces of steel that would be slotted in between them to lengthen the wheelbase, but that could wait till tomorrow. Tonight she had a date.

She didn't usually wear jewelry, in case it caught on some piece of engineering or scrap metal, but today she felt like wearing something. A symbol of her survival and her commitment to staying alive. She had scrubbed up to get the oil and grease off her hands, and changed into tight leather pants and boots with a pearlescent top. Now that she was off duty from the yard, she was wearing the only piece of jewelry Hal, or anyone else, had ever seen on her: a bracelet in the shape of two dolphins, hinged where their tails met. He had given it to her for her birthday last year. They hadn't been together then, nor had even thought of being together, but they were friends. He was a regular customer, she a trusted supplier. It was a small token of appreciation for a professional relationship, but today it felt like something else entirely.

There was a small group of people standing vigil outside the North Hollywood home of Hal Ward when Jim Castle pulled into the neighborhood. At first he didn't think anything of it; the guy was a sports celebrity and he must have fans of one kind or another.

Then he saw the little wreaths being laid, and the photographs with a strip of black satin across the corner. As the automobile stopped, he could hear sobbing and the murmur of voices talking with melancholic softness. Jim didn't like the look of this at all.

He got out of the car and went over to the nearest man. "Excuse me," he said, "but isn't that Hal Ward's house?"

"It was," the man said.

Zack Halloran was happy this morning. The sun was playing a stealth game, peeking out from behind wisps of angelic cloud, and then hiding again. He didn't mind the white clouds, as they didn't threaten rain, and no rain meant a good working day on the site of the new home of Red Salmon Software.

The building was a twenty story honeycomb of smooth stone and concrete, half-shrouded in scaffolding and the veils of tarpaulin that kept birds out of the working area and the dust in. Thankfully the elevators were already operational, having been fixed up from the dilapidated condition that the previous owners had gotten them into. Enjoying the sight of work—who was that had said he loved work, and could watch it all day? WC Fields, probably. It sounded like his kind of thing—Zack rode up in the nearest one, and found the roof to be a cluttered construction site, as it damn well should be, he reflected with satisfaction.

Cement mixers churned, while carpenters hammered, and electricians threaded wiring through the air conditioning units. A few small cranes were set up near the edge of the roof on all four sides. They weren't lifting stuff up, but lowering pieces of marble facing, and sheets of window glass, down to the upper levels of the building. There, dusty and sweating workers toiled to pull these items inwards, and set them into place.

Zack moved over to help out with the crew of one hoist, who seemed to be having trouble with their cables. The cable was well-oiled, with a sheen that almost slithered clean away. Zack's cellular rang, and he answered it cheerfully. It was Irma, calling to see if he'd be home at the usual time today. "I have a pot roast," she explained. "I need to know when it'll be needed for."

Zack glanced at his watch, and felt a sudden chill. Something dark and shadowy crept past, but when he turned, it was just a cloud passing over the sun and casting a shadow over this part of the roof. "I'll be home around eight, okay?"

"Okay. I love you."

"I love you," Zack said in return, because he did. Most men would say it anyway, to their wives or girlfriends, but Zack didn't believe in using the L-word when it wasn't true. He had said it what felt like millions of times to Irma, but had meant every single one of them.

He put the cellular away, and returned to helping tense the cable on the shadowed hoist.

* * *

Jim Castle made it to the Highway Patrol headquarters in record time, and ran in like a man looking to stop a countdown. He collared the nearest patrolman and demanded to know who had found Hal Ward, where, and when. The patrolman sent him to a sergeant's office near the motor pool.

The sergeant was in his shirt-sleeves, working on a dusty cruiser. "Hi," Jim began. "Jim Castle, ATF."

"Pleased to meet you." The sergeant stuck out an oil-stained hand and pumped Jim's hand vigorously. "What can I do you for?"

"Hal Ward."

The sergeant's expression sobered. "Yeah, poor guy. I won on every one of his races."

"What happened?"

"A family heading back from Laughlin spotted a dirt bike lying near the roadside out by the old sixty-six. They called it in and we found him in the creek."

"He took a fall?"

"He drowned. Flash flood. The weight of his helmet must have dragged his head down."

"He drowned? In the Mojave?"

"Happens more often than you'd think," the sergeant said. "It don't rain worth a bead of a rattler's sweat on the ground there, but it does rain on the mountains. And it snows on the mountaintops. When that rain flows, or snow melts, the water has to go somewhere, and that somewhere is down creek beds. Maybe a dozen people a year drown that way. Folks who don't know any better think a dry creek bed is the best place to camp in the desert, then sometime in the middle of the night, when they're tucked in nice and tight, the melt water that came off the mountaintop that afternoon finally reaches the desert floor and..." He finished off with a sweeping motion of the hand. "Wash out. People who respect the desert know better than to go into creek beds, however dried out they might look."

Jim drove more slowly west. The next name on his list for re-canvassing was a girl, Susan Fries, who ran an auto yard out in Venice Beach. He took the freeway over there, whiling away the time with a CD by The Vipers.

Susan was just backing her Dodge Ram out of the yard gates when Jim got there. He tried to put the disturbing news of Hal Ward's death out of his mind, and a professional smile on his face. "Excuse me," he called out to Susan. "Agent Castle, ATF. You might remember we spoke the other day, at Parker Center?"

"I remember," she said chirpily. "What's up?"

"Oh, nothing much. This is just a routine follow-up. Sometimes things that people see get buried in their memory and take some time to come out, so we like to come back after a few days just to see whether anything else has come into the conscious memory."

Susan smiled, strapping a yellow and red surfboard to the Dodge. "Right... I'm sorry, I can't think of anything that's come upon me."

"No suspicious characters, unusual electrical equipment..."

"No, there was nothing like that. It was just a normal day with normal people. Well, apart from that crazy woman that Will Sax is seeing now."

"You know Will?"

"Knew. Dated him for three years back in high school. Does that have any relevance?"

"No, it doesn't, sorry. Okay, I guess I'm sorry to bother you. You have a nice day and great evening, okay?"

"Will do," she said as she climbed into the Dodge. "I have a date with Hal Ward." Jim froze, and his face must have betrayed his twisting gut, as she paused. "Are you alright?"

"Yeah... Um," He wondered whether he should even bring this up, but decided that he could think of worse ways she could learn about what happened. "Hal... You haven't heard?"

She went white. "Heard what?"

At work, Will was relieved to see the customers start to thin out as the afternoon wore on. He had already been startled too many times by people asking his advice on speakers or HDTVs, when he had zoned out. Normally he was all right with the public, but today—since the bombing, actually—he found that he just wasn't in a people mood. People were something he would have to ease back into dealing with, a little bit at a time.

He took a moment to visit the water cooler. His throat was dry and he hoped it was just tiredness rather than some kind of virus. Flu was the last thing he needed these days. Either way, the tickle at the back of his throat wasn't so much an irritant as a disturbing reminder of the dust and soot that filled the air back in the Metroline station.

Sometimes he wondered if he would ever be free of that tickle, but he didn't want to worry Patti with it. He heard a soccer ball behind him, and steeled himself to face the public again.

"Will? It's Susan... Susan Fries."

He turned, shocked, and recognized her, barely. She was still as curvaceous as she had ever been, and wore the same style of clothes, but the rings around her eyes made her look as if she had aged about four years for every calendar year that had actually passed since they broke up. Will didn't know whether to laugh or cry. "I don't believe it! Susan?" She grabbed him and hugged him. "It is you! This is amazing..." He trailed off when he realized she was sobbing into his collar.

"I saw you at the Metroline station," she said, snuffling. "I was about to say hi, and introduce Hal, when... when it happened."

"Damn, I thought you looked familiar, but you had your back to me– What is it? What's up?"

"It's Hal..."

"Hal Ward?" Will slapped his forehead. "That's who that guy was! I thought I recognized him. He's the demolition derby guy, right?" Will grinned, thinking about knowing someone who knew a guy who trashed cars for a living, legally. "That is so cool—"

"Will," Susan snapped, and this time he heard the strain in her voice. Not just strain, but anguish too. He wasn't sure what exactly Susan wanted tonight, but he suddenly knew it wasn't going to be something pleasant. Susan's eyes brimmed with tears. "He's dead, Will."

"Dead? I didn't think he was that badly hurt. It was just a scratch—"

"It wasn't the bombing. He was out dirt-biking in the desert yesterday, and... Well, I don't know exactly what happened, but he was in a dry creek bed and there was some kind of flash-flood."

"Flood? You mean he got caught in it?"

She nodded. "He drowned. Oh, Will, I think I'd just fallen in love with him, and he's gone... He's gone."

Will held her, and shushed her. If Flanagan saw this, he could be fired on the spot. He waved to his nearest team member. "Shaun, tell Flanagan I'm taking a personal, okay? I've got to deal with this..."

"Is she someone from the bombing?"

"Yeah."

"Okay," Shaun promised.

"Good man." Will swiftly guided Susan out of the shop, trying to wrap his head around what was going on. Patti would be better able to handle this, he thought. A woman knows a woman, maybe. He led the distraught Susan out to the parking lot, and called for a cab on his cellular. One arrived in only a couple of minutes, and he directed the driver to Patti's house.

The last thing Patti expected to see while trying to edit the article on the TR3 airplane project was the man she loved ushering the first girl *he* had loved in through the front door. It never crossed Patti's mind to demand to know what he was doing, as she had noticed immediately that she was in tears.

"Trouble?" she asked.

"Sort of. You've met Susan a couple of times, haven't you?"

"Yeah... She was at Hill Street too, wasn't she?" Patti had thought the other woman familiar at the time, but didn't recognize her, being too intent on the vision that had warned her.

"Her boyfriend was there too. The black guy with the glasses. He died yesterday."

"From the bombing?"

"Flash flood in a creek bed."

"Jesus," Patti said. "The poor bastard. I mean, surviving the bombing, and then this... It's the sort of think the *Borderlands Patrol* would love." She meant it too, and part of her both wanted and expected to see the story told there. She knew that if she was quick, she could be the one to tell it, but found that she didn't really want to be quick.

Cops and doctors, and sometimes journalists too, had rules about personal involvement and the conflicts of interest that could arise. Patti didn't feel particularly conflicted, but she knew that she wouldn't feel comfortable turning in the story either. It would just be too damned incestuous for its–or her–own good. Let Pete handle it, he'd get the right mix of astonishment and respect.

It was getting near sunset, and Zack still hadn't had lunch yet. Rather than send somebody for take-out, he volunteered to go himself. God knows, he wasn't paying these people enough to ensure their loyalty, so camaraderie would have to do the job instead.

He rode the elevator down to street level, and strolled out towards where his pickup was parked. He'd be gone and back within ten minutes. It was darker than he expected on the edge of the site, and he looked upwards to see if more storm clouds had come in. El Fucking Nino had a lot to answer for. There were dark clouds in sight, but they were low and localized, like the little black cloud that rains on a character in a cartoon when he's depressed. Zack got his mind back on the job in hand, trying to remember the workers' orders.

He had only gone a few steps when he heard a strange popping sound and a yell from somewhere above him. He paused in mid-step, looking up. There was a hoist sticking out from the roof of the building, thirty stories up, but he couldn't see anything wrong with it. It wasn't holding anything anyway.

There was a faint flicker in the air, somewhere between the hoist and himself. He frowned, puzzled, trying to figure out what it might be. He was still standing there gawping and wondering, when the sheet of glass hit him in the forehead.

Falling too fast to see, it had remained vertical, and hit him edge-on. It sliced clean through his body in an instant: through the skull, between the hemispheres of the brain, down the throat, ripping through the right ventricle of his heart, down through stomach and intestine to emerge from his groin and hit the sidewalk.

The two halves of Zack hadn't even begun to topple when the glass edge cracked against the ground, and the whole pane shattered. It sprang apart in a spray of tiny razor edged fragments, peppering the bisected man. Blood and tiny gobbets of meat splashed across the street, mixed with the glass in a silver and red seasoning that dusted the halves where they had fallen.

The whole thing took less than a second, and it was several stunned moments longer before someone on the street began to scream.

Susan screamed when Patti turned on the news. There had been some kind of construction accident up in Van Nuys, and a man had been killed. Apparently the casualty was one Zack Halloran, according to the news anchor. His next of kin–a wife and two kids–had been informed.

Although the news anchor on the scene was stating there was only one casualty, two body bags were being carried to the ambulance behind her. Will frowned as the story changed to something about a court case between celebrities. "Zack Halloran? I know that name..."

"He was at the Metroline station with us," Patti said softly. "He was one of the ones my vision saved. Like Hal Ward."

Jim Castle dragged himself out of his car and up to the office. None of the witnesses had remembered anything new, and one was dead. What a fucking day, he thought. Needing a boost, he snagged himself a coffee from the machine on the corner, but immediately had to put it down as a printout began streaming from the fax machine on his desk. It was the analysis of the explosive used in the Metro bombing, sent over from the Bureau's Chemical Analysis facility. Since the lab was in the business of testing explosives and other dangerous chemical agents, it was hosted off-site in case of accidents. Tony Chang noticed his dash for the fax, and followed. "The bomb analysis? Please tell me it's something we can work with."

Jim nodded, holding up a sheet of paper. "PETN with a Torpex booster. Commercial, not military."

"Traceable?"

"Well, there are several suppliers to the demolition and construction trades in California alone. Maybe a hundred nationwide."

"A hundred? Jeez."

Chang tilted his head, half shrugging. "Could be worse. Checking them all's a big job, but it's not a needle in a haystack kind of job. This kind of stuff can only be sold to qualified and carded pros, so we'll be checking out who bought every ounce in the country."

Jim hated to look on the negative side, but it was pretty much his job. "Could it be stolen?"

Change shrugged. "Anything's possible. We're checking back to see if any supplier or manufacturers have reported any explosives going AWOL this year."

"Oh," Chang held out an *LA Times*. "Did you see this?"

Jim took the paper. "No, but I know what happened. I went to visit him today and found out."

"Nice of the CHP to let us in on this. Witness to a major federal case with every agency on the books needing to talk to him, and they don't think it worth mentioning that he dies." Chang said. "Less than a week gone and he's dead. Poor bastard; Fate has a funny sense of humor."

Jim looked at the picture on the front page, and shuddered. Even being blown to bits in the bombing would surely have been better than this? "How does the line from the poem go? 'This is the way the world ends...' Most people don't give a shit how–or even if–the world ends. They only care about how they themselves, personally, end."

"With a bang or a whimper?"

"Yeah."

Chang paused a moment in his report reading, and looked over his nose at Jim. "This is a morbid train of thought you're on, Jim."

"Can you blame me?"

"Law enforcement jobs of any kind are ones where a man comes face to face with all manner of reminders of his mortality." He hesitated. "Was it the bombing scene? It was pretty overwhelming for anyone—"

"I don't need on the job counseling if that's what you're suggesting. I just... I just find it weird that two survivors of the bombing have been killed in freak accidents within a matter of days."

"Ah." Chang pushed the report away from him. "It makes you wonder what's the point, huh? What sort of sick fate is it to be spared one violent death, just to meet another so soon?"

"That's about the size of it, Tony. You feel that way too?"

"Nope. It makes me wonder whether one or more of these people weren't specific targets of the terrorists. It makes me wonder if those sick fucks are now finishing off the job the bomb didn't. And it makes me wonder whether keeping an eye on that little group might not lead the terrorists to us."

"You're thinking of using them as bait?"

"I'm thinking of exploiting a flaw in the terrorists' planning, Jim. I'm thinking of making the best of a bad situation."

SIX

Patti screamed as fire roiled around inside the carriage, kissing her with pain. The carriage itself dissolved into a storm of shrapnel in which metal, plastic, Naugahyde and glass were bouncing around too fast to see, cutting and slashing at her. It was like being inside the barrel of a shotgun when a load of double-ought buck-shot was fired.

Suddenly, that's just where Patti was, raising her hands in an ineffectual attempt to shield her eyes against the oncoming blizzard of metal.

Then she sat bolt upright, shaking, gasping for breath in the warm darkness of her own bed. There were no screams or shots, just the distant rumble and whoosh of traffic from the 405 a couple of blocks over. Will slumbered next to her. Lucky him, he was sleeping like a baby.

She stumbled into the shower to wash off the cold sweat, and the stink of fear that had ridden it out. It had been a bizarre night. The sun that had been unseen behind a gray veil all day faded, the cloud turning faintly pink. The sky looked like undercooked and badly preserved meat, and Patti didn't like it any more than she had in the morning. Together, she and Will had managed to calm Susan. Will was good at that. Watching him comfort her, Patti felt a warmth about him; his ability to look after a woman in distress was a rare thing in her experience, and was a major part of why she loved him. The fact that this girl was an ex of his didn't matter; there was no law that you had to stop loving someone because they didn't love you back. There was no law that said you could only feel love for one person at a time. Any such law would imply people could pick and choose who to love, and when, and how. There were enough different kinds of love to go round.

They had called Susan's brother to go and sit at the house in Encino, and then Patti had driven her home. When she had returned, Will was curled up on the couch, looking into space. "I'm sorry," he said. "But she's still a friend–"

"Will, there's having love for, and love of, and being in love with. I know you still have love for Susan, and there's no shame in that. But I also know you have love for me, and I can feel your love of me radiating like the sun, and I know you're as in love with me as I'm in love with you."

He blushed. "I know, I know... But most people wouldn't think that way. Most people would think 'Uh-oh, conflict of interests, possible ménage-a-trois...'" He blushed brighter at the last, and Patti could practically read his fantasy like a book.

"Don't sweat it, honey," she said. "You did the right thing. You did the only thing you could have done."

He nodded, but still wasn't convinced. He'd be saying more than a few Hail Mary's after his next confession, she thought. They had gone to bed then, and held each other until they fell asleep.

Patti briefly wondered how the others who hadn't boarded the train were doing. Did they dream their deaths every night? She doubted it. None of them had experienced it the way she had. It might have been just a warning in her head, but it was as real as anything else she had ever experienced. Sitting her SATs, losing her virginity, having breakfast yesterday morning, dying in a bombed metro train. They were all the same, all as real as each other.

She turned the shower off. Screw nightmares, she thought. Letting them rule her life was a victory for whoever had put that bomb on the train, and she wasn't in a mood to give them the satisfaction, even if they never knew about it.

Patti stepped out of the shower again. The noise of it still hadn't woken Will, lucky bastard that he was. She was half tempted to deliberately wake him up just for the company, or even to prove that he could be wakened. She didn't do it, though. He looked too handsome and peaceful to disturb like that.

Instead, she went through to the little living room where she kept the PC and laptop, and switched on the former. If she was going to be awake in the middle of the night she might as well make some use of it. the *Borderlands Patrol* could always use another article or review, and something about being up at night got her creative juices flowing.

The bombing made her think as well, or the nightmare recurrence of it a few minutes ago did. Somebody had planted that bomb, and they no doubt had demands or threats to make. She wondered who they were, and how they operated. Did they target people or places? Did they target anything specific or was it all just down to random luck?

Maybe there was a *Borderlands Patrol* piece in that, she thought. They had covered the likes of the Oklahoma City bombing, though that was before her time on the magazine, and the attack on the Twin Towers, so why not the LA Metroline attack? Terrorist attacks and paper-selling conspiracy headlines went together like any of the things in Sammy Cahn's "Love and Marriage" song. Where there was terrorism on American soil, there was also, at least in the fears of the general public, corruption and/or incompetence to be exposed.

Now fully awake, she began to type notes, spooling off her thoughts as they tripped blithely into her forebrain. She would pitch this to Matt in the morning.

Will rose with the sun, and shuffled naked into the living room, bearing orange juice and coffee. "You're working already?"

"I was thinking about conspiracies, actually."

He blinked. "What, JFK? That kind of thing?"

"The terrorists who planted the bomb. How did they get here without being caught? How are they keeping out of sight?"

"Hey, Patti, you ain't going all Michael Moore on me are you?"

"'Course not!" She shifted slightly, rubbing up against him. "Well, maybe just a bit."

"A bit?"

"A tiny bit."

"I dunno Patti," Matt Lawson said. "It doesn't sound very, well, borderland to me." She held his gaze, daring him to go further. "I mean, it's good thoughts, but more a *Sixty Minutes* kind of thing, isn't it?" They were standing next to the water cooler in the *Borderlands Patrol*'s offices, next to some framed examples of the past year's cover artworks.

"Oh, come on, what about 9/11 then? That wasn't exactly a supernatural UFO occurrence, but we've ran a lot of pieces on it."

"True..."

"Conspiracies by their nature contain the possibility to uncover hidden truths and connections to things that we might not expect. They're all about the unexpected."

Lawson chewed on his lower lip, visibly torn between two reactions. "Okay," he said at last. "Start working it up as a fallback piece. If any of the scheduled features falls through, we'll put yours in its place."

"Thanks, Matt," Patti said. It was as good as a yes; in this business something always fell through and had to be replaced. He returned to his office, and Patti took a cup of water from the cooler, draining it in front of the framed cover art. Her mouth suddenly felt dry, despite the water, as her eyes fell upon the cover for last December's issue.

She looked at the cover, and then darted back to her desk. She rarely used it, preferring to work at home and telecommute, but she spent a few hours a week there when it was really necessary.

"December... December..." She rooted through her desk drawers. There was an archive room further down the corridor, which contained every issue published since the magazine was founded in 1973, for the use of writers who might need to refer back to something in a previous issue. December was recent enough that a copy should still be floating around in the office.

She found one, not in her own drawer, but in Pete Cochrane's. She wondered what he had wanted it for. The answer to that question was staring her in the face, on a yellow legal pad on the desk.

What Pete had in mind was utterly insane. It was crazy, and it was scary, and it gave Patti a feeling she hadn't had since the bombing. In fact it gave Patti the exact same feeling that her vision had given her. She knew at once that she had to tell Will. Hell, she had to tell all the remaining survivors, but she would start with Will. They had been together for three years, and he knew her better than anyone. He would be her litmus test for belief.

She took her Saturn over to Circuit City in Northridge, and virtually abducted him from the store as soon as it was his lunch break. He got in the car and she took him home. "Patti, what's eating you?"

"I was thinking about the wrong thing last night. The terrorists, I mean. I was looking in completely the wrong direction, and had no idea."

"The wrong direction from what?" He looked into her eyes, tilting his head as if trying to see the loose screws in her brain.

"Did you know that Pete Cochrane is doing a story on us?"

"On you and me?"

"On the six of us who survived the bombing."

"Eight," Will corrected her. "There were two cops, remember?"

"Transit cops on the station. They weren't going to board the train. Only the six of us were going to board, but didn't because of me. You, me, Susan, Hal, Zack Halloran and some Hollywood agent called Al Kinsey."

"So?"

"So... Something happened a few months ago, right here in SoCal. A rock club collapsed, and a number of the survivors all died in the space of a couple of weeks, from accidents."

"So?"

"So, Pete Cochrane seems to think the same thing is happening to us."

"He said that?"

"Well, no, not actually. He... He's working on a piece about Hal Ward. He's brought Zack Halloran into it as well, and tied his death into it. *Borderlands Patrol* readers love stories about synchronicity. Coincidences and weird patterns–"

"Like two bombing survivors getting killed in the same week?"

"Bingo. Remember The Vipers?"

"Yeah. They were pretty good."

Patti threw a file on the table. "The Vipers. Jess Golden on lead guitar. She had a vision on stage at a gig about a year ago, that the building would collapse. She tried to tell the audience to get out, but was thrown out by security herself. Then the building did collapse. The weird thing is, of the people who got thrown out because of Golden, several died in spectacular freak accidents over the following week or so."

Will looked pale and shocked. "Coincidence..." He broke off as she tossed another file of clippings on the table. Will looked at it. There was a picture of a Marine Corps unit grinning against a desert background.

"Afghanistan, three years ago. Eight Marines miraculously survived a chopper crash after their gunny had, he says, a vision of what was about to happen. They were all rotated home immediately and within a month they were all dead."

"Soldiers get killed."

"They were on leave back here in the States. All the deaths were written off as accidental: a hit and run, a kitchen fire, a boating accident..." Another file hit the table. "Australia, 1996. Five surfers would have drowned when a freak wave hit, but for one of them warning the others away at the last minute because he'd fallen asleep and had a dream of disaster. All five die in 'accidents' over the following two weeks."

Slap on the table. Another file. "Japan, 1994, seven medical students abandon their yacht minutes before a faulty gas stove blows and sinks it. Four of them die in freak accidents within the week." File. Slap. "Ontario, 1991. Six people in a camper van stop at the end of a bridge that then collapses when they'd be halfway along. The driver tells a TV reporter he just saw it happen before it actually did happen. He and four others from the van are killed in accidents before the month is out."

Will sat in silence, running a hand through his hair. Patti hadn't seen him do that since went for the job interview at Circuit City. "So maybe those people were just unlucky. I mean, not all of them get killed, right? You keep saying 'six guys, and four get killed' or whatever. What about the ones that survive?"

"They seem to disappear. The Vipers' guitarist, Jess Golden? I tried to get a hold of her, pick her brains for some ideas on what this shit is all about. She's gone."

"Gone?"

"No one who knew her has heard from her in over six months. It's like she dropped off the face of the Earth."

"Just like Richie from Manic Street Preachers."

"The three Japanese medical students, the last guy from the Canadian camper van... All gone without a trace."

Will shivered. "Could they be dead too?"

"They could, but there's no mention of any bodies being found, and all the deaths were pretty public."

"Then they're... hiding?"

"That would be my guess. The question is, hiding from what?"

"Or who?"

Patti breathed in and out slowly. "Hiding from what," she repeated. "The Vipers didn't worry about terrorists. Neither did the Japanese students. I think Pete is on to something with this. There are just too many cases."

"This can't be happening with the survivors of every accident in the world."

"No, it can't. There has to be some other connection between them." She looked at the files again. She had been doing so for hours without result, while waiting for Will. Now, however, perhaps buoyed by the presence of the most special person in her world, things were different. The words blurred in front of her eyes, until only the few common repetitions would stick in her brain: "accident," "miraculous escape," "killed," "dream," "vision." Over and over they tumbled through her head, until she thought that she'd be dreaming them when she finally felt able to go to bed.

Something flashed in her head, the closest she had ever experienced to a cartoon light bulb blazing with an idea. She might dream about the word. Dream. Have dreams, see visions...

She started sifting through the files and cuttings, locking on to those words with more accuracy than any guided missile could have. She would find them at a glance, and toss the file aside to look at the next one, and always with the same result.

In every case, in every file, someone had foreseen a disaster, either in a waking vision, or in a dream. Just like Patti's own vision of hell aboard the Metro train. She looked at Will. "Precognition."

"What?"

"Forewarning, Will! In every case, the people who survived the original disaster survived because one of their number had some kind of forewarning in a dream, or a vision."

"So how come Kreskin isn't Public Enemy Number One?"

"I'm serious, Will. We have to tell the others about this."

His face darkened. "We can't do that; they'll laugh in our faces. Except Susan, who'll probably have a nervous breakdown."

It was frustrating, but he was probably right. At the same time, Patti thought, she had saved them once against their skepticism, so she could do it again. At least, she hoped she could do it again. "What about that ATF guy?"

"You want to spend the rest of your life in a funny farm?"

"He seemed open-minded."

"Hey, who's the conspiriologist here? That's what they want you to think!"

She shivered at the thought of how dumb an idea she had just had. "Yeah, point."

"Maybe it's not all bad," Will went on. "Even if this stuff is true, some of them must have survived. Not in every group, but in some of them, somebody must have figured out what was going on, and how to stop it."

"Then they disappear?" She frowned. "Witness protection? I mean, if someone's coming after you, maybe it's some sort of cult that wants to finish off accident survivors. You know, like those religious fruit-loops that won't allow treatment of their own sick kids. Maybe somebody thinks dodging your fate deserves a fatwa on you or something."

Will had leaned forward to leaf through the papers in the file. Some of them were old and yellowed. "Patti, how far back do these files go?"

Patti hesitated. "I'm not sure. They're not in order..." She started to shuffle through them, and he joined her. "1968," she said at one point. "1965... 1959... 1957..."

"Jesus fucking Christ," Will suddenly whispered, pale. He held a file out to her, eyes wide.

"Check this out. It must be old–it has fucking drawings, not photos."

Patti took it from him. It was a photocopy of a creased old newspaper, the *London Times*, no less. The front page was indeed adorned with a pen and ink portrait of a man in some kind of uniform. Above him, a headline read "Unsolved Murders Baffle Chief Constable."

Halfway down, on the right hand side, was a small column headed "Vision saves Spiritualists from Blast."

"How old is that?" Will asked, awestruck.

Patti looked for the date under the elaborate banner, and nearly choked. The dateline read "15 October 1888."

Will took it back. "Survivors of the Mornington Crescent disaster," he read, skimming it. "Bill Sangster... Matthew Upton... Juliet Collins... Dr Stewart Tubbs..."

"Hang on," Patti interrupted. "Back up. Did you say Juliet Collins?"

"Yeah."

"Juliet Collins..." Patti murmured. "Weird."

"What's weird? It's a just a name."

"Grandma's maiden name was Collins, and she came over to the US from England in the Thirties. And her grandmother was called Juliet. My dad did the whole 'family tree' thing back when I was a kid. That is too spooky for words." She forced a nervous laugh.

Will swallowed. "More than spooky. It says here she was eighteen. Daughter of the Reverend–"

"Gilbert Collins," Patti whispered.
"Gilbert," Will confirmed.
"Oh shit," they said together.

SEVEN

Winter had come early to London, or so Juliet Collins felt. There hadn't been snow or ice yet, but it was cold for October and the mist that drifted through the streets on a breeze made it feel colder and damper than ever.

The mist was light, not yet the billowing clouds of what Charles Dickens had twenty years earlier christened a "London Particular," but there was smell of coal tar in it, falling from the factories and workhouses in Lambeth, on the southern side of the Thames.

Juliet emerged onto Golden Square from the terraced house. For all that the upstairs windows were dark, the curtains closed like the eyelids of a slumbering giant, she could feel her father's disapproval burning into her back. She closed the door as quietly as she could.

She descended the few steps to the roadside, and started off in a south-easterly direction. Although the sky was darkening behind the clouds, the buildings themselves cast the deepest shadows across the road.

The street was quiet, with only a few people around. Gas workers were lighting the lamps for the night. Boys pushed carts with milk, cheese and eggs, or called at side doors with loaves still steaming where the snow landed on them.

The cold made the smells richer, whether it was the welcoming warm smell of bread fresh from the oven, or the alkaline stink of manure and horse urine that still hadn't been cleared.

Rather than take Gibraltar Street, which was already busy with omnibuses and delivery carts, down to Piccadilly, Juliet kept to the residential streets. High stone buildings lined either side of the cobbled roads, and narrow ginnels and alleyways edged between them like deep crevasses. The snow abutting against walls and buildings was still pale and smooth, not yet tainted by the holes that would appear as the day wore on, where men stopped to urinate in the street.

She was pleased with her neat escape. Her father would have fallen into his customary after-dinner slumber, and her mother would be busy supervising the servants as they laundered clothes for the family. Neither of them would come looking for their daughter, whom they no doubt presumed to be reading by gaslight in her bedroom.

Juliet had nothing against reading, but to read about something was not to experience it for oneself, and how could one learn without experiencing? Juliet wasn't stupid, of course; she had no desire to experience the life of a lady of the night in the East End, or the life of a chimney sweep, or a drayman... She did, however, very much desire to experience more of life than church and Sunday school, even though she enjoyed those things as well.

She had first discovered tonight's adventure in print, of course. *The Strand Magazine* had run an article recently on the latest scientific fad from North America; that of spiritualistic mediums. It seemed pretty far fetched to Juliet, this idea that people could somehow speak to the dead, to ghosts, and give their living relatives advice and counsel from the next life, but the article said that the high societies in New York and Boston swore by it. She had been surprised to read that the whole thing had been started off by two girls no older than herself, named Fox. That had only slightly piqued Juliet's interest, and she might never have thought any more about it, save for the reaction her father had to the article.

A man of great passion and single-mindedness, Gilbert Collins, vicar of the church at the end of their street, had torn the pages bodily from the magazine and thrown them into the fire, proclaiming that such nonsense was an offence against both God and reason.

Naturally, Juliet was hooked from then on. She simply had to learn more about this spiritualistic fashion, no matter what. Thankfully not everyone took the same view as the Reverend Collins, and Juliet had persuaded the cook to talk about her experiences with the new science, if science it was. Nobody seemed quite sure whether it was a new science or a new religion. Juliet was fascinated still further.

The cook had told Juliet that she herself had attended several séances, and been given messages from "The Other Side" –and Juliet could hear the capitalization in the cook's awe-struck tones–from her late lamented husband, who had died of smallpox a few years previously. Apparently the unfortunate man was enjoying himself immensely in heaven, though the cook foreswore that he had shown no interest in such heavenly pursuits as music and philosophy when he was alive. The cook didn't seem to think that such a transformation was suspicious, saying that closeness to God and Jesus Christ had probably turned her Neville away from the cock-fighting and the whisky.

Juliet had agreed politely, as a young lady should, and, in return for the friendly ear, the cook agreed to recommend a medium should Juliet wish. Juliet wished very much, and the cook said she would have a cab meet Juliet at the end of the road on Tuesday night, to take her to a terraced house where Madame Adrienne conducted the best séances in London.

So, here Juliet was, waiting at the end of the road for a Hansom cab. She didn't have to wait long before two horses pulled a carriage to a halt in front of her. She looked up at the cabbie. "Four, Mornington Crescent, please," she said, and climbed in before he could step down to assist her. Once she was settled in the seat, the cabbie set the horses in motion.

The journey was perhaps fifteen minutes long, and quite uneventful. The cab was not heated, of course, and Juliet was more than glad of her winter coat, muffler, gloves and hat.

When the cab stopped, the driver jumped down to help Juliet step down onto the ground. Juliet looked around. The Crescent was a nice set of Regency terraced houses, and only the narrowest of lights peeked out from between curtains in the large windows. Juliet moved toward the nearest house, squinting to see if the door had a number four on it, as that was the house of Madame Adrienne.

Nearby, some workmen were throwing their tools into the back of a cart, while others secured the ropes and chains on some steam-driven cranes and pulleys that rimmed a deep black pit.

The stench that rose up from the pit suggested that they had perhaps managed to penetrate some level of Hades itself, though Juliet supposed it was more likely just the sewers. As she paid off the cabbie, she pointed to the pit. "Are they working on the sewers again?"

The cabbie looked, squinting. "Nah, Miss. It's this new underground railway. The first four stations have been so successful that they're building new ones all over the Smoke." He sniffed, and spat.

"That can't be good news for you," Juliet said perceptively.

"Well, it'll take years for people to get used to 'em, but I can't see as how my boy will follow in his old dad's footsteps."

"Perhaps they will have underground cabs too?" she suggested. She didn't believe it, but felt that she ought to offer the man some words of hope.

He chuckled. "Drawn by pit ponies, mayhap, eh?" She tipped him handsomely for his courtesy in helping her down from the carriage. He touched his cap-brim in return.

Juliet was alone now, but in a well-lit and safe area. She had no need to fear the killer whom the newspapers had been printing scare stories about lately, who stalked Whitechapel over in the East End.

In the distance, Big Ben chimed eight bells, the sound carrying further than usual in the thick fog. Though clear, the bells sounded softer yet more drawn out. It reminded Juliet of the old quotation, "Ask not for whom the bell tolls. It tolls for thee."

Suddenly less excited by the prospect of the new experience than just keen to get off the sinister street, Juliet darted up the steps of the terraced house which she had now identified as number four.

A pretty little maid, younger than Juliet, answered the door when Juliet rang the bell. "Yes, ma'am," the maid said.

"Is this number four? I'm looking for Madame Adrienne," she explained.

The maid smiled. "This is Madame Adrienne's home, yes, ma'am. Will you come in?" Juliet nodded and, thrilled, entered the house. The maid took her hat and coat, glover and muffler, leaving Juliet in a well-cut tweed jacket and appropriate skirt. The maid then led Juliet upstairs and into an ante-room where several people were helping themselves to little triangular sandwiches and cups of tea. "Madame Adrienne will be along in a few minutes," the maid promised. "In the meantime, please help yourself to refreshments."

"Thank you." The maid disappeared through a door, and Juliet nervously approached the others. They were quite a mixture of ages and genders, and she circulated to effect introductions to each, just as her mother had always taught her.

Bill Sangster was a young-looking man with an angular jaw, wide cheekbones and a narrow mouth. His hair was not cut short enough to disguise the natural sweeping waves in it.

Though he almost had a local accent, Juliet could discern a hint of a more northern tone in voice. Manchester, she was almost sure. He had obviously been born and bred in one place, and assimilated part of an accent elsewhere, but Juliet couldn't tell whether he was a Londoner who had spent time in Manchester, or a Mancunian who had gone native in London. He didn't strike Juliet as the sort of person who would be interested in the occult, and she said as much.

"I'm neither interested nor disinterested," he admitted. "It's the social thing I like. This bit before the séance, when I can catch up on all the gossip that's not fit to print. I mean, it's not as if Her Majesty is going to invite me to one of her garden parties."

"Oh," Juliet said. "I see."

He paused and looked her up and down, then waggled a finger. "Let me guess," Sangster said. "Your parents still treat you like you're six years old."

"Something like that. Six, not eighteen."

"Ah, so this is by way of your first steps into a wider world? Well done, Miss Collins." He sniffed and nodded towards a man of vast bulk, which stretched out in front of him like the slope of a gentle hill. For all that he wore the coat and cravat of a gentlemen, his beard was a tangled mat, and a smell like a wet dog in wrapping paper hung around him. "Master Matthew Upton," Bill said. "Writes for some newspaper down Grubb Street. Over there, at the sherry already, is Hector Barnes. He's a professor of Egyptology. Probably wants to talk to some great pharaoh or other." Barnes wore a tweed suit that was as gray as his hair and moustache. It made him look positively dusty, in Juliet's opinion.

"The woman with him is Mrs Stanley; you probably know her."

"Sir Norman's wife?" She was bright and freckled, with auburn hair and an overly showy frill to her blouse.

"That's the one. The boy with them is Andrew Caine. Next big thing in Egyptology, they say."

"Who says?"

"Hector, Mrs Stanley and himself, mainly. Finally, the young buck over trying to get into the séance room early is Mister Stewart Tubbs."

Stewart Tubbs was still a young man, in his early twenties, but Juliet could see that he was one of those people who wished to seem older, jealous of the deference that Upton and Barnes were accorded simply because they had seen more summers than he had. Tubbs turned from the door whose handle he had been impatiently rattling. "I prefer to be addressed as Doctor Tubbs. It is a title and mark of respect that I worked hard to earn, and I do not appreciate being referred to by the same pronoun as a lesser man who has not worked so hard."

"I'm sorry, I didn't know that you were a doctor."

"I have a practice in Bermondsey, as it happens."

"Keep practicing," Bill suggested, "and maybe you'll get it right."

Juliet was shocked. "How rude," she said. "Shame on you, Mister Sangster."

Bill merely grinned. "No doctor under thirty 'has' a practice of their own. He'll be the junior tonic-salesman, hoping to bootlick his way up to a real medical job."

The conversation fell silent then, as a maid—a different one, who seemed to be half-caste—opened a door and said "Madame Adrienne will see you now." At her words, another woman walked in. She was perhaps in her mid-forties, but still utterly striking, and wore a silken gown that accentuated the fact that her hips and breasts were as full as could be.

Adrienne had hair as pale as her skin, large eyes that still held a trace of wonder at the world, and an elaborate coiffure that looked like a tall nest of serpents.

"Thank you," she said to the maid. "Ah, I see we have a new face among our regulars." She nodded to Juliet. "Miss....?"

"Juliet Collins."

"Oh, the Reverend Collins' daughter? Your cook recommended me, I imagine."

"That's right."

Adrienne chuckled. "Well then, we must endeavor to make sure that you do not report back to her any disappointments." She turned then, and unlocked the double doors that Tubbs had been fiddling with a few moments earlier. She went through, followed by the others.

The room was dim, illuminated only by candlelight rather than gas mantles. Thick drapes hid the windows, another layer of drapes inside matching the upholstery of the chairs. The chairs themselves were arrayed evenly around a polished mahogany table. "Please be seated," Adrienne said.

Juliet found herself seated between Bill and Tubbs. "Would you all please hold the hands of the people on either side of you?" This they did, Bill's strong grip in her right hand, and Tubbs's clammy paw in her left.

Suddenly, the room was filled with light, from all around. The shadows of the people sat round the table crisscrossed sharply, dancing as the brightness of the light shifted and flickered.

Juliet was frozen to the spot, unable to comprehend what she was seeing. Only when the thick cords of ectoplasm emerging from Adrienne's mouth and nose began to burn did she realize the light was a wall of fire.

Then Juliet screamed, as she felt the heat climb up her back, and her hair began to shrivel. The others were all screaming too, as they burned in their chairs. They thrashed as their skin bubbled red.

A gigantic invisible hand swatted them, and Juliet, through the room. The fire was snuffed out as blackened bodies and charred furniture tumbled into the wall. A wall which then crumbled, splitting open with a sound like the Earth itself cracking in half, and then Juliet was falling.

She woke in her seat at the séance table with a sharp slap, as if she had fallen into it from a great height. Perhaps she had, though no one in the room was looking at the ceiling. Juliet looked up, and saw no hole through which she could have landed from the heavens above.

She looked around, now completely at a loss as to what had just happened. Everyone was looking at her with varying degrees of concern, varying from the mildly interested in Tubbs's case to the desperately shocked of Sangster. "Are you all right, miss?" Hector Barnes asked.

"I... I think so," Juliet said uncertainly. She wasn't sure whether she was all right or not, but thought that perhaps giving a positive answer would help reassure everyone, herself most of all.

"What happened?" Upton asked, his breath strong enough to bring her round fully, with more ease than a dose of smelling salts.

"I just saw something." What was it? A flash? A fire? Whatever it was, it was hot, and it burned and it killed. It killed everyone in this very room. "I saw us all die."

Adrienne started. "You saw what?"

"I saw us all die." The memory came into clearer focus, summoned up by the words, as if they gave the image the power to become more real. "We were all sitting here, and you started to extrude this strange substance."

"Ectoplasm, of course."

"I suppose so. But it had hardly begun, when there was a flash from over there." Juliet pointed to the corner of the room. "Then the flash got bigger and brighter like *that*!" She snapped her fingers. "And the whole room was on fire, and so were all of us..." Her voice collapsed into great racking sobs and mumbled syllables that even she couldn't understand. She sniffed and stood up on quivering legs. "I'm sorry, but I can't stay here. I just can't. And I don't think anyone should."

"Why ever not, dear?" Adrienne asked. She gave a reassuring smile. "Whatever you saw was obviously powerful, and has had a great effect on you, but it wasn't real." She gestured to her maid and the other members of the group. "We're all still here." She paused in thought for a moment. "When someone comes into contact with the power of the spirits for the first time, they may often have a reaction that is strange or upsetting, but you mustn't worry about it. It's simply that you are adjusting to the truth of a wider world."

Juliet understood why Adrienne would see the matter that way, but she just knew, in her heart of hearts, that this wasn't the right answer. What she had seen and felt must have been real. If it wasn't real now, then it must be real at some other time, perhaps in the future. Something in Juliet instinctively recognized the truth of that. "It wasn't real now, but it will be."

"Will be?" Mrs Stanley raised an eyebrow.

Yes," Juliet said, her stomach knotting up with a sudden urgency. "I don't know when. Perhaps tomorrow or another day, but we were all here, and we were all wearing the same clothes as we are now."

Andrew Caine laughed. "Well, then, that's an easy premonition to circumvent. We just wear different clothes next time."

Bill Sangster shot him a withering look that could have drained several years from Caine's young life. "What she's saying, you narrow-minded pyramid-urchin, is that what she saw is something that, if it were real, would happen today."

"Exactly," Juliet said. "Don't you see? It will happen tonight. In an hour or this very minute I don't know, but I can... feel it." She could certainly feel a throbbing in her temples, the way she often did when the barometer at home moved to point to an oncoming thunderstorm. And with that, she turned and ran to the door. "Please, let us leave here now, while we still have the opportunity. I beg you."

Sangster stood first. "Well, I can't in good conscience refuse a lady."

"What about the lady asking you to stay?" Adrienne asked. "I mean no offence to Miss Collins, but she is mistaken."

"Maybe," Sangster allowed. "But she's also afraid, and someone ought to do something about that. It's a weakness of mine, Madamme Adrienne." He stood, and joined Juliet at the door. "Don't worry, lass," he said. "I believe you." She looked relieved and slightly reinvigorated. She looked challengingly at the others seated around the table, and gathered herself to try to sound rational and convincing. She didn't want anyone to stay in danger because they felt she was just a jittery little girl.

"I believe we are all in the most terrible danger," she said in a quavering voice. "I cannot explain how or why, but I do implore you to come away from this house for tonight. If I'm wrong, we can always come back tomorrow. In different attire if need be."

Matthew Upton rose next. "Frankly, ladies and gentlemen, the way tonight has gone I almost need a change of clothes already." Juliet, who could smell his odor from the other corner of the room, found it impossible to disagree.

Doctor Tubbs shrugged and stood as well. "I'm afraid the night is already spoiled for me." Mrs Stanley, Barnes and Caine all rose too, looking like children whose favorite toys had been taken away.

Adrienne sighed. "All right, go on then. We shall reconvene tomorrow night at the same hour," she said primly, as if they were members of some kind of board of businessmen. "Those of us who truly have an interest in the spirit world, at least," she added, glaring at Juliet.

Juliet was relieved to see most people collecting their hats and coats, but she hadn't intended to simply rob their hostess of her circle. "Madamme Adrienne, I do not mean just your visitors. You and your servants have to come too. I saw everyone in the house die!"

"This is my house," Adrienne said coldly. "And if die I must, this is where I should choose to do so. Now I bid you goodnight, and shall pray for your better understanding when next we meet." She nodded to the hatchet-faced maid, who came over to escort the visitors downstairs. Juliet wasn't offended by Adrienne's rather waspish tone; in fact she understood it perfectly. She did, however, feel a sense of dismay that Adrienne wasn't listening to her, and that nor was she taking heed of the others' decision. When it came right down to it, Juliet was also surprised and disappointed that someone supposedly so in tune with the spirits couldn't see or feel the truth of what Juliet was saying. If there were spirits that came in the evenings to whisper messages into the ears of mediums, every one of them who visited Adrienne should be yelling at her to get out before she became one of them.

Perhaps that was what the spirits wanted, she thought. Maybe they wanted Adrienne for a new recruit. When the front door of the house closed behind her, and she could hear the bolts being thrown, Juliet wanted to hurl herself to the ground and cry for the waste of life that was about to happen. If she had the strength she ought to break down the door and drag the servants, at least, to safety. She was just the daughter of a vicar, though, not a circus strongman who bent iron bars into coat hangers, so such a violent rescue was not an option. Instead, like the others, she walked into the street, and began to look for a Hansom cab, listening out for the clip-clop of the horses that drew them.

Inside, Adrienne closed her eyes, and tried to stabilize her mixed emotions. What potential that girl had, radiating from her like the glow from a lighthouse—and what rudeness to try to usurp Adrienne's séance like that.

Her foot nudged the damp muslin hidden under the table. She wouldn't be needing that tonight; there would be no ectoplasm to impress the audience.

Although everyone who had left Adrienne's was walking in different directions, they were all still in sight of each other when it happened.

There was a small explosion from somewhere in the vicinity of the excavation for the underground railway, followed by a whip crack sound. Then fire splashed against the wall of the tenement. Searing flame rushed through the downstairs rooms, and up the stairwells, like water following the pipe to a faucet.

Adrienne never saw or heard it coming. She had bent to pick up the muslin and put it and her other props away for the night, when the room brightened as if a thousand candles had suddenly self-ignited. The room was immediately filled with light, from all around. The shadows of Adrienne and her servants, busy taking down the impedimenta of a séance, crisscrossed sharply, flickering as the brightness of the light shifted and flickered.

Madamme Adrienne was frozen to the spot, unable to comprehend what she was seeing. Only when her mouth and nose began to burn, and searing liquid agony poured itself down her throat as easily as gin, did she the realize the light was a wall of fire.

Then Adrienne screamed as she felt the heat climb up her back, and her hair began to shrivel. The servants were all screaming too, as they burned where they fell. They thrashed on the floor as their skin bubbled red and stuck to the smoldering carpet.

A gigantic invisible hand swatted them all clear through the room like bright shooting stars. The fire was snuffed out as blackened bodies and charred furniture tumbled into the wall.

Every window erupted outwards, heat and fire sending shards of glass across the street like shotgun pellets, peppering the houses opposite. An omnibus was caught in the blast, and blown clean over. One of the horses drawing it fell with all too human shrieks of pain, and toppled into the other. The second dray horse whinnied in fear and tried to bolt, but it was weighed down by its injured colleague and the omnibus. It strained against its harness, but couldn't really move. In the end it stopped moving, and stood screaming.

Juliet found herself on the cobbled road, downed by a vast and invisible slap. She felt herself shaking and hoped that the noise she could hear so close wasn't her own whimpering. She drew up her knees and held them, still lying on her side. A few inches away, some straw was host to a couple of small fires, like candle flames. She stared at the flames, almost hypnotized by the way they danced, and delighted that they weren't coming any closer.

Her throat was dry, and she had to swallow a couple of times before she could breathe normally.

She tensed, almost screaming, when a hand took hers. She held back the cry long enough to see that it was the young poet, Bill Sangster. "I'm sorry about the familiarity," he said, "but it's not safe here, is it? Let me help you up."

She nodded, not trusting her voice to sound normal, and pulled herself up his arm until she was standing. Above her, the stars were being blotted out by smoke from the burning building, spreading its stinking wings across the night sky like a triumphant oily dragon.

EIGHT

Bill looked back at the inferno that number four had become. "Whatever happened to you in there, we're grateful to you. You saved our lives, I think."

"I just... I was just frightened."

"How did you know what was going to happen?" Upton asked.

"I don't know. I saw it, I think."

"Saw it?"

"When we were sitting around the table. When you all looked at me as if I was mad. It was repulsive," Juliet said, fighting down a wave of nausea at the thought of it. "I closed my eyes like Madame Adrienne told us to. When I did, I saw... I saw the whole room on fire, and we were all burning. Then there was a bang, and we were all thrown against a wall, and the wall fell in—"

"She fell asleep," Tubbs exclaimed. "Doesn't say much for the powers of the supernatural that someone dozes off in the middle of the show."

"Or went into a trance," Hector Barnes countered. "She certainly got something out of it, didn't she? She saw the room on fire and exploded, and that's what just happened to it. If it was a dream it was a damnably prophetic one, wouldn't you say?"

"As a matter of fact I would not. More likely she smelled gas while dozing off, and her brain translated it into a warning dream for her."

"Perhaps," Barnes agreed. "I'm still pretty dashed grateful to her all the same."

Flames licked at the walls of Mornington Crescent, illuminating a crowd of people in fitful light. The blast had shattered windows halfway along the street, and shaken everyone in the neighborhood out of their beds. Women watched with fearful eyes, and children stared in fascinated awe, as the men of this and several neighboring streets flowed out into the road like a shoal of fish.

Water chains were soon formed, while runners went to fetch the horse-drawn fire engines that were stationed half a mile distant. As well as the fire wagons, several uniformed coppers had turned up, wrapped up warmly against the chilly fog with military-style greatcoats over their blue serge uniforms, and their conical helmets pulled down low about their ears.

Beams from the front of bull's-eye lanterns crisscrossed, making patterns in the mixture of fog and smoke from the smoldering buildings. The fire engines arrived, drawn by carthorses, and firemen swarmed over the wagons using great levers to manually pump the water onto the fire. Once the fires were extinguished, men started clambering over the wreckage, pulling chunks of brick and mortar.

With a tearing, clattering boom, the front wall of the house collapsed. Most of it hit the cobbled road in one piece with an explosive bang, while loose bricks clattered and thudded around the street. The flames inside the exposed rooms flattened themselves against the scorched and peeling walls, as if seeking shelter from the breeze.

Juliet couldn't bear to look. She had never seen anything like this before. In fact the only dead body she had ever seen before was her aunt, who had been taken by a canker three years ago. Even now her father only ever dressed in black, and, although he behaved normally, she suspected that he had never really got over his sister's death, and that he never really would.

The firemen and policemen had moved survivors and residents alike to a safe distance while the rescue efforts went on. Householders from the Crescent brought out blankets and hot tea to warm the survivors, while policemen took statements from everyone.

A sergeant had taken Juliet's statement, and didn't bat an eyelid at her tale of the vision she had seen. "Don't you think that's odd?" she had asked him. The sergeant merely gave a noncommittal shrug. "Isn't that what all this spiritualism business is supposed to be about?" he replied. In truth, Juliet didn't know, but she hoped not. She had only come to see a spiritualist, not to become one.

Of all the survivors, she felt the most confused, though she suspected that each and every one of the others also felt that they were the most confused.

Bill Sangster had been the most practical, and the first to get his hands dirty by joining a bucket chain and attempting to fight the fire that consumed number four from the inside out. Surprisingly spry despite his girth, Upton had been the second to join in the rescue effort, followed by Stewart Tubbs. Something about Tubbs's expression had suggested to Juliet that he had only really joined in because the other two men had, and that he didn't want to be looked upon with scorn by the people who were watching both on the street and from their windows.

Hector Barnes and Andrew Caine didn't seem to mind being scorned, as they blithely stood and watched, the only men in sight—bar the constables who were performing their sworn duty by other means—who weren't either pumping water, carrying buckets, or clearing the rubble. Neither Mrs Stanley nor Juliet herself could be expected to join in the physical work, of course.

After a couple of hours, the fires were quenched with what looked like half the contents of the Thames. Four bodies had been pulled from the rubble. Juliet hadn't turned away in time to not look, but the bodies were relatively shapeless forms, neither recognizably human nor mutilated and gory.

The crowd of people began to break up then. A coach took Hector Barnes, Andrew Caine, and Mrs Stanley away first. Bill Sangster had eventually walked off into the night, whistling a melancholy tune that seemed apt to the aftermath of the evening. Upton had persuaded someone to fetch a cab for him, though he had to walk along to the end of the road, as the horse refused to go near the dead and wounded omnibus horses. Tubbs had grimaced as if he had fallen into a cesspit, and taken directions from one of the Crescent's residents to the nearby branch line. From there he apparently intended to travel back to Bermondsey and return either to his lodgings or to the hospital at which he worked.

Juliet herself walked for a bit, wanting the chill night air to clear her nostrils of the scent of dust and smoke. After a few hundred yards, she too was able to hail a Hansom cab and return home.

The coach in which the three students of Egyptological history had departed brought them eventually to the Stanley's residence: a three-story Georgian house set back from the road. A low wall enclosed an outer ring of lawn and herbaceous border and an inner ring of gravel drive.

As the driver stabled the horses, the trio entered the grand old house handing their hats and overcoats to Fitch, the butler. The house was a marvel of the traveler's souvenir-collecting habits. Most of the objets-d'art were Egyptian in origin although there were a few pieces from other parts of Africa, Greece and the Mediterranean.

Mrs Stanley yawned, and pulled a velvet cord to summon the butler. When the venerable Fitch appeared, she instructed him to prepare strong hot tea for herself, Caine, and Barnes. "Yes, ma'am," Fitch had creaked, and retired to the kitchens. The cook would have gone home for the night several hours ago, so he would have to make the tea himself. Mrs Stanley didn't mind that; Fitch had been a sergeant-major in the army many years ago, before he became a butler, and he made that sort of strong, sweet tea that was peculiar to the British army, the sort that was almost thick enough and sweet enough to spread on toast and eat as a sandwich.

While Fitch busied himself in the kitchen, Mrs Stanley picked up a note from the silver platter that was on the table just inside the front door. She read it and smiled triumphantly. "Excellent news, Hector: our latest find from Egypt has arrived at the docks. It is being unloaded and will be delivered later in the day."

Caine beamed with youthful exuberance. "The sarcophagus of Amenkharis IV," he said, practically drooling.

"Just in time for a mummy party, eh, Jane?" Hector said.

"Exactly. I'll have a cold collation set out, and we can unwrap and examine Amenkharis at our leisure. His dissection will have Wallis in apoplexy, but his won't be the name on the paper."

"It'll be Sir Norman's?"

"It will be both our names, Hector—my husband's and my own."

"If you don't mind my saying so, Jane, you might think about putting in a dedication to that young girl who came to Adrienne's tonight. Without her, you wouldn't be here to write such a book."

Mrs Stanley crossed her legs casually. "Yes, I agree, young Miss Collins deserves our thanks. Like myself, she has sharp senses and a quick wit. She should go far," Mrs Stanley added pointedly.

"Like you?" Andrew Caine asked, obviously not getting the double meaning.

Mrs Stanley looked at him as if he were a simpleton. "Of course. Like myself, she recognized the danger and acted upon it. Of course her youth is an advantage in terms of physical reaction—"

Hector sipped the tea that Fitch had brought. "Oh, I see, you were about to give the alarm as well?"

"Well, of course. I could hardly just sit there and let us get..." She broke off, her voice now trembling. "Killed," she finished, her mask of composure slipping.

"What I'd like to know," Caine interrupted, "is how she could have known what was going to happen."

"Maybe she smelled gas," Hector suggested. "Though no one else did."

"It doesn't seem so odd that someone would

have a vision of danger," Mrs Stanley said. "Odd that it should be this young lady rather than Adrienne herself..."

Hector drew his watch, a gold Hunter, from his vest pocket and opened it. "Good grief," he exclaimed. "I had no idea it was so late."

"That's no matter," Mrs Stanley said. "Why don't you both stay here tonight? I'll have Jensen take you home by pony and trap in the morning."

Hector looked sad. "I'd love to, Jane, but I have a prior appointment. I'm late already and I really must dash." As if telepathic, Fitch appeared at Hector's side with his hat and overcoat. "Thank you for the tea," he said to Mrs Stanley. "Fitch."

"I'll see you out, sir," Fitch said, and escorted Hector away.

"I'd be happy to stay," Caine said. He blushed slightly, an amusing trait, Mrs Stanley thought. "But I'm afraid I brought no nightshirt or pajamas."

"Don't worry, Andrew. Don't worry about that." She went to the window and teased the drapes open a little, but not enough to let the reflection of the lamplight from inside the room interfere with her view of Hector walking down the street. He was going in an eastwards direction.

"What sort of appointment needs to be kept in the wee small hours?" she wondered aloud.

Stewart Tubbs returned to his lodgings in Bermondsey long after midnight. He had taken a train most of the way, the last one that puffed and chugged through the night, and then hailed a passing cab to take him the rest of the way.

Once home, all he really wanted was to have a bath drawn, but there was little point in waking any of the landlady's family to do so, as they would only resent having been roused at such an ungodly hour. It occurred to him that once they read the reports of his narrow escape in the morning papers, they would probably be his willing slaves for a day or two, until his unfortunate celebrity wore off.

That was still several hours off, so he didn't bother to call for them. Instead he settled for undressing, and giving himself a basic wash with a cloth and some cold water from the large jug and basin on the dresser. The water and the rough cloth did well enough in dealing with the soot and dirt from the fire, but it didn't make the slightest bit of difference to the taint of superstition and religious irrationality that had been so infectious at the séance.

It clung to him like the odor of stale sweat, and made him feel unsettled in his stomach. Damn that insidious young girl with her premonitions, harbinger of doom that she had actually turned out to be, and the damn fool drinking-class workers who had cracked a gas main. If the séance had been allowed to go ahead as planned, he would have overturned the table when Adrienne had started extruding ectoplasm and exposed the muslin that he was sure the substance was really made of. He had been to eight of her little theatrical séances and, over that time, had taken careful note of everything that happened at them. It had then been a simple enough matter to work out with pen and paper exactly how the old fraud had staged every single "supernatural" event.

The exposé, when sold to the serious scientific journals, would have raised his standing in academia and perhaps helped him get out of the rut of being a glorified dispensary aide in Bermondsey. It would have helped him get a practice of his own.

Then this Juliet Collins person had come along and his ambition went, literally, up in smoke. She would pay for that. Like the others who got in his way, she would learn the lesson that it wasn't wise to interfere with Stewart Tubbs.

Matthew Upton let himself into the house in Piccadilly, and retired to his apartments. Despite his size and requirement of a silver-topped cane to assist him in walking, he could move quite silently when the occasion demanded. Returning to the house past two in the morning without prompting a mother-hen reaction from his housekeeper most certainly required a subtlety and decorum in his movements.

She was a dear old soul, but just a little too overbearing at night, when she seemed to assume that people got up to things they shouldn't, and insisted upon lecturing him on this matter.

Upton took careful, measured steps, while gulping in as much air as he could. If he could just breathe a little easier as he climbed the stairs to the second floor of the terraced house, his mastery of stealth would be complete.

Despite the hour, Upton felt refreshed and invigorated once he had thrown off his coat, jacket and vest and settled into his wine-stained favorite armchair in his shirtsleeves. Whether it was simply his muse seducing him in the darkest hours of the night, as she often did, or whether his brush with death had caused him to rebound into waking life, he neither knew nor cared. Either way, he knew that he ought to marshal his thoughts, and the best way to do that was to write them down.

Gilbert Collins was no taller than his daughter, and dressed conservatively in dark clothes and coat. He was compact rather than short, and carried himself with a natural pride, like a general who ruled over everything from horizon to horizon. He almost crackled with contained power, but only his eyes gave a real glimpse of it.

He was waiting for her in the sitting room when she returned home. She didn't notice at first, assuming he and her mother would be in bed by this hour. It gave her quite a start to turn round and see him looking at her, inscrutable, but with a slight cant to one eyebrow. It was an opening, she knew; an invitation to tell all and accept his judgment and inevitable sermon. It was as much a trap as the feint made by a swordsman, pretending to give his opponent a weak point to attack, luring him into losing the duel.

Juliet had never fenced with anyone, unless playing with wooden swords against her brother when they were children counted, but she knew how to recognize a lure, and when to take one.

"I'm sorry, papa."

"Sorry?"

She rushed into his arms, and held him. "I'm sorry I went to the silly séance thing, I thought it would be harmless..."

"When I instruct you to do or not certain things, Juliet, it is invariably with good reason. This ungodly Spiritualistic nonsense is–" He broke off, sniffing. "What is that? Have you been gallivanting down a coal mine as well?"

"There was an explosion, daddy, and a fire. The whole house was destroyed, the moment I walked out the door."

"What?" He looked stunned, or even awe-struck. He started patting her head, looking for bumps or wounds. "Are you all right? Did you come to any harm?"

"I'm fine, papa. It's just... I could have died," she wailed.

Gilbert hugged Juliet tightly, tears squeezing out from his eyes. "Dearest child," he sobbed. "Why did you go? Why?"

Juliet wept too, letting go of the hurt that had been bottled up inside her since the blast. "I just wanted to see what sort of people went, Daddy. I just wanted to do something different."

"Oh, Juliet..." He looked at her with great love. "You should probably rest. I'll call Doctor Layton in the morning, to make sure you are really unharmed. In the meantime I shall have to think of how to break this news to your mother without giving her a seizure."

"You're right," she said. She did feel tired, and it was late. "I shall see you at breakfast."

Gilbert nodded. "Don't forget to say your prayers. Prayers of thanks tonight, I should think."

"I will," Juliet promised, and made her way upstairs to her bedroom. Once inside, Juliet locked the door and leaned back against it, half-afraid that her father would barge in after her. It was bad enough that she had gone to a séance—a function of the Spiritualist Church, which her father had called satanic often enough—but she herself had had some kind of vision there. A vision of hell, which had then come true. She didn't dare tell him that part of the night's story. She knew what he would think if she did: that she had been corrupted by Adrienne's occult powers, and, by extension, tainted by the devil.

Juliet knew better and reminded herself of that with every breath. All the same, she couldn't shake the nagging worry that perhaps father was right. Maybe she had been touched by the devil.

The word "medium" meant someone who provided a channel from one world to another. Perhaps hell was one such world. That thought led to a far more disturbing one: what if she had caused the inferno that consumed Adrienne and her building?

Could her mind have somehow projected the fires of hell that she had seen out—perhaps through Adrienne's powers of mediumship–into the real world?

Bill Sangster didn't feel like sleeping when he returned to his garret. If anything, the events of the night had inspired him. This was a night on which to work, to perform and to create. His muse had been awakened by the noise of the blast and by the light of the fires, and she had found it good.

She had also been as intrigued as Bill by the newest member of the circle, Juliet Collins. He would have to look her up later, and see what she had thought and felt about he night's events. First though, he had the urge to work.

The lateness of the hour taunted him, however. It paraded itself through his mind, reminding him of how tired he would be if he stayed at the easel, daring him to try to leave. He had been painting with as much passion as he could muster, but all that looked back at him from the canvas were random patches of wet paint. There was no life there, no death, no anything worth calling art.

The canvas was as mocking as the hour, defying him, and making him regret choosing it as his medium for the thoughts and feelings that threatened to overwhelm him. He kicked the easel over with a snarl, offended by his own idiocy in choosing the wrong medium. He should have known better than to work on canvas, and he should have recognized the error sooner.

He slumped into a battered chair, whose stuffing was bursting forth from the arms, and which was spattered with flecks of paint. If the canvas wasn't the right medium for tonight, then what was?

The poetry folio? Clay? The clarinet that was jammed into the elephant's foot umbrella stand? Depressed, he slumped and looked at the fog that wafted and churned outside the garret window. There was constant art, constant tireless creation, forever generating new patterns and new images and new realities in the very air.

He smiled, thinking that this was the answer to his mood, provided, as usual, by the greatest artist, Nature herself.

Dr Stewart Tubbs didn't feel like being alone just yet, nor did he want to suffer the company of others. There was only one suitable compromise than came to mind, so he dressed and left his lodgings again. Because a number of doctors lived in the building, there was always a cab waiting in the road in case any of them needed to go to the hospital to work. He boarded the cab, tapped the ceiling of the cab with his cane, and called out to the driver to take him to Pall Mall and drop him off next to the Carlton.

From there, he walked a few doors down, and entered a door that led to a quiet hall with a deep carpet and dark wood paneling. The wall on the far side was made of opaque glass panels through which the shapes of chairs and a few seated men could be made out. A manservant appeared silently beside Tubbs, and took his hat, coat, gloves and scarf. Tubbs asked for a large brandy and proceeded through into the club proper.

The room was large and luxurious and mostly unpopulated at this hour. A small group of men sat in plush leather armchairs reading books or newspapers, almost all under a small cloud of cigar or pipe smoke. None of them looked up as Tubbs entered, and took a seat in a bow window that overlooked the street.

This was the best seat in the club as far as Tubbs was concerned. A good view, and with his back to the other members, none of them would see how pale he was or how his hands shook. Even if they had, the rules of the club stated that it was strictly forbidden for any member to notice or acknowledge the presence of any other member, so Tubbs knew that tonight he could be alone here, in suitable company for it.

He looked at the backs of his hands, wondering how such slim and youthful hands, the hands of an artisan of his chosen craft, could quiver like the hands of a worn-out old man who needed a nurse to raise his brandy to his lips for him.

When Tubbs's hands became steady again, he knew it was time to complete his ritual cleansing. He needed a woman, and quickly. He left the club and hailed another cab.

"Whitechapel," he told the driver.

The next morning dawned as cold and pale gray as a corpse's skin. George Frederick Abberline had been a member of London's Metropolitan Police, and latterly Scotland Yard, for almost as long as he could remember and he was getting little enough sleep these days as it was, without being roused at the crack of dawn to come and see a house that had been burst from within by tremendous explosive force.

Abberline picked his way carefully through the charred wreckage. The dead had been removed, thank God, but it was still a sobering experience. The damage done to solid brick and stone was so complete that it suggested a human being, a person of mere flesh and bone would have been utterly destroyed had it been hit by the same force.

This wasn't literally true, Abberline knew, but the remains—he couldn't in all conscience call what was left "bodies"—were in such a condition that their own mothers or spouses wouldn't recognize them. Thankfully there were witnesses who would be able to give statements with the names of the other people present.

"Oh, dear God, not the Fenians. Bad enough what happened to the Yard in '84, without a tenement getting bombed."

A uniformed sergeant who was with him shook his head. "No, inspector, it wasn't the Fenians this time. Workers digging on the new underground railway line struck a gas pipe sometime in the morning. It's been leaking all afternoon and evening, and finally built up enough density that the fire for the building's boiler ignited it."

"Then why the hell was I called here?" With that, he stomped off. Somewhere in London, Jack the Ripper was waiting for Abberline to catch him.

* * *

Doctor Layton had given Juliet a clean bill of health, and, after a healthy breakfast of smoked kippers, Juliet was off to Knightsbridge to fetch some reams of cloth for her mother. The blast was big news in the papers, but luckily no one recognized her as being one of the people involved.

At lunchtime, as she rested in a fashionable tea room, she was surprised to see Mr Sangster approach. He looked as surprised as she was, but also delighted. He came over, paying for a small cake for her.

"We didn't get much chance to talk last night," he said. "Much to my regret."

"Don't you work, Mister Sangster? I should have thought most men to be at work at this hour."

"I write poetry and I paint. The page and the canvas are both very different, but I love them both."

"You were whistling when you left Mornington Crescent last night. Didn't almost dying bother you?"

"I've been dead before," Sangster said with a shrug. "It wasn't frightening. In fact the most frightening thing about it was that it actually was... nice."

"Nice? You must have gone to heaven."

"I doubt that," Sangster said with a chuckle. "I didn't see any clouds or harps. Mind you, there were no toasting forks either."

Fascinated, Juliet leaned in closer. "What was it like?"

"It was like..." He trailed off in concentration. Juliet wasn't surprised, and knew it couldn't be easy to explain something like this. They had no common frame of reference, and she just hoped she understood whatever description he did give.

"It's like being an ant, at the foot of the Tower of London. You know there's something there, and it's something huge and wonderful, but you're too small to take it all in. You just know there's something so astonishing to learn about, and for you to grow as you do it."

"It sounds strange but not unpleasant."

"That's the most disturbing thing, Miss Collins. It's not unpleasant. It's intriguing, and alluring and in many ways quite attractive."

"Attractive? You can't mean you'd want to... be dead?"

"No, of course not. But I don't fear it. I don't mind admitting that there's plenty I still want to see and do in this life, but I know there's plenty to stimulate the mind in the next world as well. That's comforting, to me."

"Maybe that's heaven, then. I mean, maybe it's heaven for you."

"Perhaps, though I can't say as I expect to be going that way. I've had a few too many whiskies and–though I probably shouldn't soil your shell-like ears with such tales–maybe one or two women too many as well."

Juliet felt herself blush, and he grinned at the sight. "Don't pay attention to me," he recommended. "I like to give out advice about people that's seldom worth listening to."

"And what advice would you give me about our fellow survivors?"

Bill's face took on a more serious cast. "Don't trust Upton. He's a newspaper type and showman, and in my experience showmen may have papers, but they never have any real news in them."

"That smell..."

"I think our Mister Upton is a little old-fashioned. He probably clings on to some medieval superstitions about bathing causing you catch a spot of Black Death."

Juliet looked sidelong at him. "And what about you, Mister Sangster? Should I trust you?"

Bill smiled, a diamond-like glitter in his eye. "Course not. I'm a bachelor wordsmith and you're a beautiful girl, with, if I may be so bold, the most beautiful eyes I've ever looked into. Trust me least of all."

NINE

Dawn seeped over the city, rather than breaking over it. The darkness of an early winter night faded to the thick gray of fog. It was, thought Matthew Upton, a "London Particular," and no mistake. Letting the plain drapes fall closed again, Upton noticed Percy coiled nearby on the piano, and patted his head, as most people would pat a dog. Percy only tasted the air in return.

Upton had never quite decided whether Percy was a pet or a family heirloom, but he loved the beast nevertheless. Keeping the apartments warm enough for Percy's comfort was expensive, but not so much that Upton would ever consider not keeping him. Upton finished dressing, putting on a vest and frocked coat. He took an overcoat from the rack, and folded it over his arm. Even in vest and frock coat he was sweating like a pig, thanks to the temperature that Percy required, and he didn't want to add yet another layer of clothing until he got into a nice comfortable chill outside.

Upton gathered the sheets of notepaper from last night with satisfaction, and thundered downstairs. He knew that luck was with him when he saw a Hansom cab waiting outside the door. "The Clarion," he told the driver, as he pulled on his overcoat. He took up the entire seat, but at least it was comfortable. Once settled, he rapped on the cab's ceiling with the end of his cane, signaling the driver to set off. It was a good twenty minutes' journey before the cabbie reined in the two horses, and Upton could squeeze himself back out of the cab. He paid off the driver, further tipping him with a ha'penny.

The Clarion's offices and printing press were opposite the home of *The Times*, but held tight between a firm of solicitors and a public house. The cobbles, paving stones and walls were damp from the morning's fog. Upton pushed through the slightly warped wooden door, and was immediately assailed by the noise of the printing machines in the basement. He ascended the stairs to the offices.

"It's a sad loss," Gibson sighed. "One of England's greatest mediums. Or one of England's greatest confidence tricksters. Either way she'd have kept us on the gravy train till the cows come home."

Upton chuckled. "Don't start giving this rag the last rites yet, my lad. Madame Adrienne might now be playing for the other side, but at least she went out in a fashion that gives us her natural successor. I speak, of course, of none other than Juliet Collins."

"She a medium too?"

"Of that I can't be certain, but she has all the qualifications to be the biggest star of the Spiritualist circuit since the Fox sisters themselves."

"What qualifications?"

"The ability to experience–and pass on to an audience who are all ears–visions of the future."

"She ain't just another pikey fortune-teller?" Gibson asked suspiciously.

Upton felt momentarily outraged, and told himself that it was on Juliet's behalf. Even though she would never know of the insult, it was a slur on his own character that he would promote and publicize such a common person. "Miss Collins is no gyppo! She is the sole daughter–and a proper lady in the making, I might add–of one of London's most respected clergymen."

That piqued Gibson's interest, and he smiled a greedy and crooked rat-like smile. "A clergyman's pup? That has promise, I'll grant you. Especially if he's a real hardliner who likes to take a crack at the Spiritualists..."

"Spiritualists, Darwinists, Catholics... Our Reverend Collins plays no favorites. He is, and always has been, a most non-discriminatory bigot."

Eastwards along the River Thames, in the Pool of London, clippers and steamships were tethered to the north bank by thick and ancient piers. Despite the chill in the air, stevedores toiled bare-chested, sweating rivers as they hauled on ropes to unload cargoes brought from all over the world.

Whether it was bulk cargo such as tea from China, India or the Americas, or exotic goods brought from the strangest corners of the Empire, it would come here or up the Medway to be unloaded, and stored for excise. The wide roads between the warehouses and the piers were jammed solid with men bearing heavy crates, and with carts drawn by powerful Shire and Clydesdale horses. The streets between were narrow winding alleys, whose floors seemed cut deep into the ground, if only because the stained and filthy walls on either side rose two or three stories high. The light from the gas lamps on the main streets didn't reach far into these noisome crevices, and only the occasional escape of candlelight from a greasy window allowed a traveler to see what he was stepping in. Despite this, the streets and alleys were far from empty, even at this hour of the night.

It was gone one in the morning, and Louis Diemschutz was looking forward to finally getting to bed after a long day trawling round Lambeth and Whitechapel with his rag and bone cart. He huddled on the driver's board, keeping his secondhand peacoat wrapped tightly around him, and his black Derby hat pulled down over his ears. The pony that pulled the cart looked just as tired as he felt, trudging along with its head weighed down with oncoming sleep. Diemschutz had just a couple more stops to make along Berner Street.

The street was dark and narrow, almost too narrow for the pony and cart, but he and the pony had been along it enough times to know how to slip through and into the various yards that opened onto the street.

His next stop was at a working men's club, and the pony knew the way well. It started to turn in through the gateway to the yard, then shied. Diemschutz cursed it, but the pony would go no further. Momentarily forgetting the cold and his tiredness, Diemschutz jumped down to the cobbles to see what was in the pony's way. It was a woman, slumped in the gateway. She looked to be completely unconscious and the air above her was an alcoholic haze of juniper. Diemschutz groaned. Just his luck that some gin-addled soak should fall into a drunken stupor right in his path.

There was a sudden noise from the far corner of the yard, and Diemschutz balled his hands into fists, half expecting a rushing attack from some thief or other. The clattering footsteps went the other way, fading into the night like a bad dream. Relieved, Diemschutz returned to his cart and found a candle from among the bric-a-brac that was there. He lit it with a Lucifer match, and walked back to the stupefied woman. "Come on, dolly. Time to go home, eh?"

He reached down to shake her awake by the shoulder, and grimaced at the feel of something warm and sticky against his hand. God only knew what repulsive filth she had been lying in. "Good grief, woman," he exclaimed. He brought the candle closer to her, expecting to see her blink in the light. Instead he saw a lifeless gray face, smeared with dried blood. Below her slack jaw, her throat was opened like a thirsty mouth. Her collar and shoulder was damp with blood. One ear hung half off the side of her head. Diemschutz recoiled with a yell. The woman was dead, and his mind could only form one thought: the Ripper. Revolted, he stumbled backwards, "Help!" he shouted. "Police! Murder!"

The source of footsteps that Louis Diemschutz had been so rightly afraid of, ran, as excited by the thrill of having almost been seen at his work as he was frightened and angry about almost having been caught. He turned from Berner Street onto Commercial Road, chasing the shadows cast by the flickering gas lamps all the way to Houndsditch. After ten minutes, his legs ached, and he had developed a stitch in his side, but he was happy enough to have evaded whomever it was that had so nearly stumbled upon him. He slowed, as he could hear footsteps up ahead. They were slow and a little uneven; certainly not the steady footfalls of a copper walking his beat. Pausing, he slipped into the shadows, but was too late.

"'Ere," a female voice said. "You couldn't help a lady, could you?"

He decided to play it confident, and stepped towards her. From her tatty yet revealing clothes and the scent of gin, she could only be a whore. "I might."

She giggled. "Good. Only, the Peelers just turfed me out on my arse, and I ain't even got tuppence for a bed for the night."

"I suppose I could be persuaded to give you one. A tuppence, I mean."

"I knows what you mean, mister," she said with a grin. "And if you know of a place..."

"I have a room..." He thought quickly: where was he, and what would she believe? "A room in Mitre Square." That was just around the corner. The shorter the distance, the more likely she would be to acquiesce. To his surprise, she did more than that. She grabbed his arm and started pulling him in the direction of the square.

"Come on then," she said. "No sense waiting, is there? Life's too short for that."

Constable Watkin was bored and looking forward to the end of his shift. The sooner he could put his feet up and get some sleep, the happier he would be. It wasn't so much the lateness of the hour, or the length of his patrol that was so tiring, but the repetitiveness of it. He walked the same small patch in Houndsditch, so small that it took only fifteen minutes to have come full circle and started a new lap. He had passed through Mitre Square at one-fifteen, and again at one-thirty. By now he was used to seeing the wet cobbles, iron gratings and stonewalls as empty as a politician's head. One-forty-five and something was different. This time there was something lying in a heap near a wall. If Watkin didn't know better he would have thought it was a collection of rags fallen from a rag-and-bone man's cart.

He stepped closer to the mound of rags, adjusting the aperture of his bull's-eye lamp, so that it would cover the entire ragged shape.

It was a woman, lying in front of a cellar grate, her dress flung up from her naked waist. Watkin's gut clenched at the sight. It was just what every policeman in London was half dreading and half expecting. The oily metal scent of blood and meat reached him immediately, as if the lamplight had alerted it to greet its visitor. Watkin couldn't think of anything he would prefer less than approaching the body. The pose and the smell was enough to tell him that this was no longer a woman, with a personality and thought, but just a shattered vessel left behind by a departed soul. He forced himself anyway, using his free hand to put his whistle to his mouth. He blew three sharp blasts on the whistle as he walked further into the square, but the breath was sapped from his lungs by a sudden sickness as he reached the body.

Her face was torn and bloody, sliced into strips by long deep slashes, and her throat had been deeply cut from ear to ear. There was a bloody mess at one side of her head where one ear seemed to be have been torn off. Her stomach had been laid open from the hair between her legs to the ribs. She was still warm enough for steam to rise faintly from the stew of glistening meat in the red cauldron of her abdomen.

"Look, Miss Collins. I'm not out to discredit you, or to imply any wrongdoing on your part. I'm genuinely keen to know how you knew what was going to happen."

"I just *knew*," Juliet insisted.

"What I mean is, was it a literal vision, or did a voice tell you? Was it simply that the knowledge was suddenly there."

"It was... a vision," she admitted. "I saw the blast and the flame, and all of us being hurled against the wall—" her voice broke then, and she choked back a sob, resisting the urge to shudder. "What's happening to me?" she wailed. "Am I becoming a witch?"

"No, not at all. I'm sure that's a conscious choice that witches make."

"Then it must be madness then. I shall end up in Bedlam!"

Upton closed his eyes, and again heard the screams of the dying, and smelled the acrid odor of burning human flesh. The view in his head wasn't that of a fog-bound London street, however, but of a small fort in the virtually airless mountains of Afghanistan. The tribesmen there didn't seem to mind the disparity between their scimitars and Napoleonic muskets, and the British Army's repeating rifles and Maxim machine guns. They popping up from under rocks in the most unexpected places to slaughter men in their billets and set fire to the buildings. Upton had thought he had put the things he saw and did there to rest in his mind, and for a dozen years this had been true. Then had come the explosion at Madame Adrienne's.

In a city as crowded as London there was always death, but it was a refined and structured death.

There were rules about how everyone should react, and fixed limits on who should feel what and when. What had happened at Adrienne's was something the rules couldn't cope with; not to Upton's way of thinking, anyway. The only time he had seen such horrors inflicted upon human bodies has been back in Afghanistan when the tribesmen—devils that they must have been, though they bled like men, and wept like women when captured—overthrew a camp or a fort. Those incidents had affected Upton, of course, but he hadn't thought of them in years, and he certainly hadn't felt the shakes and the loosening of the guts that he did now.

The difference was most likely that in the hill country the men who died had gone into it with their eyes open. They knew that, as soldiers, someone may try to harm them some day, and they accepted the risk. Adrienne and her servants, now they were a different matter. Innocents going about their daily lives in central London, they had accepted no risk, or even recognized it.

"Why did you want to talk to me?"

Juliet, if she were to admit the truth to herself, didn't really know herself why she had sought out Upton. He seemed to have believed her about having a vision of the explosion before it happened, so perhaps it was simply that she felt better about talking to someone who had shown a hint of a willingness to listen.

"When I said I saw a vision before the explosion... you seemed to believe me. In fact you didn't seem surprised at all. I wondered... I wondered if you knew about such things before."

Upton lowered his chins to his chest, peering over his pince-nez at her. "It's true I have a passing familiarity with those who profess such powers." He relaxed. "As a matter of fact, I have been making a study of this ability for several years. I believe it is a faculty that many people possess."

"Mister Upton, I profess no such power–"

"I'm sorry, Miss Collins, let me rephrase that. Many people display the traits of such ability. Some exploit it for the purposes of business or entertainment. Others deny it and seek to quash the spiritual abilities out of fear or misapprehension. The majority–including, if you don't mind my saying so–yourself, simply don't recognize the fact, and live out their lives giving it no thought, or believing themselves simply lucky. Or cursed."

He sounded sincere enough, and she had heard such tales, even from her father. "And you believe I have some sort of... power?"

"As a matter of fact, I believe that everyone does, but that relatively few people ever experience it.

TEN

From *The London Clarion*, 1888.

Ripper's Dark Arts Threaten London
By Matthew Upton

Although some old heads and wise heads are calling most vociferously for the resignations of Sir Melville McNaughten and his fearless assistant, Inspector Abberline of Scotland Yard, perhaps the angry correspondents to London's premier newspapers are venting their ire upon the wrong targets.

McNaughten and Abberline are policemen, men of the law, who are experienced and, I should sincerely hope, trained, in the practices of upholding the law and bringing the members of the city's criminal underworld to justice. Why then, have they not yet caught this nefarious madman who has been terrorizing women of a certain kind in Whitechapel and the East End?

The Whitechapel killer is, after all, one must presume a criminal. Murder is a crime, so he is logically a criminal, and a member of the criminal underworld. I refuse to describe them, gentle reader, as the criminal underclass as some do, for the simple reason that there is no such thing as a class made up entirely of criminals. Crime is endemic to our industrialized society at all levels, from the corrupt members of Parliament who accept bribes from rich landowners, to the poor who beg or threaten good citizens for money.

These are the wretches and leeches that feed off the great British Empire and all her works, and these are the types of people whom our wonderful (and not-so-wonderful) guardians of law and order such as McNaughten and Abberline are most assuredly equipped to deal with.

The so-called Ripper who has been so brutally cutting a swathe through London's dedicated members of the world's oldest profession may not be the type of miscreant that these staunch servants of Her Majesty are experienced in taking to task for their crimes. Indeed this Whitechapel butcher may even be a manner of man completely alien to McNaughten and Abberline's ability to imagine, let alone comprehend.

What do I mean by this? What sort of criminal can be so unusual and strange to those very people whose entire lives are dedicated to studying the criminal makeup. Quite simply put, the sort of criminal who is not a criminal at all, but a far baser creature, a veritable devil who has taken human form and sent to create havoc on God's Earth.

Nay, do not dismiss my words so lightly, though I confess I do not mean to cast the Whitechapel murderer as a literal, supernatural figure risen from the depths of hell. Such fancies are for the superstitious, or perhaps the readers of the esteemed Monsieur Verne.

I do suggest, however, that the Whitechapel murderer may in fact believe himself to be such a creature of myth or legend. Furthermore, I speculate that this foul fiend who stalks the East End by night may not even have come to this belief through the action of clinical madness or vapors of the brain, but has chosen this insanity, coldly and deliberately as a means to end.

I spoke of corruption earlier, and mentioned the Honorable Members of Her Majesty's Parliament, many of whom are willing to accept filthy lucre in exchange for favors, in order to further their ambitions for power and prestige. There are other forms of power than that granted by God and Her Majesty, and there are other forms of ambition than the purely temporal one of seeking governmental power over the citizenry.

There is such a thing as spiritual ambition, in which a man (they are almost always men, women having been dissuaded from the pursuit of such ambitions by Matthew Hopkins, et al. in centuries past) seeks to gain power by aligning himself with forces opposed to God himself.

I speak of the Magus, the warlock and the magician. There are still many such men abroad in the world, carrying out foul and depraved rituals with the intent of gaining the power of supernatural entities. Whether there truly are such satanic entities, waiting to be summoned to corporeal existence by these men, is a matter for conjecture and debate, but is not a matter of relevance to my argument. It is not a matter of relevance because, even should these diabolic homunculi not exist, the Magus will behave as if it does, and carry out the fearful wishes that such a being would, in the opinions of the Magus, desire.

In short then, my assertion is that the Whitechapel killer, Jack the Ripper, Jolly Jack, or whatever name you may know him by, is such a Magus, conducting a bloody and murderous ritual which encompasses the whole of the East End, with the aim of gaining for himself some form of dark power.

This is why McNaughten and Abberline will never, I believe, catch the fiend: They have no knowledge or experience of the Dark Arts, nor do they know or comprehend the minds of the men who seek to become Magi. And until they seek out the knowledge of those who are experienced in such matters, they will fail in their quest.

So, to McNaughten and Abberline I say this: seek out the spiritualists who can guide you in your quest. Only with the assistance of this new and wondrous science can these awful crimes be solved, and the residents of Whitechapel sleep soundly in their beds once more.

* * *

"The horrendous hyperbole of Grubb Street," Abberline rumbled darkly in his office, tossing the morning's *Clarion* into a corner. Abberline sat at his desk and took out the file he had been collating on this maniacal killer in Whitechapel, whom the papers and the general public referred to as "Jack the Ripper". Abberline hated the name and would prefer to discuss the case under a more professional term, but since the last killing even his own officers, both uniformed and detectives, had taken to calling the killer by that name.

"What's that, sir?"

"It's the esteemed columnist," Abberline's voice dripped sarcasm, "Mister Matthew Upton, causing, as usual, more trouble than he's worth. Look at these." He pushed a couple of tatty letters across to the sergeant.

"Dear Boss," the first letter began, in a crude scribble. "I keep on hearing the police have caught me but they won't fix me just yet... I am down on whores and I shan't quit ripping them till I do get buckled. Grand work the last job was. I gave the lady no time to squeal. How can they catch me now? I love my work and want to start again. You will soon hear of my funny little games and me... The next job I do I shall clip the lady's ears off and send to the police officers just for jolly... Keep this letter back till I do a bit more work, then give it out straight. My knife is nice and sharp. I want to get to work right away if I get a chance. Good luck. Yours truly, Jack the Ripper"

The second read, "You'll hear about Saucy Jack's work tomorrow. Double event this time. Number one squealed a bit. Couldn't finish her straight off. Had not time to get ears for police. Thanks for keeping last letter back till I got to work again. Jack the Ripper."

"You mean these are hoaxes?" the sergeant asked.

"Aye, lad; about as legitimate as a wooden shilling."

"They look pretty convincing to me."

"Well they wouldn't be very successful hoaxes if they didn't look convincing enough to fool people, would they?" Abberline lit a cigarillo. "Part of the problem with pests like Upton is that they don't seem to realize that the Whitechapel killer isn't that unusual. Whores are killed every other day, by their pimps or the men they service, or rivals, or... Well, none of them make the news. Why, only last week one poor mare was killed by having a crank-handle shoved up... up her."

"This Ripper is different though. Most of the killings are for money or gang disputes. The Ripper... well, he ain't like that at all."

"No, he isn't. And that's what makes Upton such a pest. The fact that he can glaze his nonsense with a dose of truth."

In the office of *The Clarion*, a very angry Upton slapped a copy of the *Courant* on the desk. "That larcenous, narrow-hipped trollop!"

Gibson looked over the headline with dismay. "New star medium found in London. Clairvoyant prophet saves scholars. Lady Stanley gives exclusive–"

"That two-faced, thieving glory-hound." Upton lowered himself into a chair, which creaked. He glowered at the paper and let his breath out through his teeth in a way that suggested he was trying to hold in more colorful words. It sounded a little like steam escaping from a dangerously overheating boiler.

Gibson had never thought there was a literal sound for someone said to be seething, but now he knew otherwise.

"Makes a change. Usually it's historical discoveries she purloins and tries to get her name on. Wallis Budge was so angry with her last year that I thought he was going to punch her in the street outside the British Museum."

"So did he. It turns out she's a nimble little minx when she has to be. Her whole little gang was there last night, actually. Boring Barnes at least didn't say much, or we might all have roasted in our slumber."

After leaving *The Clarion*, Upton decided to visit Juliet Collins again. He knew a short cut to a stand where he could more easily catch a Hansom cab and slipped through a narrow street between *The Clarion's* printing press and one belonging to the *Courant*.

He continued on through a dilapidated industrial area along the side of a crumbling, positively disintegrating old building.

Upton heard a footfall behind him, and turned, gripping his cane with both hands. If some footpad thought that Upton's bulk made him slow to react when it came to a moment of action, he was in for a shock. Upton wrapped his hand around the silver top of the cane and twisted. The sword-blade hidden inside the ebony cane sprung up by about an inch, ready for Upton to draw it and fight off any attack.

It was a homeless derelict, who looked harmless apart from the thousands of fleas and lice he was no doubt bearing. Upton locked the sword-stick closed, and turned to continue on his way, his feet thundering on the cobbles, his jaws gasping and biting at the air in a desperate attempt to get enough oxygen to keep his three-hundred-pound-plus frame in motion.

Something rolled and turned beneath his foot and Upton felt himself start to fall. He put out a hand to try to steady himself but to no avail. His entire mass tumbled sideways, onto a sloping pile of rubble that had long ago fallen from the old building.

At first he thought he was unharmed, though his chest still hurt. Then he looked down and saw the six inches of steel pipe that protruded out from his breast.

Upton looked at the pipe with disbelief. Partly he couldn't believe that it was there, sticking out from his swollen belly, slick with his blood, his own stomach jammed into the end like wadding into a musket barrel. The other part he couldn't believe was how little pain there was. Instead there was a strange and repulsive quivering in the flesh all around the pipe, as if the skin and fat were trying to shrink back in terror from the invader.

It was the strangest sensation he had ever experienced, movement inside the flesh, and in many ways it was worse than pain. Pain he could have understood, but this was incomprehensible and threatening.

He supposed he was in shock.

Bizarrely, there was a smell of burning. It was like grilled pork, with a hint of black pudding, and a markedly less appetizing undertone of darkness and decay, a leering suggestion of rotting manure.

To his astonishment, the merest heartbeat before the ravaging pain finally slashed its way into his consciousness, he saw a tiny orange flame spiral out of his skin, clinging on to the bloodied surface of the pipe.

Then he was screaming, his throat raw, his guts clenching against the metal, burning themselves against its hot surface. Instinctively, Upton tried to run away from the fire, which he imagined to be behind him and traveling along the pipe. He hauled forward, trying to pull himself off the pipe. His whole body felt like it turned to jelly, every nerve ending quivering in sick terror.

He forced himself onwards, the urge to survive overriding the urge to shake and scream. As he moved, the fire along the pipe grew brighter, licking outwards and into his skin. The flames began to melt the fat that he had carried around for so many years, and feed greedily from it.

He was sick then, and would have fallen to his knees, but the pipe wouldn't let him. It was strong and held him upright, robbing him even of the mercy of a fall. The vomit splashed onto the pipe and flashed into fire.

Too late, Upton realized that the acid in the vomit ignited the chemicals on the metal. Stomach acids. Acids that would be reacting all the way along the pipe, and which would have smeared even further along it as he tried to pull himself off the metal.

He choked on more vomit, trying to force it down and delay the process, even as he knew it must be too late by now. Coruscating flames and acrid smoke were fizzing in his heart and belly. He was beginning to cough on smoke that was filling his lungs from the inside, rather than being inhaled from the air.

Reflex spasms took over as he fought for breath, his limbs twitching as the fires consumed the fat on his arms and legs. His beard was smoldering, but he didn't have enough breath to scream.

His head was filled with pain as the blood vessels in his brain began to boil. He saw things then. There were dark figures with leathery wings approaching him from the shadows in the corners of his vision, as black as volcanic glass, with claws as sharp. His parents, dead two decades, called to him to join them and be happy. The whole world tilted and twisted in upon itself, falling into an abyss.

He never knew that they were all products of his brain being poached in its own juices. He, mercifully, didn't realize that he had gone blind just before the liquid centers of his eyes had boiled and burst.

He was dead before anyone found him. By then the physical body that had once called itself Matthew Upton was just the shriveled black heart of a colony of swarming orange flames, polluting the skies with a smoke whose stench rivaled anything the factories in Lambeth could produce.

Stewart Tubbs checked himself in his mirror, preening softly. There was a knock at the door, which proved to herald the arrival of the professor, and Sir Keith Swallow. Sir Keith was tall and well built, with silver hair cut close to the head and a soft Irish lilt to his voice. Tubbs was simultaneously excited at the prospect of some kind of acknowledgement and terrified that he was in trouble.

"Tubbs," Sir Keith began. "Have you been out to do any work at the police mortuary yet?"

"N-No, Sir Keith. The opportunity hasn't yet–"

"It has now, if you can come immediately.

The Metropolitan police headquarters at Scotland Yard was a building with turrets like a castle and a huge wrought iron archway and between two turreted wings. It had a bizarre chocolate cake coloring, being mostly brown, with thin cream lines at regular intervals.

The mortuary was on one side of an open courtyard, with the door generally left open to let the stench out when floaters from the Thames were being opened for examination.

Today, a huge mound of scorched flesh was on the dissection table. The corpse didn't seem to be bloated, but was simply that large. Tubbs had only ever seen one man so big before, and immediately rushed to look for the distinctive signet ring that Matthew Upton had worn to the séances at Madame Adrienne's. It was there, welded onto the melted flesh of the finger. Tubbs blanched, and choked down the vomit that threatened to scorch its way out up his throat. "Upton!" he croaked.

Sir Keith blinked. "Upton? Do you mean to say you know this fellow?"

Tubbs nodded carefully, feeling lightheaded and faint. "He is–was–a member of my club. He was at the séance on Saturday."

"He was one of the survivors?"

"Well, yes, of course!" Tubbs turned away. Upton had survived the explosion and fire on Saturday, but appearances suggested otherwise today.

Sir Keith harrumphed. "Normally there are rules about conflicts of interest between doctor and patient... But I don't suppose it matters when the chap's already dead. Can you go on with this?" Tubbs nodded wordlessly. "Good. Let's get to work, then."

The professor pulled the metal shaft out of the remains of Upton's abdomen. The whole abdomen collapsed, spilling ashes and organic sludge on the table. It stank of roast pork and acrid chemicals. "The fire seems to have started... inside the body," the professor said. It was clear from his tone that he could hardly believe his own theory.

"But that's impossible," Tubbs protested. "Unless you consult Dickens for your diagnoses. Didn't he have some villain burned from within?"

"Krook, in *Bleak House*," the professor confirmed. "I can't speak for the figment of Mister Dickens's imagination, but this man certainly burned from the inside out."

Sir Keith finished his examination in a little under half a hour and reported to Sir Melville McNaughte and Inspector Abberline in the Chief Constable's office, informing him of the bizarre circumstances of the man's demise. "I should like to look into this a little further, George."

Abberline wished he could help. "It's a baffling case, right enough, Sir Keith, and I wish with every fiber of my being to help... But I just don't have the manpower, what with the Fine Na Gael on one side, and the Ripper on the other. Every copper in London is already working double shifts."

"We need an expert opinion. What about that man you used before, on that business up at Wapping?"

"I suppose I could ask–"

"Please do," McNaughten said. "At once."

"Yes sir," Abberline said stiffly. He left the chief constable's office and went to find a desk sergeant who could be relied upon. As in the army, it was the sergeants who really got things done in London's Metropolitan Police. He needed to send a telegram to Baker Street.

"Hmm," the newcomer pursed his lips, making his already thin face even more cadaverous. Tubbs, Abberline and Sir Keith watched him work. There was a second visitor from Baker Street accompanying the first. He was shorter than his pallid, bright-eyed companion, and had a graying moustache. Where the tall visitor dressed like a well-dressed undertaker, the shorter man dressed like a country squire.

The taller man scraped a little of the ashen powder into a glass tube, and set it over a gas flame. He then mixed another sample of powder with some distilled water, and put it under a magnifying glass. "Yes... there's certainly blood in the mixture. Also a few flecks of paint, some woolen fibers and cotton. I should imagine the latter are from Mister Upton's clothes."

"Anything else?" Sir Keith asked. Clothes didn't just burst into flame for no reason.

"If, by that, you mean a chemical," the consultant said primly, "yes, I believe there is."

"Can you tell what it is?"

"Of course, of course... Not from microscopic examination alone, however." He straightened and indicated the glass tube being heated by the gas flame. "A chemical analysis will give us the proof we need. By heating a sample at a temperature being increased slowly, we should be able to view the different compounds burning off at different stages of the process. The color and composition of the flux will tell us precisely what metallic elements were included, and in what quantities." He tapped a thick book on the table. "Then we need only look up the recipe, so to speak, in here."

The process was a slow one; painfully and frustratingly slow as far as Abberline was concerned. The flame barely changed hue as far as he could tell, though both the consultant and the doctor occasionally muttered an "um" or "ah." Abberline hoped this actually meant they were seeing something significant, and that a result of the test would be forthcoming. He could but pray that said result came forth before he died of old age.

Suddenly, the cadaverous scientist scribbled something on a scrap of paper, and flicked through the book. "Eureka!" he cried. "Good grief. Doctor, come here; you'll find this fascinating, my dear fellow."

"What is it?" his shorter companion asked, hurrying over.

"It's the substance that was on the metal bar which so neatly impaled the unfortunate Mister Upton." As Abberline, Tubbs and Sir Keith came round to peer over the pair's shoulders at the diagrams and formulae in the book—which were as mystifying as any set of Egyptian hieroglyphs to Abberline—the scientist went on. "I use the phrase 'the unfortunate Mister Upton' advisedly, doctors, inspector, Sir Keith. It is truer than you know. As it transpires, he was the victim of a scientific misfortune the likes of which I have never previously encountered." He turned to his companion. "As a matter of fact, I feel I ought to write a monograph on the subject."

"Well, what happened to him?"

"It's actually quite simple, if rather mathematically unlikely to happen again. The pipe that impaled Upton was caked on the inside with a residue of potassium permanganate. Sir Keith, would you be so good as to inform the inspector how his stomach digests food?"

Taken aback by the sudden change of subject, the titled professor stuttered. "Well, enzymes produce acid which breaks down the food we eat, so that it can be more easily absorbed by the body."

The haughty scientific detective nodded approvingly. "What type of acid."

"Why, hydrochloric. You know that as well as I do."

"Indeed I do. I also happen to know that a reaction between potassium permanganate and hydrochloric acid produces the deadly gas, chlorine."

Abberline was lost now. "But he wasn't gassed. He was impaled and burned."

"No, that's where Upton's second, and most spectacular, piece of bad luck comes into play. While the potassium permanganate had been inside the pipe, the outside had accrued a coating of ammonia."

"So?"

The expert paused, looking as if he was tempted to not answer, as if that would assert his own superiority. Then he shrugged and smiled. "Ammoniac compounds react with chlorine to produce nitrogen trichloride, sometimes called chloride of azode. This is highly volatile, unstable and self-ignites at a temperature of sixty degrees. The living human body, of course, has a temperature of ninety-eight point four or so. More than enough to ignite the azode."

Abberline was astounded. At the same time, he could see some obvious flaws in the theory. For one thing, the pipe had been barely an inch and a half in diameter. "But there wasn't a lot of these chemicals on the pipe, surely? I mean, compared to the size of Upton–" There was no possible way the pipe could have contained enough of any inflammable compound to immolate the huge man so completely.

"The amount does not particularly matter, inspector, since the chemicals in question merely ignited the fire. His own body fats fuelled it and kept it going, in much the same way that candle wax continues to burn around the wick long after the match has been blown out."

"How could Upton have come into contact with these chemicals in the street? Surely they're quite specialized and only likely to be found in munitions factories, or–"

The pale, cadaverous man shook his head. "Come with me, gentlemen. I fancy we shall find our answers at the location where the body was found."

Within the hour, the whole group was standing at the place where Upton had fallen. The thin man from Baker Street pointed to a vast derelict hulk of brick and stone at the end of the road. Its walls had crumbled, and its ceiling collapsed inwards. "That building used to be a leper hospital, did it not?"

Abberline nodded. The old place had indeed been a hospital and hospice for lepers, from the English Civil War through until perhaps twenty years ago. When the church closed the hospital after the last leper died, they had tried to sell the building, but couldn't find a buyer. No industrialist or company wanted to risk setting up shop in what they thought of a plague area. As a result, the building had fallen in to dereliction. Only human derelicts, the flea-ridden scavengers that any city in the Empire had hiding in its darkest alleyways and under bridges would venture within its walls. "What's that got to do with it?" he asked.

"The potassium permanganate is used as a disinfectant and sometimes to treat skin sores like eczema. Ammonia is also used in for cleaning as well as for the production of fertilizer and so on. I would speculate that the pipe upon which Upton was impaled came from there, where it had been part of the impedimenta used to clean the wards when a patient died. As the building fell into disrepair, the pipe was just another part of the rubble. Upton then fell upon it, most likely by accident. You can see how uneven the road is here."

Abberline shook his head in dumb amazement. "Astonishing."

"Quite elementary, I assure you, inspector."

The Stanley's Regency town house was even grander in the daytime than it was at night, with the herbaceous borders shown off to their best effect. Andrew Caine, walking up to the front door with Hector Barnes, hoped to have such a house someday, funded by marvelous discoveries in Egypt. He had been studying the explorations of that mysterious and ancient country all his life, though he had yet to go there himself. He hoped that when he did eventually go, he would be able to test his theory about the hidden last resting place of Amenophis IV, otherwise known as Tutankhamen.

He knew that Mrs Stanley had been out there several times to visit her husband, Sir Norman, on his digs, and that more than her pretty frame attracted Caine to want to learn more from her. About everything.

Fitch, the cadaverous butler, was waiting in the hallway to take their coats, ably assisted by Jensen, his fresh-faced young apprentice. Fitch had been Norman Stanley's father's butler, and wasn't getting any young. Mr and Mrs Stanley both expected him to retire within a year, after which Jensen would be their butler.

Mrs Stanley smiled at both of them, but her look to Jensen was a lot less formal than her smile to Fitch.

The drawing room had been turned from a cozy place for reading by candlelight, to a sort of temple to the ancients that Verne's Captain Nemo might have had aboard the *Nautilus*. Thick velvet drapes hid the paneling and bookshelves on the walls. Small Egyptian statuettes were dotted throughout the room, while a kneeling sphinx kept vigil at each corner of the room's central feature.

This was not a table or piano—they had both been removed to make room—but instead a large wooden sarcophagus, almost as wide as it was long. It was large enough to hold several people in comfort, though everyone in the room knew there was but one person within.

Four clay jars were arrayed on a small plinth in front of the sarcophagus. Though they were all the same size, each had a lid carved into the shape of a different animal—a baboon, a jackal, a hawk, and a man. Canopic jars, Caine realized at once, designed to hold the mummy's organs. He wondered if these were the jars belonging to this sarcophagus, that of Amenkharis IV, or if they had simply been put there to foster an appropriate atmosphere.

"Welcome back," Mrs Stanley said.

As he began to pull the double-doors closed, Fitch saw something that made him wonder if his aged eyes were getting too rheumy to do their job properly. There was a faint haze emerging from the corner of the sarcophagus. It roiled and flowed the way fog did when it crept through an open door or window, except that this was certainly no fog. It was too black even for the tar-tinted mists of London.

"Mrs Stanley," he called uncertainly.

She couldn't take her eyes off the carved lid of the sarcophagus, and stared at it as if hypnotized. "That'll be all, Fitch," she said, without turning round.

Fitch hesitated. Normally he would obey his mistress's commands with question, but it was surely part of his duty and responsibility to look after her. "But, Mrs Stanley..."

She turned her head, the venom in her eyes a stark counterpoint to the beatific smile on her face. "I said, that will be all, Fitch."

"Yes ma'am," he acquiesced. Reluctantly, he stepped out of the room, and closed the doors.

Mrs Stanley thought for a moment, then crossed to the doors, and locked them, tossing the key onto a nearby table. She was already turning away, and didn't see the key skid along the top of the table, and off the far edge, into the shadows at the foot of a bookcase.

"He's due to retire soon," she said to the others. "You can see why." They grunted in response. "Now to the most exciting part of the day," she promised. "Hector, if you would do the honors."

Hector Barnes took up a crowbar and, helped by Caine, began to lever up the antediluvian lid of the sarcophagus.

Mrs Stanley's heart fluttered as the lid snapped open. The gap between the lid and the sarcophagus was only an inch or so at first, but it was enough to let out the foulest stench she had ever experienced.

Hector stretched out a hand reverently, his eyes wide, entranced. He touched the wrappings where they were indented over the eye sockets, and let out a tiny sigh, as if caught on the peak of sexual pleasure. Mrs Stanley understood completely. To see something no one else had seen, to touch the untouchable... "If only he could see us, when we see him."

Suddenly Hector stiffened, his arching almost enough to snap his spine. His eyes bulged with terror, and his scream was full throated, holding back not a bit of the mortal dread the human mind is capable of experiencing.

A cobra's head, its hood fully flared, was hanging from his wrist. As the others in the room added their screams to Hector's, the snake whipped itself up, coiling around his arm.

Mrs Stanley screamed again, yelling for Fitch and Jensen. They responded quickly, and the door handles rattled. "It's locked," a muffled voice called through the door. Mrs Stanley let out a most unladylike curse and looked to the table. The key wasn't there.

She scrambled around, looking for the key, whimpering while the door began to rattle under the impacts of Fitch and Jensen's attempts to break it down. This wasn't right, she thought, and wasn't fair. She tried to tear her eyes away from the snakes, but couldn't.

They had sought knowledge, and now the serpents had come for them.

She turned towards the door, and found another cobra rearing up in her path. She screamed again. "Jensen! The door! Break it down!" Her words were barely comprehensible, just waves in a primeval sea of the noise of fear.

The cobra tensed, using its body as a spring to leap upwards. Its fangs grabbed hold of her tongue, pumping venom into the root of it. She couldn't breathe for the snake's head filling her mouth. Her throat convulsed, gagging and trying to retch. Her whole body curled over, trying to bring up enough vomit to force the snake off her tongue, and the effort knocked her over sideways. Some vomit escaped around the gap between the cobra and her lips, but the rest backfilled her nose, and tried to slide back down her throat, choking her more and more.

All through this, the cobra's venom continued to take effect, sending waves of fire down from her tongue, through her neck and along her limbs. Her head was filled with what felt like boiling steam, with enough pressure to make her eyes feel as if they would be shot from her face.

Shocked and unsure what to do, Andrew Caine backed away. One of the cobras followed. Its hiss sounded like steam forced out of a boiler that was about to explode. Andrew froze, suddenly sure that there was going be another explosion somewhere, just like at the spiritualist's apartments. Surely the gas had hissed out of the pipe just like that, before it had been ignited.

The cobra reared up in front of him and Andrew reached out blindly behind him for a weapon. His fingers curled round cold hard wood, a walking stick. The cobra's head darted forward and Andrew swept the stick across to block it. He missed the snake, but it pulled back, allowing him to back away a couple of steps.

The snake followed smoothly, undeterred. Andrew swung the stick, aiming for its head, but it dodged easily, curling around and away from the stick like smoke. He raised the stick again; sure that he had now judged the snake's capabilities. He knew where it would try to dodge to, and so he wouldn't miss.

Andrew took a deep breath, trying to steady himself for the all-important strike. In that moment, the snake reared again, rocking backwards slightly and opening its jaws. For a fraction of a second, Andrew thought it was afraid, that it recognized his superiority and its own impending demise.

Then, from five feet away, the venom it spat hit his eyes. His vision went red, then black, as the burning pain from the venom felt like it was eating clean through his eyes and into his brain. His head seemed to be bulging with fire, which ate downwards towards the roots of his upper teeth, and into his ear canals.

He didn't feel himself drop the stick, or clutch his hands to his head, but he did feel the cobra sink its fangs into his ankle.

He fell, screaming, and thrashed on the floor, trying to get away from the pain within. Instead, more pain came, with another bite, this time to the arm. More fangs pierced his neck, and then, worst of all, Andrew distantly felt something sinuous and powerful slide up his pants leg.

His last scream was the worst of all.

ELEVEN

Will put down the old *London Times* on the Formica tabletop at Coco's on Sherman Way and laid a copy of the memoirs of Sir Norman Stanley on top of it. Patti had picked the latter up at Crown Books in their ancient history section, having sought out the Stanley name after reading the old paper. Since the advent of *Discovery Channel*, Ancient Egypt had become big business and just about every book ever written on the subject was back in print somewhere.

"Okay, let me see if I've got this right. Your great, great grandmother, or thereabouts, had a vision of an explosion and got people out, that was in the paper. Then three of the survivors died in this freaky snake accident that this guy—" he tapped the book with a fingertip "—wrote about in his memoirs."

"Yeah."

"So far so déjà vu."

"That's exactly what I thought when I found that first newspaper report. At first I thought it was just a hell of a coincidence, but when I found the story about the survivors of the blast starting to die—"

"Why should Hollywood have a monopoly on sequels and franchises?"

"Right. Juliet Collins lived at a time when the spiritualist church was really popular. In fact, in those days spiritualism was pretty much considered to be a real science. I did some checking on the net. Juliet and the others went and spoke to mediums. People like Helena Blavatsky. They obviously thought that these mediums had some kind of knowledge that could help them out with the situation they were in. Which is too much like the situation we're in to be a coincidence."

"What, you think maybe it's some sort of family curse?"

"I don't even know if curses exist, but if they do, then maybe it might be. Right now, though, I'm thinking more that there's some kind of set of circumstances that combine to make a cause that provokes a certain effect. I think it happened in 1888, and it's happening again now."

"Because you're from the same family? Is that part of the circumstances?" Will held her hand across the tabletop.

"Maybe. I don't know for sure."

Will swallowed. "Okay, so these Victorian dudes went to their local mediums and psychics to save their asses from this shit. And did they?"

"I don't know," Patti admitted.

"What do you mean, you don't know? I thought you were reading all this shit in those old newspapers and on the net."

"I am, but I'm getting the results of these searches out of chronological order. And the newspapers didn't tell everything anyway. It's not like they interviewed Juliet for the whole story from start to finish." She opened today's paper to the classified ad section. "Having said that, I think we can still follow their example, and maybe get ahead of the game. I've been picking out the likeliest-looking ads." She turned the paper around so he could see the ads she had circled in red ink.

"Professional psychic?" Will scoffed. "What the hell do we want with them?"

"They're the modern equivalent of mediums, Will. If Juliet Collins got any joy out of the mediums in her day, maybe we can get some results out of the modern equivalent."

Patti's choice of psychic was a Julianna Fiegl in Mission Viejo, and she and Will decided to drive there straight away. Patti tended to take a no-time-like-the-present attitude at the best of times, and this was a time when it seemed an even more apposite attitude than most days.

They had driven up towards Saddleback Mountain and then turned into housing areas that were shaded by trees. Today, the trees provided more of an umbrella function than a parasol one.

Will had expected either a fearsome looking mock-gothic castle or a cheap mini-mall unit plastered with bargain prices that shared floor space with a tattoo parlor. Instead, he found himself looking at a neat little Frank Lloyd Wright-style of house in a pleasant hillside area. It looked more like the sort of place where he would have expected to find a mid-range actor, not a professional psychic.

"Are you sure this is the place?"

"Definitely," Patti said firmly. "This is it."

"If you say so." Will got out of the car and tried to dismiss any and all expectations and preconceptions from his mind. After all, the place was completely different than he expected, so maybe the psychic and her service would be completely different too. Actually being worth anything, and not sucking, would qualify as being different from the expectations he had formed earlier.

He didn't say anything more, though. This was Patti's show and so naturally he would back her up, whatever she wanted to do.

They walked to the door, and Patti rung a discreetly placed buzzer. After a moment, a blonde woman with mousy-colored roots and blue eyes opened the door with a smile. She was barefoot, and wore jeans and a plain pastel T-shirt. Chalk another one up against expectations, Will thought. He had expected the full Goth getup or a hippy-style kaftan. The bare feet were as he expected, however, so he allowed himself a point for them. She was also curvaceous, and Will appreciated that at least he'd be able to enjoy the beauty of two women while he was here.

"Yes?"

"Uh, my name's Patti Fuller and this is Will Sax. I called earlier for an appointment..."

"Please, do come in."

The interior of the house was spacious and airy, all in pastels with chrome shelving and lamps, and the biggest kick-ass wall-mounted flat-screen TV he had ever seen. Whatever make and model it was, she hadn't bought it at Circuit City.

"Coffee, juice?" Julianna offered.

"OJ, please," Patti replied. "Two."

"I knew you'd say that." Will groaned and Julianna laughed musically. "Sorry, I always say that to my prey. Can't resist." She disappeared for a moment and returned with the juice, freshly squeezed and ice cold. It almost made up for the whole idea of visiting a psychic, in Will's opinion.

"You have a question for me. I don't have to be clairvoyant or read minds to know that."

"You're sort of right," Patti said. "It's more I'm looking for an opinion on a story, than that I have a straightforward question. Is that okay?"

"Whatever you want to tell me is fine."

"Okay. It started with the South Hill Street Metroline station..."

It took nearly an hour and a half for Patti and Will to tell Julianna their story, including as they did a condensed second hand account of what the knew about the survivors of the Mornington Crescent gas explosion of the Fall of 1888.

"Would it surprise you if I said I'd heard this story before?"

"That would depend on who told you it."

Julianna smiled, showing small even teeth. "Like a doctor, I hold dear to the principles of confidentiality. If I told you something someone else had told me, how could you trust me not to betray your confidence too?"

Patti laughed, liking the woman a lot. "Maybe I can surprise you. It was Jess Golden who told you this type of story before, wasn't it?"

"I can't answer that," Julianna said, but her expression had already done so.

"So, what is it that's happening? It feels evil, like I'd imagine Satan to feel."

"What's after you isn't evil. Not in the sense you mean."

"Well, it's hardly what I'd call good."

"It's neither. Your doom is no more evil than a hurricane, or an earthquake.

"Does it know that?" Will asked. "It seems to take a sentient and perverse delight in killing us as horribly as possible. If we have to die, that's one thing, but where's the nature in dying so horribly?"

Julianna mulled over her words carefully before she spoke again. "When man messes with his environment he creates things that are worse for himself. Acid rain, global warming, carcinogens in food. Why can't gorier deaths be part of those side effects?

"It's a part of nature," she added. "If Mother Nature is the creative force that brings life, then death is Father Nature. It's not a family to fuck with; it's a family to respect. They've been running the world since its first dawn, and who are we to interfere with them?"

Al Kinsey spent a pleasant evening cooking for his wife. It wasn't something he needed to do, but he enjoyed it anyway, maybe because it was a creative thing. It wasn't a script or a movie, or a painting or statue, but at least it was something he had created that would give pleasure to someone else as well as himself.

It was an Italian dish, a Bolognese, since that was what Gloria liked best. Al himself preferred to cook oriental food, which gave him more opportunity to play—or experiment, as he insisted on calling it—with spices and seasonings and all manner of flavors to be added to whatever the main ingredient of the dish was.

Italian was good too, though, as he could mix and match herbs in the meat and sauce. It was also a little more solid and filling than most Chinese dishes, though if someone had put a gun to his head to force a confession, he might have admitted that it could as easily be down to him not being as a good a stir-fry cook as he thought he was. After all, nobody really knew how good they were at things, because they couldn't be objective.

Gloria's face when she ate the dinner he had spent so much time on told its own story of how good a cook he was. She positively glowed with good vibes and wolfed down the lot. How she could do that and not put an inch on her waistline, Al neither knew nor cared. He had the perfect wife; one who loved to eat as much as he loved to cook but never lost her figure, and who earned just a few hundred bucks a year less than him—so they were pretty well solvent, but he never felt threatened by her breadwinning ability.

If she would just lose her inhibitions about giving him head, she really would be perfect.

Back at Patti's, Will paced back and forth, clenching and unclenching his fists. The activity didn't manage to hide the trembling that threatened to overwhelm him. "What was the point, Patti? What was the point of us still standing and breathing?"

"You know what I think? I think all this weird shit is because we're supposed to be dead."

"Weren't you listening? It's because we survived."

"Like, if there's such a thing as fate or destiny. And we were fated or destined to die in that bombing, maybe the world, fuck, even the universe, hasn't caught up with the fact that we're still here." He waved a hand in a vague spiral, indicating, Patti supposed, everything in general. "The world without us is running along on its own momentum, and sooner or later I just hope that momentum runs out so it can figure out that we're still here."

Patti managed to follow most of his line of thinking, and wondered how many beers had either fuelled or partially drowned it.

"So, if I'm right, there's one of two ways it can go, yeah? Either the world gets its shit together and accepts that we're here to stay, or..." He hesitated.

"Or it kills us."

"One way or the other." He sat beside her, and tapped her on the shoulder. "That's not the weirdest thing. I mean, I've been thinking pretty hard–"

"Too hard by the sound of it."

"– about this. What if us still being here when we should be dead is really a bad thing? I mean, really bad for the world, not just bad for us."

That stopped Patti in her tracks. "What?"

"Reality has fucked up. We're something that shouldn't be a part of it. Like an infection or a couple of cancer cells. We're not part of the body that nature specified." He saw that he had gotten her attention now. "What happens when there's bad stuff on the loose in the body?"

"The immune system fights it. Antibodies..."

"Yeah. Antibodies come out and fight the infection or whatever."

"They kill the undesirable cells."

"Yeah. "

Patti shook her head. "I don't buy it." *Won't* buy it, she corrected herself silently. "We're not an infection. An infection spreads."

"We stop being careful, anything's possible. Then we're a virus, replicating, spreading." He caught her look. "Okay, let's say we're not a virus, not spreading. It's still an inert piece of material rejected by the body."

Patti understood. "Like a pearl."

"We're the piece of grit in the oyster, except that instead of just coating us to isolate us from itself. It needs to get rid of us altogether."

When Jim Castle got home, he was both bone tired and emotionally worn out. His left leg felt about a decade older than the right, and he kept wondering if that was just a side effect of the weird hours he was pulling on this case, or if the world around him really was slightly jittery and fuzzy.

His wife, Lauren, was waiting for him and wrapped an arm around his shoulders as he finally sunk onto the couch. It was a simple gesture on her part but it felt better than being presented with a medal for his efforts.

Jim let out a long sigh, shaking his head. "Some days I wish I was a barber, or a fisherman, or anything but a Fed."

Jim managed to catch a few hours' sleep in the warmed dent that Lauren had left in the mattress when she went to work. It wasn't quite as good as having here there with him, but he could smell her shampoo on the pillow and that helped him feel connected to her.

He made dinner for her, putting it in the fridge before leaving again for South Figueroa. He wasn't working any specific duty shifts now, not since the bombing. There was sleep time, and on duty time, and nothing in between.

Tony Chang was pinning mug shots to a board in the briefing room. Jim looked at them. "Does this mean we've got a lead on the guy in the demand video?"

"Better than that," Chang said. "We got a name."

Jim blinked, his mouth agape. "A name?" God, luck or the Force, whatever, was definitely with them.

"The man in the tape is, as far as we can tell, an Irishman called Sean Reilly." Chang thumbed the remote, bringing up a police mug shot on the screen. It was a photo of a man with a mane of dark hair, thinning at the front. He had a goatee beard, graying at the sides, and eyes that said they wouldn't take any shit from anyone. Chang thumbed up another file photo. This was a candid one from covert surveillance. It showed Reilly walking into a hotel, a leather trench coat flowing out behind him.

"Who is this guy?" Jim prompted.

"He used to be with the Provisional IRA back in the 1980s," Chang said. "A real hardliner. He came to the US to raise funds to buy Stinger missiles with the intention of shooting down a British Airways flight on final approach to JFK or Dulles.

"He was allowed to escape somehow and slipped back to Ireland. The peace deal and Good Friday Agreement between the Brits and the Republicans didn't sit well with him. He wanted nothing less than the death or exile to mainland Britain of every Protestant in Ulster.

"So, when the violence tailed off, he founded a splinter group, IRAX–IRA eXtreme. Reilly was exiled from Ireland under sentence of death from the Provo IRA Council if ever he returned to the island. Rumor has it that it was because he and his followers attempted to assassinate the leaders of the Sinn Fein party and the President of Ireland. Then Reilly disappeared off the face of the Earth and the FBI and the British MI5 both thought he'd been deep-sixed by the IRA."

"So, the subway bombers are a dissident Irish Republican group?"

"I don't know. It's possible, or it could be that Reilly has started a new group. The prints we made of a surviving piece of the bomb don't match Reilly. They match *this* guy here." A click brought up an image of a handsome shaven-headed Mediterranean-looking man in his thirties. "Leon Khalid. French Lebanese, former member of Hamas. Last known to be a student of al-Zahwari."

"Bin Laden's right-hand man?"

"That's the one. The news didn't make headlines here, but according to State Department sources in Pakistan, Zahwari has issued a fatwa on Khalid, for pocketing a share of Bin Laden's family fortune that was intended to buy weapons. Khalid managed to get out of Afghanistan, but didn't get the cash out with him.

"We've seen Khalid in surveillance pictures with another man. You're gonna love this one, he's homegrown." The image on the screens looked as if he had stepped off the cover of a ZZ Top album to beat up the listener. "Dan Hoffman, late of Montana's chapter of the Aryan Nation. They've got a contract out on him for having got the chapter head's daughter pregnant and then taking her to a back street abortionist who managed to leave her with peritonitis. The abortionist turned up dead in a firebombing last month, and Hoffman's house was torched, but he'd already gone to ground."

"So what is this group?"

"Our worst nightmare. A 'Magnificent Seven' of the world's most depraved and cold-blooded murderers, disaffected from any and all causes they previously held dear, and out purely for their own gain."

"Command me and I shall obey, oh master."

"Take copies of these mug shots and show them to the surviving... survivors. See if any of these faces ring a bell."

The Borderland Patrol's offices were different than Jim had expected. It was neither shabby nor a high-tech nerve center. There were no "I Want To Believe" UFO posters on the walls, or filing cabinets filled to bursting point with dog-eared Warren Commission volumes.

Instead it was an airy open-plan area that felt more like a lounge than an office. The nearest thing to it that Castle had seen was a video game developer's suite of offices. The decorations were tasteful and subtle. The occasional bas-relief hung on the walls, and it was only on close inspection that Castle realized one was a molding of a face made out of leaves, and another a plaster cast of what he presumed to be a Bigfoot footprint.

Chromed lamps put out a soft light, while potted palms made the place a little friendlier. Which was fortunate as Patti wasn't in yet, though the editor said she was due to pop in at any minute and Jim decided to wait. He didn't want to risk going to Patti's home and maybe pass her going the other way. So he read back issues for half an hour until she showed up.

He glommed a spare desk from Matt Lawson, the editor, and spread the mug shots of Reilly, Khalid and Hoffman out on it. "I need to know if you recognize any of these men, especially if you saw them near the Metroline station."

Patti looked them over carefully, taking her time and not wanting to make any mistakes by rushing. It didn't make any difference to her eventual verdict: she had never seen any of them before, except for a TV broadcast about Khalid a couple of months earlier.

"Sorry," she told him.

"That's okay."

"Who are this group anyway? Al Qaeda?"

"No, this is a different thing altogether. I don't think we even have a word for it beyond 'trouble.'"

"Oh?"

"They don't have a political or religious cause that we can exploit for leverage. They've all got death marks on them from both the authorities of half the world, and the major terrorist organizations they used to belong to." Jim balled his hands into fists and glanced momentarily at the ceiling. "I believe these are the men who may, and I stress may, and it's just my pet theory, not ATF policy... I believe these may be the men who are hunting down and killing the survivors of the bombing. They're the men who might be after you."

TWELVE

Inspector Abberline's expert consultants were waiting outside the Stanley mansion. Today the tall and thin one was wearing the expression of a man too concentrated to keep the headaches away. He was flicking through a report with disdain. "Excellent work on that business at Wapping last month," Abberline said. "A nasty business."

"Thank you, inspector, but it is how I earn my keep, and I fear my housekeeper would be most displeased were I to prove unable to pay her the rent when it is due."

Abberline chuckled. "I've heard she's a fearsome battleaxe."

"Strong-willed and unwilling to tolerate nonsense, I should say. An attitude the good doctor and myself happen to agree with."

"Absolutely," the stouter man agreed. "She also lays out the finest cold collation in London. Invaluable for keeping up one's strength during a troublesome case."

"Exactly."

"Well, the Home Secretary was grateful for your assistance, so I imagine she'll be able to keep you in cold collations for some time to come."

"Quite so. Oh, might I enquire as to what happened to the freighter?"

"Taken out into the Solent and sunk by naval demolitions experts. I imagine you need to know that for when you write up the case, doctor?"

"For our own records, yes," the stouter man admitted, "though I don't foresee publishing the details of this particular case for some years to come. I don't think the world is really ready for such a terrible case, the Ripper murders notwithstanding."

"As for these deaths? I suppose it's possible that Sir Norman put the snakes in before the sarcophagus's transport to England, as part of some sort of over-elaborate scheme to get rid of his wife?"

"I suppose it's theoretically possible, but I doubt it's the case."

"No, nor do I. Clearly an accident, I fear."

Gilbert Collins's face wore a look of sadness and dismay at the state of the world as he read *The Times*. He always looked like that while reading the papers, and Juliet didn't pay much attention to it, until he beckoned her over.

"Juliet... The séance you went to? It was in Mornington Crescent, wasn't it?

"Yes, why?" She couldn't imagine why he wanted to bring the subject up. She would have thought he'd have been perfectly happy to never hear about it again. Unless, she thought with a cold trickle between her shoulder blades, he had heard about her vision. Bill Sangster had told her that the *Courant* had mentioned it, though thankfully it didn't mention her by name, and her father didn't get such a downmarket publication.

He passed *The Times* to her. "There's been a kind of... terrible, well I suppose you'd call it an accident. Three people died last night from the venom of Egyptian spitting cobras, which had somehow got into a sarcophagus they had brought over." Gilbert didn't sound too distressed. "I should think that might send a message to so-called scientists who practice grave-robbing and desecration, even of pagan tombs." He looked up. "It says all three were at Mornington Crescent, and so was a man called Matthew Upton." Upton? Juliet thought. Surely he wasn't dead too? "His body was identified yesterday. Burned to death, apparently, in some kind of even more bizarre accident."

Juliet sat, or, more accurately, fell, back into a chair. Four of the survivors are dead? Was there some twisted significance to that? She needed to get out and find the others. She needed to talk to them, if only to reassure herself that they were all safe and that the apparent connection of these four deaths was purely coincidental. She rose unsteadily to her feet.

"Where are you going?"

"I–I have an appointment to see some friends."

"I don't think that's necessarily wise, do you? Have you considered the possibility that four people from the séance dying so strangely might be more than a coincidence?" He sounded nervous, frightened even, and that disturbed Juliet. Her father wasn't afraid of anything. He never had been. Yet now he sounded terrified. "Yes," he continued, "I see that you have."

He stood as well. "Juliet, I don't think you should go out anywhere for the time being. At least until the police have looked into this matter and confirmed that the deaths really were accidents, and that this is not..." He trailed off.

"Not what?"

"Nemesis. Retribution for a sin."

Juliet understood exactly what he meant, but she felt that if there had been a sin at the séance then it had been her sin, not that of any of the four people who had just died. She held her father's gaze, possibly for the first time in her life. "Papa, you have always raised me to believe in atoning for sins, and in redemption."

"Yes, the gospels–"

"If there was a sin that night, it was mine." Gilbert blanched. "It wasn't Madame Adrienne who had a vision at the séance, it was me. And that vision was of the explosion." She bit her lip. "If these deaths are in any way connected to the event of the séance, then it's my responsibility to atone."

Gilbert was struck dumb by this incredible change in his daughter's behavior. She took advantage of his stupor to fetch her hat and coat and run out of the house, scarcely believing what she had just done, or what she was about to do.

Juliet's first port of call was the obvious one: Scotland Yard. It took her almost an hour to get to see Inspector Abberline. More precisely, she had been rebuffed by the desk sergeant immediately, and waited outside the door for an hour until Abberline passed through it and she could buttonhole him directly.

She showed him the morning's edition of *The Times*.

"I've read it," he said curtly.

"I think someone ought to find out who or what is killing the members of Adrienne's group."

Abberline sighed, but not unkindly. "Miss Collins, Scotland Yard has its plate full with the Ripper, to say nothing of Irish terrorism and all the other crimes in the city. We don't investigate coincidences."

Juliet wasn't going to be fobbed off so easily. "But someone or something killed Upton and those three people in that house. Don't you think it's odd—more that odd, in fact—that four people who survived an explosion are dead by other means within a week."

"Odd, yes, but the world is odd, lass. It always has been, just as it has never been fair, and as it has always been twisted and perverse." He sighed. "It's sad right enough that those people died, especially considering their escape along with your own last week, but they were accidents, just as the gas explosion was." His eyes narrowed, and he leaned forward. "Unless you're thinking that it wasn't an accident?"

"I don't know. All I know is that I have a feeling that something evil is happening."

"Accidents, Miss Collins, not evil. It's easy enough to see how you could cast the one in the light of the other, I suppose. Perhaps, after surviving the gas explosion, they thought that was as unlucky as they could get, or that they were indestructible. It happens sometimes, with people who survive disasters or acts of violence that have been perpetrated upon them. Then, so thinking, people might become a little more careless than they normally would be."

"Careless? How could three people in an English drawing room be expected to look out for poisonous cobras?"

"I should have thought someone importing a large crate from Egypt would have at least checked their new property to ensure it was all in one piece." He took a piece of paper from his desk drawer. "According to this, there was a hole in it, and a stevedore down at the docks thought he saw something slithering there while unloading it from the ship upon which it arrived."

"Why didn't he tell someone before?"

"He thought he was hallucinating after a few jugs too many the night before. After he saw the report in the papers, he came in to tell us what he saw, not that it makes a blind bit of difference to the coroner's verdict. We now know there were eight spitting cobras in the sarcophagus. All deadly."

"But how did they get in there?"

"They're native to the Valley Of The Kings, according to Sir Wallis Budge. They must have got in when the sarcophagus came out of the tomb. Accident and coincidence."

Juliet snorted in disgust. "Then it would appear that I must simply make my own investigations."

Abberline maintained a creditably straight face, but Juliet could feel the patronizing amusement coming off him in waves. "Your own investigations?"

"I shall hire a private detective."

Baker Street was her next port of call. The laughter there was a little sharper, and slightly more kindly. "My dear Miss Collins," her choice of consulting detective protested, "I deal in facts and rationally observable phenomena, not vague feeling and anxieties."

His companion had been more kindly. "He gets like this sometimes. It's the morphine solution he takes to relieve the boredom. It makes him... unpredictable." So she had left Baker Street, as disappointed as she had left Scotland Yard.

Once she had gone, the shorter man turned to the other. "That was rather rude, you know; laughing in her face like that."

"I shall write her a note of apology, perhaps. I have been thinking about this matter since we returned from the Stanley house. I am not so sure it was an accident; there is a whiff of clever design about it."

"But you said—"

"I simply did not wish to take the case. The truth would not necessarily be easy to get to."

"You've often told me that whenever you eliminate the impossible, whatever remains, however improbable, must be the truth."

"And therein lies the problem, my dear fellow. In this instance we cannot eliminate the impossible."

Disconsolate, Juliet wandered the streets, trying to cheer herself up by telling herself she could shop or take a tea at a tea rooms.

She heard running footsteps behind her and turned, prepared to at least try to hit back at whatever pickpocket or footpad might be aiming for her. To her delight, it was no pickpocket or footpad, but Bill Sangster, his pace slightly hampered by his overcoat, and a big smile of greetings on his face. She stopped to wait for him.

"I wasn't sure it was you," he said, not out of breath in the slightest. "But I thought it was, so... Well, no joy from the Peelers, eh? I told you they're pretty hopeless."

"So it would seem."

"You look like you need cheering up. Come on, I know a good pub round the corner." Juliet wasn't sure it was quite proper for a young lady to accompany a man to such an establishment, but her feet were beginning to hurt and she could use an opportunity to take the weight off them and refresh herself.

Bill's choice of public house was a relatively clean establishment in Westminster. Through a narrow gap behind the bar, she could see the tapster pouring a thick black-red liquid into a barrel of beer. Bill quaffed his black beer, apparently unconcerned by the reddish tint to the foamy head. “So, what are you going to do?”

“Someone or something killed four people who survived what happened at Adrienne’s. What if he or it hasn’t finished?”

“You mean if the deaths keep going.”

“There are several more survivors, including ourselves.” She shuddered. “Perhaps what happened to Mister Upton and the others really was just a terrible, unfortunate coincidence to come so soon after the explosion... But I find myself so frightened that it was not.”

“Fear is a survival mechanism, Juliet. It gives us information we can use to decide what to do about things. Like, if some man decides to attack you, you can decide whether to fight back, run away, or do whatever else might feel right to you. Doing what feels right is usually the right thing to do, I find.”

“What happened to the others, even if there was some design or plan to it, wasn’t the work of a man’s hand.”

“Then perhaps it was the work of something else.”

“Like what?”

“I don’t know... God, perhaps? Fate? Death himself, even.”

“That’s some damned queer thoughts you’re having, Jules,” he said. “Damned queer thoughts.”

He flashed her a grin that made her forget to reprimand him for abbreviating her name. "But I like them. This may be the age of reason, but I don't see why it should also be the age of... of lack of spirituality and art." He let out a snorting laugh. "Let's see Mister Darwin tell us what the grim reaper evolved from."

Stewart Tubbs grimaced when he saw Juliet and Bill approach him in the quadrangle that provided the hospital's patients with access to fresh air, and its doctors with a place to smoke their pipes and cigarillos.

"What do you want?"

Juliet and Bill exchanged glances. "We just wanted to see if you were all right," she said.

Tubbs looked up, so they could see the bags under his eyes. "I'm as right as I look, all right? Anyway, why wouldn't I be?"

"Don't you know what happened to Tubbs and Mrs Stanley?"

"Of course I know! I was at Tubbs's autopsy."

"Then you must have the same feeling we have. The same instinct that something isn't right. It can't be a coincidence that four of the people from Madame Adrienne's séance are dead."

"Of course it can," Tubbs scoffed. "Just because something looks a certain way doesn't mean it is that way. Not for people who can resist gullibility. You two might be fooled by all that spiritualism rubbish, but I'm not."

"You went nine times," Bill pointed out softly.

"To study her methods. Like the ectoplasm she used to produce."

"It was just muslin," Juliet said. Tubbs looked at her, mouth agape. "I saw it in the vision, burning. That's why it caught fire, when something made of ectoplasm couldn't."

"Come on," Bill said, squinting up at the slate-gray overcast. "I can think of at least one other person who might be able to help us."

"Try an alienist," Tubbs recommended.

The woman sitting in the center of the room wasn't just old; she looked as if she had been born old. She looked as if she had been old when the world was young. Despite that, her eyes were as bright as diamonds, and as deep as the mines from which those gems were unearthed.

Juliet was utterly in awe of her, in a way she hadn't been by Madame Adrienne. The woman took a drag on a hemp cigarette and coughed. "Fuck me, it's cold today." Her accent was eastern European, and very thick, and her name was Helena Petrovna Blavatsky.

In fact her real name was Helena Hahn, but who could keep track of what was real in this world? Juliet certainly couldn't any more. Blavatsky's smile was as cold as ice. "The Akashic records hold the tales of many shitty situations such as this. It is not just in this so-called age of reason that men seek to avoid their destinies and to cheat Death. It has been so since the times of Ancient Greece and Rome, and even before the sinkings of Atlantis and Lemuria."

"People's will to survive is strong," Bill said, desperately trying not to sound shocked by this outrageous and vulgar creature. "Their deaths aren't always easily accepted, and nor should they be."

Blavatsky's smile warmed up slightly. "When I speak of cheating Death, child, I do not mean simply avoiding losing one's life. I mean that sometimes the Reaper himself is cheated. He is a bad loser, you see. He despises being cheated and made to look a fool. And so he punishes those who try."

"But," Juliet began, "surely the nature of life is to fight against death?"

"Fight? That's such a misleading word. Can you fight a cloud to stop it from raining on you? Can you hold back the wind and stuff it back into wherever it came from? That's what you're trying to do now. You're trying to defy nature, and that can only make things worse for yourself."

"When you say 'You...'"

"I mean you two and the others who survived the gas explosion. The veil was thin at the séance and you were able, however unconsciously, to exploit that to cheat the reaper. But now he will make you pay."

THIRTEEN

Patti paced around the parking lot, which glistened like obsidian after the day's rain. The Aztecs, Patti recalled, used obsidian, for sacrificial knives. They would use it to cut the hearts out of people. "God knows we're getting our hearts torn out," she muttered to herself.

"Huh?" Will asked.

"Oh, I was just... just wondering whether anyone would come."

"They'll come," Will said, with a tone of confidence that Patti could only hope he really felt. "Don't worry. By now they're bound to be as freaked as we are."

"Well, here's hoping they're not too freaked to be rational." She glanced at the papers and magazines on the back seat of her Saturn. "Not that any of this is likely to sound very rational to anyone."

"You're right there," Will agreed. "But we're going to do our best anyway, right? You can't stop rock and roll, huh?"

Patti wished she could agree, but something had stopped The Vipers pretty well a few months ago. Stopped them dead.

The first to arrive was Jim Castle's Vanagon. "What the fuck is he doing here?" Will demanded.

"He's our best bet for help and protection," Patti told him.

"He's our best bet for getting locked up in a psycho ward!"

"I've been talking to him–"

"I noticed," Will said tightly.

"And I think he has an open mind."

Before Will could express any further doubts, the silver Volkswagen van had stopped and Jim emerged. "Well, this is cozy," he said. "Did you remember something about the bombing?"

"No," Patti admitted. "This is about what happened after. It's about Zack Halloran and Hal Ward."

Jim regarded her calmly and then nodded. "All right, I'd like to hear about that."

"Well," Patti said. "I hate to keep you in suspense, but we're not going to be alone here. We're waiting for the others."

"What others?" His expression cleared. "The other survivors? Fries and Kinsey?" Patti nodded.

Next to pull into the parking lot was a low-slung BMW. In the starless and moonless night, its red paintwork made it look like some slab of meat, freshly cut from a leviathan and still glistening with moisture. Al Kinsey stepped out and immediately swore. "You psychos? I came all the way out here for you?" He threw off his jacket. "You want a rematch, huh? I've been hoping for that. Been working out, ready for it."

"Put your jacket back on, Kinsey," Patti said, the tiredness she felt finally slipping into her voice. "I just want to talk about Halloran and Ward."

Al looked around, from Patti to Will to Jim, and back. "What about them?"

"It's a surprise," Will said nastily.

Finally, Susan Fries's Dodge Ram pickup rumbled to a halt, and she emerged, wearing tight boots, trousers and a leather top. She looked as if she hadn't slept in a week. "This better be good," she warned.

With everyone here, Patti cleared her throat, while Will handed out cans of cola. "I wanted to talk about what's been happening to us lately," Patti began."

"Us?" Susan echoed. "What 'us' would that be?"

"The 'us' who survived the bomb because of my..."

"Bugging out?" Al suggested.

"If you want to put it like that, yeah."

"Two of us died recently," Susan said darkly.

Al shrugged, butting in before Patti could answer. "So? The construction industry has a certain element of danger to it. So do extreme sports."

Susan stiffened, and Al held up a conciliatory hand. "None of which makes a death any less tragic, but... They do happen, you know. Both guys went into it with their eyes open, you know what I mean?"

Patti nodded understandingly. "I know, shit happens. Sometimes it happens for no reason other than that the universe is set up that way, but sometimes there's a reason. What I'm gonna tell you is going to be hard to believe and harder to accept the truth or even if you do believe it, but I... I honestly believe that this is what's going down." She took a deep breath and a long draught of cola. "I've been doing a lot of research into what's been happening to us. The deaths of Hal Ward and Zack Halloran this week were not a coincidence."

Susan gasped and made a fist. "What are you suggesting?"

"I'm suggesting that it's no coincidence that two of us have died. I'm suggesting that we were all meant to have died in that bombing, and that the job that was started there is being finished, one by one."

"You mean the terrorists?" Al said. "Why would they want to specifically kill us? I mean, it's not as if we're all rocket scientists, or military types who spend our days playing Rocky and Bullwinkle to their Boris and Natasha."

"I wouldn't discount the possibility," Jim put in. "Maybe you all saw something when you were at the station turnstiles and don't even remember it."

"Well, I didn't see shit," Al snapped, "after some psycho bitch popped me in the eye."

"Maybe you didn't," Jim admitted, "but the bombers think you did. That could be enough to put you on a death list. Or maybe they just want to be thorough, so they can make that part of their psychological strategy to try and scare us."

"If that's what they're trying, then they're succeeding."

"All right," Jim said. "Let me tell who I think is stalking you. And yes, we are talking about evil assassins, if you want to put it that way."

"Is this off the record?" Patti asked instinctively, pulling out a Dictaphone.

"Whatever. You'll see this on the news tonight anyway, along with the few pictures available."

"Okay," Susan said slowly. "Let's hear the official line."

"Well, it's not strictly speaking an official line. Not on what happened to Ward and Halloran, anyway. Look, we've provisionally identified the men behind the bombing you were caught up in. Tonight their pictures air in the hope the public can help us track them down. If anyone is targeting you specifically—and, to be honest, neither the ATF nor myself believe they are—it would most likely be them."

Jim handed out copies of the mug shots he had shown Patti earlier. "Anyone recognize these people?" There was a chorus of negatives.

"Can't we get protection?" Al demanded

Jim shrugged. "If you ask, I'll see what ourselves, the FBI or the LAPD can do, but like I said, the idea that they're hunting you is just my pet theory, not a working theory at the Bureau."

"If we ask?" Susan echoed, sounded insulted. "Shouldn't you people be offering protection? We are taxpayers, damn it!"

"If any of us thought that you were in danger from this group, we would. As it happens, we don't see the likelihood as being very high."

"You don't seem too upset that Uncle Sam here doesn't seem to give a shit about us," Al said to Patti. "Or were you and Bruce fucking Lee there just thinking of punching them out of the country?"

"That," Patti said with exaggerated patience, "is because I don't believe there are terrorists trying to hunt us down and kill us."

Susan recoiled. "What? But you said you had something important to tell us about what was going on. You promised you were going to give us all... something, about what happened to Hal. And that Halloran guy," she added as an afterthought.

"It's Death."

"No shit."

"No," Patti said, "I mean it's Death. The grim reaper. We were supposed to have died in the bombing, but we didn't. We're a rogue element in the body that is this world, and it's going to come after us with all the antibodies it can muster."

"Bullshit!" Al exclaimed. "What fucking comic book did you get this shit out of?"

"It's not bullshit," Will said quietly. "It happened before. Anybody heard of The Vipers?" Almost everybody nodded. "Remember the building collapse on the news and the miraculous survivors. A bunch of them died pretty soon after, all in freaky little accidents, just like our two boys. And it has happened lots of times before that, all the way back to fucking Victorian London. We've got stacks of documents at home?"

"Official documents?" Jim asked, his tone intrigued.

"Well, newspapers from the time, magazines..."

"Shut up!" Susan yelled, stabbing a finger at Patti. "Just shut up." She turned away and then back, as if unsure whether to get in her truck or throw a punch. "Damn it! Fuller, two people are dead, and all you can think about is how it fits with the sort of bullshit your supermarket checkout magazine publishes?" She spat on the ground. "Fuck you, I'm not listening to any more of this. And I'll be filing a complaint against your shitty magazine too."

Susan stomped angrily across to the Dodge Ram and hightailed it out.

Al, Jim, Will and Patti all looked at each other. The moment had crystallized around Susan's outburst and nobody wanted to risk being the one to shatter it and set the shrapnel flying.

"Okay," Will said slowly. "So... the grim reaper gets pissed when somebody screws with his schemes. Fine, so how come it's us who did the screwing?"

"We survived because–"

"No! Okay, we're all pre-supposing that we were fated to die in that bombing. But you said death is part of nature; it's just the way things are."

"Right," Patti agreed.

"The bomb wasn't."

"What?"

"You said that if it's your time, then it's your time. Okay, I can live with that. Or not, but you know what I mean." He paused. "How do we know that Death, fate, God, the Devil, whatever, didn't intend for us to all live to ripe old ages? We can't be born just to get killed by some other prick, because isn't there some sort of genetic marker that gives us a limited lifespan? I remember reading something about there being a kill-switch built into our cells."

Jim nodded. "Yeah, I think I remember seeing something about that on *Discovery Channel* one time..."

"Cool, because if that's right, then *that's* Death's grand design for us. That's what tells us our number's up. That means these terrorist motherfuckers are the ones who messed with Death's appointment book, not us. They're the ones who decided they wanted some people to die ahead of their time."

Patti snorted. "The question of free will versus predestination is an old one in philosophy."

"Don't get pretentious on me, not right now. I'm too drunk and too scared, and never liked that shit anyway."

Al suddenly spoke, a faraway look in his eye. "It makes some sense, I guess. But what's the problem?"

Patti couldn't believe her ears. "What's the problem? You're gonna die, that's the damn problem."

"Death, fate, whatever. I don't mind."

Patti was astounded. "How can you not mind? The very angel of death is stalking you, inescapable, implacable, and you don't mind?"

"If it was fated that I was supposed to die in that blast, then that was my time. This extra time, whether it is days or weeks, years or hours, are... bonuses. A gift that I don't intend to throw back in the faces of the powers that be." Al smiled faintly. "If someone lives even one day past his or her appointed time, that's a day that should be savored and enjoyed, not squandered in fear or regret for the days you'll miss in future. Those days would never have been yours anyway." With that, he strolled back to his Beamer, got in, grinned, waved, and drove off.

Susan Fries hadn't cooled down much by the next morning. She stomped around the auto yard performing all the necessary chores, all the while thinking about how she could get revenge on this Patti Fuller. Did the bitch that stole her first real boyfriend think that Susan's feelings were her playthings?

Or was it some sort of twisted marketing scam for that crappy magazine of hers? She would have to think of something vengeful to do to that too.

Still fuming, she picked up a metal pail full of aluminum powder and shavings that had come off a few mopeds, and started to carry it back to the office. She had a crucible out back in which she could melt it down, mould it into ingots and sell.

As she walked, something caught Susan's eye, towards the lower edge of her peripheral vision. A shadow flickered round the edge of the pail, and she looked down to see if it was a bug of some kind circling within.

She picked up the pail with both hands and peered in. There was nothing in there but powdered aluminum. The pail needed to be moved anyway so she cradled it in her arms, and started walking towards the office. The rusty pail was rubbing against her coveralls and Susan just knew they were going to stain. She could also feel tiny jagged flakes of rust coming off and tickling against the skin on her wrists, and her collarbone.

She groaned and stopped, intending to put the pail down and brush off the particles of rust. As she stopped, a stinging snap made her jump. It was a spark, static from her clothes. Then something strange happened, that she had never seen before, and never would again. The powder was glowing at the edges, where it met the inner surface of the pail.

She stared down at it, dumbfounded, wondering what the hell was happening to it. She started to take another step, to walk on, put the pail down and film it, or at least call someone and tell them about this weirdness.

Another blue spark jumped between her clothes and the pail, and this time the powder within did more than glow. Suddenly, Susan was caressing a bucketful of white heat, hotter than the surface of the sun. The old iron bucket couldn't contain that kind of power and it vaporized in her arms.

Susan would have screamed, but the spreading reaction had burned through her coverall, shirt, and chest. By the time she had opened her mouth to scream, her lungs had been seared open, their contents boiled out through the hole in her chest. Her heart caught fire, popping and hissing as it shriveled away to nothing, allowing the fire to crumble several spinal disks to ash.

The process was furiously fast and the white fire had burned itself out by the time it had emerged from the center of her back. Susan remained upright for a moment, wisps of smoke rising from the charred holes in the front and back of her coveralls. She was already dead, though, and nothing of who she was remained to feel her body fall.

She was lying on her side, a look of utmost agony and surprise on her face. Jim and Chang leaned sideways to get a better look at what had killed her.

There was a hole clean through her torso, wide enough to fit almost from nipple to nipple. Most of her lungs were gone, as was her heart. What remained of the lungs was, like the rest of the flesh that bordered the gap, dried and glazed, cauterized by the heat.

"Another one of the Metroline survivors?"

Jim nodded. "I was just talking to her yesterday." A passing cop had seen the body and the coroner had determined a probable explosives involvement in the death, so the ATF had been called.

"What happened? It looks like somebody took a blowtorch to her."

"Close enough," Jim said. "Thermite."

"Thermite?"

"The ingredients for it at least. She was carrying them in a bucket—the rim and handle are all that's left—when self-ignition occurred."

Chang was surprised. "How could it self-ignite? It's not volatile like nitro."

"Electrical spark most likely. She was dumb enough to wear clothing of artificial fibers while wearing it. They rubbed off together, a spark hit, and..."

"Boom."

"Well, more like whoosh, actually, but yeah."

"Jesus."

FOURTEEN

Helena Blavatsky was sitting upright on a chaise-lounge. Like so many elderly ladies that Juliet had met, she was hunched over. Unlike them, Madame Blavatsky seemed to be in such a pose to hold in a huge amount energy, lest it escape and do terrible harm to those around her. Her eyes were wide and clear, the pupils small. Her gaze felt like a beam of some kind of magnetism, rooting Juliet to the spot while it searched through her soul.

Juliet knew the eccentric old woman had had a wide variety of experiences, both worldly and otherworldly, but she had no idea of the scope of this life. She knew that HPB, as she was known to her Theosophist followers, had traveled to India and contacted secret Tibetan masters whom she claimed had told her of the five "root races" of man, which included Lemurians and Atlanteans.

She knew that the woman had been married to a Russian Count, and that she had recently brought out a book called *The Secret Doctrine*. She also knew that HPB had a strong connection to the world of spiritualism via her comradeship with Henry Olcott, whom *The Strand Magazine* had said recently was the world's first–and so far only–spiritualist lawyer.

Most importantly, she knew that HPB appeared to know what was happening to her. "What do I do?"

"Do?" HPB echoed. "What the hell do you mean 'do?'"

"How do I stop it? How do we get away from it?"

Madam Blavatsky looked puzzled for a moment. "Why would you wish to, child?"

"To live. To survive."

"Child... You're too young to understand. You mustn't fight it or flee from it." The old woman smiled knowingly. "When your time comes, it your time. That is nature, the way of the universe. That is your destiny, and it would sacrilegious to oppose it."

"It can't be my destiny to die now. What purpose would it serve?"

"The human mind is too small to answer that question, my child. We are all put here on this Earth for a reason and our lifespan is part of what we are. To change it would be to interfere with the purpose of our existence. That is why suicide is a sin. And so is the prolonging of life against the desires of nature." Juliet could feel tears prickle at her eyes. "Enjoy the gift of extra days you have been given. Seek forgiveness for the harm that has been done to the universe by them. And accept your destiny when it reaches you.

Bill Sangster sat and stared into his coffee for long minutes. "'Accept your destiny,' eh?" he said eventually. "Damnation to that, mate."

"But she knew what was happening... How could she tell us that?"

"Because she's biased for one thing. Bright's Disease." Juliet looked blank. "She's dying and she knows she's buggered."

Juliet blushed at his language but she could hardly criticize him for it. "She says it's Death. How do you hide from the Grim Reaper? How do you fight him?"

"Damned if I know," Sangster admitted, "but I'll tell you this: if the bony bastard comes near you or me, I'm going to make him eat his bloody scythe."

Stewart Tubbs welcomed the sight of the various ephemera of his career. Not only did they exist as silent, tangible, congratulations on a job well done, but they were all examples of solid, reasonable, practical science. Even the fully articulated skeleton in the corner was calcified proof that the dead didn't speak. It had certainly never started up any conversations with him.

He poured himself a whiskey and raised the glass to the skeleton. "Here's to us," he said, and downed the shot in one. Movement through the window by the skeleton caught his eye and Tubbs glanced out into the cobbled yard. He shuddered at what he saw there. Two rag and bone men were tugging the clothes off a dead woman in front of the morgue's open doors. A bored looking constable watched them with the curled lip of a man who smells something utterly repulsive under his shoe.

The woman's skin was gray, almost to the point of being pale blue, and a deep lipless smile beamed at Tubbs from under her chin. Just as Tubbs started to turn away, Abberline and the police surgeon strolled out from the morgue. The latter man was tying a stained apron around himself and gestured to a couple of orderlies to carry the naked corpse inside.

"A few days later," Abberline was saying to the tall detective from Baker Street, "he followed this with a gruesome package which was delivered to George Lusk, Chairman of the Whitechapel Vigilance Committee. The cardboard box contained a kidney that was previously missing from the body of Catherine Eddowes. A note addressed 'From Hell' was enclosed and contained the following message." He cleared his throat. *"Mr Lusk. Sir, I send you half the Kidne I took from one woman prasarved it for you. tother piece I fried and ate it was very nice. I may send you the bloody knif that took it out if you only wate a whil longer. Signed Catche me when you can Mister Lusk."*

The tall detective took the note and read it. "This note isn't in the same hand as the other two letters. The spelling and grammar are appalling. How interesting."

Abberline spread his hands in a gesture of appeal. "What does it suggest? Either this letter or the previous two must be a hoax."

"Not necessarily. There could be more than one killer."

"A partnership? A gang? Lord knows there are enough pimping gangs out there chopping up the ladies for not paying their protection money on time."

"Or a coincidence. Unrelated killings being linked in the minds of the police and public." The tall detective snapped a finger against the notepaper, and then examined the paper from all four edges and sniffed at it. "It all comes back to the letters, inspector. The first two notes are clearly from an educated man, who can read and write, putting his words into the vernacular of the city's working class speech. He wants us to hear the words in a particular voice and one which is therefore almost certainly not his own..."

"And the other letter? It seems genuine semi-literate."

"Indeed. Which means either it is, or the writer wants us to believe it is. 'Tother' implies a northern man. Yorkshire, perhaps.

"What sort of man are we looking for?"

"A maniac, obviously," the detective's shorter companion opined.

"Yes..." Abberline murmured. "Let's hope so, anyway."

"Hope so? What else could he be but a maniac? If you had but been there when that poor mare was still warm, you could have no doubt. She had been rent by some raging beast."

"I hope he is but a simple maniac, because a maniac acts purely on instinct, not thinking to hide his trail. If Jolly Jack isn't a maniac, then he's intelligent and deliberately trying to mislead us. That makes him a far greater danger, doctor."

"The inspector is correct, my dear fellow," the tall detective said. "No. I should say that the disparity in the letters is an excellent clue as to who and what the Ripper is not. His first letters want us to think he's a jolly Londoner of the working class, so he is not. His third letter wants us to think he's illiterate, and possibly, if we're sharp enough to notice, a Yorkshire man. Therefore he's not either of those things."

"Well then, what have we left? A lettered man of middle or upper class, from an area other than Yorkshire or London? Why, that still incriminates more than half the country!"

"Not necessarily. I think we can narrow the field still further. Our man is right handed, and well-read."

"Well-read?"

"Enough to understand grammar and structure to a degree that he can pastiche different types of communication. I'd say he's right-handed from the direction of the strokes of the blade on the victims.

The Mitre Square victim in particular gives this away. The slashes on her face and marks on her throat indicate a right-handed assailant gripping her with his left and wielding the knife in his right hand."

"And possibly a medical man. That's what they say, anyway. That he removed that woman's kidney with surgical precision."

The stocky doctor grunted. "Utter nonsense made up by someone who can't tell the difference between a scalpel and a claymore. The man's no more a surgeon than you are, though I'll admit I could point you towards some so-called surgeons whose butchery is a crude as the Ripper's."

Abberline grunted. "The newspaper gossip is having an effect, though. Nobody's willing to see a doctor in the East End. In fact, just yesterday I had to protect a doctor from a lynch mob just because he was carrying a Gladstone bag in Whitechapel on his way to a patient."

The tall detective cleared his throat. "If you force me to guess, based upon this letter–and the fact that it came with a part of one of the victims says well for it–I should say the Ripper is an educated man from the north-west. Liverpool perhaps."

Gilbert Collins had changed the locks on all the doors of the house. When Juliet returned, eager to tell the story of her adventures, she was horrified.

"What are you doing? Are you trying to lock me in a cage?"

"No, of course not. It's just that it seemed prudent, these days, to have stouter locks fitted."

"Then you'll be giving me a key?"

"Your mother and I have spoken, and we think that it would be best if we did not."

"But papa!"

"It's not that we don't love you," Gilbert went on, a strange hint of pleading in his voice, "but that we worry about you. With mad killers in the streets—"

"If you mean the Ripper, he only kills... ladies of the night, daddy," she finished pointedly. She wanted to say "whores" but couldn't bring herself to soil her lips with such language, and her father was already sufficiently shocked at her.

"That's what they say, but they could be wrong. And, frankly, since no man is infallible, who's to say this Ripper character couldn't kill a lady in error? Or that he isn't just practicing, starting at the bottom, as it were." Juliet had no answer to that, especially since it was a thought that had crossed her mind many times after dark this year. She would have been surprised if there was a woman in London who hadn't thought that at some point.

Juliet languished in her bedroom, feeling as if she was doing time in prison. Admittedly she still thought that perhaps she had committed a sin serious enough to deserve such a punishment but it did not make her feel any better.

Perhaps it was the punishment angle that was getting in the way of her acceptance of being locked in the house. If she was being punished, then that was fair and well, but to be imprisoned simply for the sake of it—to prevent her from doing something to save her own life—no, that was another matter entirely. That was a matter that she could not tolerate.

Luckily, although her parents had thought to change the locks, it had not occurred to them to make her bedroom window any more secure. She could open it as normal, sliding it up the runners until there was a wide enough gap for her to squeeze through.

She had already agreed to meet Bill Sangster again this evening, and try again to convince Tubbs—who, if truth be told, Juliet was beginning to think deserved whatever horrendous fate the world had in store for him—of the realities of the situation. It was really for his own good.

At the appointed time, Bill, in dark tweeds, appeared opposite the house. Juliet scrambled though the open window—not easy in all her skirts and petticoats, and ran across to meet him. On impulse, she kissed him on the cheek and then blushed at her forwardness. He smiled with all the warmth of the summer sun, momentarily banishing the fog that floated around them and chilled her to the bone.

They took the train to Bermondsey, and made their way to Tubbs's lodging house. As they approached, they saw him emerge from the house carrying a Gladstone bag. Bill started forward to greet him, but Juliet felt an instinct to hang back, and she stopped him.

As Juliet and Bill watched from round the corner of a hedge, Tubbs pulled a simple cloth cap and a filthy jacket out of the sack. He proceeded to put these on, and shove his dapper day clothes into the bag in their place.

"What the hell?" Bill muttered. "I'd have thought that stuck-up idiot would have rather died than worn anything so common."

"Obviously it's some kind of disguise. But why?"

"Well, to save his skin for one thing. A posh bloke in Whitechapel at night is like a mouse in a cage full of starving cats, even before the press started casting Jolly Jack as some sort of nut job in a top hat. Or he could want someone he's dealing with to think he's something other than what he is."

"*A gaudy wig and stilts...*" Juliet murmured, half to herself.

"Eh?"

"Goethe. From *Faust*."

Bill rolled his eyes. "Tauntin' me now with foreign poets. Bleedin' marvelous."

"Even if he was a murderer, why go out in the streets and commit his crimes so openly? It doesn't seem rational."

"Cutting the kidneys out of people, eating them and sending the leftovers to the press isn't what I'd call rational. The man's a maniac. You know what 'mania' means? Look it up in the dictionary, and you'll find it's quite a long way from rationality."

"Fifteen letters, or thereabouts."

"Very clever."

"You'd think a true maniac would be obvious to his friends and neighbors. He'd be ranting and raving, obviously deranged. We wouldn't be sitting here waiting to see when or if he strikes again."

Bill huffed. "He seems to be quite deranged when in the presence of his victims, if what I saw at the morgue today is anything to go by. Perhaps there's some sort of trigger for his mania that causes a brief explosion... Being asked to pay for it? Maybe he's tight-fisted, like a Scotsman."

"Do you think Mister Tubbs could be...?"

"The Ripper?" Bill finished. "Never, not a ponce like him."

"Perhaps we should follow him and find out. If he is the Ripper, we can send for the police..."

Bill looked at her for a long moment. "You've got a touch of the madness about you, but I like that. You'd make a fine muse." They watched Tubbs vanish into the mist.

Juliet couldn't tear her eyes away from the point in the gloom into which the disguised doctor had vanished. She didn't dare move a muscle for fear that she would faint or run away despite herself. Could it be true that she had been sitting next to Jack the Ripper at Adrienne's spiritualist meeting? Was the hand she had held the same one that had wielded the most feared knife in England? Had she grasped the fingers that had torn Annie Chapman's liver from her body and shoveled pieces of it into his throat?

She wished she could decide "no." She wished she couldn't believe it so easily of Dr Stewart Tubbs but believe it she did.

FIFTEEN

Susan Fries was buried in a Jewish cemetary adjunct to Forest Lawn, in a family plot. Will and Patti attended, as did Jim Castle, Susan's brother and about two dozen other friends and relatives. Will didn't feel like mixing much, but held onto Patti for support, which she in turn was happy to give.

The weather had improved slightly; the cemetery was crisp and peaceful under blue skies and sunshine. Bands of putrescent darkness remained on the horizon to the north and west.

Susan's brother had chatted briefly with Patti and Will, thanking them for coming, and expressing gratitude that Will's friendship had stayed strong enough to bring him here. He also thanked Patti.

"What for?" she asked.

"For saving my sister from the bomb," he said. "It's cruel that she was taken from us anyway, but... but she graced our presence on this Earth for a couple of weeks more than she would have otherwise. She was my baby sister and every moment that she lived beyond the detonation of that bomb is a gift more valuable than all the gold and diamonds in the world."

"I didn't really do anything," Patti protested, embarrassed.

"If you can't see that, then I'm sad for you too," Fries said. "But if you can't see the good you did on the Metroline, then thank you also for driving her home the other night."

"Anybody would have done the same."

It was only once they returned home to Patti's house in Sherman Oaks that Will felt comfortable to let go and weep. He dropped backwards into a chair. His head felt light and dizzy, and he knew if he tried to turn to check the position of the chair, he'd lose his balance and fall.

He grabbed for Patti's hand, pulling her close, so he could hold onto her. He looked out at the faces in his mind's eye, floating past, oblivious to his pain or to the effort it was taking to not let tears get onto his face. "The first person you fall in love with most likely won't be the only one... But they're still special."

"I know. It's okay."

"She was the first person I ever knew that I fell in love with. I mean, maybe I'd been in love before but didn't quite recognize it." He closed his eyes, and was back in the theater in Encino. He didn't remember what the movie was, but he remembered the smell of her hair, and the warmth of her shoulders under a thin T-shirt when he took her in his arms. When they kissed it was almost as if she were trying to knock his teeth out with her own. He didn't mind because it was part of what made her so vibrant.

As their mouths parted, Will heard—aloud, reverberating from all around the theater—a voice say, "Oh, fuck, I love her." It wasn't a line from the movie and nobody else in the theater showed any sign of having heard it. Will knew he hadn't said it aloud either, but it couldn't just have been in his imagination, surely?

Susan had smiled, and leaned in close for another kiss. She was beautiful, and Will knew that, regardless of whether the booming voice was imaginary, the love in his nineteen year-old heart was not.

Will opened his eyes, letting the tears fall from them. He couldn't think of anything else to do. "If someone, a person, had killed Susan, it wouldn't be so bad. At least then I could do something: call the cops, attack the person, fight, whatever." His voice was thick, and he wiped his eyes with a napkin. "Even if it had been some sort of disease, I could donate to, like, some charity devoted to getting rid of it. You know?"

"Yeah, I know."

"But just... just an accident? Just a 'shit happens?' What's the point of that?"

"It's not 'just an accident,' or a 'shit happens.' It's Death. Fate. It's stalking us, one by one. And if you want someone to blame, or an enemy to fight, then there he is."

Will leaned back, squeezing his wet eyes shut, and forcing the grief and pain to turn around and metamorphose into anger. "Bring him on," he said. "Bring on the Reaper and I'll show him what it's like to be left behind." His heart and his mind suddenly cleared, focused. "I mean it, Patti. We've been rolling over for too long, we can't go on doing that. We need to get more... proactive. Like that great-great-grandmother of yours."

Like her great-great-grandmother. Patti nodded. She hadn't known Susan Fries that well, but had nothing against her having been Will's previous girlfriend. All that mattered was whether a person was good or bad, whether they deserved respect or did not.

Patti stood, pacing around the room. "Death isn't a man or even a manlike spirit. It's not a walking skeleton, or a psycho, or a sociopath that kills for kicks. It's part of what we are, part of what the universe is. Without death, how do you define life? When I say Death is someone to blame... It's a misleading term. It's not something we can fight. It's not like some movie serial killer, or a rabid wolf."

It was tempting to anthropomorphize their stalker into something more bearable. A skeletal, black-clad professional with ice water for blood, the first horseman of the Apocalypse, updated to driving a sinister limo with blacked-out windows.

Patti could feel the image trying to settle in her head. Its voice was seductive, keen to lull her into thinking her opponent was a mere mortal, or at least something that could be safely run from or fought against with fists and feet. She gritted her teeth, and told it to fuck off out of her head.

Death wasn't a person. No calcified assassin walked the rain-slicked streets with bone clicking against the sidewalk.

"All I know is that if that bony motherfucker comes near me, I'm going to make him eat his scythe," Will said. He went through to the bathroom to splash some water on his face. It woke him up a little from the puffy heat that his face felt when he wept.

"That theory of yours," Patti said slowly. "The one about us being rejected by the body, by reality? What if it's because we've been wrongly tagged as something bad?"

"Wrongly tagged?" Will echoed.

"Yes... We need to get ourselves re-tagged."

"What the hell are you talking about?"

Patti dug in her magazine rack for a copy of *Scientific American*. It was folded open to a story: some conspiracy tract about how gene therapy should be either banned or not unrestricted. Even Patti couldn't figure out which it was, just that the columnist thought it should be the opposite of whatever the government's line was.

Will looked blank. "And this has what relevance to our situation?"

"Gene therapy affects the body by altering the genetic markers. You can mark, say, a fat cell as a viral cell so that the immune system will attack it."

"So?"

"So, you can also do the reverse. Mark a viral cell with a gene that says it's a healthy red blood cell, so the immune system won't attack it. That's what the article's about, I think. It'd make a repulsive form of biological warfare."

"Cool," Will said absently. "Hey, I get it. You're thinking we can mark ourselves to reality as healthy... guys."

"That's what I'm thinking."

Will grinned broadly. "Fucking-A! What do we do?"

Patti gave the tiniest shrug. "Damned if I know."

"Yeah... You do know?" She shook her head. "You don't? Shit. Who's left out of the group, apart from us?"

"Al Kinsey. He's some sort of talent agent."

Will looked none the wiser. "Which one was he?"

"The one you hit," she reminded him

"That spiky-haired yuppie creep?"

"That's the guy."

"Shit." His face said he didn't want to waste time saving a guy like Kinsey. Then he straightened up. "Okay. Kinsey."

"We have to get to him."

"And... what?"

"And warn him. Everything that's happened, happened to us separately. Maybe if we're together, we keep an eye out. Watch for each other, at least long enough to work out how to set this right."

"You're going to tell him all that you just told me?"

"Yeah."

Will laughed harshly. "He's a high-flying Hollywood type, Patti. He'll call the cops and tell them you're a stalker or something. He'll never believe all that stuff."

"Do you believe me?"

"Yes. Yes I do. But I'm biased. I've known you for a long time and I happen to love you. That means I'm more automatically predisposed to believe you or at least agree with you because quite frankly I can't think of anything else to do. This guy, Al, seemed like a big-headed jackass."

"I can be persuasive. I'll make him listen, and I'll make him believe."

"What are you going to do? Put a gun to his head and tell him to believe you or you'll blow him away?"

"Maybe," she said grimly. "Hey, you never know; maybe killing him off, like a sacrifice, will mess with Death's design the other way, and make the trail go cold." Will sat stunned, scarcely able to believe his ears. His Patti was a peace-loving, love-loving babe, not Charles Bronson. She looked sideways at him, finally catching his expression. "I'm joking, Will. Deadpan, you know. The only sort of dead I plan to be for a while."

They changed from their somber funeral outfits into more casual cloths. Will wore denims and a plaid shirt over an Iron Maiden T-shirt. Patti was back in black jeans, black halter and black leather blazer.

They ate, then got in Patti's Saturn and drove to Hollywood, past the *Borderlands Patrol*'s office, and on along to the building where the newspapers had said Al Kinsey had his office. A blonde receptionist was sitting in the outer office, typing speedily on a high-end PC. "Can I help you?" she asked, without looking up.

"We're looking for Al Kinsey."

The receptionist looked up. Faced with two fit twenty-somethings in smart but casual clothes that radiated confidence and suspicion, she said, "You've come to the right place, officers, but he isn't in right now."

Patti and Will exchanged a look. "Will he be back soon? This is a very important matter."

"Life and death," Will added.

The receptionist gave them a skeptical look, but checked her book anyway. "He's due back at two. Not that he's likely to appear then."

"Where is he likely to be?"

"I don't know."

"Listen, this is important. His life is in danger and we have to find him." Patti took a deep breath. "We're... we're also targets of the same killer."

"Shit!" the receptionist blanched, and looked at the glass door as if she expected *The Terminator* to burst in and start blasting. "And you're trying to lead him here?"

"It's not so much a him as—" Patti gave up. She couldn't think of a way to explain to the receptionist that would be understood, let alone believed. "Al's next, then us."

"I wish I could help, really. I'm sorry."

"All right, thanks anyway." Crestfallen, Patti and Will left the office and returned to the Saturn. Will pulled off the ticket that had miraculously appeared on the windscreen, and tore it into confetti.

"What now?" Patti wondered aloud.

"His phone," Will suggested.

"Cellular? Try to tag it from its signal?"

"It works in the movies."

"This isn't a movie."

"I could hear a 'but' in that tone."

"But, there's always Eddie at the phone company. He's been very co-operative with the *Borderlands Patrol*, since he thinks we're like, I dunno, the Lone Gunmen or something..." She pulled out her own cellular as she slid into the driving seat.

"What are you doing?"

"Driving." As if it wasn't patently obvious.

"You're using your cellular at the same time."

She tossed him the phone, and he caught it awkwardly. "You call, I'll drive."

"The guy at the phone company knows you, not me." He tossed it back.

"Fuck." Patti slid across the hood, *Starsky and Hutch* style, to the passenger door, while Will ran round to the driver's side. Will threw the Saturn into gear, and peeled away.

Patti dialed, rapping the fingers of her other hand on the dash. She hated being a passenger. If she was in a car, she wanted to be in control of it. “I need a favor, she said into the phone”

“For the magazine?”

“Yeah,” Patti lied. “There’s something I need to try out.”

“Like what?”

“Can you track a cellular phone’s location and pass it on to another person.”

“The person being you?”

“I gotta test it myself, yeah.”

“Yes we can, if–and only if–the cellular is switched on.”

“Can you try it now?”

“What phone?” Patti rattled off the cellular number from Al’s business card, which she had snitched from the holder on the receptionist’s desk. “Hold on.” The line went static for a moment, and then Eddie came back. “Got it. It’s in Malibu.” Patti snapped her fingers, pointing west, and Will swung the car around at the next cross street.

“Keep me informed, Eddie.” She broke the connection, and looked at the business card again. “First I’ll try calling him.”

“We broke his nose, Patti; he’s not going to want to talk to you.”

She knew he was right, but she dialed anyway. What else was she supposed to do? “Well, breaking his nose saved his ass, so maybe we’ll get lucky on balance.”

* * *

Al Kinsey smiled at the blonde girl in the tank top and jeans as she eased her perfect ass into the Ferrari he had just picked up from the auto shop. She was leggy and her breasts were middling but perfectly formed. She wasn't quite as pretty as his wife, but she was surely more inventive. It would all benefit his marriage in the long run, when he brought a new experience home. "Al," he said.

"Candi," she replied. She took his outstretched hand and put in on her breast. "Like it?"

"I do," he said. "And I even like the price."

"Is there somewhere you want to go? A motel or somewhere?"

Al shook his head. "How about we just cruise down the PCH. It's a nice day for a drive."

Candi smiled. "It's your money."

"And there's plenty of it." He started the car; enjoying the sound of the engine and the vibration he could feel through the leather seat and the foot pedals. He never heard his cellular phone ring, because it was set to vibrate silently. He never felt it either, because it was in the glove box so that nobody could disturb him by calling him on it.

Patti closed her phone. "Voicemail—shit." She had only just done so when it trilled, and vibrated in her hand. She flipped it open, and said, "Fuller, go."

"Patti, it's Eddie. That cellular? It's moving."

"Moving?" That wasn't good, but it was typical of her shitty luck. Some would say she had great luck, surviving the bomb and all, but she knew they would be wrong. Somebody with great luck would never have been near a bombing.

"It's still switched on, but definitely moving. It's heading onto PCH, southbound."

"Gah!" Patti closed her eyes, wondering where the idiot was going.

"Try calling again," Will suggested.

"No," Patti said curtly. "If he's driving, I don't want to risk distracting him and causing a crash." She reached into her bag, pulling out a Palm Pilot. "Eddie, can you link your tracking over the net?"

"Sure, but—"

"If I put my Palm Pilot online, could you keep a live feed running to it, of that signal track?"

"Jesus, Patti! What the hell are you on? I could get fired for even discussing whether this shit's possible."

"It is though, isn't it?" Her tone was definitely not that of a question. Eddie remained silent. "That's what I thought." She took a deep breath, hoping she wasn't about to make an ass of herself. Being deceitful just didn't sit right with her, no matter how crazy the truth sounded. "Eddie, this isn't just for the magazine, it's a matter of life and death. Literally. The owner of that cellular is likely to be the next victim of... in a series."

"What do you mean? Like a serial killer?"

"You read the *Borderlands Patrol*?"

"You know I do."

"December issue. The Reaper's Harvest?"

"Woah. He was here?"

"No. It's happening again. The same thing, but this time it's the survivors of the Hill Street Metroline bombing."

"Cool. I mean, not cool that it happened, but... Oh hell, you know what I mean, right?"

"I know what you mean, Eddie. You just keep that location online for me, okay."

There was another long silence. "Okay, you got it." The line went dead. She put the phone away, and brought up a Multi-Map display of LA's road network on her Palm Pilot. A few moments later, a smaller window opened, with a street name and giving the direction as "southbound."

"Stop the car."

Will stood on the brakes. "What's up?"

"I'm driving." She handed him the Palm Pilot. "You get to navigate. We need to intercept him." She got out and slid over the car. Will shifted across into the right-hand seat, looking at the display.

"Get ahead of him on PCH, from here?" Will shook his head. "That's impossible."

"It's not impossible, just illegal." Patti gave him a look that desperately wanted to have a glint in its eye, but was too frightened to dare. "Buckle up," she suggested, doing exactly that. Then she threw the car into gear, and hit the gas.

Cruising on the Pacific Coast Highway was probably Al Kinsey's favorite thing in the world. There was always a great view, there were lots of pretty little towns on the way, and driving the open highway with music playing on the classic car's CD player was just the sweetest and most relaxing thing he could think of.

He was relaxed, and de-stressing with every moment, as Springsteen serenaded him from the in-car speakers, and Candi's soft lips enveloped the most sensitive part of him. He was in heaven.

Patti threw the Saturn around the highway, swooping between lanes and cutting in front of other vehicles with an inch to spare. Horns were sounding every time she made a lane change, and Will didn't dare look back in case he saw wrecked cars burning on the blacktop.

A wailing cut the air behind Patti's speeding Saturn, and Will risked a glance in the mirror. Sure enough, red and blue lights were flashing there. "Maybe we should pull over."

"Like hell."

"Patti, the cops have cameras, they have choppers... They most likely already know who's driving the car."

"I've always wanted to be on *America's Wildest Police Videos*."

"Shit."

"If there's a chance of stopping what's killing us, the traffic laws are not what I'd call important."

"You're gonna get us killed!"

"Not a chance. If Death's got a plan, we're safe until Al gets his." She yanked the wheel hard to the right, cutting off the traffic that was trying to come through the on-ramp.

* * *

Al allowed himself to relax, keeping his hands firm on the wheel, but not too tight. It wouldn't do to steer into the wrong lane due to a shiver of pleasure winding its way through the autonomic nervous system.

Ahead, the blacktop shimmered under the cloud-broken sunlight, and, for a second, Al thought the road was slithering on its own, the way a sidewinder might cross the desert, only scaled up to be far slower and more massive.

He told himself it was just the heat haze, and maybe a bit of Freudian imagery, seeing as his mind and body were so concentrating on the trouser snake action being delivered from the right-hand seat.

The highway was starting to go uphill, so he reached past the bobbing blonde head with some difficulty, to shift gears.

There were now three police cruisers behind Patti's Saturn, and both Patti and Will knew there would be others converging on their position from ahead.

Will looked at her, and Patti knew he was scared. Scared that she had lost her mind, scared that they would be caught and scared that they would be killed. Patti wished she had the words to reassure him that none of those things were true. She felt they were true—more than that, she knew it, as she had known there was a bomb on the Metro train—but she had no idea how to convey that convincingly.

If actions spoke louder than words, then just doing what it took would prove her point better than any speech would. She knew Death was stalking them, and knew Death was fussy about how things went. She had the suspicion that even if she drove the Saturn into a gas tanker truck and blew it to bits, that she and Will would walk out unharmed.

She didn't want to waste time trying it, though.

If Death, Fate, the universe wanted things done a certain way, who was she, a mere mortal, to argue? If that certain way meant she wasn't to die until after someone else, then where was the shame in taking advantage of that? It was sauce for the goose.

Hell, if she could keep Al Kinsey alive long enough, she and Will were probably indestructible. In a comic book they'd be superheroes, but Patti would settle for not having to worry about counting calories or tracking allergens.

Al had spotted an identical Ferrari model to his own just up ahead, the only difference being color: the other car was gloss black. It was waiting at a set of lights, and Al pulled in alongside, grinning at the two guys in it, who obviously shared his love of the sports car, or at least his love of speed.

The other guys grinned back, and the driver revved his engine with a wicked look. Al responded by revving his. He was on his favorite drive, being blown, so why not smoke these turkeys as well to make his day complete? In a contest of equal cars, only bravery and skill would take the prize. Besides, the two guys were beefier than himself and Candi, so he should be able to squeeze an extra mile or two per hour out of his engine.

The lights went green, and Al floored it.

Patti was grinning madly, her hair flying, and the laughter that was emanating from her sounded like the shrieking of the insane in some old Italian horror movie.

Will had never seen her like this, and it both frightened him and turned him on like mad. And then the Palm Pilot's screen went black. "Fuck! I've lost the signal."

"Great," Patti grumbled, as she swung onto PCH, and turned right, northbound.

It was too close to call. The black Ferrari was neck and neck with Al's the whole time, neither car edging more than an inch ahead of the other.

Up ahead, the road surface changed, to accommodate rails for tourist trolleybuses, like the ones in San Francisco. There were no trolleybuses in sight at the moment, but Al saw blackness writhing along the steel tracks that were inset into grooves in the road. He blinked and they were gone. He supposed they must have been a trick of the light on the shiny metal. The black Ferrari glistened like crude oil, though its surface must actually be as bone dry as Al's car.

Al swore as the other car edged ahead, getting to the rail track first. Then he laughed, as one of its rear tires blew out on a piece of broken metal that was wedged into the groove for one of the rails. Rubber burst and disintegrated in a cloud of stinking blue smoke, the wheel rim crashing down onto the shining steel. Al's laughter was the last sound he ever made. Sparks flew as the black Ferrari's hubcap was prized off by the rail, and flicked through the air.

It takes a tenth of a second for the brain to register what the eye sees. The last thing Al's eyes saw was the glinting hubcap sliding through his disintegrating windshield, but the sight never got to register in his brain.

Candi felt something pass overhead, and Al most definitely lose interest in what she was doing with her tongue. She looked up and screamed. Al's body was squirting blood from the neck; his lifeless arms drooped on the wheel.

Al's head, wearing an expression of bizarre glee, was lying on its side in the narrow back seat, trickles of gelatinous blood drooling from his mouth and nose. Next to it, a red-slicked hubcap was buried half in and half out of the leather upholstery.

Screaming as if every nerve ending in her body was on fire, Candi tried to wipe Al's blood from her face. It was still warm, and that made her scream even more. A car horn blared—no competition for Candi's Olympic-class lungs—and something large and black swerved around the Ferrari.

This was enough to remind Candi that she was still in a moving car. A car that was moving very fast on a busy freeway stretch of PCH. Her screams fell briefly silent as her terror exceeded her lungs' capacity for air, and she gasped for breath. As if the indrawn air reinvigorated her, she thought to grab the wheel, and steer the Ferrari left out of the path of a slowing RV.

The RV flashed swept past on the Ferrari's right, but there was another car, a four-door sedan–a couple of hundred yards ahead. It was going at a steady sixty, but the Ferrari was still accelerating. Dumbstruck, Candi realized the headless corpse next to her still had its foot on the gas pedal.

Either the late Al's legs had twitched like a chicken's when he was decapitated, or the now literally dead weight of them was holding the gas pedal down. Either way, Candi knew the car was gaining speed.

Desperately, no longer even taking the time to scream, she tried to pull the leg off the pedal. From the passenger seat, though, she wasn't at a good angle to get leverage for load bearing and the cadaver's foot wouldn't come up. The trunk of the sedan was only about twenty yards in front and closing, so she tried to get her own foot onto the Ferrari's brake pedal.

She just about managed it, but her spike heel turned, twisting her ankle instead of fully depressing the brake pedal.

The sedan's trunk was now only ten yards ahead, and, through the rear windshield, Candi could see the backs of four heads that were blissfully unaware of her approach. The only thing Candi could think of to try was to hit the horn, repeatedly. It blasted out, startling the people in the sedan.

For some reason, be it instinct or stupidity, the sedan's driver hit the brakes in response to the horn. Candi screamed again, twisting the wheel.

The Ferrari hit the concrete center divider at about ninety-two miles per hour. The hood crumpled inwards as if it was made of nothing more substantial than paper. The engine itself was more solid, and punched clean through the concrete barrier in an explosion of dust and gravel chips. The car emerged, spinning, into northbound traffic on the other side, and if Candi was still screaming, she couldn't even hear herself over the noise of the impact.

Patti stomped hard on the brakes as the center divider on her left burst open. A red car, its hood torn to shreds and exposing a battered and steaming engine, bounced into the lane right ahead of her, and spun a full 360 as if it was on ice as it swept across the northbound road. It came to halt about four feet in front of the Saturn, smoking, steaming and screaming.

Will and Patti sat dumbfounded in the Saturn trying to remember how to breathe. They shook like palm leaves in a storm.

"Oh shit," Patti said at last. "I think we found him."

Tony Chang and Jim Castle looked up at the unfinished building from which a window had guillotined Zack Halloran. "What have we got, Kemo Sabe?" Chang asked Jim.

"A possible connection between Reilly's group and the death of at least one of the Metroline survivors. I originally came over to interview Halloran, but he was dead by that time. When I spoke to his men, they said they'd reported the theft of some equipment and explosives to Van Nuys PD a couple of weeks ago."

"Oh?"

"According to their report, what went missing was PETN with Torpex boosters."

"A familiar formula."

"Yep." Jim handed Chang a demolition charge, made of the same waxy explosive material. I had the lab analyze this. It's exactly the same constituency as the bomb, and so was manufactured at the same plant." Jim led Chang into an elevator, and up to the roof.

"Did anybody see anything?"

"A couple of people reported seeing a truck with airport security pass stickers on the windshield." He took Chang over to the eastern side of the roof. "Van Nuys Airport."

Chang nodded slowly. "Let's have it checked out, quietly.

Will could hear screams from the red Ferrari. It was a female scream, and he was out of the Saturn like a shot, and over to the wrecked car. He could smell concrete dust and gasoline, and hoped the car wouldn't ignite. The story of what had happened to Mrs Stanley, Andrew Caine and Hector Barnes was still fresh in his mind, and he didn't like the idea that Death might go for a two-for-one.

He couldn't not respond to the screams of a woman in distress, though, and neither could Patti, who was right on his heels.

The screaming woman was a lithe blonde, who was pressing herself into the inside of the passenger door, trying to keep as far away as she could from a headless corpse that was in the driver's seat. A familiar spiky-haired head was lolling in the tiny backseat, its spectacles hanging off its ears. It was just too much for Will, and, biting back yells, he turned, fell to his knees and threw up.

Patti envied him. Her own stomach was all but exploding with the desire to vomit, but it just wouldn't come. Her limbs and head buzzing with the sort of vibration that extreme tension provokes–she had always thought of it as an orange sort of sensation–she pulled the blonde woman clear.

All she could think of was not that she had failed, or that she had saved another person to put in danger–the woman had obviously survived on her own–but that there was now only her and Will left, and she didn't think either of them could live without the other.

Jim and Chang burned the midnight oil in Suite 800, waiting tensely for a report from the undercover agents Chang had sent to Van Nuys Airport that afternoon. Waiting on the delivery of a family's first baby could hardly be more nerve-wracking, Jim thought.

The phone did eventually ring and Chang snatched it up. He listened for several minutes, smiling grimly, then said, and "You know what to do."

He looked at Jim. "It's them. They're in the customs' bonded warehouse, posing as customs workers.

"Then let's get them."

SIXTEEN

Juliet and Bill took a horsedrawn cab to Scotland Yard to report their suspicions, as Juliet had been brought up to believe a good Christian lady should. Bill either acknowledged the reality that it would be foolhardy in the extreme to follow Jack The Ripper in the fog, or else he simply preferred her company to that of a demented murderous maniac.

She was beginning to hope that the latter was the case and found the idea sweet and flattering. Truth to tell, she didn't mind where they were actually going so long as the company was as pleasant. He was not always so polite, but he interested her, and surprised her every time he opened his mouth.

Most of the boys she met of roughly her own age were from the Sunday school, or the choristers at papa's church, or otherwise restrained and conservative. She had never before met a man who could be a charming gentleman one moment, a lewd and satirical jester the next and a man in touch with everything that was esoteric and mysterious in the world.

She wasn't sure whether this was just because she had only met boys from her parents' circle before, or whether it was because she had never met an artist or poet before.

Either way, she was glad of having met him, and his company even made the frights and danger she had faced at Mornington Crescent seem worthwhile, as something good had come out of the disaster. It was still a terrible thing that four people had died–eight if she included the four remarkable accidents–and of course her burgeoning friendship with Bill was not an exchange she would have willingly made for people's lives.

Scotland Yard was still open at night, of course, as crime did not end at sunset. Quite the opposite, in fact, and the two-tone building with its distinctive turrets was still working at all hands to stations when the cab dropped them off there.

Juliet had hoped to see Inspector Abberline again, and even though the desk sergeant at night seemed more personable and co-operative, nothing could get round the fact that Abberline worked during the day and had gone home several hours ago.

They settled for trying to get the desk sergeant to mobilize a search for Tubbs. They told him everything that they knew and had seen, and insisted that he must surely be considered a viable Ripper suspect.

The desk sergeant took down their concerns dutifully in his notebook, and then folded his arms on the desk and spoke to them in a quiet voice. "All right, all right. I get the message that you think this bloke is Jolly Jack. I've taken down all your details and they'll go into the case file. A constable will be sent along to interview this Mister Tubbs tomorrow."

"But he could have committed another murder by tomorrow," Bill said forcefully. "He could have done it by now, as a matter of fact."

"That's as may be, sir, but I'll make no secret of the fact that we get forty suspected identifications of the Ripper in here every day and it takes time to go through them and investigate all those suspects."

"Oh, to hell with it," Bill snarled, and turned and walked out. Juliet apologized to the desk sergeant and hurried out after him. "We should have followed him after all," he said. "You were right all along." He made a fist. "That smart arse swine's got it coming," Bill said. "I swear, he's got it coming."

For a moment, Juliet saw anger in Bill's eyes. Not just the anger that made men swear or shout, or lash out thoughtlessly, but a deep and primeval anger that burned like frostbite. It cast its own dark light over him, and suddenly he looked poised rather than relaxed, though he hadn't shifted his position. The angles of his nose and chin were like flint knives, his teeth sharp, like Varney The Vampire, or something equally predatory out of a yellow paged "Penny Dreadful".

Then it was gone, and he was just rangy, relaxed Bill Sangster. At least, Juliet hoped it was gone, but a small part of her, somewhere deep in the back of her mind–the part of humanity that remembers being on the menu for saber-toothed cats–whispered to her with another possibility. What if it wasn't gone, this voice asked. What if it was just hidden and covered up, the way the lips hid teeth?

"We can still get a cab to Whitechapel..." she said.

"All right. The East End's a big place, though. I'd be happier if we had some idea of where he was."

Tubbs grunted and groaned as he writhed on top of the bored whore. She was doing her best to sound enthusiastic and caring, but that wasn't saying much. Tubbs wasn't surprised, since God alone knew how many men had already mounted her today. Familiarity bred contempt, or at least desensitization. Maybe the first man of the day had piqued her interest a little, but it wasn't Tubbs.

Not that it mattered; sex was sex, and the physical sensation was good enough for Tubbs. If he wanted tenderness and lovemaking he would have taken his wife in their own home, rather than wander the streets looking for a spur-of-the-moment burst of physical pleasure.

There was a slam of wood against plaster, and a roar that could have come from some ancient and terrible beast of legend. "What the *fuck*?" it blared.

Tubbs looked up to find a large man standing over him. More than just a large or burly man, he seemed to be a veritable ape-man with hair like a Scotch terrier's on his arms. He stank like the cattle that he butchered in the local abattoir, filling the air with acrid sweat, coppery blood, and the scent of cow dung.

He was Tubbs's worst nightmare: a walking disease factory with hands that could crush a man's skull like a rotten egg and the vengeful glint of the cuckold in his eye. "Who in the blazes are you?" he demanded.

The whore tried to explain, saying, "He's just a little ducky, love. He paid two shillings–"

"Shut up, you tart!" the ape-man snarled, backhanding her across the face. "I thought I told you to stay off the game until this Ripper is put away. Pulling pints might not pay as well as spreading your legs for gents from up west, but being a carcass in the Peelers' mortuary would leave us all threadbare in Carey Street." The whore stayed silent, pressing a corner of the stained bed sheet to her bloody nose. The ape-man glanced down at Tubbs's clothes, scattered on the floor next to the bed. "For all we know, our bencull 'ere might even be the bloody Ripper."

He bent to rifle through Tubbs's belongings, extracting all the money from the young doctor's clothes, and shoving into his own pockets. He froze, then, noticing something under the bed.

Tubbs's blood ran cold. His Gladstone bag must have been knocked under there. It had all his medical tools inside and they were all valuable.

The ape-man picked up the Gladstone bag in one massive paw and glared at it. Then he opened it and, amazingly, went white as if he had just seen old Spring-heeled Jack leap out of the bag. "Upon my oath," he said in a slightly strangled voice. "Knives like I've ne'er seen and scalpels... He is the Ripper right enough!"

Terror struck Tubbs. The only thing worse than being a victim of Jack the Ripper these days was being accused of being him. The police had several times had to rescue gentlemen from lynch mobs just because they had walked into a slum that no gentleman on legitimate business would go near, or even because of the clothes they wore resembling the fanciful illustrations printed in the various broadsheets.

The whore had also screamed wordlessly, pointing at him and trying to cover herself at the same time.

"No!" Tubbs protested. "You don't understand. I'm a doctor. I work at the hospital in Bermondsey—"

"You hear that?" the whore squeaked. "A gentleman doctor, just like in the papers!"

"Yerr..." the ape-man rumbled. Tubbs felt his stomach clench up, and realized that he had just made the biggest, worst, and potentially last mistake of his life. He scrambled backwards, desperate to reach the window as the ape-man advanced on him. Behind the oncoming leviathan, the whore goaded him on squealing, "Smack him. He's a rapist and a murderer! Smack him one for me!"

Tubbs tumbled through the window, clutching a small thin bed sheet to his breast, and ran for his life. The cobbles were hard and slick underfoot, but his bare soles and toes gave him better purchase on them than the leather sole of a shoe would have. Naked and terrified, he ran, set only on outpacing the primordial bellowing that echoed around the foggy street.

It was easily the worst night of Stewart Tubbs's life. He was naked, penniless, and trapped in Whitechapel, home of twisted murderers, lynch mobs, and coppers who wouldn't look too kindly on a naked man wandering the streets in the middle of the night.

Tubbs held the sheet around his chest. It was too thin to provide any warmth and too small to give much in the way of modesty. Already he could hardly feel his feet, the wet cobbles were so cold. Walking was like trying to use his hips to swing lead weights from the ends of his legs. He kept hearing voices approach from all angles, and having to hide until they had gone. He could see the beams of bull's-eye lanterns poking though the mist and tried to dodge or duck them. Every evasion was another delay to his return to sanity and civilization, and another degree of temperature dropped. It could surely only be a matter of time before he was struck down with hypothermia.

Then, a stroke of luck: the mists parted to let a tunnel of clear night though, and, at the end of it a window set into the wall of a local hospital. That would be his salvation, as there would be spare clothes for doctors inside. Looking around to make sure there was no one around, he tossed the sheet into the gutter, and pushed the window up. It moved easily, allowing him to climb in.

Inside, he stood regaining his breath for a minute. With a startling thud, the window fell closed behind him. He tried to open it again but it was stuck fast. In his efforts, his elbow struck something, a wooden shelf by the agonizingly solid feel of it. He turned to seek confirmation, just in time to see a glass jar lean out and tumble through the air. It hit the stone floor and exploded like a bursting soap bubble.

"Damn it!" Tubbs snarled. He started to turn back and then froze. He could smell something that hadn't been in the air a moment ago. He looked for the source, and his eyes cast downwards toward the shattered glass vessel. Some sort of colorless liquid had spread itself across the flagstones. Tiny fragments of glass spiked up from the pool like miniature icebergs, but that wasn't what worried Tubbs.

Ethereal wisps of white vapor were surfacing from the liquid, and curling upwards into the air. The individual streamers of vapor were joining together into almost corporeal forms. They filled out like billowing silken sheets, or the ghosts in Dickens's Christmas Carol.

As if they were paying attention to his thoughts and fears, some of the insubstantial arrivals seemed to look at him, with blank eye-sockets that appeared as he watched.

Tubbs staggered back, telling himself that it was just some sort of liquid evaporating into gas, and the eye-sockets were just the way his brain was interpreting the sight of vortices in the vapor. Icy glass briefly touched his bare back and buttocks, before exploding on the floor. Tubbs yelped in shock and danced sideways in an attempt to avoid planting his bare soles smack in the middle of a field of jagged glass shards that now separated him from the window.

From each of the newly broken jars, more gaseous wraiths arose, floating into the air with a lazy confidence that seemed calculated to tease him. Whether guided by currents of air creeping in under the door, or by some malign intelligence, the misty forms slithered towards him through the air. He tried to wave them away–or hit them, he wasn't sure which, but either would do–without success. His fists passed through them without touching anything other that a freezing chill that stiffened the hairs on his arms. The vapors themselves simply wrapped around his swinging arms and, if anything, were drawn to him even more quickly.

Then they were upon him, their wintry touch numbing his nose and ears and lips as they swirled into the openings of his head like water into a plughole. Tubbs thought he was screaming, but since no one came to open the door and investigate, he would never know whether or not he really was.

His whole head throbbed with the burning that only the coldest frostbite can inflict, and his throat tightened, refusing to let any air in to thin out the condensing vapor. There was a rushing in his head that sounded like distant voices, thousands upon untold thousands of them, just beyond the verge of hearing. He wasn't sure whether they were reassuring him or taunting him. He wasn't sure there was a difference.

He realized belatedly that he couldn't see the door for a thick white fog that filled the room. When he, with great effort, pulled his hand up to touch his face, and still couldn't see it, he screamed because now he knew the freezing fog had filled the inside of his eyes, not the room.

He didn't feel himself fall, in the end. He didn't feel anything else at all. Not yet.

Juliet and Bill walked together through the streets of Whitechapel. So far they had seen neither hide nor hair of Tubbs. Juliet could feel eyes upon them from every direction. Bill's assertion that they had only robbers to fear didn't reassure her. At least they personally weren't likely to be at risk from the Ripper. Not only were they chasing him but he had never attacked a man or a couple. In fact he had always fled when men threatened to approach.

As they walked, Juliet steered the conversation back to the matter of the deaths of Upton and the others. Madame Blavatsky had seemed to think that something similar would happen to them too.

Bill would have none of it. "I'm a fighter, Jules," he said. "Maybe not with fists, pistols or whatever, but I'm not going to back down. I'll fight."

"How? How do you fight... a storm? It's a force of nature, Bill. It's like the wind and the rain. You can't hit it, or shoot it, or stab it. You can't grab it to wrestle with it. All you can do is take shelter."

"You can't shelter for your whole life. Sooner or later you'll be outside and feel the wind in your hair or the rain in your face. You have to stand your ground."

"Turn the other cheek, is that it?"

"I suppose you could look at it like that. Father would certainly say so. You might not fight with your fists, but your heart and soul can fight against the darkness."

"Trust me on this: if you turn the other cheek, you simply end up with two black eyes instead of one."

"That's a horribly saddening viewpoint."

"That's the voice of experience speaking."

She hesitated, suddenly feeling sorry for him. Whatever had forced that viewpoint upon him must have been painful.

Sir Keith Swallow strode into the hall wearing a bloodstained leather apron, and faced three-dozen fresh-faced young medical students, eager to learn. He chuckled to himself; they wouldn't be either eager or fresh-faced for long.

"I have a treat for you today," he began. "This corpse is very fresh, having succumbed to death here in this very hospital only last night. As such it is only in the very early stages of rigor mortis, and so today I shall exploit the opportunity to lecture you upon this process."

He turned and pulled the sheet off the nude body that lay on the dissection table. He almost dropped his scalpel when he saw that it was Stewart Tubbs. He recovered quickly, not letting his surprise show to his students. It came to all men, he reminded himself, even young doctors.

"As you can see this is a cadaver of younger chronological age than normal. No obvious outward signs of trauma, so we'll have to go inside the body, to see if we can find out what killed him."

Sir Keith made the first incision neatly, opening Tubbs from crotch to ribs with a single fluid stroke. There was a little more blood flow than he had expected, but he wasn't too concerned. The corpse was utterly fresh, after all, and the blood probably hadn't finished pooling.

When he had cracked open the chest, Sir Keith splayed the ribs out in order to gain access to the pulmonary system. He lifted out one lung, which was as wet and heavy as any he had ever removed from a body.

Then there was a faint movement, a change to the glistening fluids that coated the heart inside its sac. It was impossible, Sir Keith knew, but it was almost as if it had moved in some reflex action. He raised the scalpel, preparing to cut the heart free, when it did it again. This time it was a definite pulsation. Worse still, it was a beat, and with it blood squirted from what seemed like everywhere in the open chest cavity.

Sir Keith realized he couldn't feel the scalpel in his hand. He looked down and saw that it had fallen to the floor without his knowledge. He tried to call out to his students to send someone for help, but his voice wouldn't come. In truth, he couldn't think what help could be given anyway. Dumb and paralyzed, Sir Keith simply couldn't think what to do.

Stewart Tubbs solved his dilemma for him, by regaining consciousness there and then. His eyes snapped open, and a second later his bowels filled the lecture theatre with a foul stench. He sat bolt upright, looking around like a hunted animal, and tried to scream. With only one lung, and the other backfilling with blood, an eerie whooping bubble was the best he could manage.

He could see the organs that had already been removed from his body, the sensation literally indescribable. Sir Keith Swallow was looking down at him aghast, covered in fresh blood: Tubbs's blood.

Tubbs had thought that yesterday had been the worst day he could imagine. He was wrong.

SEVENTEEN

Jim Castle and Tony Chang emerged onto the roof of the LA field office of the ATF. A dark blue Blackhawk helicopter was flaring in towards the roof, where ten men in blue jumpsuits, black body armor and ATF patches were waiting. They all wore Fritz-style Kevlar helmets and carried a variety of weapons. There was roughly a fifty-fifty split between MP5/10s and FN P-2000s. There were two Remington sniper rifles with scopes and everyone also wore at least one pistol, either a SiG or M92F.

Flak vests and Fritz helmets were waiting for Jim and Chang on the seats in the chopper. They started to pull them on as the armed and armored men mounted up. The Blackhawk was back in the air within fifteen seconds and banking west.

"Where are we going?" Jim asked, checking his SiG 226. "Van Nuys?"

Chang, doing likewise but with a Walther P99, shook his head. "Not quite. Burbank Airport. We'll rendezvous with the FBI and LAPD SWAT there before heading to Van Nuys."

Although most people thought of LAX, Los Angeles International, as LA's airport, there were actually several airports in the city. John Wayne Airport down in Orange was capable of handling large domestic jets, whilst other airports at Van Nuys, Malibu and Burbank all catered for executive jets, helicopters and private planes. Van Nuys and Burbank airports in particular were quite close together, a little over five miles apart.

The flight from South Figueroa to Burbank took a bare twenty minutes, a fraction of the time it would have taken to drive, even in the best possible traffic. Through the open door of the chopper, Jim could see a second Blackhawk in formation with the ATF bird. The other Blackhawk sported police markings. Since most police choppers tended to be smaller machines designed for lighting up suspects on the ground with spotlights and cameras, and the Blackhawk was more of a troop carrier, Jim was certain that it was ferrying an LAPD SWAT team. The local Van Nuys team would be en route in a truck or van.

On approach to what was more properly called Burbank-Glendale-Pasadena Airport, Jim could even make out Van Nuys Airport in the distance, with the two stubby towers of its attached hotel, the Airtel Plaza, on the south-western corner of the field. The tiny dots of commercial and private helicopters floated around the airport, whilst colored flecks that were light aircraft came and went along the main east-west runway. Then the Blackhawks were descending into Burbank, and slipping over towards a cordoned-off hangar as far as possible from Burbank's small terminal.

Several police vans were waiting a safe distance away, alongside various unmarked cars. About a hundred yards further away, a Learjet was waiting, its steps lowered, and the engines already turning.

Ducking under the spinning rotors, Jim and Chang hopped to the ground and ran across to the hangar. The bulky shapes of a couple of planes loomed in the darkness at the back of the hangar, draped with protective tarpaulins for some reason.

A series of lightweight metal tables had been set up in the front part of the hangar, with powerful PCs and communications equipment on them. Freestanding frames held aerial photos of Van Nuys airport and flipcharts with hastily scribbled notes and diagrams that looked more like football plays than strategies for assaulting part of an airport.

Chang shook hands with his opposite numbers in the FBI and LAPD SWAT, and introduced Jim, who did the same. "How are we doing?" Chang asked.

The SWAT captain looked to the FBI suit, who nodded. "Van Nuys units are on scene already, as are the FBI. They're keeping an eye on each other to make sure everybody keeps their head down until we're all set. We don't want to spook these guys and scare them off.

"Here's how it's going to work. Assault teams in choppers will come in low and drop onto and around the suspect warehouse. There are choppers coming and going from the airport all the time, so the noise shouldn't spook them. However, we don't want them to look up and see what kind of helicopters are coming in, so we'll give them something else to watch."

"The Lear?"

"The Lear. We recommend you guys go in that. By the time you reach the bad guys' hangar, they'll be bushwhacked by airborne SWAT and ATF teams."

Chang nodded, and Jim could tell he approved. Jim could see a problem, though. "Shouldn't we evacuate the airport and the hotel there?"

"We do that, and they'll suspect that we're onto them. Unless of course we were to include them in the evacuation, which would kind of defeat the purpose. Van Nuys PD will be mounting an evac op as soon as the assault teams make their move, but in any case we're lucky that the terrorists have picked a fairly remote warehouse to hole up in. There's two hundred yards of open ground between them and either the airport proper or the hotel. No cover; they're screwed."

"What sort of resistance will the assault teams–and ourselves when we get off the Lear–be up against?" Chang asked.

"Fully auto assault rifles and subguns. Pistols, maybe hand grenades. No rocket launchers as far as we can tell."

Chang and Jim exchanged glances. "Here's hoping your people have good eyesight."

"They're the best," the SWAT captain promised.

With barely time for a sip of bottled water, Jim and Chang were aboard the Learjet, and hurtling into the sky. They had both strapped themselves into comfortable seats, along with a couple of members of the ATF assault team. The rest would be going in the Blackhawk.

This wasn't the first time Jim had flown, but it was the first time he would spend the whole trip with his safety belt fastened, since the flight–if it was even worthy of the name–was just a couple of minute turnaround, the takeoff and landing coming back to back. The plane began to descend almost as soon as the thought had crossed his mind.

Sean Reilly glanced up at the sound of helicopters overhead. Helicopters flew over the little airport all the time but there was something about this sound that set his teeth on edge. One chopper could easily be innocent, but two, in formation? That was suspicious. He walked to the bonded warehouse's side door and peered out. The sound of rotors was louder, though the only chopper he could see was a two-man job floating over the Airtel.

A Learjet had just touched down on the runway and was taxiing towards the small terminal and airport office, a route that would take it past the warehouse. Reilly ignored it, craning his neck around to search for the helicopters. To be so loud and yet impossible to see from the doorway, they must be very low, he realized.

Low enough to almost land on the roof, in fact. "Ah, crap," he muttered. "Khalid! We're going to have company!"

"Let them come," Khalid shouted back, unshipping the AK74 from his back and cocking it.

The Blackhawks kicked up sand and dust and soot from the warehouse roof as the SWAT teams leapt from them.

Skylights were blown with sharp cracks, and SWAT men swarmed inside. Jim was first out of the Lear when it stopped, and already he could hear shooting. The terrorist's had already seen the SWAT teams, and engaged. The game was up; the authorities' cover blown.

The door Jim was making for was a side door. Observers had reported vehicles parked inside the bonded warehouse's main door, and those would be guarded. The side door offered a better chance of penetrating the building without running into any of Reilly's group coming the other way.

No battle plan, however, survives first contact with the enemy, and Jim walked almost straight into Leon Khalid.

Khalid's eyes widened and he let rip with his AK. Jim dove keeping his face down so he wouldn't be blinded by shards or splinters. Inside the warehouse, the terrorist gunmen were giving it all they had, blasting away on full auto from their AKs and MP5s, but they didn't seem to be aiming true. The SWAT teams, highly trained and disciplined, were firing fewer shots, but better aimed and more effective.

The barrage of terrorist fire blew sparks and chips of concrete from the walls and floor, and occasionally clipped a Kevlar helmet. A three-round burst from a SWAT MP5 dropped a terrorist in his tracks when he let himself creep a little too far out of cover.

Jim glanced round the side of the doorjamb and saw Khalid pulling the banana clip from his AK74. Without waiting for the man to reload, Castle popped out from cover, gun arm straight and support arm crooked, and let him have four rounds in the chest. The terrorist fell and didn't get up. Either he wasn't wearing body amour, or he had taken the hint and decided that discretion was the better part of valor.

Chang grinned at him. "Well done, kid," he said, and moved into the warehouse. Like most bonded warehouses, it was a vast space filled with crates and containers of various sizes, with several sections of the floor area partitioned off by chain-link for storing more sensitive goods, or items on which duty would have to be collected. This forced both SWAT and terrorists to break down into smaller units, each fighting separately from the rest.

Wooden and metal catwalks lined the interior walls, and there were several large wooden crates on a high platform in the center. Suddenly, with a thunderous crack, a flimsy office halfway up one wall, used for controlling the cranes that lifted cargo around the floor, exploded into fragments. Its windows disintegrated into a hailstorm of glass shards. No one in the warehouse, terrorist or lawman, could resist the impulse to look up, squinting and holding their hands up to protect their eyes against the razor-sharp blizzard.

Almost impossibly, a motorcycle was at the heart of the glittering storm, its rider standing in a half crouch on the footrests, an Uzi in each hand and a flaming red ponytail peeking out from under his helmet. It was Sean Reilly.

Before anyone on the ground could get off a shot, and before the bike dropped to earth, Reilly opened up with two outward arcs of automatic fire. Jim, Chang, and everyone around hit the cement or took cover behind crates or the two pickups that were parked near the main doors.

Sirens were getting louder and a police cruiser nudged its way in between the pickups just as Reilly's jump came to its natural end, unfortunately for the cops inside.

The gunman's bike bounced when it hit the cement floor and leapt like a salmon, thumping onto the hood of the black and white, and speeding for the runway.

Jim Castle rolled to his feet and let off a couple of shots at the back of the fleeing biker, then the slide on his SiG locked open, the clip empty.

There was another motorbike parked nearby, chrome and scarlet, wearing the logos of a Triumph Daytona 650 with pride. Like the bike Reilly had just fled on, Jim supposed it was an import machine waiting for duty to be paid. Hoping that being outside its shipping crate meant the terrorists had illegally fuelled it, Jim ran for the bike, swapping magazines on his SiG as he went. A SWAT man was standing next to it, and Jim snatched the Kevlar helmet off his head and leapt onto the bike.

More cops were heading towards the warehouse from the main part of the airport, so that was not an option as far as Reilly was concerned. He spun his motorbike, a BMW K1200S, on a dime, and started for the chain-link fence that separated the airport's tie-down spots from the Airtel's parking lot. Something snapped and whined from the tarmac nearby, a sniper round. He was glad he wasn't trying to cross the two hundred yard kill-zone on foot.

Reilly weaved the bike, zig-zagging slightly to throw off the cop snipers. When he approached the fence, he risked straightening out, aiming for a half-forgotten crate that lay there. The wood was just strong enough and at just the right angle. The BMW leapt the chain-link fence with ease, and Reilly held it steady until it was confident enough in its grip on the blacktop to gain speed in a straight line. That line took it across the parking lot, and straight for the glass double doors of the Airtel's north tower entrance.

Reilly let rip with the Uzi, all but disintegrating the doors in an instant before he would have hit them. He sped inside.

Jim held onto both grips as the Triumph leapt the fence between the airport and the hotel parking lot. The man he suspected to be Sean Reilly was easily within shooting distance of him, but Jim didn't dare spare a hand to pull his gun. All he could think of right now was to catch him.

The Airtel north tower's ground floor corridor flashed past Sean Reilly in a couple of seconds at over one hundred and fifty miles per hour.

Reilly gunned the BMW across the lobby, sending clutches of people, most dressed in strange science fiction costumes, diving over the plush sofas. The Uzi loosed a burst down the main building's ground floor corridor, removing the glass from another pair of double doors at the far end.

Then Reilly was out in the daylight again, bursting through the hedge that separated the Airtel from Sepulveda Boulevard. The BMW skidded across both westbound lanes. The tire of a small hatchback just clipped the rear wheel, sending a jolt through every bone in Reilly's body.

He managed to recover from the slide, pulling the bike upright despite the pain in his back and shoulders. Then he was off again, eastbound.

Jim Castle hit the ruined north tower door at about fifty miles per hour, and jerked right to avoid slamming into the kink in the corridor.

The occupants of the lobby were still under cover when Jim reached it. At the far end of the corridor on the opposite side of the lobby, he could see another wrecked door, and a torn hedge. Movement out of the corner of his eye to the left was traffic on Sepulveda, and he just registered Reilly's helmet in the eastbound lane.

Jim sideslipped left, out the hotel's main doors. The doors weren't fast enough to open for him, nor did he shoot out the glass. Instead he hunched down, pulled a low wheelie, and hoped for the best. The Triumph's front wheel pulverized the glass, and he burst through it. He could feel his sleeves and pants' leg tear, and hear the screech of glass scratch across his helmet. There was a sudden line of red pain across his cheek.

Then he was out of the hotel's driveway and onto Sepulveda, accelerating into the oncoming traffic in the westbound lane. Cars whipped past, their blaring horns lost behind him, drowned out by the Triumph's engine and the wind in his ears.

Jim threw his bodyweight this way and that, darting the bike between oncoming vehicles at such short notice that half the time he thought the blasts of wind pummeling him were the impact of his own death rather than just a wall of slipstream trying to swat him from his mount.

Jim tried not to let his mind dwell on the fact that he was speeding into traffic on the wrong side of the road. There just wasn't time to be scared, because the time it took to imagine a fiery crash would be more than the time it would take to have one.

He had to get to his right, across to the eastbound lane. Doing so, however, was like attempting a slalom in which all the markers were moving at least as fast as he was. Slipping and hitting a car or truck would be a lot more likely to end his run today than hitting a flexible plastic pole did on a downhill slope in Aspen.

There was a crossroads up ahead, letting traffic out from both sides. Jim took advantage of the gap, cutting across in front of an SUV that clipped a sedan when it swerved to avoid his near-suicidal dash. A chorus of horns erupted behind him, but Jim ignored them. He was now eastbound in the right lane and he could see Reilly's bike ahead of him, just passing the big post office building.

Abruptly, the sound of sirens became audible, and police cars appeared in the westbound lane, probably coming in from Burbank. A police chopper swooped in overhead and Jim felt overwhelming relief that he was no longer alone. Tony Chang must have got the word out. Jim waved at the police helicopter, pointing the observers aboard in the direction of Reilly's fleeing bike. Immediately, the various police cars, a mixture of State, LAPD and Highway Patrol, started making U-turns, closing in on Reilly.

Reilly glanced back to see CHP police cruisers and an LAPD 4x4 behind him already. Above, a news chopper was jostling with an LAPD bird for the best view of the chase. Behind his visor, Reilly grinned. He'd give them a show worth watching all right.

Ahead, a tanker was in the center lane. Reilly reached inside his jacket pocket, and pulled out a smooth green sphere about the size of a small apple: a hand grenade. Grinning, Reilly slid his bike closer to the rear of the tanker truck.

Once he had matched speeds with the tanker, he got in tight by its rear wheel. He doubted the driver could see him from here. The cops following could see where he was, but they wouldn't be able to quite make out what he was doing... which was unfortunate for them.

He managed to pull the pin on the grenade, lifting his index finger off the handlebar just long enough to do so, but kept his fingers firmly down on the safety lever. Then, carefully, he stretched out his arm and shoved the grenade snugly into a gap between the wheel arch and the container tank itself. When he took his hand off the grenade, the safety lever sprung off, disappearing into the air.

Reilly immediately grabbed the bike's throttle and opened it up all the way. The BMW surged forward under him, leaving the tanker behind.

The grenade went off with a sharp crack that was audible over the roar and rumble of the traffic. The blast blew out the left rear tires of the tanker trailer and punched a hole in the tank.

The trailer jackknifed, sending smaller cars scrambling out of the way as it slewed across the lanes, and began to roll. In a matter of instants it was tumbling, spilling out hundreds of gallons of gas across the highway. The cops in pursuit all stepped on their brakes as the exposed wheel rims struck golden and white-hot sparks amidst the flowing gasoline. The bloom of flame that erupted from the tanker was inevitable.

The steel tank momentarily inflated like a balloon then burst. Liquid fire hit the freeway like red and gold breakers on a blacktop beach. The choppers wheeled away as a fireball seared the sky and turned to a roiling black cloud so thick that it looked as if the helicopters might dash themselves to pieces on its surface.

A white Ford sedan, one of the police cruisers, and a pickup with three surfboards propped against the cab, didn't manage to stop in time. The sedan and cruiser hit the tanker head on, while the pickup overturned, spilling the surfboards amid the wreckage. The other cruiser dug its nose to the ground and stopped in time, blowing out both front tires in the process.

Jim almost crushed the Triumph's brake levers in his hands as he hurtled toward the burning wreckage that completely blocked the highway, but then saw a way through. It was a surfboard, tilted against the hood of the cruiser with the two front flats.

Ignoring the part of his brain that was screaming at him to think rationally, Jim Castle gunned the Triumph's four-cylinder engine for all it was worth, aiming it at the sloping board. As he hit the board, he leaped up off the seat as he took to the air. He had no idea if doing so would really make the bike any lighter or help it fly any easier, but at least he felt he was doing something to make a difference, and that was better than just trusting to fate.

The Triumph soared. For a moment the world turned hot and black, and Jim had the uncomfortable suspicion that he knew how it must feel to ride across the plains of hell. Unseen flames cloaked in the black smoke slid around his legs, tantalized by the prey that was so close to falling into their loving embrace. Even through the helmet, he couldn't breathe, and the smell of burning gas made him want to puke.

All thoughts of Patricia Fuller, Will Sax and the other Metroline survivors had gone from Jim's mind as if they had never been. Instead he was thinking of the dead in the train, now passengers in an electrified Metro transit rail system belonging to a twenty-first century Charon. The only name he could think of to hold on to was Lauren's. She would keep him not just safe but also victorious, just by being in his heart.

Then he was through, dazzled by sunshine that was suddenly brilliant in spite of the tinted visor, and falling towards the blacktop.

Having a jackhammer slam into the tailbone, driving the spine into the base of the skull, could hardly be worse than the impact Jim felt. For a gut-churning second he thought the bike's aluminum frame was coming apart under him, to the sound of shattering metal and plastic, but then it bounced back to life and sped after the fleeing Reilly. Jim wished he had a police radio on the bike so that he could know whether more cops were on the way. From the way things had been going so far, he half expected the National Guard to be the next wave, maybe with an air strike.

If wishes were horses, he reminded himself, beggars would ride. He'd just have to stay in pursuit and hope that somebody in charge was smart enough to not just leave the situation to him. At least he himself wouldn't have to break off anytime soon; the terrorists seemed to believe in keeping their bikes well fueled, if the gauge in front of him was actually working and hadn't been fried by the jump he had made.

Reilly kept his attention in front now. The wrecked tanker should have put a stop to the police who were chasing him. If he could just work out where he was, he could figure a way to slip away to some safe area and lie low until things settled down a little. Then he could get out of California for a while. He had plenty of friends—or at least friends of his former cause—on the Eastern Seaboard. Boston or Baltimore, he thought to himself. Either of those places would provide a good measure of sanctuary for him.

First things first: get onto the freeway. A turn on to Highway 170 should be coming up soon; he had seen a couple of signs for it already. As he throttled back a little—save the gas for when it was most needed, he thought—he caught a flash of blue in his mirror. For a moment he thought it was the light on top of a police cruiser, being guided by the chopper that still floated above and behind him, out of pistol range but within camera range. When he could see the blue more clearly, he realized it was a motorbike. It looked like the Triumph that Khalid had bought, but it certainly wasn't Khalid riding it. From the blue windbreaker and Kevlar it was a cop or a Fed.

The guy must be good to have made it past the tanker, and Reilly appreciated that. At the same time, he had no intention of being caught, whether by a worthy adversary or anyone else. He opened up the throttle again, speeding for the turn on to the highway.

He got there in seconds, and swept up onto the 170, which headed southeast, back towards LA. His elation was short-lived, however. Two armored cars, ex-military Greyhound wheeled tanks adapted for police use, blocked the road ahead. From behind, sirens screamed at him. It was a trap.

Reilly wasn't beaten yet. Still three hundred yards from the tanks, he tipped the BMW forward into a nose-wheelie, and spun, almost on the spot, so that it was now moving back towards the pursuing black and white cruisers that had come along the highway behind him. Reilly hooked the toes of his boots under the footrests and leaned back against the rising seat. For an instant he looked almost as if he were crucified on the nose-down bike, arms akimbo. Then he squeezed off a whole clip from the Uzi in each hand just as he passed between the cars' noses.

The windshields and side windows on both police cruisers disintegrated, metal craters erupting in the doors. Red puffed out onto the shattered glass, as the heads of one car's driver and the other's passenger took direct hits.

Then the terrorist was past and behind them, his rear wheel returning to the ground at high rev, the spent Uzis clattering to the road as he gripped the handlebars. By this time, the car with the dead driver slewed across, ramming into the other car, whose driver was too shocked to react in time. Metal screeched and tires exploded as both police cruisers crumpled into the concrete center divide, their sirens dying into sad wails.

Jim Castle powered onto the highway just in time to see Reilly trash the police cruisers. The Irishman was now heading straight toward him. Jim gave a moment's thought to getting out of the way, but didn't, for three reasons. Firstly, Lauren didn't marry a man who would quit. Secondly, the terrorist needed to be taken down. Thirdly, Jim realized that his opponent had no way to reload. He was out of ammo and, in effect, weaponless.

Speeding towards the oncoming bike at a combined velocity of over a hundred miles per hour,

Jim risked steering one-handed and drawing his gun with the other.

As the two bikes closed like medieval knights on the jousting field, Jim fired again and again at the oncoming terrorist, until he had emptied the gun and its slide locked back. Jim's "Fuck!" was lost to the winds of speed, and he dropped the gun so that he could grab the Triumph's handgrip again.

Then Reilly was upon him, reaching towards his boot for some kind of weapon. With no weapon at his disposal, Jim leaned left and twisted the throttle, toppling the bike into a power slide. Sparks coruscated past his leg and hip, as the bike hurtled belly-first towards the oncoming motorcycle. Sean Reilly tried to lean back, bringing his BMW up on its rear wheel in the hope of getting over Jim's Triumph. It was a big mistake, as the belly of the Triumph caught his rear wheel and tripped the BMW. The front wheel smashed down into the ground almost to the forks, and the whole bike flipped forward. The terrorist was thrown clear off his bike, slamming head first into the tarmac. His BMW, completing its own forward revolution, crashed down upon him, tail first.

The sudden silence, bar distant sirens, was a jarring shock to Jim's system. He rolled onto his back, which felt like it was on fire, and roared with rage and pain. As if that sated the fire on his back, he felt a little better and managed to stand. He limped over to where his SiG had fallen, retrieved it and loaded a new clip. Working the slide to jack a round into the chamber, Jim approached the wreckage of the BMW. He approached cautiously, keeping his pistol trained on the sprawled body that lay a few feet from the mangled bike.

Reilly was having difficulty breathing, but he was still alive. He looked at Castle dazedly and then seemed to remember where he was. "Ah," he said tightly. "So much for that, then."

"You're going down, Reilly."

Reilly forced a laugh, then his face contorted in pain. "Don't be so sure. For once the Good Friday Agreement comes in handy. You'll have to hand me to the Brits, and under the deal your Mister Clinton helped set up, they'll have to let me go as soon as they've sentenced me."

"They might have to wait a while. You'll be tried for your crimes here first."

"That's true, but we have quite a lobby here. Politics always gets in the way of a fair trial, one way or the other."

"You're forgetting that your 'lobby' isn't best pleased with you. A rogue agent isn't their favorite kind of man. There's no 'I' in team, Reilly, even if there's one in IRA."

EIGHTEEN

Will and Patti held each other in bed. Neither of them quite knew what to say. Neither of them had ever thought about how they might react if they were ever faced with death, in the form of a terminal illness or whatever. Not many people thought about imminent mortality, until they reached the age at which has-been TV stars tried to sell them life insurance to pay for burial.

Diseases could be treated, men or animals could be fought off, and even old age could be combated to some degree in the hope of staving off the inevitable. Certainty was a different matter. Neither of them had thought about how to deal with the certainty of death.

"Okay, angel of death, reality's antibodies or this Reilly motherfucker. Whichever it is, it's after everybody who you stopped from getting on that train?"

"Right," she said.

"We have to try to set things right."

"Isn't that what cops are for?"

"Look, this is my fault. I stopped us all getting on the train–"

"You saved everybody's lives!"

"For later? For an even more gruesome and painful death? I didn't save any of us, Will. I tagged us all for a worse death. Besides, what if we'd boarded the train and just been wounded? Maybe I've killed us all."

"Wait a minute... We compared this to messing with the environment. What about cloud seeding in droughts?"

"What about it?"

"Well, you know it's going to rain sooner or later, but you make it happen when you want, to improve the situation. Then there are, I don't know... Firebreaks. You set a fire to burn an area so that wildfire can't spread beyond it. You fight fire with fire."

"Are you suggesting we fight Death with death?" He could see where she was going with this, and he knew she wasn't the type to suggest they started sacrificing strangers to the grim reaper to sate his lust.

"If we have to die, we should do it on our terms."

"Fuck! Patti, we're trying to avoid dying at all, at least until old age–"

"I'm not talking about dying permanently. What about temporarily."

"Temporarily? What the fuck are you talking about? Death isn't a holiday, it's not just a condition to be cured..."

"There's a thing called a near-death experience. You must have seen it on TV or read it in the tabloids."

"Yeah... People die on the operating table or whatever, they see a tunnel of light, then get resuscitated." A sudden understanding dawned upon him. It was as sickening and terrifying as it was meant to be reassuring. "You don't mean we..."

"Did you ever see that movie with Kiefer Sutherland, *Flatliners*?"

"They were med students. They had access to immediate resuscitation. And it was Hollywood bullshit."

"We need to find a way to die just long enough, and to be revived in time."

Jim gritted his teeth for the ride to the emergency room. He hadn't stopped any bullets, but half the ligaments in both his legs had been ripped and twisted around, and several ribs busted when he pulled off the power slide.

The ambulance that sped Jim Castle to the emergency room had a driver who seemed even crazier than Jim had been on the Triumph. He weaved in and out of traffic like a complete madman, sirens blaring.

Jim, despite the painkillers that were kicking in to turn his perceptions of the world into soft gray fuzz, loved every second of it. It was utterly fabulous. He told himself that this opinion was probably a result of the medication taking effet, but it didn't matter. The bastards who bombed South Hill Street were out of the picture for good, and he had survived the most insane and scary day of his life. When he was back on his feet, he would take Lauren dancing somewhere ridiculous and dance a tango with her. They'd let people watch, so that they would all know that life was good.

The doctors in the ER wasted no time cutting Jim's clothes free, and strapping up his ribs. They applied various gels and ointments to his back and legs, and strapped his knees and ankles so that they wouldn't swell too much and prevent him from walking.

One of the doctors, a young black guy, had used those exact words. Jim nearly laughed in his face. The last thing he felt like doing was trying to walk; it was just too damn painful and every joint of every limb felt like it wanted to go off and do it's own thing, rather than flex strongly and smoothly in the direction he wanted them to go in. Walk? Maybe tomorrow, but for now Jim just wanted to sleep.

He resisted the urge to fall into the relief of sleep. His clothes were in the little closet beside the bed. Chang had taken his gun and ammo back to the office–best not to leave that lying around a public hospital–but everything else was there, including his cellular.

He dug out the phone, and called Patti Fuller.

Patti arrived about an hour later, looking tired. Her eyes filled with sympathy when she saw him. "Hi, G-man. What can the *Borderlands Patrol* do for you today."

He laughed, which hurt, and then forced it down to just a smile. "You're safe now," Jim said. "Fate, Death, whatever you call it, was just a group of men who weren't as clever or as badass as they thought they were."

"I..." She forced a smile, but Jim could see the tears it masked. She still didn't believe him either, he saw. She never would, because that was how people's minds worked; they believed in what helped them get on with their lives. The problem some people had was that they sometimes got turned around somehow, and believed in things that got in the way of their lives. Patti was too smart to be one of those latter people, but all the evidence showed that she was one anyway.

So he believed, anyhow, and he wasn't blind to the irony of that. Belief kept his mind on the job; belief that it was right, that he was good at it, and that man was fouler and more evil than anything an imaginary supernatural could throw at the world. Lauren believed that too, and that, more than anything else, kept him going.

"I guess I should thank you."

"For getting those guys, not for helping you out." It wasn't a question, and Patti didn't say anything by way of reply. Jim closed his eyes and felt the urge to sleep. Healing came faster when the body was asleep. He forced himself awake again. "Tell me something, Patti, how do you fight against death? What is death?"

"The opposite of life?"

"The absence of life," Jim corrected. "It's pretty obvious, isn't it? You stand against death, fight it if you like, by living."

"Define living," she challenged him.

"Well, that's different for different people, isn't it?

"What about us teenage hippy chicks?"

"You're not a teenager any more," Jim said. That stung Patti, and he could see it. "Sorry, I didn't mean it that way..."

"Twenty-two," she said, mock-thoughtfully. "That's a teen by porn industry standards."

"You're not a porn star either. I hope."

Where the hell was this guy coming from, she wondered? It was a hell of a roundabout way to talk to her about terrorism on the subway, or her health, whichever he had supposedly called her in about. "No," she said slowly and carefully. "I've always managed to keep my clothes on in everything I've done for the magazine."

His eyes twinkled. "I'm not sure whether that's the best news I've heard all day, or the worst."

"Either way I guess it's bad news for the newsstand outside, if it means you won't be buying now."

"Not necessarily, I'm a sucker for all that paranormal conspiracy stuff."

"Professional interest?"

"Science fiction and fantasy fan." He raised an eyebrow. "That is what goes in those things, right?"

By time Patti got back home, Will had gone to work.

Any big store feels like a ghost town in miniature when there are only a handful of employees prowling the aisles and stockrooms long after the last customer has gone. Not that Will disliked that. In fact he thought it was kind of cool. It was all too easy to imagine the occasional other employee that was glimpsed in the distance being a shuffling zombie like in *Dawn of the Dead* or *The Beyond*. Will sometimes amused himself by hiding from the other members of his shift and pretending to shoot at them with an imaginary shotgun.

It was also a relief not to have to smile and be polite to assholes who came in to buy stuff. Not all the customers were assholes, and most even deserved a smile and a "Have a nice day," but it was frustrating and annoying to still have to give the assholes the same treatment as everyone else.

When the retail day was finished, and the shoppers—assholes or otherwise—gone, Will and the others could loosen up. They still had work to do, like restocking, pricing or cleaning, but they could do it like normal, real people, not like brainwashed machines.

As Will went past the staff changing room on his way to the john, he saw the game in progress. Kay Franks was messing with something in the locker, while Mark Bell crept up behind her.

Mark raised his hands as if holding a pump action shotgun. Will bit his lower lip to stop himself from laughing out loud, in case the sound stopped the little performance he was sure was about to follow. Sure enough, Mark swept his left hand down and back, as if pumping a shell into the chamber of the imaginary shotgun.

"*Pow!*" Mark said, startling Kay, who shrieked, then gave him a sour look. She briefly mimed a zombie-like gait as she moved towards him. "You're supposed to destroy the brain," she warned him.

"Only if the target has one."

Will harrumphed loudly, startling both of them. "You do know we don't pay overtime here?"

"Huh?" Mark vocalized.

"It's three minutes past the end of your shift, Mister Brain. Go on, get outta here and leave the real work to me."

"If you need a hand..." Kay offered.

Will held up a manila folder. "Inventory."

"See you tomorrow," Kay said.

The rain was colder than usual. It hissed through the leaves around the apartment block like a besieging army of serpents and darkened the normally oatmeal-colored sidewalks to the same leaden shade as the sky.

Out of the darkness, a man walked, the tails of a leather trench floating out from behind him. He was at least six feet tall, with graying red hair worn in a ponytail. A dark beard, edged with silver, lined his jawbone. His pants were black combats, and he wore heavy biker boots.

Patti, sitting on the decking of her patio, recognized him immediately. It was Sean Reilly. He smiled a crooked smile, the gray edges of his beard glinting like the edges of a knife blade.

"Hi Patti," he said in greeting. "Sorry I couldn't get to see you earlier."

Patti stammered, with no idea what to say. "Reilly..."

"At your service, dear heart. I've heard a lot about you. I couldn't resist the urge to come and see for myself." He tilted his head, clearly making a judgment on her body, but matter-of-factly, not in a sleazy, undressing her with his eyes kind of way. "Not bad," he said. "Your friend Will is a fucking lucky guy, isn't he? Or lucky fucking, considering that you're the one he's doing."

"Did you come here just to talk dirty to me?" She felt frozen, like a jackrabbit in the glare of headlights. There must be something she could do, some way to get away from this motherfucker who had killed so many people. Hell, she wouldn't mind killing him herself if not for the slight problem that she had no weapons.

She had never been interested in guns and never owned one. She wouldn't know what to do with it. Swords were a different matter but she owned only a pair of bokken, wooden training swords. It was said that Miyamoto Musashi, the greatest samurai who had ever lived, had won several duels with bokken, even killing men with them. She believed it, but she also knew that she wasn't him.

"Actually I just came to talk, and to enjoy the weather."

"You like this piss?"

"Reminds me of home," he said. "I hate the heat. I mean, the colder it gets, you can always put more clothes on. But when it's hot... Once you're naked that's as far as you can go, and then you're fucked aren't you? Sorry, I'll try to avoid putting the words 'naked' and 'fucked' together like that."

"Get to the point. If you came here to kill me like you killed the others."

"Ah, straight to business. I like that. Most women can't do it." He sat back and crossed his legs. "I haven't killed anybody." He frowned. "Let me rephrase that. I haven't killed Hal Ward, Susan Fries, Al Kinsey, Zack Halloran–"

"How do you know–"

"Or Will Sax."

"What?"

"Oh, I know Jim Castle and various other people have tried to tell you that I did, but let me put it this way." He drew a massive Desert Eagle pistol from under his coat, cocked it, and pointed it at Patti's forehead with the safety off. "If I wanted to kill you, all I'd have to do is pull the trigger." He thumbed the safety on, de-cocked it and put the gun away. "So why didn't I?" He stood up. "Keep working out," he advised. "You look great." Then he vanished.

She sat alone for a moment, and then something he had said reached her consciousness. "What do you mean, you didn't kill Will?"

And she woke, sheathed in cold sweat, in her bed. "Oh fuck!" she yelled, grabbed her clothes, and ran.

Will Sax was alone at last. Just himself, the inventory sheets and the best home entertainment sound systems that other people's money would buy. The only thing missing was Patti and she would be picking him up later anyway.

He went through into the customer service office and pulled the bland and soulless muzak CD out of the player. Then he returned to the home entertainment section and starting setting the levels on a prime display of speakers, all of which he hooked up to the most expensive player in stock. "Try before you buy," he said to himself, and slid a Rammstein CD into it. Pressed *play*.

He was, damn near literally, blown away. The bass and sheer volume should have blown out the store windows, but all the settings on the system were also working at peak efficiency, carrying every layer, every frequency and every note in just exactly the way that Christophe Doom-Schneider and the boys would cream themselves over. It was beyond awesome, and well into heaven on Earth.

* * *

The lights throughout the store flickered, plunging the displays into a second of darkness before coming on again. Oddly enough, the music didn't pause, but flowed relentlessly on through the shadows. Will wondered if he should check the store's breakers, and started across the shop floor towards what he thought of as the backstage area.

As he passed by an array of flat screen TV's, something caught his eye, and he looked around. The TVs were on, and muted, but some of them looked very dull. Someone must have been screwing with the brightness and contrast settings, he thought. He went over to check them, and found that the images on the screens were wavering with ripples of darkness. That was worrying, as Flanagan would go ballistic if a whole set of top-of-the-range TVs turned out to be no good. He started to turn them off, and, in the suddenly blank glass, he saw something flit across it. It was just a shadow, flitting across TV screen like the reflection of someone in another part of the room.

Although the first couple of TVs he had touched were now switched off, Will started to note an unpleasant humming sound. It was a deep throbbing buzz, almost calculated to set hackles raising. It was primal, or as primal as a technological sound could be.

Will didn't like it at all. Considering all the stuff that had been happening lately, he wasn't going to mess with something that sounded the way he imagined a reactor on overload would sound. He stepped back from the TVs, and decided that the breakers were definitely the things to look at. An electrical fault in an electrical goods store was ironic and faintly ridiculous, but it happened every other day.

He had taken two steps when the strip-light above him burst, showering him with stinging sparks. Another one burst, plunging the store into a world of darkness and shadows. As if some unseen entity had thrown the switches, the strip-lights in the ceiling continued to burst. This wasn't a problem with the breakers, Will decided. This was... it. Death, the thing that had claimed Susan and the others, was here. It was here for him. He shivered, his stomach churning. He had to get out of here, if it wasn't too late.

The interior of the store was bathed in semi-darkness, lit only by the TV screens on display, the LEDs on other pieces of equipment and the occasional piece of concealed floor-level lighting used to highlight a display. It was like being on the spaceship set for a movie or TV show. As he tried to decide the best way out, the TV screens, one by one, went to static.

Sparkling gray and white bled out of the screens, and in it, Will thought he could make out faces. Susan, Hal Ward, lots of people he didn't recognize and skulls. Lots of skulls, even fractal skulls within skulls and they were all laughing at him. He forced himself to look away, taking all of his willpower to do so. The faces were his imagination, he told himself. People always saw patterns in things, like figures dancing in campfire flames.

There was a discreet plastic click and Will looked towards the source of the sound. It was a slimline DVD player, the disk tray sliding out only a fraction of the distance it should do. The edge of a disk glinted inside, curving wide and gently like the smile of a shark. He watched it for a moment, lulled into wondering what was happening.

The disk tray snapped open faster than he could see, the force of it flicking the disk towards him. A flicker of red pain seared his cheek open. His hand darted to his face, which stung. He touched his fingers to his cheek, and they came away glistening red.

"Oh shit," he whispered.

As if that was the signal to go, another disk flashed out of the darkness, nicking his ear. A third flitted past his back, cutting into his shirt. Will ran, legs pumping like jackhammers, trying to keep his head down. The air was filled with soft clicks and silver flashes. Slashes of icy fire, painted red, winked into existence across his left bicep and right calf. Will looked, stupefied, at the cut on his leg. The pants leg was sliced neatly with no tearing. So was his skin, half an inch into the muscle.

He tried to get out of the department, but disks caught him in a crossfire, driving him back. He scrambled for cover, thinking that if he could just stay alive until the machines ran out of disks, he might yet walk out of here. Or limp, even. The display stand he dived behind was not the right one for that aim. A big new CD player, capable of holding a couple of dozen disks, was sitting there in front of his nose. The card next to it read "Home Jukebox."

He lunged forward, reaching to pull the plug on the machine. The machine struck first, spitting out a silver flash. He didn't actually feel his hand come off, but he saw it, and the sight was even more disturbing than mere pain could ever be. Losing his ability to think straight, he reverted, screaming, to primeval instinct. He ran.

It was his last mistake. A glinting disk sent him to his knees by slicing through his Achilles tendon, and, in less than a second, a half dozen of them embedded themselves like shuriken into his back. They all hit at the same time, at various points along his spine, sliding in between the discs and severing his spinal cord in several places. He fell to both knees, arms flung out by sheer momentum, a stairway of silver curves sticking out of his back—a human CD rack.

Before he could fall, one last disk hurtled out of the shadows, sinking through between the neck and base of the skull and out through his throat. Will slumped forwards, the last beat of his heart pumping his blood onto the carpet.

Patti's Saturn screamed into the parking lot and screeched to a halt. She leapt from the car and ran towards the store. It was closed at this hour and steel shutters were pulled down over the main doors, but Patti went round to the staff door at the side as a matter of course.

The door was ajar, which was unusual. Her instincts began to try to convince her to turn around, get in the Saturn and leave. They hinted that dialing 911 might be a good idea as well. She ignored them, wanting only to find Will and be reassured that he was safe and well.

Half of her wish was granted.

The air on the main shop floor was thick with the smell of blood and the acrid tang of burnt insulation. Her heart sinking, Patti ran through the dim interior to the home entertainments section. The tableau she found was arc-lit by static from TVs that surrounded the body like rubbernecking ghouls. He was lying face down, with gleaming silver curves embedded in his back and legs. His head hung limply, held on only by two flaps of skin, one under each ear. His right hand was a yard or so from the rest of the corpse, still sporting the eternity ring she had given him at Christmas.

Patti ran out into the parking lot and back to the Saturn. The thought of driving couldn't even make itself heard over the tumult of loss that filled her head, deafening her from the inside out.

She slumped against the side of the car, grabbing her head in her hands and wailing. If Death were the skeletal stalker of myth she would have hunted him down and ripped him to pieces, bone by bone. Patti looked for a bright side, because she had always believed that everything, no matter how bad, had a bright side. The only one she could think of was that at least Will wouldn't have to experience the raging grief that she was now suffering. Having already lost one friend, it would have utterly destroyed the great guy if he lost his beloved as well.

NINETEEN

The next night, Bill and Juliet returned to Whitechapel, in search of Stewart Tubbs. One problem that occurred to Juliet was that they could not be sure that he would be wearing the same disguise again. They knew his build and features well enough, however, Juliet was sure they could spot him regardless of what disguise he wore. "No matter how grand the wig," Bill reminded her.

"Exactly."

"There's something else we should consider," Bill said. "The Ripper has only struck a few times in a whole year. He may only come here rarely. We could find ourselves going round and round this district forever, like the bloody Wandering Jew or something."

Juliet looked around, hoping that she might see Tubbs walk out of the fog and prove him wrong.

There was a laugh to be sure—a woman walking in Whitechapel, hoping that Jack the Ripper would show his face. Perhaps her father was right after all, and she wasn't sane enough to be allowed out on her own. Perhaps she should just go home and stay there.

Then again, she still had that oppressive sense of threat hanging over her, which had been there since the night of the gas explosion. She had performed a heretical act then, foretelling the future even without knowing that she was doing so. The atonement and redemption that she had spoken of to her father still had to be fulfilled. She could only hope that it didn't mean she had to die. She had been looking over her shoulder ever since she and Bill had spoken to Helena Blavatsky, and yet nothing had befallen her. Perhaps the policemen and detectives were right all along, and the deaths of Upton and the trio at the Stanley house had been purely coincidental.

She also worried that perhaps some evil force had wanted her to think that, to lull her into a false sense of security. Most likely, Bill had suggested at one point, they were just cosmic pawns being played with the gods of Olympus. "It makes sense when you think about it," he had said. "The Greeks believed that the gods were greatly interested in human emotions, and that's why they kept coming down from Olympus and meddling.

"Every time the gods meddled, people, mortals, got shafted and went through the predictable responses that people go through: love, betrayal, loss... Angst seemed to be their favorite though. I dunno if that was intentional or just a handy effect that the gods happened to like. People would worry and fret and get their knickerbockers in a twist, worrying about what the gods were going to do next. And the gods loved this, so what usually happened is the gods would wind some poor bugger up something horrible, and watch them squirm–"

Juliet shivered. "That's horrible. I thought God was supposed to be good."

"Well, the Greek gods weren't our God–who, by the way, is a damnable swine in the Old Testament, before he got all jollied up later–so why should they be? They were people writ large and they had all the emotions and appetites of people writ large, including the desire to get entertainment from worry and angst."

"That isn't a mortal desire!"

"Isn't it? Haven't you seen a cockfight or watched some sprog scoop some pond life into a bucket and poke 'em with a stick to make 'em jump? Nah, we like it, but on a human level; the old Greek gods were way bigger. Anyway, so they liked the worry and the angst because it gave them a thrill. Then, when the people didn't worry or suffer from angst, that's when they'd get blasted."

"Because they weren't any good to the gods any more?"

"Exactly, my pretty little doll. So you just keep worrying about whether something horrible involving fire or snakes is going to happen to us, and, with any luck, it won't." He sniffed and looked around. "I wonder..."

"What?"

"There's a Gladstone bag lying over there." They went over to it. It was empty, but it bore the initials "S.T." "It's his," he said.

"Are you certain of that?"

Bill nodded. "It's the one he was carrying last night."

"He must have dropped it."

"Or been lynched."

Patti screwed up her eyes, half expecting to see a corpse swinging from the nearest gas lamp. He picked up the bag and handed it to her. "We probably need to get this to the police."

"I'll take it straight away," she volunteered. "The Ripper only attacks... women of a certain kind. You stay here and keep watch on this spot. There might be clues."

"Very well," he agreed at last, after about five minutes of arguing. She didn't actually persuade him, she just ran into the fog with the bag.

Ten minutes later she was hopelessly lost, stumbling around in the fog, and felt her way along the walls of factories with her hands. After almost an hour she found herself in a cramped little square. The sign above her head read "Miller's Court." A light was on in one of the rooms on the corner, and she rushed over to it. At least she could get directions.

Juliet froze in the doorway, blushing. "I'm sorry," she stammered, "I didn't know–I mean I thought–" The words tumbled out so fast that she couldn't stop them, even though she knew that the naked girl in the bed wouldn't feel particularly forgiving for her intrusion, and that she should just back out.

"Sorry," she said again, and reached out a hand behind her for the door handle. The girl in the bed still didn't reply, though her eyes were fixed glassily on Juliet. "Are you all right?" Juliet asked, almost in spite of herself. There was still no answer. Juliet was torn, unsure whether to get out before she caused any more offence, or to step forward and see whether she was ill. Perhaps getting a doctor would be an appropriate compromise, she thought.

The smell reached her then. It was thick and rank, heavy with copper. It was the scent of an abattoir or the back room of a butcher's shop. A fire burned low in the grate, almost out, but giving enough light to see by.

The sheets weren't red silk or satin after all; they were red with congealed blood. The girl's abdomen was completely hollowed out, her right hand drooping inside the cavity as if it was testing out a sour stomach. What used to be her pretty head–before its nose had been sliced off–was severed, in all but name, remaining attached to the torso by only a thread of skin. Her heart lay on the pillow next to it. Her left arm was equally loose, again only the tiniest strip of skin holding it on to her shoulder. A breast had been removed, leaving only a huge red scab, while her splayed legs had been skinned. A picture frame above the bed was smeared with blood and offal, a length of intestine draped over it like celebration bunting for the mentally sick.

Juliet screamed, partly in revulsion, and partly in that prescient way that animals led to the slaughterhouse do. She stumbled backwards out of the little room, the smell of hot blood and offal clinging on to her nose and soaking itself into her clothes. She ran blindly, trying to get away from the stink and the sight as well as from whoever was responsible. The Ripper, she knew. He must have been literally moments earlier. Possibly he was even still there, watching her reaction through a crack in the interior door.

There was a splashing from the opposite corner of the court. Tubbs, she thought. Her blood turned as cold and sluggish as the Thames in her veins. She had found the Ripper, and the only thing in her favor was not a gun or a knife, but the simple fact that she was not a whore. The man was bent over a water butt, washing his hands and arms. The figure looked familiar, but it didn't remind her of Tubbs. In fact it more resembled Bill. Juliet peered around the corner, trying to focus on the face that was so barely illuminated.

"Bill, is that you?"

He turned, and Juliet was relieved to see that it was, in fact, Bill Sangster. He too must have been lost in the fog. She let out the long breath she had been holding, and her smile followed it naturally. Bill looked surprised, and, worse, shocked, though Juliet couldn't imagine why.

Then she saw what was in his hand: a long narrow-bladed knife, which looked strong and sharp. It wasn't the steel itself that worried Juliet, it was the wetness that glistened on it. In the dark, there was no way to tell what color the liquid was, but Juliet knew instinctively that it would be red.

"Oh no..." he said. "Why didn't you just go to the police, Juliet? You would have been safe with them. You would always be safe on these streets with me to protect you." He looked over her shoulder at the door in the corner, number 13. "Oh no," he repeated. "I'm so sorry, I didn't want this. Not ever; I could never hurt you."

She started to back away, back out into Dorset Street. "You're the Ripper? You're Jack the Ripper?" She wanted to vomit more now than when she had come face to face with the mutilated corpse in number 13. She had been sitting hand in hand with the Ripper at Madame Adrienne's after all. And many times since. "You killed Tubbs!"

He shook his head. "I haven't seen Tubbs. Doctors aren't safe here, thanks to the reprehensible behavior of the gutter press. He may have been lynched, like I said earlier."

A worse thought occurred to Juliet; one of those accidents, a gruesome and spectacular accident for another of Madame Adrienne's survivors. Now there was only herself and Sangster left, and she couldn't foresee an accidental death for herself, not from the Ripper. As if reading her thoughts, he stepped towards her.

"If it's any consolation, you won't end up like Upton or the others. It'll be quick and painless."

"Have any of your victims died quickly or painlessly?"

"You won't be a Ripper victim. This is just self-preservation. I told you before, I'm a fighter. I will fight for my ongoing existence, whether that means attacking a horde of soldiers or killing you."

She remembered what he had said after their visit to Helena Blavatsky, and his opinion of her advice to accept their fates. "Bollocks to that," she snapped as best she could and kicked him squarely in the articles referred to. He doubled over with a squeal, dropping the knife. She kicked it into a corner, hoping it fall down a drain or be lost in the gutter and then she ran like the very Devil himself was after her.

Because he was.

Bill Sangster fell onto his side, gasping for breath. When the pain subsided, he scrambled around in the gutter for his knife. He found it quickly, the hilt sticky with manure, but she had got a head start on him.

Nevertheless, he set off in pursuit. He couldn't see her too well in the mist, but fog was a better conductor of sound than regular air on a clear day, and he could follow her footsteps with ease.

Juliet ran blindly, her strides as long as she could manage while her heavy skirt threatened to foul her ankles and trip her. She could hear Bill Sangster's steady pace behind her. The worst of that sound was that it wasn't the sound of someone running flat out, but of someone pacing themselves. She knew he could run her down at any time, but was holding back.

She wished she could believe his hesitance had something to do with the feelings he had seemed to have for her. With all her heart, she wished that, but she couldn't. This was the fiend the newspapers had named Jack the Ripper. This was a killer who took passionate pleasure in the frenzy of destruction he wrought upon women's bodies. Such a person could only be toying with her, and seeking to prolong and heighten her fear and suffering.

She had no idea where she was running. The buildings around her were getting higher and more ornate, but the channels through which she ran were still narrow. It was as if every step took her not just further into the labyrinth, but also deeper into the earth. Little light could squeeze down past the walls, and each new short alleyway felt more like a freshly dug grave. There was no way to climb out, so Juliet had no choice but to keep her feet pounding, running on from grave to grave with the prayer that she would be interred in none of them tonight.

Juliet, perversely, was almost relieved and not really scared. A man, however insane, and with however much blood on his hands, coming after her with a knife wasn't her idea of a good time, but at least it was a situation that was somehow more real, and therefore easier to deal with, than what had been happening to the people she had met at Madame Adrienne's. She could run from a man with a knife.

She could run, and that simple positive ability felt like a massive freedom.

There she is, Sangster thought. She can run, but she can't hide. It would be a shame to end the life of someone so sweet and innocent, but, while he would take no pleasure from it, he knew that it was necessary.

Juliet emerged from an alley half a block along the street, in the same dress and overcoat. Sangster launched himself after her.

Juliet ran, her lungs burning hotter with every strained breath she managed to take. Her feet hit the pavement more heavily with each step. How much did they weigh now? A hundredweight? A ton? The thought didn't cheer her up any.

A narrow iron footbridge ahead straddled the railway line. She crossed it, turned, and slipped in a puddle. Pain exploded in her shoulder and a clatter of toppled milk churns made her grimace. She wanted to scream with frustration; not that it would have helped, but maybe it would have made her feel better.

The churns were at the entrance to another, narrower, road. She turned along it, her flight funneled by the damp redbrick walls of cramped tenements on either side.

The street was like an obstacle course, with the hulks of old wagons and carts, potholes, puddles and more milk churns as obstacles to be dodged or clambered over.

Belatedly, she looked at the ground, dreading to think what her fine shoes might have already stepped in.

Footsteps clattered behind her, but she didn't look back to see how close Sangster–the Ripper, she corrected herself–was. Ahead, a wall appeared as if by magic: another tenement block, studded with many square dark eyes, blocked her path. For a moment she was certain that it was a dead end. Then she skirted around a large pile of hay, and realized that she had reached a T-junction.

Juliet hesitated, looking left and right into streets that were slipways into rivers of darkness. All the buildings were dark and cold, their windows closed in sleep. She knew it was her imagination and a trick of perspective, but she couldn't help feeling that every street she turned down was a little narrower than the last.

She realized that she had already lost track of how many streets she had crossed and what direction she was running in. There seemed to be an endless progression of tenement buildings, closed pubs and empty factories no matter where she turned.

She wished she could shake the feeling that, sooner or later, one of the yellowed streets in this maze would close in on her, catching her between its walls, and hold her in a crushing grip until

Sangster could use that knife of his to lever her out at his leisure.

She couldn't do that, but it wasn't for want of trying. All she could do was keep running, and hope that he would get as lost as she already was.

Bill Sangster swore as he tripped over an orange box and went sprawling. When he got up, he shouted after her, "Wait! You're not like the others! It'll be quick for you!" but his voice was hoarse from the effort of running more than he done since he was a child.

Desperate not to let her get out of his sight, he forced himself onward.

Juliet could hear distant voices, and the clip clop of horses, but whichever street she ran into was always black and silent.

It was too easy for Juliet to feel that she was thoroughly enclosed, running round some sort of maze. The sky was such a matt layer of charcoal that it could easily have been a flat roof laid on top of the walls that funneled Juliet's run in one direction or another.

She forced her legs to carry on, now weighing what felt like at least five tons each.

Sangster saw the road up ahead, and saw Juliet go left. He thought he could cut her off by darting though a side alley behind a small coaching inn. He ducked through the alley, and emerged a scant few feet behind her; just in time to see her run towards the distinctive shape of Tower Bridge.

The peaks of the bridge were jagged and pointed, fangs piercing the low clouds, lancing them of the rain that swelled within. Juliet kept running, realizing too late that it was a mistake. There were no side alleys crossing her path on a bridge. It was a strictly one-way journey.

She looked back and saw that Sangster was gaining on her implacably. She was sure she couldn't go any further, but she had to anyway. Whatever happened she would not quit, not when she had yet to redeem herself for what had happened at the séance.

Sangster followed briskly. Juliet was slowing and would be his prize within minutes. A whistle blast screeched to one side, and he half thought it was the Peelers. It was a steam whistle though, a signal of some kind.

There were lights on the river, heading towards the bridge: a ship intending to pass underneath.

Ahead, the road jerked, and the cantilever halves of Tower Bridge began to rise open to let the ship through. And Juliet kept running; only now she was climbing.

Juliet felt a vibration under her feet, and then the whole surface of the road began to lift into the air, taking her with it. She hurried on, but the angle of the road was becoming steeper, and soon she was climbing hand and foot, using the decorated ironwork of the railing at the side of the road as a ladder.

She made it to the top, surprised at herself, but she was now what looked like hundreds of feet above the River Thames. Behind her, Sangster reached the top.

Why do you do it?" Juliet demanded. "Why do such horrible things to those women?"

"What a piece of work is man," he quoted, a hint of mocking in his voice. Juliet wasn't sure whether he was mocking her for asking, or the quote itself as part of his answer. "You know that line, Jules?" he went on. "It's Shakespeare. Good old Will, the Bard. He's not the first to describe man as a work of art, and he won't be the last. I'm an artist, Jules, and what better canvas to work on than the viewer him or herself?"

"You think you're making art?"

"I know I'm making art, Jules. It's a new form, never tried before.

"People could make so much of their lives if they only tried. You and I have both made something of ours; we've lived up to the expectations of the supreme artist–" he pointed to the sky "–who made us all.

"Those girls in the East End, they've squandered the gift they were given, right? They were made as pieces of art, but they didn't see it, and they let themselves deteriorate into filth. Now, what happens when a painting is no good, eh? The painter washes the board clean, and paints a new picture on it.

"I give those girls back the gift; I make them into art that will be remembered as long as the Mona

Lisa or Botticelli's Venus." He looked down at his shoes momentarily. "You are a piece of art as a living woman, Juliet. I will forever regret having to take it from the world."

He lunged for her, grabbing her throat with his left hand. She looked down and immediately regretted it. The Thames was a deep mire of polluted darkness at the best of times. Only thirty years ago, Juliet's father had said, when he was a boy, the effluence was so dense that it had cast a stench over the city so terrible that Parliament was all but abandoned because nobody could stand the smell. "The Great Stink", it had been called.

The moonlight gave the river the glistening look of a slug's coat of slime. Then the moon faded behind a cloud, and the river was darker still. Juliet fancied she could see movement down there, black against blackness. If all the shadows in London emerged from the alleys and from Bazalgette's new sewer system, if they slunk out from the factories and rat-ridden docks, if they all came to the river to bask in the full moon, this is how they would be.

Juliet's heart fluttered as she saw exactly that. There were insubstantial shadows creeping out from under Parliament, and from the opium dens of Lambeth. Like oil so light they floated on the air, the shadows ran and tumbled and flowed, down into the river below her. There, they sank, but were somehow still visible, flitting together the way a shoal of fish might be seen to do in clear waters.

She realized that the last breath she had taken could be her last ever breath. Sangster's fingers wouldn't let another whisper of air through her windpipe, one way or the other. She tried to snatch at his knife hand, but he twitched it and drew a line of fire against her palm, which seemed to burn up the inside of her arm to the elbow.

She screamed with pain and slapped and scratched at the arm holding her. His forearm was as solid as a lead drainpipe, though he wasn't a very muscular man. A distant part of her mind recognized it as being product of fencing practice.

"I'm sorry, Jules," he said softly. The words seemed hollow, coming from a man who held her by the throat with a knife to her cheek, but she could see in his eyes that he meant it from the heart. Despite herself, she felt the briefest twinge of sympathy amidst her terror and rage.

She slapped at his face, trying desperately to interfere with his use of the knife. He darted his head from side to side, leaning back at the neck to keep her at arms' length. "Don't struggle, my flower, you'll only make it hurt more." She barely heard him over her own scream of defiance, and she kept slapping and smacking and clawing.

His face lost its wistful calm for a second, and he jerked her roughly sideways with a bare-toothed snarl, cracking her head against the wrought iron handrail.

Juliet's scream died in her throat, and her heart beat one last time before the knifepoint tore it apart. A metallic whoosh wafted past her face, and she wondered if it was her soul leaving her body.

Her weight shifted backwards, suddenly free though the fingers hadn't loosened their grip on her throat. Sangster's face floated in front of her, eyes wide and wet, the mouth round, skin as white as his linen shirt.

The face floated up and away from her, its eyes focused disbelievingly on the stump of his left wrist that was squirting blood into the night. Then gravity took hold, and Juliet realized she was the one falling from the lip of the raised roadway. The severed hand kept her scream squeezed down in her throat as she plunged towards the Thames.

Sangster recoiled, his balance thrown off by suddenly losing the weight of Juliet, and he fell, sliding down the tilting roadway. His mind was flooded with the burgeoning pain from his wrist, but some deep-seated animal instinct made him fling out his arms to try to catch hold of the road and stop his descent. His left arm merely exploded into more pain. His head swam and he felt as if his stomach was trying to turn itself inside out.

He managed to roll onto his back as he slid, and pressed his head and shoulders back against the near-vertical road. His head rattled, blurring his vision, but he kept struggling, trying to slow his descent to a less terrifying rate by pressing the sides of his shoes into the road.

It didn't work, and his legs pin-wheeled, trying to get purchase on the slick macadam. His back burned from the friction, and his head felt as if it was being stripped bare with every yard that he dropped. Desperately, he tried digging his heels into the road. It was the worst mistake of his life.

His heels caught, but the sudden flexing of his legs pushed him forward. His back and shoulders came away from the slope and he tumbled literally head over heels, now falling headfirst. He began to scream as the road below rushed up to meet him face to face. He spread-eagled his arms and legs, hoping to at least adhere to the slope rather than free fall through the air. The slope might still, he prayed fervently; slow him enough that he would survive this night.

Below, the line between the raised road of the bridge and the regular road was ill-defined, just a blur of shadows, like smoke. Did the raising of the bridge create smoke there? Sangster wondered. He didn't honestly know.

Hitting the ground and bouncing like a discarded doll to one side was beyond painful, and into the sheer blinding destruction of every nerve in his body. Sangster had no idea how quick the impact was, or how long he lay there, insensate, his total being a thoughtless blaze of pain instead of a thinking, feeling entity.

Eventually, after what felt like several eternities, but he suspected was really only a minute or two, the sea of pain sank just enough to allow the island that was Sangster's consciousness to taste the air once more.

He couldn't move his legs, but he could wiggle his toes, so maybe his back wasn't broken. He could taste blood, and spat some up when he coughed. Everything hurt, literally everything. He laughed anyway. It was a rasping sound, the sound of a broken machine scraping along on its way to the scrap yard, but it was loud and heartfelt.

Bill Sangster was still alive, and he was as grateful as he was surprised. He lay still for a moment, savoring his survival. That was twice he had had a miraculous escape, and he must truly have a guardian angel watching over him. His grandmother, probably—he had always been her favorite.

He started to roll over, to see whether he could push himself to his feet. He was immediately jerked to a halt. Baffled, he looked to where his remaining whole arm was, and his blood froze in its veins.

His arm had been flung into the gap between the road and the raised section of bridge and become jammed, held fast by something he couldn't see. He looked close, peering in through the gap. Something glistened in there, and moved. It slithered around, and he decided it must be oil. As if prompted by his thought, the darkness trickled away, pouring down between the rusting iron teeth of the bridge-raising mechanism. He could make out narrow parts of what were obviously large gears and cogwheels.

That was when the steam whistle and bells that signaled to the bridge operators to open or close the bridge, sounded again. This time it sounded to Sangster like a hunting horn, making a triumphant fanfare.

The cogs and gears began to turn, and Sangster began to scream "No!"

By the time the mechanism had consumed his whole arm, he was screaming for God. By the time it had begun to bite into the side of his hip and stomach, he was screaming for his mother and grandmother. By the time the great iron teeth crunched into his ribs, bursting his lung and liver like soap bubbles, he was screaming like a slaughtered pig. When that stopped, there was only a wet patch on the road, spreading like a leak of oil, to show that anything or anyone had ever been there.

On the narrow ledge under the bridge, where a dozen derelict men slept for shelter from the winter weather, it not only rained for the first time, but rained red.

TWENTY

Will was gone, and she didn't know what to do. It sounded strange, to not know what to do just because one element of your life was missing. Objectively speaking, everything else should pretty much work the same, but somehow it just didn't.

While the cops were questioning her in the Circuit City parking lot, they had given her a bottle of spring water to drink. She had stared at it, her mind numb as to what to do with it. She wanted Will to be there to open it and take the first swig, just so she could share it with him.

Every time she closed her eyes, she hoped and prayed that she might open them to see his face. Every time she opened her eyes, he hadn't been there, and something just looked wrong with the world. She couldn't even put her finger on that—it was more than just Will's absence from her line of sight, since they had separate homes and different jobs—so she had often gone a day or two without seeing him at all. Nevertheless the world looked and felt a little odd, a little skewed, as if it wasn't really her world but instead some very similar parallel world.

She didn't belong, she realized. She remembered the conversation she had with Will about the universe deciding that the survivors of the Metroline bombing no longer belonged in the world. At the time, she hadn't actually felt that way; it was purely an intellectual concept. Now it felt real. She belonged in a world where she and Will were a couple and lived out their lives as they saw fit.

This wasn't that world.

Patti took in shaky breaths with great racking sobs. This wasn't how it was supposed to be. She was supposed to love and be loved—even though it might take work—forever. Or at least until the fires of passion burned themselves out, or some garbage like that.

The cops had looked after her pretty well, all things considered. This was the third time in a week that she had turned up next to a bent, folded, spindled or otherwise mutilated corpse. She supposed Jim Castle had been pulling a few strings. He had seemed nice enough and sincere in his desire to help stop what was happening to them, but she resented that he was so damned staid and closed-minded as to believe that everything came down to a human agency. Terrorists, right? Well they were taken care of and Will was still dead, cut to pieces by fucking CDs and DVDs.

How was a rational person supposed to explain that one? It was impossible, but Patti knew from long experience, both in her own life and from articles in the *Borderlands Patrol*, that they would do it anyway, after a fashion. They would decide on something that sounded "reasonable" and then twist or ignore the facts to make them fit. They couldn't quite call it swamp gas, but she had already overheard one of the LAPD crime scene techs saying something about an unusual electromagnetic surge.

It was all bullshit and she knew it. She suspected they knew it too. That was probably why they had brought her to the hospital in Northridge. Observation, they called it, but she knew they meant suicide watch. It was an understandable precaution to take; someone whose other half—better half—was now gone might think that giving up the remaining half was less painful or less hassle than trying to go on.

If she had woken up one day with one arm, leg, eye and ear missing, it would probably be less disruptive than this was.

She didn't feel like killing herself though. She wasn't sure why; maybe it was that it would be surrendering to the force of nature that had taken Will from her, or maybe she was just too tired and too hurt to bother taking any sort of action at all. She had tried to be proactive about the situation she was in, tried to do something about it, and look where it had gotten her: the best thing in her life gone–in fact, her life gone, as he was her life–and sedated in a hospital bed about two blocks from where Will died in agony and terror.

Perhaps she should just stay in bed, and not set foot outside, for the rest of her life. Life, she thought; and just what sort of *life* would that be exactly? She wouldn't even grace her current situation with the word. It would be continued existence, sure, but no more than that.

A dark and silky voice from somewhere inside her head whispered to her then, making the point that maybe that was actually appropriate, she thought. Maybe Will and Susan and the others would have survived the bomb even if they had boarded the train, or been resuscitated by the paramedics that arrived on scene so quickly, as had at least one other person, according to the news. If by interfering she had condemned them all to death, life imprisonment was something she deserved. No remission, no parole, just solitary confinement for the crimes she had committed against her life.

Though despondent, she realized that she had actually become more awake over the past hour or so. Perhaps they hadn't sedated her after all, or maybe the dose had worn off. She couldn't honestly remember.

Her legs swung off the bed without any conscious command from her brain, and planted the soles of her bare feet flat on the linoleum floor.

Her clothes were hung over a chair next to the bed, so she pulled off the paper hospital gown, then dressed and pulled her boots on.

In something of a daze, she walked out into the beige corridors of the hospital. No one seemed to mind, so she kept walking, following the signs and the colored stripes on the wall until she found the ER entrance. Nobody challenged her, maybe because she was back in her regular clothes, and thus didn't look like a wandering patient the way she would have if she'd just walked around in the paper gown.

She went outside. A harsh wind was blowing, scattering discarded newsprint and a couple of paper cups across the ambulance delivery bays. There was a taxi stand a hundred yards away, so she started towards it, hunching her shoulders against the cutting rain and powerful gusts of wind.

The storm surrounded her, the wind carrying sibilant whispers all around. Waxen leaves and stained newsprint fluttered into the air like bats, chasing after what might have been bugs or cigarette butts. The detritus was swept into the gray skies above Patti, and she could feel the wind's chill claws tugging at her sleeves and pants legs.

For just a second, she thought she might actually be lifted off the ground whole, and carried off to Oz. That might not be so bad, though the thought did make her wonder if perhaps she had been sedated, and this was all a morphine-induced dream.

Suddenly, the clouds weren't just clouds. Every little billow and bulge was a screaming face, a desiccated corpse face vacuum-sealed in plastic, and every face's eyes were pleading to her for their first taste of air in a thousand years.

Then the wind rose, and the faces were torn apart and blasted to nothing but gray clouds. The moon glinted through a gap in the clouds, a single beady eye watching her unblinkingly from an utterly black socket. Pale moonlight picked out a vast celestial jaw and teeth and cheek and temple, all half hidden by a heavy cowl of black ashes wrapped around the implacable grin. It was a dream, she decided. She was strapped to some fucking hospital bed, doped up to the eyeballs and completely zoned out. She was fucked.

"You looking for a cab, lady?"

The voice surprised her. It was a rough-looking middle-aged guy, leaning out of a cab's window. She was standing at the taxi rank outside the hospital. The shiver she felt had nothing to do with the wind or the rain; she wasn't dreaming. For all that she had just seen in the storm, she was awake and lucid.

This made her feel more ruined than ever.

"You know the Circuit City near here?"

"Two blocks over," he said.

"Take me there."

He looked at his watch, theatrically and unnecessarily. "Store's closed, even if it wasn't full of cops."

"I know. I just left my car there." She got in, and the cabbie started off.

"You something to do with why there are cops there?"

"Yeah."

"Wanna talk about it?"

"No."

"OK." He fell silent, and in a couple of minutes the cab driver was pulling into the parking lot. Patti paid the cabbie, and returned to her Saturn, ignoring the crime scene vehicles that were parked at the building's side door.

She drove home then, and went to bed.

The dawn light was gray-blue, and there was a warm amber tint to the walls and sidewalks. To Patricia Fuller, it was as if the last of an evening's whisky was ending its effects with a coloring of the morning.

She might be less drunk, but she knew, with a desire to wail against the injustice of it all, that Will was still as dead as he had been last night.

They were so close to having escaped. So close to figuring out a way to die painlessly and be resuscitated. Patti knew she couldn't really imagine how it must have felt to be cut to pieces the way Will had, but she also couldn't imagine it being anything remotely near painless.

If a paper cut stung, death by a thousand of them must have been simply unbearable. In the end, he had probably welcomed the release. The only release Patti would welcome would be the release of letting out her grief. She didn't want to just cry, she wanted to sob and shake and scream at the sky.

She wanted her love to find its voice in grief as it had in their life together. She wanted to be as passionate about missing Will as she was about being with him. He, or his memory, deserved nothing less. Her love could give nothing less.

The other deaths that had surrounded her recently had been strangers or, at best, acquaintances. Will was someone who had been part of her life—part of her—since junior high. His being gone meant part of her was gone; part of her life had been cut out.

Her eyes fell upon the Egyptology book and *The London Times*, still lying where they had fallen. They seemed to wink at her invitingly. There was a saying that every action had an equal and opposite reaction. Perhaps the opposite reaction to Will's death was her meeting—at some remove, and in a virtual way—her great-great-grandmother.

And perhaps Juliet still held the secret, if Patti could prize it out of her, of how to survive this. Not that Patti necessarily wanted to survive this today, but she was damned sure that, live or die, it would be on her own terms, not on those of Will's killer.

Patti ignored everyone at the *Borderlands Patrol* when she marched into the office. She vaguely recognized that people were saying hello, and mouthing vague words of sympathy about what had happened to Will. She let her subconscious nod her head on autopilot while she thought of the best search strategy for the archives.

Matt Lawson intercepted her before she could get into the archives. "Patti, are you okay?"

"I'm fine," she said tightly.

"Uh, yeah, look... I know you're strong, and you can handle what happened, but you don't need to come into work today. I mean, jeez, I'm not an ogre. I got feelings and I know you must need some time to yourself—"

"I'm fine," Patti repeated. She tried to imagine herself as some sort of fictional robot warrior. She felt dead enough inside to pass for a machine. "Don't worry about me."

"I worry about all my staff. I'm just saying you should take a few days off. On full pay, of course. I appreciate you coming in like this, but, really, work isn't the place for you right now."

"Yeah, yeah, well that's okay, Matt. I didn't come here to work." She unlocked the door to the archives and went on in. Matt followed, his brows knitting.

"You didn't? Then what are you doing here?"

"Genealogy."

"Genealogy? What do you mean?"

"It's the study of one's roots, Matt. Family history."

"I know what the word means, Patti. I'm a fucking publisher, after all. I just don't know what you mean by coming in to the office for it."

"I want everything you've got on the mystery of Jack the Ripper."

"You're sick," Matt exclaimed. "But anything for an easy life." He rooted around in a filing cabinet and came up with a CD-ROM. "This has everything the *Borderlands Patrol* has ever printed on the subject, as well as some public-domain documents and theories from other older sources. Whatever you want, it should be in there."

"Thanks, Matt."

The empty Sherman Halls hotel was twelve stories high, its pale pink frontage facing a park. A used car lot was on one side of it, a small shopping mart on the other. No guest had stayed in the hotel for over month, as the place had been bought over by a mid-price chain. They had closed it down temporarily for refurbishment and, more importantly, re-branding.

Work had stopped over the weekend and the construction workers, electricians, carpenters and all those involved in the remodeling had gone home to enjoy President's Day with their families.

Only shadows frequented the hotel on this national holiday. Air currents were disturbed by rodents or roaches, or whatever else men feared in the dark when the floorboards creaked and scratching sounds came from behind the walls.

As the day passed and the weather changed, light shifted across the floors and trod weightlessly on the new carpets. Fingers of darkness probed the light switches and the electrical sockets, seeking vibrant life.

Eventually life was found. Whether a rat or a mouse, or something else entirely, there were teeth behind the plasterboard walls of the hotel. Teeth that could scrape away rubber and plastic insulation. Teeth that could cut through wires. Teeth that could short out a circuit.

There was no one around to see the sparks crackle. No one saw them catch hold of the wallpaper through a wormhole in the fiberboard paneling. Nor did anyone see the miraculous virgin birth of the flames that suckled hungrily at the dry paper and fibers from which they had been delivered.

TWENTY-ONE

Juliet Collins fell.

She screamed, though even she didn't know whether she was screaming more at the fall or at the sight and feel of the severed hand that was still clamped to her wrist. Bill Sangster's artful hand. Jack the Ripper's bloody hand, following its latest prey all the way to a watery hell and never letting go.

She thrashed her limbs, trying to find a position that might grant her a softer landing from which she could swim, or at least to shake off the hand that clung to her like a terrier's jaws.

Then there was sheer agony, worse than the blast that had knocked her down in the explosion at Adrienne's. Hitting the river was almost as hard an impact as hitting solid ground, smashing her flat with the impact. The only difference was that after the bone-crushing smack, her landing spot then opened up beneath her and swallowed her whole. Her back and head exploded into blackness that swamped every sensation in her body, and every thought in her head.

There was a moment of nothing, then the pain kicked her awake.

Juliet tried to scream, but instead of sound forcing its way out of her throat, the darkness of the river flooded in. It wasn't just cold water, but dark water, filled with the smoky particulates of as many poisons as Juliet could imagine, and still more that she could not.

It forced its way into her stomach and into her lungs, which began to burn as if the water was lamp oil and had been lit. She tried to move her arms and legs in an effort to swim, but the limbs only jerked, held too fast by the grip of the thick water. There was movement all around her, and she imagined that huge fish were coming to swallow her, like in the story of Jonah and the whale that she had studied in Sunday school. Nothing bit or touched her, that she could feel, but instead the shadows enveloped and danced with her.

They had faces, bloated by being too dead, too long. Their skin flaked away to nothing at the slightest touch of a current, leaving only laughing skulls to enjoy her death. Their fingers clawed at her, forcing her to scream and scream again, losing the last of the precious air in her lungs. The silver bubbles of air danced gaily upwards in the moonlight and Juliet felt a moment's calm. The silver lights leaving her were so beautiful that they could only be pieces of her soul, freed from her doomed body and ascending to heaven.

She smiled, even though the terrors that grabbed leeringly for her became more real with the absence of oxygen. She was on her way to heaven and that was nothing to fear.

Constable Wagg had been sitting with a couple of boatmen around a burning brazier, sipping from a tin mug of hot sweet tea when he heard the splash. It had come from the direction of Tower Bridge. The two boatmen, brothers in matching sweaters and overcoats, looked at each other.

"Jumper?" one asked. They all looked at the bridge, its two halves raised as if to toast each other. The ship that had required the bridge to be opened was already fading from sight.

Wagg looked out into the darkness, trying to see if there was any froth of displaced water, white against the blackness of the river. "Sounded like it," he groaned. He had just dispatched a floating corpse to the morgue on a cart not an hour ago, and wasn't looking forward to seeing another one so soon. If it were up to Wagg, he'd stay put, warming himself by the fire and enjoying the tea.

It wasn't up to him though, and one of the brothers was already skipping with surprising lightness down the wooden steps to the water. "Come on," he said. "If we're quick, he might still be swimming." He stoked up the steam engine that squatted in the belly of the boat, and its thin iron smokestack belched a few glowing sparks among the streamer of blackness.

"Bugger it," Wagg grumbled, tossing the remains of his tea down into the water. He followed the other brother down the effluent-crusted stairs, and climbed as gingerly as ever into the boat. While the brothers cast off and got the boat moving, Wagg lit his bull's-eye lamp, and aimed the beam at the area where he thought the splash had came from.

The boat's prow pushed through the water, making a white "V" that was just visible in the lamplight. "Do you see anything?" one of the brothers asked.

"Not a thing," Wagg replied. He scanned the water with his lamp. Was this the area where the splash had been or not? The bridge was large and the river wide, and any ripples from the entry of a body would have dissipated quickly. "Go left."

The nose of the boat turned, and one of the brothers joined Wagg with another lamp. It wasn't a bull's-eye lamp, and so couldn't project a directed beam of light, but he held it out as far over the prow as he could without falling overboard.

As the minutes passed, Wagg became more and more certain that whoever had fallen from the bridge must have been swept away by the current. He felt relieved as well; let some other copper further downriver have all the fun of pulling the floater out. Then, almost impossibly, he saw something. A smudge of white–it could just as easily have been a discarded shirt or a soaked and mushy piece of paper–but Wagg didn't think so. "There!" the boatman beside him said, confirming his thoughts. "Hold that light on 'im."

Wagg did as he was told, while the boatman fetched a billhook. His brother slowed the boat under his direction, and the boatman stretched out with the long wooden pole to hook the body's clothes. He caught in on the second attempt, and pulled the corpse towards the boat. Wagg put his lamp down carefully, and leaned out to take the body in his arms. With some effort, he hauled it out of the water. The body was a little warmer than most but, Wagg reflected, it had only spent a few minutes in the water. By the time he had got it halfway out of the water, the boatman had put down the billhook and grabbed an arm and a leg to help.

They laid the body on deck, and the boatman nodded to his brother, who started the engine chugging again, and guided the boat back towards the little landing from which it had come.

With the body on board, Wagg relaxed a little. The worst part was over, and at least this one was fresh, and wouldn't stink the way floaters usually did after they'd been in the river for a couple of days. He set both the lamps next to the body, the better to see whom it was. To his surprise, it was a woman–no, a girl–barely out of her teens, if that. Her face was bruised, the purple swelling of one eye stark against skin that had already been fashionably pale even before the gray pallor of the drowned had taken hold.

"Poor mare," Wagg said quietly. She was very pretty, no older than his own eldest daughter, and wore what had obviously been fine clothes. He couldn't think why such a young lady would throw herself into the river and end it all. It was a bloody waste, he thought.

"Jesus, Mary and Joseph," the boatman whispered. Wagg agreed with the sentiment, and then realized that the boatman's gaze was fixed on her right arm. When he saw why, Wagg felt his heart miss a beat. A man's left hand was clamped around the girl's wrist, the stump of it still oozing blood.

Suddenly offended by the sight, and by the action of whoever had been holding her so tightly, Wagg tried to pull the hand off. For once, he didn't feel squeamish at the touch of the dead flesh—he was too angry for that.

The hand held like a macabre clamp, as immovable as a rock. However, Wagg found something new to concentrate on. As he held the girl's arm in one hand, he felt a faint tremor. It was barely noticeable, but it was a pulse, and fading fast. "Bloody hell!" he exclaimed. "She's alive."

The boatman immediately bent to roll her over, and started flexing her arms as if pumping water. A trickle oozed from her lips. Wagg shook his head. "Not good enough, mate. Give over." He rolled the girl onto her back, and took off his helmet as he knelt beside her. "When I come up for air, you press on her chest, all right?" The boatman nodded, putting both hands on the girl's sternum. Wagg could tell it wasn't the first time he'd dealt with a near-drowning.

He bent his head to hers, pinched her nose shut, and began to try to breathe air into her lungs. The boatman did his part too. In a few seconds the body convulsed, and the girl suddenly twisted in their hands. Both men scuttled back just in time as the girl's whole body undulated, and then spewed forth black water from her nose and mouth. She dragged in a deep breath, the air shrieking into her lungs.

Wagg grinned despite himself. "Welcome back, lass," he said, almost in tears with the thought of how far gone she had been. "Welcome back."

There was a pale light, a rather flesh-toned patch materializing out of the darkness. Juliet didn't understand it at first, and wondered whether it was Saint Peter himself, or just an angel come to greet her and welcome her to heaven.

It was a face, of that she was certain. As it resolved itself, she saw that it was looking at her, the lines around the mouth and eyes tight with worry. As the face came into focus, it relaxed into a look of relief. She recognized it now: it was her father. Juliet felt a pang of sorrow and a wave of confusion. She had thought some relative who had died—grandmamma, perhaps—would welcome her into the hereafter, but father wasn't dead, was he? Had he too passed on?

There was a tight squeeze of her hand, and she let out a hint of a yelp. Bill's hand, she thought, it would never let her go! The squeeze came again, and she could see it was her father's hand, and it was as solid as her own. She snapped fully awake, sitting bolt upright. She was alive, wearing her nightdress, and in her own bedroom! Her dolls were looking down from their shelves, their eyes bright with reflected candlelight, silently welcoming her back to the land of the living.

"Papa!" she cried and hugged him.

"It's all right, Juliet," he whispered. "It's all right."

She slept a dreamless sleep after that. The next morning was crisp, with frost on the edges of the windows, and a clear sky. She hadn't thought she would be able to face food so soon, but the cook had prepared some devilled eggs and toast, and Juliet wolfed them down as soon as they were put in front of her.

In the afternoon, two visitors called to the house. Inspector Abberline, and a uniformed police constable. Terence Collins bade them to sit, and had the maid bring tea and scones to the drawing room. Though Abbeline sat, the constable remained standing, settling for doffing his helmet. Juliet started to excuse herself so that her father and the policemen could speak in private, but Inspector Abberline shook his head. "Actually, Miss Collins, it's yourself we called to see."

"Me?"

Abberline nodded, and put what looked like a box, wrapped in plain paper, on a small table.

"Don't worry, you're not in any trouble. We came for two reasons. Firstly, I thought you might like to meet PC Wagg." He nodded towards the constable. "It was he, and a couple of boatmen who assist the police's river patrol, who pulled you out of the River Thames two nights ago."

Juliet looked at the constable, and smiled. "Thank you... I really don't know what else to say." She blushed, wondering how indecent she had been with her clothes all wet, and how much of her exposed flesh he touched to save her. She decided it was best not to think about such things.

"That's all right, miss," he said quietly. "All part of the service."

"Er, yes..."

"The other matter," Abberline continued, "is a little more delicate. It's about this." He lifted the paper off what Juliet had thought was a box. It was a small glass jar, and inside, floating in formaldehyde was a man's hand, neatly sliced off at the wrist. Its fingers were curled into a claw, as if still grasping something of about the same thickness as a girl's wrist. Juliet took a deep, shaking, breath. "You recognize it, I see."

Juliet nodded. "I do."

"Can you tell me who it belongs to?"

Juliet looked at him sadly, unsure whether to miss Bill's smile, or be relieved to be free of it. She hoped she would know one way or the other some day. "Jack the Ripper," she said simply.

Abberline nodded thoughtfully. "We found a– We found the remains of a man. There was no identification. I wondered if you could tell us who he was."

It would be so easy to say the words, Juliet knew, but then she looked at her father, and thought of Bill's parents, back in Manchester. She wondered if he had had brothers or sisters as well. If so, how would any of them react to the news that he had been the most depraved and evil killer that England had ever seen? What good would it do to put them through that, when he was already beyond the reach of the courts?

"Does it matter?" she asked. "He won't be killing any more women. Not ever. If I gave you a name and the newspapers learned of it, they would turn on his family since they can't get at him. That would be adding more misery and more victims to the Ripper's tally. I hope you can understand why I can't do that, inspector."

Abberline shrugged. "So long as he's gone, that's good enough for me."

TWENTY-TWO

The PC monitor flashed, and then went to the blue screen of death. She ejected the CD-ROM, and pulled the plug on the piece of junk. She knew she should be ecstatic at the revelation that there was a solution to the sword of Damocles that hung over her, but as far as Patti was concerned, it was too late.

She and Will had been more than just him plus her. Without him, there was no Patti, not as she knew herself. Juliet Collins had been lucky in a way; her salvation had been as much from human evil as from the forces of nature's progress.

She had read enough *Borderlands Patrol* letters and articles, and watched enough A&E documentaries, to know that there had never been a stated clear solution to the Ripper murders of Victorian London. The tale on the disc could just as easily be a fanfic, with Juliet Collins's appearance added purely because her surviving the gas blast at Mornington Crescent had attracted the writer's eye. If so, she couldn't take its solution to her problem at face value.

She wasn't even sure whether she wanted a solution now. She sat on the sofa and tried to focus through the tears. She held a picture of herself and Will at San Diego Zoo a couple of years ago, and still expected to hear the phone ring and his voice to reassure her that he was really okay.

The phone remained silent, and she sat on the sofa, staring at a frozen moment of life, and telling herself that he would always exist so long as these paused moments did. It wasn't reassuring. Even the weather hadn't improved. The temperature was barely seventy, and there were still squalls perpetrating drive-bys of rain across the city.

No wonder Jess Golden had fled. If Patti could think of a place to go that would shelter her from the sorrow and the pain, she'd be on the first plane out. It wasn't as if there was anything in LA for her any more, besides bad memories and terrible nightmares, assuming that she even lived to sleep another night.

She closed her eyes for a moment and, when she opened them again, she saw that there was a faint glowing light from somewhere. It was the TV; she had forgotten it was still on, the sound muted. A local weather forecast was being screened; its digital map of the area surprised Patti. Despite the gray light coming in through the windows with great reluctance, the map forecast sunshine and a seventy-four degrees temperature. The only cloud on the map was the one placed over Sherman Oaks.

One cloud. One single cloud.

One remaining victim.

It was an insane thought, but that cloud was over her. Maybe it had come for her, maybe it had come from her– she was depressed enough–or maybe it was just all a coincidence. It seemed like her whole life, at least in this borrowed section of time she had been living on, was driven by coincidence. Maybe this one was the coincidence that proved there was *no* coincidence, the exception that proved the rule.

More likely it just proved that it was her turn next.

Fine, she decided. Who was she to rail against nature? She had signed ecological petitions by the bushel, yet here her very existence was, perhaps, environmentally harmful. If Patti was to be true to who she was then she would have to die and be done with it. As a woman, a living human woman, she had a duty to survive. That was the purpose of all life, wasn't it?

The CD-ROM, if its unsubstantiated tale about Jack the Ripper was true, gave a solution to the paradox: die and be revived.

It happened all the time on the highways and the freeways, in water and in hospitals, but it had always seemed so random when mentioned on a news report. Choosing the right way to die, with a fair chance of being revived, was her top priority. Drowning was a good choice, if there were people around to see it and take action in time. Unfortunately, people would almost certainly pull her from any public water– a pool, marina, whatever– before she had died. They would just be handing her back to that fact of nature that caught up with every last person on the planet. Besides, she thought, perhaps the killer she was trying to avoid would be wise to that. Fool me once, the old saying went; shame on you but fool me twice and shame on me.

Don't think, she told herself, just do. She jumped up and looked towards the kitchen. Lots of opportunity for death there, but what would be best? Whatever it was, it ought to be painless and not do any physical damage that would interfere with being resuscitated. That brought up her next concern: being rescued in, and not before, the proverbial nick of time. It wasn't as if crash-carts could be booked in advance. People didn't phone for an appointment–

People dialed 911 and asked for an ambulance and paramedics. Patti thought about this; was there any reason why she couldn't dial 911, specify a place, and then get it over with in the right window of time? Traffic might be a problem, but she could factor that in. Perhaps only do the deed when she heard the sirens come into earshot. That would mean a quick death, though; she didn't want a prevention.

Quick, she decided. Quick was probably better anyway, and less likely to be painful. That was fine by her.

Her mind made up, Patti ran into the kitchen and dropped to her knees, sliding across to the low closet under the washbasin. There were chemicals–bleach, disinfectants and God knew what else. Surely they were fatal. They all had hazard warnings printed on them.

She hefted a bottle of Drano, and hesitated. If she had to die to get out of this shit, then fine, she'd die. But a slow and agonizing death wasn't the way she had in mind to go. Ideally, she would have preferred to die in her sleep; to be blissfully unaware of her shuffling of this mortal coil. What was it Poe had written? "Sleep, those little slices of death. How I loathe them." Patti sighed and shoved the Drano back in the closet, and stood up. Through the kitchen window she could see a part of the low roof of the local pound.

The pound, she thought. Didn't they kill strays there after they'd been caged for a set time limit? She was sure they did, she had signed petitions against putting animals to sleep there, not that it had done any good.

She wondered what sort of chemicals they used. Was there a specific drug or poison, or did they use whatever was to hand? Was it something a human could be revived from, if the paramedics were notified in time? There certainly wouldn't be a problem calling for an ambulance, since that could be done in advance. There was one obvious problem. The veterinary staff wouldn't be exactly co-operative about giving a person the needle and Patti didn't know enough to do it herself. She would just have to persuade them.

Outside the house, the sky was impassive and inscrutable. It pressed down upon her with a weight that she felt between her ears, and it was the color of a blunt but strong knife. "I get the message," she whispered under her breath.

She turned, jogging round the corner, past a couple of well-kept lawns, to the highway. Before she even reached it, she half expected some drunk driver to come up behind her, mount the sidewalk, and bang, dead. Nothing like that happened. Instead, she slowed to a walk at the edge of the highway. She turned onto the sidewalk that edged the road like a rind, and started walking towards the minimart that was along there. As she went, she studied the traffic.

The highway was sheer madness. It wasn't rush hour, so vehicles could travel at speed. Hatchbacks and curved-topped sedans and sports cars ran down all four lanes like super-powered insects racing to get to the next piece of decaying flesh. Between them, motorcycles darted, and buses and huge trucks lumbered as if they were just looking to crush such insects underfoot.

Trying to cross on foot was almost certain death, but Patti was willing to take "almost" over "certain" any day of the week. She fought down the thought that she might be making it easier for Death to claim her. That would be too easy, she told herself. Death wants something more showy, something more of a warning to others. If she was wrong, well, what had she lost? A few minutes, perhaps. Most likely less than a day of fear that she probably would have spent in the bathroom. If she misjudged here, at least her fate would be quick enough that she probably wouldn't even notice it. "You can't fight a storm," she had told Will. Well, she could damn well piss into the wind and hope to have moved fast enough to get out of the way when it blew back.

She watched the traffic for several minutes, trying not to think about the chances of something large and fast mounting the sidewalk and squishing her like a juicy bug. She told herself that she would judge the right moment, but that it might take a few more seconds. And a few more. And a few... She cursed herself, suddenly seeing that some part of her would never let her say, "Okay, this is it."

"Fuck it!" she snapped to herself. Her foot started moving before she knew she had decided to go for it.

Dodging in and out of traffic was hard enough in a car going at the same kind speeds as the rest. On foot, it was a physical impossibility. She hadn't even reached the middle of the first lane when there was a blaring horn from her left. She snapped her head round without stopping, and saw a low-slung sports car van braking hard, but not in time.

Rather than be hit, Patti jumped, putting one foot on the car's fender, and the next on its hood. She leapt from it into the next lane, just behind a FedEx truck that barely made it past in time. A suburban screeched to a halt about an inch from her, but she ignored it and kept going.

She was almost at the other side when one leg was jerked up short and she fell. As she tumbled on the road, she saw a curl of something black and serpentine whiplash away from her left foot. It was a bootlace that had tripped her. She started to get back up, but had only reached one knee when she felt the bow-wave of displaced air that heralded a semi and trailer failing to stop. Patti was sure she was dead. She had failed, and Death had caught up with her. All she could do was fall back and let it happen.

There was a strong smell of burning rubber from either side of her, and she turned her head to see smoke bursting forth from huge tires as they skidded to a screeching halt. The blackened and oily underside of the truck was about two inches above her face, and, by some miracle, the tires had passed on either side of her.

Her breathing strained by sheer disbelief at being able to do it at all, Patti rolled out from under the side of the truck and got to her feet on the sidewalk. The truck driver was looking at her, slack-jawed, so she gave him a grin to show that she was okay. That seemed to shock him more, so she got on with checking her bearings. The pound was on the opposite corner of this block, but there was a grid of little alleys that would allow her to just go diagonally there rather than circumnavigate the block.

She started running.

In the Sherman Halls Hotel, there were dozens of new residents thronging the corridors by the moment. Dancing flames, they swelled into existence and filed up the stairs. On every floor, they fanned out along the manmade fiber carpeting and slunk under the doors of rooms.

There were no beds left in any of the rooms, but there was plenty of air to feed the fire. There was paint and wallpaper and dusty plasterboard, all welcoming the heat. Flames that tapered like KKK hoods ascended from floor to floor on a platform of liquid heat until they reached the topmost door in the building. It was steel and wouldn't burn, so the fire lodged into the ceiling, the underside of the roof, and began to spread outwards like an army of burning spiders.

Outside, on the roof proper, there was the usual setup of ventilation boxes, phone cables, TV antennae and so on. As the fire below grew hotter, so heat rose up through the gravel in waves. Electrical insulation in the air conditioning units began to melt. Fumes rose invisibly from the lining under the gravel.

In one corner, the aluminum of a large TV antenna began to soften at the base. After a very short while, the heat had become so intense that the antenna first groaned, then buckled. Finally, the stressed metal at the base of it gave up the ghost altogether, and, with a loud snap, the antenna toppled.

Various metal branches of it snapped off as it hit the gravel on the roof, and scattered around it like needles from a long-dead pine tree. The main antenna pole settled, hanging half off the edge of the roof. As it went, it pushed against an old phone cable, which stretched, and caught on the corner of an air conditioning unit.

Patti could hear the pound long before she saw it. The barking didn't bother her so much, but some of the temporary inmates howled and whined as if every torture known to vivisection was being tried out on them, even though they were just sitting in a kennel awaiting an owner.

Most of the howlers and whiners didn't have owners, of course. Who wanted to bring an animal home to the kids when it looked like it was ready to beat itself to death against the cement walls of its kennel? Their fears led them to go mad, and then their madness led them to be put to death. They called it putting them to sleep, but by now Patti was well aware of the difference.

There were a couple of cars parked in the pound's lot, which meant visitors as well as staff. That might make things harder for her, but she wanted to get out of the public areas and into the back rooms anyway.

She walked into the pound's main building that was festooned with pictures of cute kittens, puppies, the occasional iguana, and Scooby-Doo, all crayoned by kids. Thankfully there didn't seem to be any children in here today. She wouldn't want to upset them or give them nightmares for life. There were plenty of people in the world who were willing to do that, without her joining in as well.

There were no people in the reception area, which was a good start to her plan. Most likely they were touring the kennel blocks, picking a pet that didn't whine or howl. So far, so good. Ignoring the leaflets and posters about pet care and animal treatment on the walls, she walked up to the heavyset woman behind the desk, who must have weighed as much as a silverback gorilla. "Can I see one of the veterinary staff, please?"

"What for?" the woman demanded.

"I hit a dog on the highway about half a block south of here. I don't know where the nearest veterinary surgery is, but when I saw this place, I figured you could help. I think it's a stray anyway."

The huge woman looked doubtful, but lifted a phone from the counter. "Doctor Reese, could you come out front? There's a lady here says she hit a stray... No, I don't know how badly hurt."

"I think its leg's broken," Patti offered helpfully.

"Leg broke," the woman relayed. "Okay." She put the phone down. "Doctor Reese will be right out."

So tense she could barely stand still without wanting to scream and rage, Patti looked closely at some of the leaflets on the stand, without seeing a single one of them. She didn't want the fat woman seeing her facial expression and figuring out what sort of state she was in. After a couple of excruciating minutes, an interior door opened, and a middle aged man came out, wearing a white lab coat over slacks and a sweater.

"Doctor Reese, I presume," Patti said with a weak attempt at a vaguely sickened expression. "It's about this dog. I was–"

"Where exactly is this dog?" Reese hadn't intended to be cold–hostile even–just down to business at hand.

"On the back seat of my car," Patti said, leading him out into the parking lot. "I wrapped him in a blanket. There was nothing I could do, he just ran out the very instant the lights turned green..."

Reese nodded understandingly. "Sometimes it's unavoidable, but you did the right thing by bringing him here–" Reese didn't get any further, as Patti grabbed his arm and twisted it, in the sort of barhold that cops weren't allowed to use any more.

"Listen to me carefully, okay? I don't want to hurt you, but I need you to take me into a room with some special contents."

"You want drugs?" He sounded more disgusted than afraid.

"Not exactly. What do you use to put animals to sleep?"

"Ah, you're an animal rights fanatic?"

"No! Now just answer the fucking question or I'll twist a little harder and you'll never scratch Spot behind the ears again, okay?"

"There isn't a specific drug. We give terminal patients an overdose of anesthetic. The muscles relax, they drift off, and eventually the autonomic systems relax to the point where they no longer function either..."

"Sounds what the good doctor ordered. How much would you need for something my size?"

"What?"

"How much would you need to snuff an animal of my size and weight?"

"I... I should think about fifty CCs."

"Cool. Let's go get some." She shoved Reese, keeping up the pressure on the lock. The fat woman started to rise as they re-entered the building, but Patti caught her eye. "Keep your butt in its seat or I break his arm."

"I'm calling 911," she replied.

"Good. Make sure you request an ambulance and paramedics. We're going to need a crash-cart."

The fat woman's face clouded more than anything the sky had done lately. "Don't you hurt Doctor Reese, bitch! Whatever you freaks think, he's a good man!"

"Don't sweat it," Patti told her. "It's for me, not for him." Then they were inside. Patti saw a door marked "Dispensary" and steered Reese towards it. "Will they have what I need in there?"

"Yes, but–" Patti choked him off, and pushed in through the door. It was a small room full of jars and vials stacked on steel shelving. There was a desk and chair with a phone and some log books in one corner. Opposite, a window gave a view of the Sherman Halls hotel on the block across the way. Once inside, Patti locked and bolted the door.

"Point me to the stuff."

"On your left, third shelf..."

"Thanks." With that, she released him and kicked him squarely in the groin. He sank to the floor in agony, and she felt guilt wash over her. It didn't stop her opening up a box of disposable syringes and sticking one into a small glass bottle of anesthetic. "I'm sorry I had to do that, but you might get some funny ideas about not letting me harm myself."

"If you want to commit suicide, I can recommend some good counseling," he gasped.

"I know what I'm doing," Patti insisted. "Don't you watch the news?"

"I know who you are, lady. You survived the Metroline bomb, some of your friends died... What you're feeling now must be some kind of really hyper survivor-guilt." The vet spread his hands in a gesture of appeal. "I know what it's like; I had it myself in Desert Storm. I know the pain of losing a loved one makes life hard to go on with but—"

Patti forced a laugh. "All you need to know is how to dial 911. You know that?"

"Yeah."

"Good boy. Go do it now."

"What?"

"Dial nine-one-fucking-one, now!"

His face drained of blood, and he picked up the phone, punching the buttons. "Tell them you need paramedics on the scene right away, because some dumb ass bitch has gone and mainlined this shit, and she doesn't really want to be dead very long. Got that?"

Keeping the metal desk between Reese and herself, Patti took a last look out at Sherman Oaks and the duck-egg blue that was appearing through the broken clouds. Then she stabbed herself in the left bicep with the syringe and depressed the plunger.

Out the dispensary window, diagonally across the block, and up on the roof, the phone cable creaked alarmingly, creeping up the corner of the silver air conditioning box.

When it reached the top, it snapped back like a bowstring, and hit the broken base of the TV antenna as it went taut. The antenna shot off the edge of the roof, zipping through the air with deadly efficiency as quickly and silently as anything an English longbow launched towards the French at the battle of Agincourt.

Patti hadn't expected to suffer much in the way of pain. Dogs didn't seem to feel any when they got the needle. Then again, she wasn't a dog, and she had gone for the closest artery she could think of near the heart, rather than the hand or foot.

She couldn't breathe, and her chest felt as if it was in a car crusher. It didn't feel anything like going to sleep as far as she was concerned. She could hear voices in the distance, shouting and wailing. There was a crash of glass somewhere, so faint it was like the tinkling of an old fashioned music box, and she felt a current of air drift overhead. Perhaps it was the cloud she would be playing her harp upon. Then there was nothing.

Patti crumpled to the floor, sprawling limply under a flash of silver that stopped with a crunching thud.

Doctor Reese's jaw dropped, stunned by the four-foot shaft of metal that had suddenly appeared, half-buried in the plasterboard office wall. The glass from the window it had broken on its descent was still falling to the carpet. Most astonishing of all was the lock of the woman's hair that the gleaming shaft had pinned to the wall, having passed through it as she fell.

The vet crossed himself, shaking and shivering. He couldn't tear his eyes away from it. It resembled a bizarre and macabre variation of a television antenna and he couldn't imagine where the hell it might have come from.

In the distance, he could hear sirens belonging to both the cops that the receptionist had called, and the paramedics he had just dialed. Dropping the phone, he knelt beside Patti, careful not to touch the antenna in case it was hot or sharp.

He felt for a pulse at Patti's throat—just in time to feel it stop.

TWENTY-THREE

"Watch this." Tony Chang held up a tape. He and Jim Castle were alone in the briefing room. Chang had locked the door as well, though Jim couldn't imagine why. "The LAPD took it from what they described as a suspicious death at Circuit City."

"CCTV? Another candidate for *America's Wildest Videos*?" Jim would never cease to be amazed by people's capacity for that crap. He collapsed into a chair, exhaling a long sound of relief for resting his aching legs. He could just about walk without a cane today, but it wasn't easy and it wasn't comfortable.

Chang shook his head, but didn't laugh. "This one will never be seen in public. The LAPD will be lucky to bury it themselves before the government steps and stashes it in Area 51 or something."

Chang pressed the *Play* button, and Jim Castle's life would never be the same again.

Patti Fuller died.

She didn't remember all of it. She didn't remember meeting any of her family, or Will or Susan or any of the others. She didn't even remember seeing the legendary tunnel of light that people always talked about in the tabloids or on those stupid television psychic shows. Maybe the living just weren't meant to remember that stuff, or perhaps the pain of being reborn screwed it all up in her head. Or maybe the people on TV just talk a lot of crap because they don't really know what it's all about.

Imagine being an ant, pressed right up against the wall of something huge, like the Empire State Building or the Colosseum. You know there's something there—some environment—but it's way too vast for you to get the shape of, let alone understand. Being dead is like being that ant. It's calm, and calming. Wondrous rather than peaceful.

That's all she remembered about it, because she came back.

Dying was easy. The coming back part hurt like sheer fucking hell.

Whether the pain woke her, or her waking kicked it into life, she didn't know. All she did know was that every breath was sending fire around her ribs, across her shoulders and down her back. The fire paused in her chest to gather itself, psyching itself up to come out fighting with each new breath. The body's organs–heart, lungs, liver, kidneys–didn't much like being switched off and then back on again, it seemed.

The fire was white hot, but didn't cast any light. Patti wondered if she still had eyes, or if they'd melted. The thought of blindness terrified her more than the pain. Pain she could deal with, either mentally, or with painkillers. To not be able to see just sounded horrible beyond words, a literal fate worse than death.

Finally, an arc of white cracked the darkness. Her eyeballs were still intact and they were finally opening. For a moment she thought that she was going to see that tunnel of light crap after all. Then the brightness faded, and she could see lines stretched faintly across it. Cracks in ceiling plaster.

All by themselves, her eyes focused, with sudden, dizzying clarity. Her hands clenched onto something soft and giving, holding on in case she fell. White-painted walls met the ceiling, and white light came in through a window. A band of pale wood was belted around the walls at waist height. A smell went with the white: overly powerful disinfectant.

Something was stuck into her nostrils, but couldn't quite block out the institutional smell. The chirping she could hear was not a cartoon bird flying round her head, but a white machine to one side.

Patti's hands eased their grip on the mattress. She was lying in a hospital bed, and she had no idea how she had got there. Her only experience with hospitals was from television and films, and she had always thought hospitals were for old people, not someone who was only twenty-two years old.

Correction: only twenty-two when she died. She supposed she was really only a day old in this new life.

The doctor was kind of cute. Black, young—only in his early thirties—and friendly. He was tired, too, and didn't look a lot better than Patti felt after a night's heavy work. A nurse had fetched him after she noticed Patti was awake. He shone a light into his patient's eyes. She looked away, but he looked satisfied with whatever he saw in them. "Do you know where you are?"

"Hospital." What a word with which to discover you can talk, she thought. "Don't know which one."

"St Joseph's." She knew the one. "Do you know who you are?"

That gave her pause for thought. For a moment—just a moment, but it was gut strangling—she didn't have a clue. She had never felt anything quite like that sudden loss of identity. It was weird as hell, and she thought she must be having a nightmare, or going crazy. That moment was probably the most scared she had ever been.

It didn't last, thank God. "Patti. Patricia Fuller"

He nodded. "Do you know why you're here?"

Pain. That's one hell of a good reason, and Patti decided she would rather he took it away than talked incessantly. "Well, my ribs, back, shoulder and chest all hurt like crap, and this is a hospital."

The doctor grinned. "Yeah. Do you know why you hurt like crap? What made that happen?"

"I died."

The doctor made a so-so gesture. "Only for a minute, if that." Patti couldn't tell whether he was joking. He took a deep breath, putting on his best serious expression. He still had humor in eyes despite the attempt at gravitas. She liked him. "Overdoses of anesthetic, luckily for you, are recoverable from, if the paramedics get to you in time."

Patti relaxed. Even though she had barely woken up, she felt sleepy already. Either he'd given her a sedative, or there was a big difference between an evening's healthy sleep, and waking from death.

Between being poked and prodded, and all kinds of samples taken, Patti slept. In sleep, she dreamt of going clubbing with Will and Susan, and of taking tea with a spry old woman in 1940s-era clothes.

Somehow she felt rested by morning, though she didn't feel up to breakfast.

The black doctor from the previous day came in to see her again. His name was Russ, but at first she misheard it as Ross and had a George Clooney-related fit of giggles. "If you're up to it, you have visitors," he said.

"Well, you're the doc, doc. Am I up to it?"

"Absolutely." He beckoned two people forward. It was Jim Castle and a red-haired woman with green eyes. From the way they stayed in orbit of each other's personal space, this was obviously Mrs Castle.

"Hi," Patti said. "Your wife thinks you're doing me?" she whispered, for Jim's ears only.

He laughed. "No, she knows me better than that. The bureau's the other party in our love triangle." He became more serious. "I saw what happened at... at the store. The CCTV tape." He shook his head. "I don't even know how describe it. All I can do is believe in it."

"A little too late, don't you think?" She winced, realizing that that might have come across as sounding a little more bitter than she had meant it to. "I mean... Who could believe something like that? I couldn't, if our situations were reversed. Better if it had been the terrorists..."

"Well, Reilly's not going to see daylight again. Most of his group are dead, and–"

"And I've now been dead like I should have been all along."

"So, one way or the other, I guess it's over. Time to start rebuilding your life."

She shook her head. "That life's gone. It not being gone was the problem."

"A new life, then?"

"Yeah. A new reincarnation, if you believe that kind of thing."

"Don't you?"

"In this life?" She shrugged. "Maybe."

ABOUT THE AUTHOR

David A McIntee has written more *Dr Who* novels than he can count these days. A seasoned traveller, he is married to Ambassador Mollari and lives in Yorkshire, in the UK, with B'Elanna, Seven of Nine, a live cannonball and a stripy git. When not writing books, he explores historical sites, researches Fortean subjects, teaches stage-fighting workshops, and collects SF weaponry. His role models in life are the Fourth Doctor, Kerr Avon, Graeme Garden and Eddie Hitler, so members of the public should be wary of approaching him. One of the statements on this page is untrue.

Also available from Black Flame

FINAL DESTINATION:
DEAD RECKONING

by Natasha Rhodes

If there was one thing Jess Golden had learned at school, it was this: never trust a guy who can run faster than you.

Not even if they're nice to you. Not even if they buy you dinner and drinks and tell you that they love you.

And certainly not if you think they'll ever have reason to chase you.

That thought was now at the forefront of Jess's mind as she tore across the lonely concrete parking lot towards the lights and safety of the buildings nearby. Her muscles burned with exhaustion and her lungs felt fit to burst, but she kept going. It wasn't as if she had any other choice. It was past midnight in downtown LA, and the empty streets were filled with the kind of shadows that moved when you looked at them. Orange sodium lamps did little more than accentuate the darkness and dogs barked as she flew past gated compounds strewn with razor wire.

From somewhere behind her came the sound of pounding footsteps, punctuated by heavy breathing and the occasional shouted obscenity. Jess ignored the sound and concentrated on running. Running was a really good thing to do right now.

The three-inch heels were a mistake, she saw it now. And the leather miniskirt? Just asking for trouble. She felt the heels of her expensive boots giving way as she ran and silently cursed herself. She'd spent a long time dressing up for dinner with this guy, and she'd got it wrong yet again. Why did looking good mean wearing stuff you couldn't run in?

She blamed men in general. She was sure they had something to do with it.

Still, she was nearly at the brightly lit cluster of buildings on the corner, which meant that she was almost safe.

Almost...

Jess skidded round a corner and nearly ran headfirst into the fence that blocked the walkway. The sidewalk was completely cordoned off for roadworks. Thick chicken wire was tied across it, strung in place with heavy ropes. A sign read "Diversion", and pointed back the way she had just come. There was no way around.

Jess swore loudly.

Glancing feverishly back over her shoulder, Jess began searching for a way around the blockade.

There had to be a way through. Fueled by adrenaline, she grabbed the barrier in both hands and yanked on it as hard as she could.

It stayed firmly in place.

There was only one thing for it. Jess kicked off her high heels, scooped them up in one hand and started climbing. There was no time to go around. Reaching the top, she threw herself over, feeling the edge of the fence draw blood from her bare stomach as she half climbed, half fell down the other side. She dropped heavily to the ground and then it was back to the running.

Seconds later, she heard her pursuer hit the fence with a sound like a shopping cart being dropped onto concrete. He gave a bellow of frustration and began shaking the fence in fury, yelling at Jess to come back.

Jess allowed herself a small smile. That would hold him for at least a minute, giving her precious time to escape.

She ran flat out for another couple of blocks, before slowing to a walk. She was wheezing. Boy, was she out of shape. She made a mental note to get her butt down to the gym after the weekend, instead of bitching to her friends that she looked obscene in Lycra.

Jess paused and stood for a moment with her hands on her knees, then took a deep breath and straightened, flicking her long dark hair out of her face. She leaned back on the wall and stole a glance behind her.

There was no sign of her pursuer.

Good.

Reaching into the pocket of her denim jacket, Jess carefully pulled out a large leather-bound wallet and regarded it with a great deal of satisfaction. She already knew what it contained—platinum credit cards, Diners Club card, a couple of hundred dollars in cash and a photo of Bill and his wife. Bill was the name of the irate man currently pursuing her, and he had good reason to do so. His illicit date had turned out to be very costly to him, in more ways than one.

Jess tucked the wallet back inside her jacket and patted it in a friendly fashion. There was easily enough money to pay a couple of months' rent in there, although she'd probably have to toss out the cards once Bill had reported them as "missing." Hell, the guy could sue her if he wanted the rest of his stuff back, although she was pretty sure that he wouldn't dare. If he wanted to mess around behind his wife's back, especially with her, then he deserved everything he got.

Jess gazed across the road, her eyes searching the street. *Ah—there.* On the roof of a derelict warehouse, a neon sign in the shape of a cat burned, lighting up the darkness with a deep crimson glow. Beneath it, a long line of clubgoers waited patiently outside the door, smoking and chatting.

Smoothing out her jacket, Jess took a deep breath and started making her way across the road towards the club. With everything she'd been through tonight, she could sure as hell use a drink.

The interior of Club Kitty was dark, dirty and loud. Jess yawned as she pushed her way through the heavy industrial doors and clanked down the metal steps in her high heeled boots.

There were countless such places in LA, clustered around the major intersections like flies on a corpse, attracting a diverse mix of tourists, high-lifers and even the odd celebrity. They were universally tacky and as transient as the town that housed them. What was Club X one week would be resprayed and turned into a pizza joint the next, leaving a lot of confused patrons scratching their heads and wondering what had happened to their favorite nightspot, and why on earth their pizza had glitter in it.

But in LA, the City of Angels, this was just how the game was played.

Out with the old, in with the new.

It didn't matter that the old had been new just a few days or hours ago. The constant ebb and flow of trade was the lifeblood of the city.

Jess looked around her in amusement as she reached the bottom of the steps. She'd not been wrong about this place. Everything about it screamed "cheap!" from the bare-board seating to the graffiti-covered brick walls. Judging by the state of it, the club owners had read somewhere that minimalism was coming back in again, and had decided to decorate the place by, well, not decorating it at all. It was as stark and bare as the derelict warehouse above it. Tea light candles flickered on the rickety metal tables, filling the dank air with a jumping orange light, and the bar area was illuminated by a single bare bulb, which had been painted black in the mistaken belief that this made it look cool.

Over by the main stairway, a scruffy dog dozed peacefully on a pile of discarded jackets, occasionally awaking to snap at the ankles of those stepping over it.

But despite the air of general neglect, the place was packed to bursting. Dozens of too-cool-to-be-conscious teens and twenty-somethings jammed the place from wall to wall, all in various stages of inebriation and undress. Over by the far wall, a gaggle of girls burst into shrill peels of laughter over their ten-dollar apple martinis, eyeing up the guys in the designer jeans who were draped artfully over the sofas and chairs by the bar, pretending not to notice them. The general atmosphere was one of careless affluence, of seeing and being seen.

Toad the Wet Sprocket's "When Will We Fall Down?" was playing on the PA. A tall, willowy man in a tattered cowboy jacket was dancing to it all alone in a corner, lost in the music.

"This place really sucks, huh?"

Jess looked up to see a sandy-haired frat boy gazing at her appreciatively. She glanced around her, then shrugged, feeling expansive. "Nothing that a couple of hundred pounds of TNT wouldn't fix."

The boy snorted with laughter.

Jess walked past a handful of stoned-looking older guys dressed in black who were lounging against the wall, wearing leather jackets and eternally hopeful expressions, and entered the main bar area, trying to make herself look respectable. The room was dark and low ceilinged, lit only by the tangled neon display behind the bar. A giant disco ball lit the room with spinning red and blue reflections, further adding to the general air of tackiness. At the end of the room, a muffled thumping came from behind a heavy iron door labeled, "Enter Here". Above the sign, some wag had added, "Abandon hope all ye who..."

Jess's heel skidded on the floor. She looked down. The floor was scattered with heaps of glossy cards and band flyers. She peered down, trying to read the names of the bands listed on them.

"ID, please."

"Sure." Jess fished out her expertly doctored California driver's license and handed it over, taking care not to drop Bill's credit cards all over the floor. That would not be a good start to the evening. She paid the bouncer the six bucks cover charge and glanced behind her, hoping that Bill hadn't been so stupid as to follow her in here. He knew as well as she did that she could make a scene as well as anyone.

The scary-looking punk bouncer checked her card over carefully, paying particular attention to her date of birth. Jess surreptitiously studied him out of the corner of her eye.

She had been to this club once or twice before, and this particular doorman never failed to fascinate her. He always put Jess in mind of some primal and predatory beast forced to wear a suit and keep regular hours. He had a pierced eyebrow and a jaw like a piranha, and was so muscular that his arms no longer rested comfortably at his sides, hanging instead at an angle to his body. What was visible of his neck was covered in swirling tribal tattoos, and he had an impressive black and white striped Mohawk.

Jess wasn't afraid of the guy like some people around here were, but still, she made sure that she never went to the restrooms alone when he was on duty. It was just common sense. She always had the weirdest feeling that he was watching her...

The bouncer scratched a dirty thumbnail over Jess's license card, checking for telltale seams in the plastic, but couldn't find anything wrong with it. He gave Jess a sharp look and grudgingly handed it back. Then he took her hand and stamped it with the club logo, muttering something under his breath that she chose to ignore.

Moving on down the room as quickly as she could, Jess bought herself an overpriced drink at the bar, then picked up one of the scattered flyers. There were three bands on tonight—the Drills, the Vipers and some kind of rock-ska band named Mors Mortis.

Jess squinted at the fine print on the flyer. They'd spelt her name wrong again. Typical. Picking up her drink with a sigh, Jess smoothed down her hair and opened the main door onto a wall of sound.

The main dance floor of Club Kitty was packed, filled from wall to wall by a heaving throng of club-goers, all dressed up in glam rock gear. Jess frowned for a second, then remembered it was Friday. Friday meant Eighties Night. *Great*. Jess glanced down at her attire, and gave a smirk. At least she'd fit in here for once.

She shut the bar door behind her and peered into the crowd, trying to get her bearings. Strobe lighting flickered across the walls, making the clubbers look like badly animated puppets. The room was hot and the air thrummed with blast after blast of sound. The stage was book-ended by two enormous speakers, which pumped out arena-volume sound in the living room-sized club. Jess fished in her bag for earplugs.

Some local rock band was playing, presumably the Drills, a lively trio lead by a tough-looking guy with an eyebrow ring and skin-tight black jeans. His T-shirt bore the legend *"It Ain't Gonna Lick Itself,"* which for some reason Jess found highly amusing.

She paused in the doorway to watch as the band slammed into a crazy rock breakdown, the lead singer belting out a volley of insane high-speed licks on his guitar, jumping and spinning and expertly driving the crowd into a frenzy. Behind him, the tattooed drummer added a high-octane double bassdrum solo to the mix, his red-streaked hair whipping around him as he played.

The funky young bass player joined the others in an amp-smashing finale, stepping back hurriedly as the singer hurled his guitar into the air mid-solo as the final notes rang out. Then the lights went down and the audience went wild, applauding and cheering and shouting for an encore.

Jess shook her head in wonder, joining in the applause, then began pushing her way through the crowd, wiping her forehead as she walked. Empty bottles and soda cans clanked and crunched under her feet as she walked, and her heels stuck slightly to the floor with every step.

She grimaced. This place was pure class.

As the curtain closed and the filler music came on, Jess saw a familiar black-clad figure standing by the side of the stage, facing away from her, seemingly absorbed in the music. She squeezed her way through the throng and poked him in the ribs with a finger. "Hey."

The figure didn't turn round. Jess grinned and tugged on the end of his studded belt. "Aren't you glad I made it?"

The figure glanced over its shoulder, looked Jess up and down, and turned away again.

Jess pouted. "Oh, come on. I'm here, aren't I?"

The figure appeared to consider this. "Yes, you're here," he agreed. He daintily pulled back a black satin sleeve to reveal a Mickey Mouse watch. "You're here exactly one minute and thirty-two seconds before we are due to go onstage."

"Jamie. Baby. You know I'd never let you down." Jess beamed up at him, playfully trailing a white-painted fingernail down the muscle of his back.

Jamie reached around to catch her finger, then turned around fully. He was wearing a jeweled eyebrow-ring, which cast complicated highlights over his open, high-cheek boned face. His hair was spiked up with hair gel and he wore a black wireless headset over one ear. He did not look amused.

He stared at Jess for a couple of seconds, taking in her flushed appearance and sweat-streaked makeup. Then the corner of his mouth twitched up. "That's what you said last time."

Jess took his hand in hers. "You still have my word," she said.

Jamie gazed at her for a moment, then shook his head ruefully. "You know what? I'm not even going to ask." He winked at her. "Come on. Let's go wake up the others."

The story continues in

FINAL DESTINATION

DEAD RECKONING

by Natasha Rhodes

ISBN 1-84416-106-4 $7.99/£6.99

The vampire apocalypse looms as a desperate battle unfolds to end the secret war between the vampires and the few humans who know of their existence. The only person who stands between the ultimate vampire and the enslavement of humanity is the daywalker, Blade!

WWW.BLACKFLAME.COM

TOUGH FICTION FOR A TOUGH PLANET

BLADE
TRINITY
A novel by Natasha Rhodes

2000 AD
THE UNQUIET GRAVE
PETER J EVANS

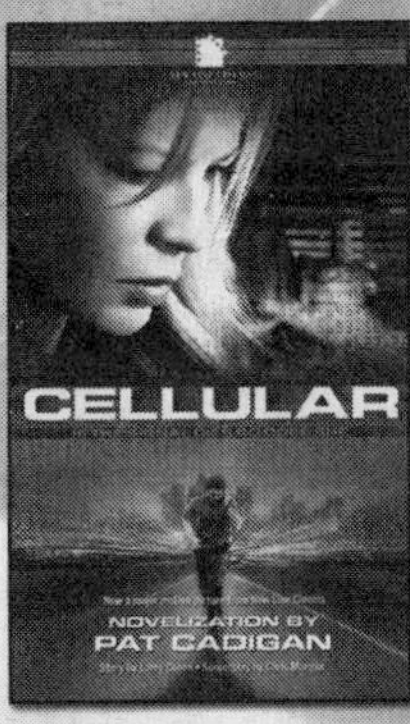
CELLULAR
NOVELIZATION BY
PAT CADIGAN

JUDGE DREDD
THE FINAL CUT
MATTHEW SMITH

NEW LINE CINEMA
THE TEXAS CHAINSAW MASSACRE

2000 AD
Hard-hitting action from the war-torn future!
ROGUE TROOPER
CRUCIBLE
GORDON RENNIE